Praise for Caroline Montague

'A moving, sweeping saga of love and loss'
Dinah Jefferies, bestselling author of *The Tuscan Contessa*

'Enthralling and wonderfully romantic, with gorgeous characters, this is perfect to curl up and get lost in'
Katie Fforde, bestselling author of *A Springtime Affair*

'Thoroughly engrossing'
Julian Fellowes, creator of *Downton Abbey*

'Enthralling … *An Italian Affair* snares us in an ever-tightening circle of love and despair, secrets and forgiveness'
Joanna Lumley

'Just wonderful'
Sun

'*Shadows Over the Spanish Sun* is scorching. It was a joy to ride across the Andalusian hills and to be transported by parallel, truly heart-wrenching love stories, past and present'
Carl Hester, Dressage Olympic Gold Medallist

Caroline Montague won her first National Poetry competition at 10 years old and from that moment dreamed of being a writer. After juggling motherhood with modelling assignments, she founded an interior design company, working on many projects in the UK and abroad. Her second marriage to the widowed Conroy Harrowby brought four stepchildren into her life, giving her a wider audience for her imaginative bedtime stories. As a family they all live at the Harrowby ancestral home, Burnt Norton, which famously inspired T S Eliot to write the first of his *Four Quartets*. At last Caroline has the time to fulfil her dream of becoming a full-time author.

Also by Caroline Montague

An Italian Affair
A Paris Secret

SHADOWS *Over the* SPANISH SUN

Caroline
Montague

First published in Great Britain in 2021 by Orion Fiction,
an imprint of The Orion Publishing Group Ltd
Carmelite House, 50 Victoria Embankment
London EC4Y 0DZ

An Hachette UK Company

3 5 7 9 10 8 6 4 2

All the characters in this book are fictitious, and any resemblance to
actual persons, living or dead, is purely coincidental.

A CIP catalogue record for this book is
available from the British Library.

ISBN (Mass Market Paperback) 978 1 4091 9807 9
ISBN (eBook) 978 1 4091 9808 6

Typeset at The Spartan Press Ltd,
Lymington, Hants

Printed in Great Britain by Clays Ltd,
Elcograf S.p.A.

www.orionbooks.co.uk

This is dedicated to my great friend and one-time dressage teacher Carl Hester, Olympic gold medallist and the man whose extraordinary talent has inspired so much of this book.

Part One

Chapter One

April 2000, Andalucía

Don Leonardo Palamera de Santos pushed back his thick silver hair, pulled on his riding boots and came down the wide staircase to the oak front door. He stood for a moment on the step, his eyes roaming past the whitewashed wall that enclosed the hacienda, towards the distant hills, as if seeing them for the very first time.

'So beautiful,' he murmured, breathing in the scent of pomegranate and orange blossom drifting through the air from the orchard below. Even now, the smell still reminded him of Valeria. He shook his head, banishing the memory, and strode across the forecourt with a vigour that belied his years. As he neared the stable block, the aroma changed; it was pungent and sweet, unique to horses and stables. His heart quickened in anticipation.

'You,' he called to Dante, the stable boy, who was walking through the arched cloister, a bucket in hand.

The teenager blinked as he emerged into the bright sunlight. '*Buenos días, señor.*'

'Tack up Seferino,' Leonardo instructed. 'And use the Vaquera saddle.'

'Seferino?' the boy asked, his brow wrinkled in concern. '*Está Seguro, señor?*'

'Of course I'm sure,' Leonardo roared, turning his dark eyes on the boy. 'Run boy, run.'

Dante turned and soon Leonardo could hear voices in the background, full of consternation.

'The idiot – what is he thinking of?' came the gravelly tone of Dante's father, Javier.

'But he insisted, Papa.'

'Well, it's his head that will be broken. Silly old fool.'

Leonardo smiled. Did they think he couldn't hear? Well, he would show them. He might be eighty-five, but he could still ride with the best of them. He was fed up with caution: he wanted to feel the extraordinary power of the young stallion beneath him; he wished to create that unique partnership once more. As he climbed the mounting block, he paused to catch his breath before the last step. His eyes darted to the tack room. Had the lad and his father noticed this display of weakness? Were they laughing at him now? He pushed on and leant against the wall at the top. Old age was something that Leonardo despised. Not his looks – he was proud of his mane of silver hair, and his wrinkles were testament to a life well lived – but he hated the way his physique had deteriorated; how his joints were not as supple as they had once been. He needed to prove that he could still ride the most difficult of horses, to show that he was still a virile man.

As the strident clop of hooves echoed down the corridor from the stables, Leonardo frowned, fear twisting in his gut. Javier was right, he was a stubborn, pathetic old man. But when the gleaming black stallion came into the sunlight, Leonardo's fear dissipated. He could feel the blood stir in his veins and the familiar excitement building inside him. The horse was all muscle, his powerful neck arched, his hindquarters were strong.

Seferino certainly had attitude. Leonardo recognised the way his eyes studied him, assessing him. Leonardo had ridden so many horses like him before and had managed to form a rapport with every one of them. Nothing had changed. He ran his hand over the branding on Seferino's quarters and slipped his foot into the stirrup. Pain shot through his hip and he grimaced, breathing sharply, but with his usual force of will, he swung his leg over the wide saddle. As the horse snorted, dancing on the spot, all thoughts of his own discomfort disappeared. He picked up the reins, feeling the horse's mouth responding through his fingers, and nudged the stallion into a trot over the cobbles and out through the ancient archway, to the white road that snaked across the vast hillside beyond.

He was halfway up the lane when he drew Seferino to a halt. A black kite circled the sky above him, its grace belying the strength of its deadly talons. Somewhere in the vegetation a rabbit was about to breathe its last, thought Leonardo. Birds of prey had always fascinated him. They could be tamed, forced to do man's bidding, but they were never truly mastered.

A flock of scraggy sheep grazed on the scrubby grass, and below him, the white walls of the hacienda were dazzling in the early morning light. He could see the entire property from here, the long two-storey house with the servants' quarters and stable yard in a quadrangle behind, the drive lined with stately Spanish fir trees. He could see the bell tower, where he had once scrambled up with Valeria, and the lush green gardens watered by sprinklers, which would soon be in contrast to the parched landscape beyond. He spotted Dante, a tiny figure brushing the yard, and the mares in the paddocks wandering towards the shade of the oak trees as the sun rose in the sky. He sighed and gazed into the distance where a line of pylons were strung across the barren hillside. In his lifetime everything had changed, he thought wistfully. When he was a child, the land had been covered with olive trees, now most of them had gone. In those days a car had been cause for excitement, now it was the donkey carts that were a rarity. But, despite the infernal pylons, the harsh beauty remained.

He rode for an hour into the hills. Occasionally, the young horse shied, leaping sideways, but Leonardo sat straight and supple, his back absorbing the movement. When they reached a long grassy plateau at the top, he spurred the horse on.

'Come on, Seferino,' he whispered, letting out the rein. 'It's you and me now. Let's go.'

He could feel the wind in his hair as the horse picked up speed, the exhilaration flooding through his body. This was what it was like to be truly alive, he thought, a laugh escaping his throat. This was what he had always lived for.

Leonardo didn't see the wild boar in the undergrowth until it was too late. Seferino reacted immediately with primeval terror. He squealed, rising on his hind legs, his front legs pawing the air, then lunged forward and bolted, unbalancing his rider. Though Leonardo tried frantically to gain control, there was no stopping the horse. He kept pulling at the reins, with no effect. He felt himself slipping further and further sideways. He flung out his hand and grasped hold of the pommel, managing to struggle upright, while Seferino thundered faster and faster across the rocky ground. The horse was in flight mode now, nothing could stop him.

Even Leonardo's lifetime of experience couldn't quell the panic welling in his chest. As Leonardo leant backwards in the saddle, trying in vain to use his seat to slow the stallion down, a thousand thoughts went through his mind. Despite modulating his voice to calm the horse, he knew full well that Seferino was now blind and deaf to anything he did. Adrenalin coursed through his veins. It was imperative he remained on Seferino. He couldn't bale out; he was too old to fall. As the scenery flashed past, he recognised with a lurch that they were fast approaching the rocky outcrop where the hillside ended in a vast drop. His only hope was to turn Seferino in a large circle to the left. His mind raced as he calculated the immense danger of the situation. If he was to save the horse, he would have to steer him away from the rapidly approaching void and it would require every ounce of his limited energy. His thoughts were now only for Seferino.

In one last desperate attempt, he leant forward and to the left, grabbing hold of the rein next to the horse's mouth. With every vestige of remaining strength, he hauled on the single rein and sent a silent prayer to Valeria. At the final moment Seferino veered sharply, rocks cascading into the chasm below. Leonardo's last conscious thought before he hit the ground was that this was the end.

Chapter Two

April 2000, London

At night when the traffic hummed outside my bedroom window, and the glare of headlights moved across the blinds, I often imagined myself far from London, from the fumes and the crowds. I would return to the Hacienda de los Santos, my grandfather's house in Andalucía. Throughout my erratic childhood it had been a haven of tranquillity, a golden sanctuary. Papa Leonardo had wrapped me up in his world of horses, orange groves and fireflies. Memories of my holidays there were full of the two of us listening to the cicadas chirping or waiting for the song of the nightingale, as we sat under the pergola in the scented night air. I still visited every August – a summer escape that seemed worlds away from my job at the magazine, my small London flat, from Matt.

I didn't know that what happened that day would change everything.

It was the usual Friday-morning rush at work, and I was frantically trying to finish my copy on the best beauty products for ageing skin when my editor called me in. Actually, it was more of a summons; she rapped on the window of her glass cage, calling out, 'Mia, I've got something for you. I know you'll love it.'

I shot a glance at Cara on the other side of the office and rolled my eyes. Dale always used that condescending tone of voice when she knew it was something I would hate. As usual, she did all the talking while I hovered awkwardly in front of her immaculately clean desk. 'A three-page spread on the best slimming products of the year. Try them yourself, if you like,' she finished with a smirk.

Dale was never one for subtlety. I tugged at my Union Jack miniskirt, which I'd bought for a millennium party and which still caused a stir four months later. I'd always felt good in it – at five foot ten, I thought I may as well make the most of my long legs – but one snide comment from Dale and my confidence evaporated.

'Are you all right, sugar?' Cara asked, as I stopped by her desk.

'That woman, she defies all – ugh, I can't even think of the word.'

'You mean she's a bitch,' Cara replied with a smile and an offhand wave. 'Don't let it get to you.'

'Why does she have to be so bloody rude?' I bristled, shuffling some papers on her desk and wishing I had the ability to brush Dale's comments aside so easily.

'I'll buy you a drink after work, before you see that gorgeous fiancé of yours,' Cara said with a wink, and I agreed, hoping that one drink would turn into two or even three. I had a feeling I'd need them.

I was doing a quick edit on the beauty-product article, when my mobile rang. It was my mother.

'Darling—' she uttered as soon as I answered, the phone jammed between my shoulder and ear as I kept typing.

'Mama, I'm at work; can this wait? I'm on a deadline.'

'No. It's about your grandfather.'

I knew immediately from the tone of my mother's voice that something dreadful had happened. My fingers stilled on the keyboard and I felt a tightness in my chest as I held my breath.

'Papa Leonardo has had an accident on Seferino. He is in hospital – in a coma. The specialists say the next twenty-four hours are crucial.'

'Oh my God,' I gasped. 'What on earth was he doing on the stallion?' I could see Cara looking across the divider with concern.

'I have no idea, it's just like your grandfather.' Her tone was tight and frustrated but also filled with panic. 'The horse came back on his own, so they sent out a search party. He was found unconscious near the edge of the canyon. He has been airlifted to Seville.'

'We need to go immediately, Mama.' I was on my feet, sweeping anything I might need into my bag.

'Yes, yes. Peter has already booked tickets. We have to be at Gatwick by six.'

I nodded, despite her not being able to see me. I had always appreciated my stepfather's cool head in a crisis.

'And have you told Poppy?' I asked, picking up the snow globe of Chamonix Matt had given me. I shook it hard, and as the white flakes fell on Mont Blanc and the tiny chalets below, my mother confirmed that Peter was ringing my stepsister and we should share a taxi to the airport. I rang off, feeling the tears well in my eyes.

As I accepted the proffered tissue from Cara, I dialled my fiancé. Perhaps he would offer to come with me, I thought, sniffing loudly, but the minute I heard his voice I knew it wouldn't happen.

'Matt—'

'Mia, sorry, in a meeting. Is it urgent?'

'It's my grandfather, he's in a coma. I'm flying out tonight.'

'That's terrible,' he exclaimed. 'Are you OK? You know I'd love to support you, sweetheart, but we're at the crucial stage of closing the deal with Gazco. I'll fly over as soon as I can—'

'Of course,' I interrupted. 'I'll call you from Spain.'

*

Late that evening we arrived at San Pablo airport, ten kilometres from Seville. As we walked into the warm evening air, I could see Ramon, my grandfather's driver, waiting for us. His eyes were ringed with fatigue and his black jacket hung limp from his once-stocky frame.

'*Buenas noches,*' he uttered, leading us to the car.

'I'm so sorry.' I touched his arm.

Ramon blinked, and through a haze of my own exhaustion I realised the depth of his despair. He was, and had always been, devoted to my grandfather. As Peter opened the door for my mother, and helped her into the ancient Mercedes, Ramon arranged the bags in the boot. Poppy threw her rucksack on the back seat, and together we clambered in after it.

'Ramon, tell us, what state is he in? Will he recognise us?' I asked, leaning forward as the car drew away from the kerb.

'I'm afraid not at the moment, Señorita Mia.' Apart from being my grandfather's driver, butler and odd-job man, Ramon was also his greatest friend. His eyes met mine in the rear-view mirror and I knew he would tell me the truth. 'Your grandfather has suffered severe injuries and they are not sure that he will ever wake up. It is terrible, señorita.'

I swallowed hard. 'Thank you, Ramon.'

I battled tears away as my mother squeezed my hand on one side and Poppy reached out for the other.

'It will be all right, Mia,' Mama said with a confidence I was sure she wasn't feeling. But I knew that if he died nothing would be all right again.

It was dark when we arrived at the University Hospital of *Virgen del Rocío* and every light in the building seemed to be blazing. While Poppy and Peter went to find coffee, my mother and I were directed to Intensive Care. We were waiting by the nurses' station when a doctor in a white coat came through the swing doors.

'You must be Señor Palamera de Santos' daughter,' he said, putting out his hand to shake.

My mother inclined her head, glancing at the label on his white coat, 'Dr Canovas?' There was hesitation in her voice and I could tell that she was scared.

'I am so sorry about the accident,' he continued in an authoritative and kindly tone. 'Your father is alive, but he has sustained severe injuries and trauma to the head. He is in a coma and these next few days are critical. We have managed to stabilise him, but his age is obviously against him.'

'Of course, I understand,' my mother murmured.

'I am told he was riding a young stallion. We treat many equestrian injuries but—'

'The patients aren't usually eighty-five years old,' I interrupted.

'*Exactamente*,' the doctor agreed, turning his attention to me.

'He's very obstinate,' I blurted out. 'He might surprise us all.'

'I can assure you we will do everything we can. He has one of the best teams in Spain working in this unit.'

'We have no doubt of that, thank you, doctor,' my mother said and shot me a look that shut off any further observations.

'At the moment our priority is the coma,' Dr Canovas continued. 'We are draining fluid to relieve pressure on the brain. I am afraid he will appear like an octopus, with tubes everywhere.' This was obviously his effort at humour before he gave the final blow.

He looked at me again, his brown eyes full of pity. 'I am afraid, señorita, that if he should regain consciousness, it is unlikely that he will walk again. With the extent of his injuries he may require constant nursing for the rest of his life. There is, of course, the state in between where the patient is only minimally conscious and remains so.'

'Minimally conscious?' I whispered. All the way on the plane I had assured myself that my grandfather would either get well, or he would die. I had never imagined there was something in between. This would be the worst possible outcome.

Dr Canovas turned back to my mother, the consummate professional. 'You will wish to see him. Forgive me, señora, it must be for a few minutes only and you will have to wear a mask and gown.'

'Can we talk to him?' I asked. 'I mean, can he hear us?'

The doctor smiled, and I knew he was trying to be kind. 'It is accepted by many of my colleagues that no amount of external stimuli can prompt the brain to wake up, but' – he shrugged his slim shoulders – 'who says we should always believe the accepted? There is no harm in talking or reading to the patient; you can even sing to him, if you like. It is possible that he will hear you. Now please come this way. The nurses are busy working with him, so you will need to go in just one at a time. We should have a better idea by tomorrow afternoon.'

I was huddled in a waiting-room chair when a nurse approached me, carrying a plastic bag.

'These are your grandfather's clothes,' she murmured, sitting down beside me. 'I imagine it was a shock seeing him like that.'

I raised my eyes and nodded slowly.

'I have seen cases that have seemed hopeless, but the patients have woken up and gone home.' She patted my hand. 'They often remember the past first, so over the next few weeks, why don't you look for things that mean something to him, photographs, perhaps, of people he once knew, tactile objects, anything that might stimulate his brain.'

'Thank you,' I said, grateful for her positivity, 'I'll see what I can find.'

Half an hour later, my mother and I retraced our steps from the ward.

'I know you are not particularly religious,' she murmured at last, 'but please hold him in your prayers.'

'I think he may need more than our prayers,' I responded, unable to obliterate the image of my grandfather reduced to a frail shell of a man.

'He is a stubborn old thing,' she squeezed my arm, 'you said so yourself, *querida*. You know his indomitable spirit. He will make it, he has to.' She shook her head suddenly and sighed. '*Viejo tonto*,' she murmured. 'What was he thinking of?'

My mother rarely used swear words and if she did, they were always in Spanish. I gave a small smile; my grandfather was a silly old bugger and we were paying for his reckless behaviour. Though her relationship with her father had been troubled in recent years, when she was a child, they had been inseparable. It was quite obvious to me that she loved him deeply.

'You're right, Mama, but Papa Leonardo has always lived by his own rules.'

We had reached the glass front doors of the lobby, when my mother drew in her breath.

'And look who is here to cheer us – your Great-Aunt Gracia.'

I groaned as my mother's maternal aunt advanced through the reception area towards us, scattering everyone in her wake.

'Ah, *mis queridos*, what a tragedy. Poor Leonardo. And now you have had to come all the way from England. You must be devastated, what a worry. But what was he doing on a horse?' She stopped abruptly, having run out of breath, and fanned herself with her hand.

What my great-aunt lacked in stature she made up for in everything else. She put her plump, ringed fingers around my cheeks, hugged me, and progressed to my mother, cradling her in her arms.

'What a terrible shock, *mi pequeña.* Ramon told me you were here.' Aunt Gracia, who seemed to lack a stop valve, ploughed on. 'Since Paloma has gone, Rafaela, I feel responsible for you both. My sister would have wanted me to care for you and her granddaughter. And now—' She pulled a handkerchief from the interior of her crocodile bag. 'But it is my belief a man as strong as your grandfather will survive. I remember the incident with the snake.' At this point my mother interjected, cutting off any possibility of Tía Gracia's favourite reptilian story.

'You're so kind to come, Gracia, though I am not sure if you will be allowed to see him tonight.'

'*Querido* Rafaela, I came to see you. I understand the trauma for you both, particularly after your father, Mia. Tomorrow I will come again and hopefully I can see him through the glass. It will be enough just to have a glimpse of Leonardo. I will come in every day and be here for as long as I am needed.'

Papa Leonardo had always found his sister-in-law tiresome. Whatever her good intentions, she was the last person he would want at his side.

'Well, then,' my mother said. 'We will have the pleasure of your company. We must arrange to see you at the hacienda during our stay. Ramon will collect you.'

When my mother had extricated herself from Aunt Gracia's embrace, we joined Peter and Poppy outside.

'How did it go?' Poppy asked, linking her arm through mine.

'Not good,' I replied, leaning into her, grateful for her presence.

Ramon shook his head. '*Donde hay vida hay esperanza*, where there is life there is hope,' he said with a sad smile.

Within an hour, we had left the outskirts of the city behind us. The flat plains of Seville had given way to olive trees with gnarled trunks and almonds with feathery blossom, clinging to the hillsides in ghostly ranks. The odd light blinked from the farmhouses dotting the landscape and, in the distance, dramatic rocky outcrops stood black against the sky. At this time of night the scenery was particularly dramatic, and it was precious to both my mother and me. It was part of our heritage, in our blood.

My mother was fiddling with the strap of her bag when I glanced at her. At sixty-two years old she was still elegant, but now in the half-light, her face was gaunt with concern.

'I'm so sorry, Mia,' she said.

I bit my lip to stop it trembling. 'He is your father, I don't have a monopoly on grief.'

'But you have a very special relationship, and that is what you need to hold on to. We have to believe that your grandfather will defy the doctors and recover. It is not over yet.'

'I'll try,' I whispered, thinking how much he would hate being dependent on anyone. Until the moment I had seen him in Intensive Care, I had convinced myself that my grandfather was strong; he could defeat anything and prove everyone wrong. But as the staff had hovered around him, peering at the monitors and checking on the tubes that were attached to every part of his body, I realised it was no longer his will that mattered, only the whooshing and sucking of the ventilator that was breathing for him and keeping him alive.

My hands were twisted in my lap as I tried to keep my emotions in check. I had been so close to my grandfather, he had been my rock when my father had died and my refuge when my mother had married Peter, and Poppy had come into my life. I looked across at my stepsister. She was five years younger than me and at twenty-three she was quite beautiful. How I had hated the red-haired seven-year-old who had been forced upon me and whom everyone adored. Now I would kill anyone who tried to hurt her. She was my sister, my soulmate and my best friend.

'I know he isn't my grandfather, but we'll get through this together,' Poppy whispered in my ear, and I knew she was right.

Chapter Three

From early childhood, my arrival at the hacienda for the summer holidays was something I would dream of. Each year I would close my eyes at the end of the lane, opening them only as we swept through the gateposts to the drive beyond. If my grandfather hadn't come to the airport to greet me, he would be waiting on the steps, his arms open to catch me as I hurtled towards him. Tonight, only a single light was on downstairs and a strange melancholy appeared to have settled on the house.

As I stepped from the car, silence lingered in the air around me and for once even my stepfather was quiet. I looked upwards. Though shaded in darkness, the façade of the long two-storey white house was just as it had always been. The marble angel continued her solemn gaze over the garden from her niche above the oak front door and the elaborate bell tower still rose above the ancient terracotta roof. The wrought-iron grills on the blue-painted windows were the same, but the house felt different somehow. Sadness seemed to seep from the walls. The life force had gone.

I turned suddenly, shaken from my reverie.

'Shall I take your bag, señora?' Ramon was saying to my mother and the mood was broken. At that moment the lights flicked on inside the hall and the door was opened by Manuela, my grandfather's housekeeper.

'*Bienvenidos*, you must be exhausted. Please come, supper will be ready in the loggia in ten minutes,' she said.

While the others trooped to the colonnaded loggia for a drink, I took my grandfather's clothes to the laundry room.

As I opened the bag, my hands were shaking. The dirt on his riding trousers and *vaquera* jacket told their own story. For a brief second, I imagined my grandfather crashing to the ground, the dust swirling, Seferino galloping home. I was putting the jacket over the chair when I thought to check in the pockets. I found the obligatory packet of mints, but there was also a crumpled envelope, with a note from me inside.

Dear Papa Leonardo,
I have had the best summer in the world and I miss you already. As much as I longed to see Mama, I really didn't want to leave. I can't wait to see you again and I am sending lots of hugs.
Muchos besos a Abuela Paloma,
Mia xxxxxx

I folded the paper and put it back in the envelope, swallowing hard. It was obviously precious to my grandfather because he had kept it for all these years.

The mood at supper was lightened by Manuela who had laid the long table with candles and flowers.

'So,' she said, putting a delicious chicken and olive casserole in front of my mother. 'In *España* we realise good food is the first step towards mending a broken heart.' She gave a pointed look at my very English stepfather. 'But I also know it won't be broken for long. The señor will come home.'

'Thank you,' my mother murmured with a smile, but Manuela had not finished yet.

'Tonight you are tired; tomorrow will be different, you'll see. *No puede ver el bosque por los árboles.*'

'You can't see the wood for the trees,' I translated to a perplexed Poppy

'I understood perfectly,' she lied.

When my mother and Peter had retired to bed, I fetched another bottle of wine from the rack in the cellar and sank onto the wicker sofa beside Poppy. I filled up her glass and took a large slug of my own.

'Thank you for being here,' I said, leaning against her.

'Idiot.' She laughed affectionately. 'Where else would I be? Do you think I would let you do this without me? Anyway, it gave me an excuse to miss the last day of law school.' She giggled suddenly. 'I fell asleep in my land law tutorial last week. Mr Shelburne was *not* amused. *Poppy Aitcheson, are you with us or without us?* I mean, Mia, what century is he in?'

'Poppy.' I pretended to look stern.

'You have to take some responsibility! It was after our night out.'

I smiled, remembering our pub crawl where we had ended up in a bar in Kensington and had to ward off the attentions of two young Italians, finally falling into bed at three in the morning.

'You're the best tonic, Poppy.' It was true, she was. Our shared flat was a haven for both of us; evenings were spent lolling on the sofa in our pyjamas while I talked endlessly about Matt, or listened enthralled while Poppy described the antics of various male students vying for her attention. Poppy knew more about me than anyone.

'He'll recover, Mia,' she said, drawing me back to the present. 'I know your grandfather.' She squeezed my hand. 'When is Matt flying over?'

I fiddled with the large diamond ring on my finger. 'He's involved in a big negotiation at work; he can't be away at the moment. Anyway, I've got you to look after me.'

Poppy frowned. 'Where has the excited bride gone, Mia?'

'I'm not sure,' I replied, thinking of the hurried call from Matt at the airport where he had seemed more concerned about his deal than my grandfather's condition.

I grimaced at Poppy. 'But Manuela is right; I'll feel better after a good night's sleep.'

As I lay between the crisp white sheets, the familiar sounds echoing through the house, I tried to sleep, but failed. The hall clock that had gently recorded the passing of my childhood seemed strident tonight, relentless. Somewhere a tap was dripping. Putting on my kimono, I tiptoed downstairs. Even in the dark I could see my grandfather everywhere, the riding crops in the hall stand, his panama hat on a marble bust of his father. In his study I turned on a lamp, picking up one object after another. Would the small fragment of blue tile stimulate his memory, or the fossil of a snail? I had assembled a pile of objects and photographs when I decided to look through his desk. I had reached the second drawer when my hand closed around a tin. Afterwards I would wonder if this was an infringement of my grandfather's privacy, but it was already too late. I pulled it out and put it on the leather blotter. The tin was oblong in shape and smelt vaguely of tobacco. Specks of rust were eating at the corners. Hesitating only for a second, I tried to prise open the lid. At last it gave, and the contents spilled out. The first object I examined was a half-medallion on a silver chain engraved with the letter L, the second, a small sprig of lavender pressed between some tracing paper. Last came a postcard of the Duomo in Florence. I turned it over and started to read.

Dearest Leonardo,

You are my best friend. It is you that I have thought of most while I have been away. I have missed you and I have many things to tell you.

Please be at home when I return.

With my love,

Valeria

I am not sure how long I sat there, the moonlight illuminating the objects on the desk, but my curiosity was ignited. What did each of them mean to my grandfather and why had I never seen them before?

The following morning, I was outside before the rest of the household was awake. As I crossed the cobbles to the stable yard, the moon had descended below the horizon, and the sun was rising, casting a pink glow on the whitewashed walls and paddocks beyond. I breathed deeply. A ride on my beloved Lyra in the stillness of the glorious Andalusian countryside would give me the strength I needed to face the day ahead.

Horses were everything to me, as they were to my grandfather. There was a time in my childhood when my ambition was to be a dressage rider with the goal of taking one of my grandfather's stallions to the Olympics. This was hardly surprising since many of my waking hours in Spain were spent in the stables or riding out with him. It was a sad moment when I had realised that I would never have my grandfather's talent. You can recognise excellence easily; it is that extraordinary fluidity, when horse and rider become one. Despite this revelation, riding remained my passion.

I could hear Lyra before I saw her. She was a feisty redhead, who hadn't learnt that kicking your stable door was unnecessary behaviour. However demanding she was, I loved her with all my heart. I would never forget the moment my grandfather had given her to me five years before.

'So what will you name her?' Papa Leo had queried, when the little foal had finally arrived.

'I'm allowed to choose?' I'd questioned in awe, staring at the delicate creature in front of me tottering on wobbly legs.

'You should always name your own horse,' he had replied. It was so typical of my grandfather, no ceremony and no build-up to this unexpected present.

'Lyra,' I said without hesitation.

'The girl in the book you've been carrying round all summer?' my grandfather murmured, kneeling beside me in the golden straw.

'Yes, Lyra Belacqua from *Northern Lights*.'

'Are you sure you want her? She's chestnut, and you know what they say about chestnut mares,' he reminded me.

'Fiery and unpredictable. That's *exactly* why I want her,' I replied.

I was in Lyra's stable when Dante stuck his head over the door. 'You wish to ride before breakfast?' he asked.

By that I presumed he meant the horse's breakfast, not my own. Horses came first at the hacienda.

'*Seguro*,' I responded, and in less than ten minutes we were riding out through the oak doors, with Estrella, Dante's lurcher, loping behind.

The Sierra Norte Natural Park was only a ten-minute ride from our own boundaries, and at its most glorious in spring. We had taken this route automatically, each of us wanting to avoid the plateau where my grandfather had taken his fall, but as we rode along in silence, my mind refused to be still. To distract myself, I tried to identify the different species of trees, the small animals inhabiting the sunlit glades. I listened to the birdsong, so pure it made my heart turn over, and the sound of water tumbling over rocks into the pools below. I even noticed the rhythmic tapping of beetles as they feasted on the dead wood.

We had come out of the forest and were riding upwards along a rocky trail when I recognised an eagle soaring in the sky above me. Watching the magnificent raptor, I remembered identifying a solitary lynx on one of my walks with my grandfather.

'Papa Leo, look, Iberian Lynx,' I had whispered, tugging at his sleeve, and for one enchanted moment, the yellow, spotted creature with extraordinary whiskers and compelling eyes had stared at us, before disappearing into the undergrowth.

'You have no idea how lucky we are, Little Mia,' he said. 'There are less than ten adults in the wild, and you have spotted one of them.' Afterwards my grandmother, Paloma, rewarded me with an ice cream. Now Paloma was dead, and my grandfather was fighting for his life and would probably never walk here with me again.

We were unsaddling in the yard when Dante turned his dark gaze upon me.

'I hope this has helped a little, Señorita Mia?'

'It certainly has,' I replied.

And it was true; by the time I had joined the others in the loggia for breakfast, I was able to face the day ahead of us. Just like my grandfather, it was only on a horse and in the open air that I felt completely free.

My mother and I soon established a routine, visiting the hospital each morning driven by either Peter or Ramon. As we greeted the nurses the answer was always the same. There was still no change. While I sat at his bedside, my mother left to complete tasks in Seville. There were meetings with my grandfather's lawyer to arrange power of attorney, and appointments at the bank. She would return flushed with exertion, and I would leave them alone. It is hard to describe my feelings in those early days, but I can say I was exhausted, not from actually physically doing anything, because that bit came later, but from watching someone, whom I loved so deeply, in a vacuum between life and death.

Poppy was my saviour; sometimes she would come to the hospital with us, and I would find her curled up in a waiting room chair with her law books and a notepad, her brow furrowed in concentration. When she saw me, she would jump up and fling her arms around me and drag me off to one museum or other, giving life a window of normality.

'Thank God, you saved me from Professor Winton's *Law of Tort*,' she said on one occasion, stuffing her book in her rucksack. 'Let's go and have some fun.'

Before long I became a familiar face at the tapas bars near the river, where I would sit and work on my copy for Dale before returning to the hospital. As the ventilator continued to deliver breath to my grandfather, I talked to him, sang to him, read from the same story books that he had read me when I was a child. One afternoon after falling asleep at his bedside, his hand enclosed in mine, I awoke with a start, filled with anxiety.

'Please, Papa Leo,' I begged him. 'Please wake up. You mustn't leave me, don't give up. Not now.'

Sometimes I was ashamed, realising I was not the only one who grieved. My mother would come out of his room ashen faced, tears sparkling in her eyes, and I wondered what had gone so badly wrong with my grandfather all those years ago. Some afternoons Ramon would visit his friend and as I glimpsed him through the glass panel, I hoped he was reminding Leonardo of a past shared and a life well lived.

Chapter Four

While the days blended into each other, there was nothing we could do but wait. Easter week would have slipped by unnoticed – an extraordinary departure for my mother – had it not been for the *Semana Santa* processions taking place in Seville.

On Holy Saturday, Poppy and Peter watched the last of the brotherhoods make their way to the cathedral to mark the end of the Holy Week celebrations, while we spent the day in the hospital.

In the past, I had always loved the pomp and pageantry of the processions, the lifelike wooden sculptures being drawn by gloriously decorated floats, but today neither my mother nor I were in the mood. Our only nod to the occasion was the traditional dinner on our return that evening with Aunt Gracia. Manuela had laid the table in the dining room, producing her famous Easter menu, while Gracia gave us a non-stop flow of anecdotes and stories. We had just finished Manuela's *Mona de Pascua* cake when Peter produced a bottle of Spanish honey-rum liqueur.

'So,' he said, swilling the amber liquid around his glass. 'What are your plans, girls? I need to be back at the office in a week's time and I'm booking your mother and myself on the Sunday evening flight.'

Poppy grimaced. 'I have to get back for my exams in the first week in May, so could you get mine too?'

I had been trying to forget the increasingly persistent emails I had received from Dale, asking me if sitting at the bedside of an unconscious relative was going to save his life. If I had disliked Dale before, my negative feelings towards her had gone into overdrive.

I fiddled with my glass. 'I know the doctors say he is out of danger, but I really don't want to leave Papa Leonardo.'

My mother leant across the table and squeezed my hand. 'You can always stay behind, *cariño*, tell that dreadful boss of yours to get back in her box and behave.'

'Rafaela!' Peter frowned at my mother, but I wanted to laugh. This was the mother I missed, the daredevil girl from the flower power era, who had run away with my father when she was only eighteen.

'As much as I would love to, Mama, there is a project in the office that I need to finish, which Dale has to sign off.'

'Oh well, if you are sure.'

After supper Poppy and I retreated to our usual position on the wicker sofa with the unfinished bottle of liqueur. She had just refilled my glass when she looked at me.

'You don't have to come back, you know. I will survive without you for a few weeks. I could even let the room!' she joked.

She ducked as I lobbed a cushion at her head and we both laughed.

'Seriously, Mia, I think you need to be here, your mother is right. I know Matt wants you home, but he can wait for a change.'

'My grandfather has always been there for me, now I want to be at his side.'

'Then you must stay.'

I looked at my sister for a long moment. 'You are absolutely right,' I declared, my confidence growing, 'I'll break the news to everyone in the morning.'

Once the decision to stay was made, I had some unpleasant calls to make. Dale was the first on my list.

'You're what?' she exploded down the phone. 'I've just given you two weeks' leave, and you have the nerve to give in your notice. And what about the anorexia editorial?'

I was about to remind her that I had been working throughout my time in Spain, when I thought the better of it.

'I'll complete that, Dale,' I said, for once standing up to her. 'Because at least this project is meaningful.' The call ended badly, of course, but it bolstered my courage to tell Matt that I wouldn't be coming home for a while.

'I know how much your grandfather means to you, sweetheart, but you can't just put your life on hold. What about the wedding plans – about us?'

'You can always fly out on the weekends,' I said after a long pause. 'And I can collect you from Seville.'

'It's not that easy, Mia – some of us have important careers, and it's still the football season, if you hadn't remembered.'

I held back any rude retort as Matt was obviously upset.

The night before my mother's departure, Gracia returned to the hacienda for a farewell dinner. This time she was unusually subdued.

'It has been so good to be with my beloved niece,' she uttered, pushing her pudding around her plate.

'It's been lovely for me too,' my mother said with a smile. 'And now I have a big favour to ask, Gracia. I need you to keep an eye on both my father and Mia, while I am in England.'

I was about to object when my mother gave me an artful wink.

'You know I will, *querida*,' my aunt said, her face lighting up. 'I shall give you regular updates; Mia may be grown up, but she will always be your child.'

'That's settled, then.' My mother folded her napkin and I understood how kind she was, putting everyone else's emotional needs above her own. With a few thoughtful words she had dispelled Gracia's insecurity.

While everyone was having coffee in the salon, I drew my great-aunt aside.

'Would it be possible to have a quiet word?' I asked. 'Perhaps we could go into Papa Leo's study.'

She followed me across the hall, her cane in one hand, her bag in the other. When I pulled out a chair for her, she sank into it.

'Is there anything wrong, Mia?' she asked. 'I haven't done anything to offend you?'

I smiled. 'You could never offend me, Gracia. It's just that—'

'Yes dear?'

'I found a tin in Papa Leo's study, I probably shouldn't have opened it but the contents made me realise I know nothing about Papa Leo's early life, or about his sister Valeria's.' I took the medallion from the pocket of my skirt. 'Do you know anything about this?' I asked, holding it out.

Gracia looked up at me and sighed. 'I wondered if you would ever come to me with these questions and yes, there are things you should know, things that worried Paloma as she was nearing the end.'

'And my mother isn't aware of these things?' I queried.

Gracia shook her head. 'I don't believe she is.' She stared at the floor and I could tell she felt uncomfortable, but I had to persist.

'Please Tía.'

She looked at me and smiled. 'You are so like your mother, she had to know everything.'

'But not this?' I queried.

'Not this,' she replied.

The conversation came to an abrupt halt when my mother entered the room.

'Everything all right?' she asked, and I knew she believed she was rescuing me.

'Fine, Mama,' I volunteered.

She gave me a conspiratorial smile. 'If you are ready to go back to Seville, Gracia, Ramon has brought the car to the front door.'

My great-aunt slowly rose to her feet. 'Thank you so much *querida*, you have been so kind.'

'Remember our agreement,' my mother said, kissing her cheeks. 'I am relying on you.'

'Never forgotten.' Gracia beamed.

I went towards her and hugged her hard.

'We will talk another time,' I whispered in her ear.

Chapter Five

When my mother arrived at breakfast wearing a smart dress, and her vintage Manolo Blahniks, I groaned inwardly. Those particular shoes meant only one thing: we were about to be invited to church.

'Who's for Mass?' she asked.

I winked at Poppy and an hour later we found ourselves attending the morning service at the *Iglesia de la Caridad*, in the Arenal neighbourhood of Seville. We were filing into our pew when my mother nudged me.

'That row is reserved for the members of the brotherhood,' she whispered, indicating the trio of elderly men who were huddled together at the front.

'Brotherhood?' At once I had visions of illuminati and secret societies – I'd recently read *Angels and Demons*, but these characters looked pretty ordinary to me.

'Brotherhood of Holy Charity,' she confirmed. 'There is a hospital attached to the church for the sick and destitute. The brotherhood looks after the patients.' She placed a prayer book firmly into my hand, her face innocent. 'Just an observation, you didn't think you would get away with not attending Mass while we were in Spain?'

'Of course not,' I replied, grinning.

The doors had closed, and the priest had begun his procession up the aisle, swinging the incense burner back and forth, when she added another layer of intrigue. 'I thought you would be interested to come to the church where your grandfather was married,' she whispered.

'Papa Leo was married here?' I asked, unable to contain my surprise.

'During the Civil War.'

I looked at my mother. There were things that were never mentioned at the hacienda and the Spanish Civil War was one of them. If it had ever come up, my grandfather had skilfully steered the conversation away. As we knelt for prayer, my mother's slim fingers touching the cross at her neck, I realised it wasn't only my grandfather's life that was shrouded in mystery. I recalled a quarrel I had witnessed between them shortly after my grandmother Paloma had died. I had been eight at the time and it had left me confused and upset.

'Why are you taking the child to Mass, Rafaela?' my grandfather had yelled. 'You are only filling her head with hypocritical nonsense. Where was God in *la guerra civil*?' He had stormed from the room, banging the door behind him. Now all these years later I wondered what had driven my grandfather's rage, and why he believed that God had deserted him. Perhaps some of the answers were hidden in the small metal tin. Whatever the consequences, it was time to find out.

When the church service was finally over, Poppy and I fled to the car, avoiding introductions to the members of the brotherhood. Then it was straight to the hospital for my mother to say goodbye.

'You cannot leave me, Papa,' she murmured, leaning over him, an expression of tenderness and regret crossing her face. In that moment I realised it often takes tragedy to heal wounds. I just hoped my mother wasn't too late.

*

The bell-tower clock was striking midday as we piled into the house.

While Poppy went in search of a shady spot with her battered copy of *Ulysses*, making the most of her last day in Spain, my mother returned to the office at the back of the house to finish off some paperwork. I could just make out Peter walking down a rocky path. I was on my way to fetch a glass of Manuela's homemade lemonade, when I paused at the foot of the sweeping staircase, reminded of the day when a small girl in pink dungarees had hovered on the landing above. Even now I could see the bright sunlight streaming through the circular window, bleaching the walls to a bright white and the spacious hallway below where my grandfather was waiting. I could see the spangles of fairy dust filtering onto the marble floor.

'You can do it, Mia, slide down!' he had encouraged, in his rich voice. With my heart fluttering in my chest, I had finally let go of the bannisters. The fear and jubilation as I had slid to the bottom was still with me.

'My brave little Mia,' he had laughed, catching me in his arms.

The drink now forgotten, I wandered through the maze of rooms, each one evoking a different memory. How I had loved standing with him in front of the muralled dining-room walls, listening to him bring the characters and animals to life. 'Do you see that monkey Mia?' he had chuckled. 'Well, that little mischief maker is called Panto, and the parrot, now that is Polonius ...'

The dining room had a special significance because it was where he had given me my first glass of wine. I had felt so grown up that evening, my head a little dizzy.

I recollected the games of hide-and-seek, the smothered giggles, the laughter, but today there was no Papa Leonardo to find me, no shoes tapping on the terracotta floor.

I leant against the flaking plaster walls of the loggia and closed my eyes, remembering the adventures we had shared. Everything had been a first: rock climbing at sunrise, riding in the hills, swimming in the river. I had done things I had never dreamed I was capable of.

If I opened my eyes again, would I see Papa Leo sitting in his usual chair, a glass of wine at his side? Would he be reading to me from my favourite book or weaving stories about Spain's exotic past?

I recalled the occasions when a sadness had seemed to settle on him and he had fallen silent, as if lost in his memories. In those days I had curbed my curiosity, but now I needed to understand why his face had sometimes closed at my questions, and why the room at the end of the corridor was forbidden to me. It was a strange day when he had taken me by the hand and had led me to the end of the passage.

'This is a room that you must never go into, Mia.'

'But why, Papa Leo?' I had asked.

'I do not have to tell you why, Mia, only that on this you shall obey me. Do you understand what I mean by integrity?'

I had shaken my head.

'It means that I trust you not to go into this room. Is that understood?'

I had nodded, knowing that whatever the reason it had to be important to my grandfather.

'I promise, Papa Leo.'

Now all these years later I was still intrigued. I climbed the stairs, and instead of going to my bedroom, I crossed the landing and walked along the passage. I could see the door was slightly ajar and as I got closer, I could feel a breeze coming from within, and the distinct smell of fresh flowers. I was tempted to enter, but the memory of my grandfather's words held me back. *Integrity, Mia.*

I paused for a moment, my heart quickening, then I turned and walked back the way I had come. Who would have opened the windows? I wondered, and why had they been in the room?

In the salon I found my stepfather scrutinising a small painting in a heavy gilt frame.

'I see you're admiring Goya's *Lady with a Fan*,' I observed. 'Not the original, I'm afraid, but it meant a lot to my grandfather. His father allegedly won it in a game of cards.'

'The original is in the Louvre.' Peter looked at me over the top of his bifocals and progressed to a French side table where he picked up an enamelled egg with a large jewel on the side. 'Did Leonardo ever tell you anything about this, Mia?'

The egg had always been a favourite of mine, and when I was a child its story had captured my imagination.

'It was given to Papa Leonardo's aunt, by a Russian countess when she came to stay,' I told him. 'His aunt had to offer her a foal in return.'

'If it's a genuine Fabergé, then it's worth a fortune. It really ought to be kept in the safe.'

I had extracted the egg from Peter and was opening the safe, when we were interrupted by my mother.

'Will you come into Papa Leo's office for a moment, Mia, there are some things we need to discuss before I leave.'

I could tell my mother was distracted so I sat down near my grandfather's desk and waited for her to speak.

'So much to sort out,' she said, turning her back on the mountain of paperwork to stare out of the window. 'Most of it can wait until I return, but I have arranged with the bank to continue paying the wages, and the utilities are up to date so the only money you will need is for food.' She handed me my grandfather's credit card with a wry smile. 'Manuela won't like it, but her housekeeping expenses may need to be curbed a little.'

'Is everything all right?' I asked.

'Just be sparing, my love, Papa Leo's book keeping has not improved over the years.'

With the time of their departure approaching, my mother and I ambled up our favourite track.

'I remember when the olive trees were cut down,' she murmured, gazing out over the empty fields. 'It was just after my twelfth birthday. Men came with axes and began to hack at the trunks, hundreds of ancient olives destroyed in a matter of days. Papa Leonardo had to restrain me from running to stop them.' She shaded her eyes and looked into the distance. 'I didn't realise he had given that parcel of land to the workers, rightly believing they deserved to own property, but what devastation—' She sighed, and I could feel her sadness at the loss of the trees all these years later.

We retraced our tracks down the hill and, after a quick stop at the stable yard to say goodbye to the horses, my mother opened the garden gate. I was trailing behind her when she picked a white flower with a dark-pink centre and put it in my hair. 'Hibiscus for my beautiful child,' she murmured.

'I'm twenty-eight. Hardly a child.'

She smiled at me. 'You will always be my precious child.' Her eyes had a faraway look and I wondered if she was thinking of her own father who loved her fiercely and was now lying in a coma.

She brought her gaze back to me, a soft smile on her face. 'Did you know that in Tahiti, a single red hibiscus flower tucked behind the ear signifies you are ready for marriage? But if I am correct, I don't think you are, *cariño*?'

I smiled at my insightful mother.

'I admit I am a little confused,' I whispered.

'I know I haven't made a brilliant job of it myself,' my mother said with a wry smile, 'but marriage is for life. Don't be pushed into anything if you are not sure, Mia.'

Relief flooded through me. I had been afraid to tell her my misgivings, in case she thought I was being foolish. I should have known her better. Her first life choice certainly hadn't been wise. Running away with my father when she was eighteen and then having a fling with him years after she had left him, had not been sensible, but despite the difficulties of being a single mother in a strange country, she had never regretted having me.

'Look what a jewel that mad moment brought me,' she had always said.

How I treasured those words. Perhaps her own youthful mistakes had made her into this wise and tender woman whom I loved so very much.

After promises of phone calls and letters, I watched my small family climb into the car and then returned to the stables for my ride with Dante. We had reached the promontory of the hill when we pulled up our horses, both of us aware of the sheer drop ahead of us.

'I imagine it was here,' I murmured, working out the scenario. 'Papa Leonardo would have done anything to save the horse.'

Dante patted his gelding's neck. '*Si, Señorita Mia*, I am sure this is the place. I warned your grandfather not to ride Seferino, and when the horse galloped into the yard lathered with sweat, I knew what had happened. Marte, he is steady and old, but the stallion ...' He shrugged his shoulders and sighed.

'It was not your fault. When my grandfather gets something into his head, nothing will stop him.'

'Seferino wasn't to blame.' He met my gaze. 'He is strong and powerful, but something must have scared him. My grandfather told me that Señor Leonardo was once the best horseman in Spain. But we all grow old.'

I smiled then, thinking of the man who challenged old age as he challenged so many things in his life.

'If Papa Leo doesn't wake up, Dante, then we must pray he goes quickly. At least he would have been doing what he loved best.'

Dante's face brightened. 'That is what my mama keeps telling me, Señorita Mia.'

Chapter Six

By the middle of May I had finished the only rewarding piece I had ever written for Dale. My obligations to her were now over, but Matt still hadn't come to Spain. Every time we spoke it was the same excuse.

'Sorry, Mia, it's the last match on Saturday and I also have a stack of work. Why can't you come home, then we can fix a date for the wedding?'

But the awful thing was, I didn't want to return. Surely I should be longing for a weekend break, trawling through the bridal shops with my mother and Poppy? But the thought of trying on wedding dresses filled me with dread. Nor did I relish standing on the side-lines for the match, followed by an evening in the pub with his football friends.

I was in the hospital corridor reading a text from Matt, when Angelina, the nurse who had comforted me that first night, sailed past me with a cheerful wave and Dr Canovas stopped at my side.

'I am pleased to say, your grandfather has had another good night. His vital signs are improving; he has a remarkable will to live.'

'Does that mean he could soon come round?'

'There are definitely hopeful indications. Now if you will excuse me, I have some patients to attend to.'

As I made my way to the hospital café to meet Tía Gracia later that morning, I sensed the subtle change. Perhaps it was the energy in his room or Nurse Angelina's optimism, but I felt a lightness within me as I pushed open the doors.

'I have ordered coffee and a *rosco frito* for both of us,' my great aunt said, her face lighting up as I pulled out a chair. 'Is that all right with you, *querida*?'

It was more than all right; the small doughnut-like pastries had been a favourite since my childhood. I had put my coffee-cup down and was wondering if the moment was right to ask my aunt about the tin, when she pre-empted me.

'Mia,' she started, 'I am sure you still have a lot of questions. May I suggest you come back for lunch at my apartment where it is a little more private.'

'That would be perfect,' I agreed.

After Gracia had looked in on my grandfather, Ramon dropped us outside a nineteenth-century building in the San Bernado district of Seville, before returning to spend time with his employer and friend.

I held my aunt's elbow as we walked from the lobby to the caged lift.

'Forgive me, the apartment is rather small,' she apologised, leading me through the dark hall to the sitting room. 'But this is all that I need.'

The apartment was by no means large but the amount of furniture certainly made it look even smaller.

'I am not very good at throwing things away,' she explained. 'Everything has a memory and I can't bear to let it go.'

There were photographs and Lladró porcelain figures on every available surface. Needlepoint cushions were piled on the burgundy velvet sofa.

'Paloma and my mother made those,' she said, plumping them up. 'If you will excuse me, I will make us something to eat. What about *Ensalada Murciana*? I remember you don't eat meat.'

'Tuna is one of my all-time favourites,' I reassured her, but when I offered to help she declined.

'You haven't seen the size of my kitchen, just stay where you are, *querida*,' she instructed, bustling from the room.

While preparation for lunch continued, I picked up some of the photographs. There were several of Grandmother Paloma as a young woman and family photographs in the garden of a large white house. As I gazed into the smiling face of a pretty girl with a bow in her hair, presumably Gracia, I was sure that the lonely flat in Seville was not how she imagined her future. I was looking at a photograph of a handsome young man in an RAF uniform when Gracia returned, wheeling a trolley.

'I see you have found Geoffrey,' she murmured.

'I hope you don't mind...'

'We were engaged to be married, you know.' Her head was on one side as she talked, and there was a wistful look in her eyes. 'I met him when I was working in England. I was a governess in a large house in Sussex, tutoring the twins for their higher school certificates. They were such a charming family. Tangmere airbase was nearby and we, that is, Sir Joseph's secretary and I, used to meet the pilots in the pub on their evenings off. They would come and relax before they went out on their sorties. I couldn't help but notice Geoffrey the first time I saw him, he was so handsome in his uniform, Mia, and very tall, I only came up to his shoulder. It wasn't long before he asked me out to dinner. After that we spent every available moment we could together and were so happy. Then one day he asked me to be his wife. I couldn't believe this kind, brave and good-looking man wanted to marry a girl like me. He was killed on his way back from the port of Brest. He went down with his plane somewhere over the English Channel. It was the twenty-ninth of March, 1941. The date is engraved in my heart. I never met anyone else that I could love, there was only Geoffrey.' She looked at me and the grief was etched on her face all these years later.

'I'm so sorry.' I wished I could hold the old woman in my arms, but she turned away.

'It was a long time ago.'

As we ate lunch at the oval mahogany table, I felt ashamed that I had never really got to know my mother's aunt. On the rare occasions I'd met Aunt Gracia when I was growing up, I'd found her trivial chatter annoying. I never knew she had been a teacher, engaged to a fighter pilot in the Second World War only to have her heart broken. There was so much I didn't know about my own family's history – I couldn't let these secrets go unsaid any longer, but for some reason the moment wasn't right.

I reached over and took her hand. 'Why don't you come back with me to the hacienda and stay overnight? We would have masses of time to talk after dinner.'

Gracia's eyes lit up. '*Estas segura querida?*'

'I have never been so sure of anything,' I replied.

I settled Tía Gracia in the guest bedroom downstairs, and afterwards we had supper together at a small table in the internal courtyard, the tin on the table between us.

We had finished our *crema catalana*, when she lifted her glass.

'Geoffrey always said an illicit thimble of sherry gave him Dutch courage before the pilots were scrambled. So, here's to Dutch courage.'

'Here's to the past,' I said, with a smile.

'You may wish I had never told you, so be warned, *querida*.'

'Don't spare me, Tía, I have to know everything,' I replied.

She laughed then, a soft melancholy laugh, and I held my breath, aware that something momentous was about to happen.

'Well,' she said, 'this is how your great-grandmother told the story to Paloma, and how she told it to me in turn. It all started a very long time ago when a small boy came over the hill…'

Part Two

Chapter Seven

July 1923, Andalucía

Leonardo slipped from his bed, pulled on his clothes and went out into the dawn. He knew where the horses would be. Last night he had seen them in his dream – eight of them cropping the grass, a stallion and his brood. But there was one amongst them that had captured his imagination – a grey with a coltish appearance. There was something about the proud head carriage, the promise of strength in his hind quarters that had drawn the boy. In the dream the colt had turned to look at him, encouraged Leonardo to approach him and had allowed him to spring onto his back.

Now as Leonardo ran down the veranda steps and called for his dog, he could feel his blood running faster. He was shutting the gate to the farm, when his mother leant through the bedroom window.

'Don't you be late, Leonardo, there are chores to be done; be back within an hour.' Adrianna pushed a sweep of glossy dark hair from her forehead, her face lighting up as she spoke. He blew her a kiss.

'*Madre*, for you, of course.'

*

Leonardo jogged down the lane. Even at eight his legs were long and well defined with muscle. While his father was away selling horses, he was the man of the house. It was really just the two of them, him and his mother, running the farm. Pedro didn't count. The old farmhand spent more time sitting in the sunshine on an upturned barrel than he did mucking out the stables.

Leonardo's thoughts were filled with optimism as he started up the rocky path, pausing occasionally to fill his lungs with the fresh, dawn air. How he treasured this hour of freedom before the day truly started, slipping away with his dog into the hills. The wild and untamed beauty of his surroundings fuelled his imagination and stirred something deep within his soul. By the time he reached the plateau at the top of the hill, the sun was climbing in the sky, heralding the relentless heat that would come. He gazed out over the barren scrub, his eyes skimming the landscape, but the only movement was the rustle of breeze through the tufted grass. He kicked at a pebble, sending it scurrying across the ground, disappointment blooming in his chest. He had been wrong after all. The small herd his father, Esteban, had put out the year before had moved to another part of the hill. He didn't have the time to track them and now the chance to ride the colt had gone. His father would return from the sales, and the mares would be caught, their offspring broken and sold. He was about to turn around when he caught a flash of movement out of the corner of his eye. He froze; they were ahead of him, unaware of his presence. He approached cautiously, one step at a time. He was only feet from the horses when a branch broke with a sharp crack, startling the herd. Leonardo watched in awe as the stallion took flight, the mares and foals following, but to his amazement the colt remained. For a brief moment he pawed the earth, his nostrils widened, snorting in indignation, completely unafraid. He looked at the boy, his ears pricked, then he trotted off, leaving Leonardo staring after him.

Leonardo sighed and whistled for the dog, but the lurcher was lost in a trail of scents, and it took several moments before she appeared over the horizon.

'Luna,' he scolded when the dog appeared at his side, 'you are very bad.' When Luna cowered, her head lowered to the floor, he stretched out his hand, remembering the sores that had covered her body, the lice-infested coat. 'Not that bad,' he said reassuringly. Luna had appeared one night, in the barn, a small curled-up stray, rejected from the world. It was only the light of the moon that showed the two eyes, glinting through the straw.

'We need to get home.' He started to jog. He could see the homestead below, the corral where his father kept the horses, the barn where he had found Luna. As they traversed the last stretch of the hill, he heard a noise rising from the valley floor, a scream that made the fine hair stand up on his arms.

He was running now, vaulting over boulders, leaping over streams. His lungs were bursting in his chest as he charged down the hill. He fell once, picked himself up and scrambled on. Luna, believing it to be a game, was jumping and yapping at his side.

As he reached the lane the screams grew louder. He chanted the words from the bible his mother had taught him over and over again: 'Lord, do not forsake me, my God, come quickly.'

He could hear his father's voice. Old Pedro was crying. He opened the gate to the yard and ran towards the house. He had to get to his mother.

A man was lying near the pig pens face down in the dust and, further away, his mother Adrianna was standing in the porch, her nightdress torn, her hand clasped to the side of her face.

'Mama,' he cried, reaching her at last. 'Mama, what is going on? What is wrong with Papa? Why is he holding a gun?'

For a brief moment she took her son in her arms.

'I love you, *mi querido niño*, never forget that, but now I want you to do something for me.' She was panting, her chest rising and falling, her dark eyes darting to his father on the other side of the yard. 'I want you to take Luna and run over the hill to the house of the Palamera de Santos. Ask for Doña Isabel. It is five kilometres from here, but you must ask for their help. Do not go near your papa and whatever happens, whatever you hear or see, you do not turn back.'

'But you are hurt, Mama, your face . . .'

She shook her head. 'No time for questions; go, Leonardo. Now.'

Esteban was striding towards them, his face contorted with rage.

'Get away from your mother.' He raised the shotgun.

Leonardo braced his back against his mother, protecting her from his father with his slim body.

'No, Papa, I won't,' he cried, his body trembling with fear. Luna edged nearer to Leonardo and bared her teeth at the approaching man.

'Go, Leonardo.' Adrianna gave him a push, but he turned and clung to her. She knelt briefly, and he buried his face in her shoulder, breathing in the smell of her.

'Go, Leonardo, I beg of you. Take my shawl and run!'

Leonardo ducked beneath his father's outstretched hand, gasping as the gun butt caught him in the back. He lurched forward, stumbling to his knees, but he picked himself up and sped towards the gate with Luna in hot pursuit. He had to get help for his mother. He could feel the blood pumping in his veins as he reached the lane and charged up the hill. His lungs were burning, but he pushed himself on. He had to get to the top, he had to get over the hill. He was wheezing, his sides heaving, but he kept on going. He turned for one last look back and a sob broke from his throat. He could see the small figure of Pedro below him. He was cowering on the ground, his hands covering his head.

Leonardo had reached the grassy headland when a noise echoed through the hills that made his blood run cold. It was a single shot from a twelve-gauge shotgun. He would have recognised the sound anywhere. He stopped, frozen in fear, his eyes scanning the terrain. Should he go back? But he had given his mother his word. He ran on, his temples thrumming as he raced over the top. He clutched at his side trying to ignore the sharp pain.

His father wouldn't have hurt his mother, he prayed. He would never do that. *Santo Dios*, he could never do that.

Chapter Eight

Valeria Palamera de Santos was sitting in the open doorway of the hacienda, reading a book when Leonardo appeared. One moment she was absorbed in the story, her small brow furrowed in concentration, the next, a boy was standing in front of her with a panting dog at his side. She jumped, for he had made no sound.

'You startled me,' she said, getting up from the step, taking in his dishevelled appearance, the rivulets of tears that streaked through the dust on his face.

'Is this the house of Doña Palamera?' he gasped, his chest rising and falling. 'Please, my mother – I've come from over the hill.'

'What is wrong?' she asked, longing to reach out to the boy to wipe away a tear.

'My father has a gun and . . .' His voice caught in his throat.

'What do you mean?' The girl's hand flew to her mouth.

'You have to help me, please. I think he may have hurt my mother.'

At that moment Alfonso, the butler, appeared in a stiff, black uniform. 'I apologise, Señorita Valeria.' He strode towards Leonardo and grabbed him by the collar of his shirt. '*Pilluelo,*' he said with disdain. 'Urchin, you should have come to the servants' entrance.'

Leonardo shook himself free, throwing a beseeching look at Valeria.

'Alfonso, fetch my mother.' She raised her small pointed chin and threw back her shoulders imperiously. 'Now.'

'Very well, señorita.'

When the butler had gone, an aggrieved expression on his thin face, Valeria touched the boy's knee. 'You are hurt, I ought to wash this.'

Leonardo flinched; he hadn't noticed the gash on his knee, or the blood running down his leg. 'Thank you, señorita, but there is no time.'

His head jerked up when a tall, elegant woman with auburn hair came into the hallway, accompanied by the butler. Leonardo charged towards her and tugged at her sleeve.

'Are you Doña Palamera de Santos?'

'I believe that I am.' The woman smiled, and a dimple appeared in her cheek.

'My mother told me to come here, she is in danger – my father is angry.' The boy bit his lip, his dark eyes huge in his oval face.

'And who is your mother, young man?'

'Adrianna. My father is the horse breaker.'

'I see.' Her expression changed. 'So you must be Leonardo.'

'Alfonso,' she instructed, 'run to the stables, tell Pablo to take three men and ride over the hill to the house of Esteban the horse breaker. They should take their guns. You, Leonardo, stay here with me and explain.'

'No,' he cried, trying to get away from her. 'I have to get back, don't you see? I have to help my mother.' When the señora held onto him with surprising strength, he finally collapsed into her embrace and she led him inside.

While Leonardo recounted the events to the señora, four men mounted their horses and galloped down the drive.

'I need to go with them,' he begged, breaking free and running to the window. 'I should take them to my mother.'

Isabel followed and put her arm around his shoulder.

'I promise you, my men will do their best to protect your dear mama.'

'You must know her?'

'I knew her well,' she replied, turning him to face her. 'She worked for my mother-in-law and became my friend. I loved her, Leonardo. She wrote to me when you were born and when you were christened.' Her shoulders sagged. 'She also wrote when my own son died.'

'Why did she never speak of you?' he demanded.

Isabel looked over Leonardo's head through the open window. How could she tell the boy that they had advised Adrianna not to marry the horse breaker, that her mother-in-law had tried to forbid it, but she had married him anyway. Except for three letters, Adrianna had cut her ties with the house.

She turned the boy to face her. 'You have to trust me, Leonardo, we will do everything we can.'

The next two hours seemed interminable to Leonardo. One moment he was hanging on to his dog, the next, his face was buried in the shawl his mother had instructed him to take after their last embrace. He scrunched up his eyes, trying to rid himself of the image of his mother's swollen cheek and the man lying in the dust.

When Isabel called for the housekeeper to take Leonardo to the kitchen, he made for the door. Bañu stood in his way.

'Where do you think you are going?' she questioned, her arms crossed.

'Home,' he whimpered, his eyes filling with tears.

'Would you feed this young man,' Isabel suggested. 'I don't imagine he has eaten today. And his leg needs looking at.'

Bañu marched the boy into the kitchen and pushed him down into a chair. She glared at Luna, who was glued to his side. 'And I don't want that scruffy lurcher in my kitchen. Valeria, take it to the yard.'

Leonardo held tightly on to Luna.

Bañu threw up her hands and stomped to the larder, returning with a glass of milk and a slice of tortilla. She slammed them on the table in front of Leonardo, then knelt down on the floor and ripped his trouser leg, completely exposing the wound.

'What are you doing?' he shouted. 'Those are my best trousers.'

'Not anymore, they're not.'

'My leg is fine,' he said, pulling away from her.

'I'll be the judge of that. Be still, boy. And you, Valeria, stop gawping at the *pilluelo* and make yourself useful.' She clicked her tongue at the girl. 'Get me some boiled water, salve from the medicine cupboard and a clean dressing.'

It was the second time in a day that Leonardo had been called an urchin. His chin thrust forwards and he glared at the old woman. 'My name is Leonardo, and my dog's name is Luna.'

'Your flea-ridden animal will be taken to the yard, and that is where he will remain.'

Leonardo was about to get up from the chair, when she pushed him back down. 'You will stay here until I have finished.' A smile flickered on the old woman's face. 'We can't have you dying of infection.'

While the old woman washed and dressed Leonardo's wound, Valeria stayed at his side, her gaze never wavering from his face.

'Why are you staring at me?' he asked.

'I'm trying to guess how old you are.'

Leonardo fidgeted for a moment before replying. 'I'll be nine in a month's time.'

'And I'm already nine,' she said, with a flash of triumph.

When the wound was dressed, the old woman slowly rose

from her knees. Leonardo went to help her, but she brushed him away.

'Be off with you and out of my kitchen,' she muttered. 'And take the hound with you.'

Leonardo grabbed the tortilla and bolted towards the door but found it was locked.

'That's the store cupboard, silly,' Valeria teased him. 'You had better follow me.'

Valeria led him to a bench in the courtyard outside, but Leonardo would not sit down. He threw the tortilla to Luna who leapt on it hungrily, while he paced the cobbles, stopping every so often to gaze towards the hills. Valeria kept pace with him, doing her best to distract him, trying to think of anything that could make the time pass until the men came back.

'Do you like horses?' she asked at last.

'*Por supuesto*, my father is a horse breaker.'

Valeria ignored the boy's abruptness and took hold of his hand. 'Well, then, come with me.' She led him up some wide steps and through an arched opening in the white wall. Leonardo's mouth dropped open. In front of him was the most beautiful stable yard he had ever seen.

There were twenty loose boxes facing onto an internal courtyard, with horses behind many of the green-painted doors. Carved stone pots were filled with bright geraniums and two grooms were sweeping the immaculate yard.

'Some of the horses are out in the paddocks,' Valeria explained as Leonardo went from one stable to the next, examining the occupants, patting their silken noses. He stopped outside the stall of a chestnut mare who nuzzled against his hand.

'We bred her,' Valeria told him, 'from one of our stallions. They are kept in the other block because you have to keep them away from the mares—' She giggled suddenly, her face turning pink, then skipped ahead of him. 'Come on, you will want to see this.'

Leonardo smelt the leather halfway down the passage, but he still whistled as Valeria opened the tack-room door. Dozens of saddles gleamed on wooden racks. There were shelves piled high with monogrammed blankets and saddle cloths and rugs for every possible occasion. There were indoor bandages and outdoor bandages. An entire wall was filled with bridles.

'*Santa mierda*,' he exclaimed and then it was his turn to blush. 'Sorry, my mother would kill me if she heard me swear.'

'*Holy shit* is a good expression,' Valeria said with a grin.

They were on their way to the paddocks when Leonardo shaded his eyes and pointed towards a hillside, several kilometres away.

'That's where I was this morning, before . . .' His voice trailed off and Valeria waited for him to continue.

'The plateau on the top?' he explained.

Valeria followed his gaze.

'That's where I saw the wild colt – dappled grey with a silver mane. The way he looked at me, he was fearless – I have never seen a horse like it before.'

'He sounds beautiful,' Valeria responded.

'I just wanted to get on his back, but it won't happen now, I will never see the colt again.' Leonardo bit his lip to stop his mouth trembling and Valeria took his hand.

'If you believe something strongly enough then it will happen, Leonardo.'

It was noon when the horsemen returned to the yard, their horses slicked with sweat. They dismounted silently, averting their gaze from Leonardo. When he rushed towards them, Valeria tried to hold him back.

'No, Leonardo,' she pleaded, but he shrugged her away.

Catching the man they called Pablo by the sleeve, he looked up at him. 'Tell me,' he screamed. 'Where is she, did you save her?' Tears were pouring down his face. 'You have to tell me.' He was pummelling at Pablo's chest when Señora Palamera de Santos came through the back door towards him.

'Leonardo, would you bring your beautiful dog to my sitting room?'

Finally, he let himself be led away by Isabel, but when she put her arm around his shoulders and held him close, he knew he would never see his mother again. The look in the señora's eyes had told him so, the gentleness of her voice. She shut the door of her study and gestured for him to sit beside her. Luna flopped at his feet.

'Leonardo,' she began, taking his hand, 'your mother is dead, I am so sorry.'

Leonardo drew in his breath. 'Where is she?' he said at last.

'They have taken her to the church for now.'

'I should have stayed with her, I should never have left her.' The boy was gulping for breath, his voice ragged. 'But she begged me to go, señora. She said I had to get help. I did what she told me, I ran and ran and ran. Now it is too late.' He buried his head in his knees, sobs racking his young body. 'Mama,' he wailed, rocking to and fro. 'I want my Mama.'

Isabel rubbed his back, 'I know you do,' she soothed.

He looked up at last, his eyes rimmed red. 'And my father, where is he?'

She stroked his cheek with the lightest touch. 'When the *rancheros* men arrived at the farm, your father had already gone.'

'What has he done?' he screamed, his voice echoing through the house.

Valeria was pacing outside her mother's study, when the old woman found her.

'Come,' Bañu took the child's arm, 'you'll wear out the floor, Valeria.'

'But Bañu, his mama is dead,' Valeria countered. 'What will become of him now?' She stopped her pacing, an idea coming into her mind. 'He has to stay here. Don't you see it is the only solution?'

The old woman brushed a strand of hair from the girl's forehead. 'You would take in every waif and stray if you could, Valeria. The boy must return to his own people.'

'Own people? He cannot return; what would become of him?' Her eyes were shining with passion and Bañu chuckled.

'You will have to talk to your mother, but I doubt she would need much persuading, she is nearly as soft as you. He could always live above the stables, I suppose, and work for his keep.' She wagged a finger at Valeria. 'But one thing is for sure, I will not have the boy or his dog inside.'

Valeria hugged her. 'The house has been so quiet, since Agustin died, I have no one to talk to.' Her hand flew to her mouth. 'I hope I haven't offended you, but you know what I mean.'

'I understand, *mi conejita*, and I agree, the house has been too silent since your little brother died. But you know the boy is lying,' she said, peering at Valeria. 'He's barely past his eighth birthday, of that I am sure.'

'You are probably right,' Valeria said with a giggle, 'but he has seen life, Bañu. Anyway, I am too old to be your bunny now that I am nine.'

At this Señora Bañu guffawed and took Valeria in her arms. 'You have an answer for everything, my child.'

Bañu's assumption was correct, Isabel had already made up her mind. She was sitting at her desk when Bañu knocked on her door.

'We can't send him back,' Isabel announced.

'And why not?' The old woman put her hand on her hips and faced her employer.

Isabel laughed, 'Because we can't, and you know that quite well.'

'From the moment I swaddled you as a babe in arms, I could see you were going to be impulsive,' Bañu stated.

'But you always said I should be strong and follow my heart, so I am doing just that.'

'I meant it, but this time I hope you know what you are doing. There will be consequences. And what is Don Carlos going to say?'

As the old woman walked back towards the kitchen, Valeria was in the inner courtyard comforting Leonardo. They were sitting on the edge of the fountain trailing their hands in the water. The dog was at their side. It was a touching sight, the two children with their heads together, one dark, one blonde, but as Bañu watched them, she had a moment of unease. There was no doubt the boy was fine-looking, his face a perfect oval, his eyes huge dark pools. His manners for the son of a horse trader were better than expected, but there was something wild about the boy, untamed. He would bring trouble to the house, she was sure of it. She slapped her forehead with her bony hand.

'You silly, fanciful old woman,' she said.

Chapter Nine

Leonardo's first few weeks at the hacienda were torture for the young boy. He was in a strange room, in a strange place, with only his dog to remind him of his past life. The horrific events of that late summer's day couldn't be kept at bay. Every night he would wake up screaming in the small bedroom over the stable yard, his bedclothes knotted around him, his mother's last words echoing in his ears. 'Go, Leonardo, I beg of you. Take my shawl and run!'

If only he had stayed, maybe he could have protected her, he thought, burying his face in the shawl, breathing in the fading scent of her. If only he had been a man and had stood up to his father.

When Juan, the groom, heard the boy crying at night from his quarters above the tack room, he believed the only way to help was to work him hard.

He gave the child so many jobs that he would fall into bed exhausted, but from the dark rings beneath his eyes, Juan realised sleep still eluded him. Leonardo became a silent shadow who moved through the stables doing everything without comment, only speaking to the dog and the horses. But Juan had witnessed the way the animals responded to him and soon suggested he should try his luck at exercising the quietest horse in the yard.

The moment he saw him climb into the saddle of the large bay gelding he knew he was witnessing something extraordinary. The boy was small on the horse, but the gelding responded to every gesture and direction. Before the month was out, Leonardo had advanced to schooling the youngsters. There was one horse that had caught Leonardo's attention, a young black stallion with a flowing mane and crested neck.

'I want to ride the Mad One,' he had requested, pushing the heavy wheelbarrow from the stable.

'That horse is out of bounds,' Juan had responded. 'The stallion is ridden only by Don Carlos and me. He has the name for a good reason; he is the trickiest horse in the yard.'

But every morning the question was the same. 'Can I ride him today, Señor Juan?'

It wasn't until Juan had watched him on a newly broken colt, that he had finally relented.

'You will follow my strict instructions and it will be in the ménage.'

Watching from the other side of the rails with the three other grooms, they marvelled at the boy's ability. Even though he was finally unseated, they had never seen anything like it before.

At first Valeria had kept away from Leonardo, understanding the boy's need to grieve alone, but on a fine early August evening, she found him in the stables long after the working day had finished.

'Shouldn't you be having supper with the men?' she asked. 'You can't work on an empty stomach.'

'Can't I?' he glared at her.

Valeria was not to be put off. 'I understand you feel angry, but I have done nothing to hurt you, Leonardo.'

Leonardo's head drooped.

'You are right on one thing, I am angry, Señorita Valeria.

Not with you, only with myself.' He kicked the straw with his foot and the horse turned to look at him. 'I should have stayed behind to protect my mother.'

'How could you have protected her? You did everything you could.'

Leonardo raised himself to his full height and puffed out his small chest.

'I am strong, Señorita Valeria, see.' He flexed his muscles and Valeria gritted her teeth to prevent herself from smiling.

'Extremely strong,' she agreed. 'But you are still a boy.'

Leonardo put the brushes back in the box, Valeria opened the stable door and they walked out together.

'And now what are you going to do?' she said. 'You have missed supper.'

'I'm not hungry.'

'Wait here, I am going to fetch some food from Bañu. We can go for a walk and have a picnic.'

'Is this an invitation or an order?' he grumbled.

'Definitely an order,' she said with a big smile.

A quarter of an hour later, laden with a basket and a rug, Valeria came back to the yard. Leonardo took the basket from her.

'So where are you taking me?' he asked.

'To the far pasture,' she replied.

As they ate, Valeria asked Leonardo about the silver half-medallion that hung around his neck.

'You don't have to tell me,' she said, her head to one side. 'Only if you want to.'

As Leonardo looked at her, he found he did want to tell her, for Valeria was as kind as she was pretty.

'My father wears one half of the medallion, I wear the other,' he explained. 'It was a present from my mother and she said we should never take them off.' He bit his lip and Valeria took his hand.

'Just remember whenever you are sad that I am here, Leonardo.'

After the first outing, a routine was established. Valeria would arrive at the stables just as Leonardo was finishing his work and they would walk to different parts of the estate. They would return in time for the men's supper. By telling Leonardo about her own life, Valeria gradually began to draw him out of himself. Soon some of his old humour was restored and he was laughing and joking with Valeria. They were ambling back to the hacienda one evening when she told him about Bañu.

'She is actually like a mother to the entire family,' she explained. 'And as you have seen, she runs the house with an iron hand.'

'I have seen,' Leonardo agreed, and Valeria laughed. Leonardo thought she had a beautiful laugh that crinkled the corners of her eyes.

'When my brother died three years ago, Bañu was the one who kept our family together.' Valeria shrugged her slim shoulders. 'Papa was so sad, he has never got over it. I heard Mama say he blames himself for what happened, so now he spends most of his time in Seville. You see, Papa went down first with the influenza. He eventually recovered, but Agustin didn't stand a chance. He was so little … Mama couldn't stop crying for months. She went to her room and didn't come out. Bañu told me that it happens sometimes with parents, they are so unhappy they forget they have another child.' She turned away and Leonardo wanted to hold her and never let go.

'I'm sorry, you must miss him very much,' he murmured.

'Bañu says he will always be with me, up here.' She tapped her forehead. 'Do you believe that with your mother?'

'I'm not sure anymore.'

They had reached the stables when Leonardo turned to look at Valeria.

'Aren't you sad that your father spends so much time away from home?'

'He has to leave us for work.'

'*Los caballos*, he leaves those too?' Leonardo asked, and Valeria laughed, the mood broken.

'He leaves the horses too, Leonardo.'

Chapter Ten

Carlos Palamera de Santos was proud of his lineage. He could trace it back to the Hapsburg kings. In fact, he was proud of many things in his life – his beautiful wife, his daughter, Valeria, and his estate. The hacienda and the accompanying hectares had been in his family for centuries. They had survived famine and wars, they had been on the right side in many a rebellion, but there was one thing they had not been able to prevent: the death of Agustin. Every time Carlos thought about his son, he was overcome with grief. His enchanting, fragile son had died, while he had survived.

But on this temperate September morning, as he walked to the small family palace in the old Jewish quarter in Seville, his mind was full of the immediate beauty of his surroundings. Sunshine was filtering through the narrow alleyways onto the intricately patterned pebbled floors. Though he took this route every day, he still appreciated the many secluded courtyards hidden behind ancient archways, or open wooden doors. Like its name, this area had once been home to hundreds of Jewish families, but they had been forced to flee this charming district, centuries before. He was nearing his house when he remembered the letter in his pocket. He pulled it out and tore open the envelope: '*My Dearest,*' it read. '*I know you have pressing matters to attend to, but there is something I must ask . . .*'

A smile crossed Carlos's face. What was his wife Isabel up to this time? He had never refused her anything and the 'ask' was merely a formality. He remembered the first time he had seen her, at a party given by his maternal grandmother. At first, he had refused to go, hating the stifling atmosphere at her soirees, despising the formality, the etiquette, the constant presence of her priest.

'But we must attend, *querido*,' his mother had said. 'Don't worry, I shall protect you from your grandmother's match-making.'

'Mama, I will choose whom I marry. There will be no inbreeding in my house.' He was alluding to the hapless and deformed Charles II of Spain, who was the result of the marriage between an uncle and his niece.

'I have no doubt that you will,' his mother had replied with a smile. This sentiment had prevailed, and he had arrived at the house in Granada in a defiant mood. It was not until he had walked into the *salón de baile*, and he had seen the girl sitting at his grandmother's side, that his humour had returned. Her hair was piled on her head in soft auburn curls. She was wearing a demure white dress, but the look on her heart-shaped face made him want to laugh out loud. There was a rebellious pout to her full lips and a glint of fire in her grey eyes.

He had walked across the room and had bent over her hand. 'Ghastly, I know,' he had whispered. 'But at least we can try and have fun.'

That was twelve years ago, and the seventeen-year-old girl he had met that night was now a beautiful woman. But there was the one great tragedy in their lives. No one could give them back their son.

He skimmed the letter, a frown creasing his wide forehead.

So Esteban the horse breaker had murdered his wife, and Isabel had taken in their child. But the boy had already been at the hacienda for two months, so Isabel was not really asking him. No, his beautiful wife was demanding his presence at home. He rapped on the studded oak door and, after a short wait, it was opened by a liveried footman. He nodded and gave him his hat.

'Forgive me, señor, I was ...'

Carlos cut in, '*No seas ridículo.* You don't have to be on hand for my possible arrival every moment of the day. I am sure you have better things to do.'

The man looked flustered and Carlos was momentarily ashamed. He smiled. 'You do your job well, Ruiz, there is no issue with your work.'

He walked down the corridor and into his study and drew in his breath. With rumours circulating in Seville, it was not the best time to be returning home.

Only yesterday there were whispers in his club that General Miguel Primo de Rivera, with the support of the King and the army, would overthrow the elected government by force. Carlos admired the general, but he also believed in democracy.

As he poured himself a glass of madeira, he thought of the current political climate in Spain. The Cortes, the democratically elected Spanish parliament, had found no solution to the poverty and unrest inside Spain, but now they would investigate the responsibility of the king in the crushing defeat in Morocco. Yes, the war had been costly, but this was tantamount to treason. Despite his unease, he would have to side with the generals.

He sat down in one of the comfortable armchairs and reread his wife's letter, the tension leaving his shoulders.

So this boy could ride like a *caballero*, he could apparently even speak like a gentleman – he doubted this, but he was indeed intrigued. He longed to see his wife and daughter and he couldn't make excuses forever. He would leave Seville in the morning. The coup, if there was to be one, would take place without him.

As he ate an excellent supper in the walnut-panelled dining room, he accepted he needed to be at home. The memories of Agustin were all around him there, but he could not hide forever.

After sacking his previous estate steward, Miguel de Rosa, he needed to make sure his successor, Thiago Gallego, was not committing the same indescribable wrongs. He gritted his teeth, remembering the day he had heard of de Rosa's treatment of the labourers on the estate. Apparently, they were beaten for the smallest misdemeanour, and their pay had been halved. Carlos and his father before him had always prided themselves on the favourable conditions at the hacienda. The steward could have destroyed everything they had worked so hard to achieve. Carlos drained his glass and went to sort his papers for the journey home.

Chapter Eleven

Valeria was waiting for her father at the door of the hacienda. She ran down the steps and hurled herself into his arms.

'Papa, Papa! Thank goodness you're home. I have been expecting you forever.'

'It is wonderful to see you at last, *mi corazon,* my heart.'

She caught his hand and dragged him up the steps. 'Have you heard about my new friend?'

'Nothing but,' he said with a grin.

He held Valeria close until his wife came across the hallway towards them. 'Isabel,' he breathed. 'Will you forgive me for staying away so long?'

She pulled away from him. 'This time it has been too long, Carlos.'

'I will make it up to you, I promise, it's just that—'

'I know what it is about. But we have needed you here.'

'I have failed you, Isabel.'

Her eyes sparkled. 'A little. But I might forgive you.'

He drew her close. 'How I missed you.'

Isabel's smile softened. How quickly she was won over, but then she had never been able to resist her husband.

'So,' he said, putting his arm around her waist. 'Shall we go in to lunch?'

Isabel inclined her beautiful head. 'Lunch first, and then I imagine you will want to meet Leonardo. The boy was so traumatised when he first arrived, he hardly spoke, but now…' She laughed. 'His true character is beginning to emerge. He is a very unusual boy; I think you will find him intelligent and amusing.'

'I am indeed intrigued to meet this paragon of virtue you talk about.'

She leant against him. 'You had better not tease me or there will be consequences.'

'I like consequences.' He grinned.

As Valeria chattered on, Carlos's gaze drifted around the dining-room walls. The jungle fresco had been commissioned to celebrate his son's birth. The animals were from books he had treasured as a child. There were monkeys, elephants, even a parrot called Polonius, but there was no Agustin to enjoy them. How he had loved the look on his little boy's face when he told him the stories, how infectious his gurgling laughter had been.

It was wonderful to be at home, so good to be with his beloved wife and daughter, but in his mind's eye little Agustin was everywhere and nowhere. He could see him toddling towards him across the lawn in his smocked rompers, the funny little sun hat on his head; he could hear his laughter the first time he had been put on the fat white pony. But the final image was of his pale little face as he lay gasping for breath in the nursery upstairs. When Carlos could bear it no longer he pushed back his plate.

'Will you excuse me, Isabel. I cannot contain my curiosity any longer. I wish to meet Leonardo.'

*

Luna saw the stranger approaching and careered over the cobbles, her tail wagging.

'And who are you?' Carlos asked, bending down to ruffle the creature's coat. 'If not the strangest animal I have ever seen.'

'She is not strange.' A boy had come out of the shadows and now stood in front of him. He had wide dark eyes and his hair was powdered with stable dust. So this was the boy, he thought.

'You expect me to agree that this ragged hairy beast is normal?'

'Of course she is. Luna is a queen amongst dogs,' Leonardo said with a grin.

Isabel was right, the boy was entertaining.

Juan shot out of the stable and cuffed Leonardo on the ear.

'Don Carlos, forgive this foolish child. He should know better.'

Leonardo swept a deep bow, 'Leonardo Castrellon at your service, my lord.'

Carlos wanted to laugh out loud. 'That's a fine bow, young man. And your name suggests you are from one of the oldest families in Spain.'

'I think you will find that my ancestors were servants of the oldest family and took their name.' The child had an answer for everything, he was neither subservient nor afraid.

'What else do you know, Leonardo?'

Leonardo looked at him, his head on one side. 'I know about horses, sir.'

'So I have heard.'

'Juan has given me work in the stables. Do you know, last week I even rode the Mad One and I lasted at least ten minutes before falling off.'

'You did what?' Carlos shot a furious glance at Juan, for the Mad One was the name they had given to the stallion that few could ride.

'He begged me, Don Carlos, and he is very persuasive.'

'That won't happen ever again, Juan. I'll not be responsible for the lad breaking his neck.'

'But I wanted to ride him,' Leonardo interrupted. 'It was not his fault.'

'You will not ride him again. Do you understand?' Carlos was used to being obeyed.

Before Carlos left, he leant down so that his eyes were level with the child's. 'I am so sorry about the loss of your mother,' he murmured.

The boy met his kind gaze, tears immediately springing to his eyes. He wiped them on his sleeve and drew back his shoulders. 'Thank you, señor, but today I am trying not to think about it,' he said.

As Carlos walked back towards the house, he turned to see Leonardo receiving a second cuff around the ear from Juan.

'Juan, you will refrain from hitting the boy,' Carlos instructed, a faint smile playing on his lips. He wasn't sure who looked more insulted, Leonardo or Juan.

Chapter Twelve

Years later, Carlos would look back on those days at the hacienda as a golden world, before the storm came. Despite the tragedy of Agustin, he would still consider them to be some of the happiest of his life. Each morning before breakfast he would ride out with Leonardo and Valeria, Luna loping behind. While his daughter rode Balada, a pretty grey pony, Leonardo always rode one of the larger horses.

'Ponies are for girls,' he taunted.

'I'm not a girl,' Valeria had cried out in her defence.

'Well, then, why are you wearing a skirt?'

At the time Carlos had difficulty keeping a straight face, recognising the growing confidence and plucky nature of the boy. He had brought happiness back to the house and even the impossible Bañu made allowances for him.

Carlos had always been a little wary of Bañu. Her loyalty was unquestionable, and indeed her honesty, but for him she was a bossy old witch. He tolerated her because he knew she would die for Isabel and Valeria.

'I am not the master in my own house,' he had once complained to his wife.

'None of us are masters in this house,' she had laughed. 'Except Bañu, of course.'

Carlos considered himself an excellent horseman, but he marvelled at the way Leonardo handled even the trickiest stallion or mare with just the lightest touch of his hands or an imperceptible movement of his leg. His body was a miracle of fluidity and his commands were almost impossible to detect, yet the horses always did his bidding.

'I use my seat and my mind,' he explained. 'I realise that you should never command a horse, you should request politely, and then he will try to please you.' Carlos would remember these words for the rest of his life.

But beneath the boy's fearlessness, he was still a child, longing for the home he'd lost. That night Carlos took his glass of port onto the terrace after dinner, and heard a faint, strange moaning from the direction of the barn. He found the boy curled up in the straw with his dog, his shoulders heaving in misery. Leonardo seemed unaware of his presence, so Carlos sat down in the straw beside him.

'Port?' he asked, offering him the glass.

The boy sat up and sniffed. 'But señor, I am only nine.'

'Are you?' he said. 'I had quite forgotten. I was about to offer you a cigar.'

The boy giggled through his tears. 'You must know you should never smoke near stables, let alone in the straw. And besides, I don't like cigars.'

'So you have tried them?'

'Mama let me try one of Papa's once, and it made me cough so much I wanted to be sick.'

'Perhaps she thought it would put you off for a while,' Carlos said with a smile.

'Oh no,' Leonardo said, brightening. 'Quite the opposite, she told me that a man should learn to smoke a cigar correctly!'

Carlos roared with laughter and the barriers were down. As

the dog put his head on his immaculate black evening trousers, Carlos put his arm around Leonardo's shoulders. 'I can feel you're missing your mother.'

Leonardo looked at him for a moment, his eyes glistening in the darkness.

'I miss her every single moment of the day, señor.' His narrow shoulders started to shake again. 'You see, it was my fault, I shouldn't have left her with my father. If I had stayed behind—'

'Leonardo, *mi querido niño*, your mother was trying to save you. You couldn't have changed anything except that you may have been hurt too.'

'I dream about her, señor, terrible dreams when she is begging me to stay, and I leave her because I am a coward.'

He gripped the boy by the shoulders. 'You're not a coward. You're the bravest boy I know. You were only doing what your mother asked. And it was right that you came over the hill to us, Leonardo. It was what your mother would have wanted.'

'Do you think so, señor?'

'I know so, Leonardo. You have come into our lives and have made our family so happy.' Carlos's voice thickened. 'If my own son, Agustin, had lived, I hope he would have been as brave as you.'

Leonardo wiped his eyes with his sleeve.

'Thank you, Leonardo,' Carlos said finally, standing up and brushing the straw off his trousers.

'I should thank you, señor. You have been so kind to me, and I do feel a little better most of the time. But then it catches up on you, doesn't it?'

'It certainly does,' Carlos agreed.

'Well, you know you can always talk to me, señor,' he had said. 'I understand what it is like to lose someone so important that you think your heart will burst with misery and never ever heal.'

As Carlos walked back to the house, he had raised his face to the sky. It was as if a huge weight had been lifted from his shoulders too; something had healed in his own heart.

Two weeks after his arrival home, Carlos and Isabel were having breakfast together.

He glanced at his beautiful wife. 'Why don't you take Valeria to Seville to buy her some clothes?'

'Your daughter cares not a fig for dresses.'

'Well, then, buy her some pantaloons instead,' Carlos jested.

Isabel put down her coffee. 'Is there anything I should know, *my love*?'

He sighed. 'I would like to take Leonardo for a ride, just the two of us. It is easy to forget that it is only a few months since his mother's death, and I would like another chance to talk to him, man to man.'

Isabel leant across and put her hand over her husband's. 'You mean man to nine-year-old.'

Carlos smiled. 'You are right, that is what I'm trying to say.'

'You're a good man, Carlos. I will tell our daughter we are going on an outing to Seville.'

On the morning of their ride together, Carlos was up early, surprised at how eager he was to be with the boy once more. He would show him the lake where his own father had taken him so many years before. He drained his coffee and went out to the stables to find Leonardo.

After a leisurely ride through the oak woods in the *parque natural*, they stopped at the side of the lake, letting out the reins for the horses to drink.

Carlos reached out his hand, touching the boy's shoulder. 'I enjoyed our talk in the barn.'

'It is the first time since my mama died that I have slept well, señor.'

'And I slept well too, Leonardo.'

When the horses had drunk their fill they rode on, and Carlos told him about his own father who had lost a leg in the Spanish American war in 1898 but had continued to ride with a tin replacement until he was ninety.

'I inherited my love of horses from my father,' he explained.

'It is the same for me, señor.' Leonardo turned to Carlos, his eyes clouding. 'Do you think my father was all bad, señor?'

'I don't believe he was. Sometimes men can do terrible things in the heat of the moment and they spend the rest of their life regretting them.'

'But supposing I am like him? What if I do something like that?' Leonardo asked.

'I can put my hand on my heart and say you will never do anything like that, Leonardo.'

While Carlos was riding in the Sierra Norte with Leonardo, Isabel and Valeria were driven to Seville.

As they walked past the cathedral, Valeria held onto her mother's hand. 'Why is everyone looking at me, Mama?' she asked.

'It is your colouring; golden hair and blue eyes are most unusual in Spain.'

'But you are fair, so why aren't they looking at you?'

Isabel laughed, 'Because I am getting older, but you are as pretty as an angel, *querida*.'

'You are beautiful to me.'

After a spoiling lunch, they wandered down to the *Guadalquivir* river and watched the ships go by.

'Perhaps I shall be a pirate when I grow up,' Valeria informed her mother.

'I think I'd rather you were not,' Isabel said with a chuckle, 'but if you were a pirate, Seville would be the right place.'

'Really?' Valeria's eyes were round.

'For two hundred years, Seville was the trading centre of the western world and our river the most important route for Atlantic ships. So where would you find the richest ships to plunder?'.

'Ships coming from Seville,' Valeria shouted in reply.

The remainder of the day was spent in *Calle Sierpes* looking at the shops.

Before the driver came to pick them up, Valeria tugged at her mother's sleeve.

'We must buy a present for Leonardo, he has no one but us.'

'That is a lovely thought.' Isabel kissed the top of her daughter's head. 'You have a generous soul.'

They found the Indian headdress at the best toy shop in Seville.

'This is perfect,' Valeria said, parading in front of the shop mirror. 'He will love it, Mama.'

Leonardo had finished in the stables when the family invited him for lemonade in the loggia.

'We have a present for you,' Valeria cried, hopping from one foot to the other as she held on to the box.

Leonardo's face lit up when she handed it to him. 'For me?'

'For you,' Valeria replied, as he undid the ribbons.

Carlos bent down and slipped the headdress over his hair. 'My, what a formidable Red Indian you make,' he announced, stepping back.

Leonardo giggled, and Valeria sped from the loggia towards the garden.

'Don't imagine you can catch me,' she taunted.

Carlos and Isabel smiled as the youngsters' whoops rang through the air.

*

Later that evening at supper, with both children now in bed, Isabel put down her fork.

'How did you get on today with Leonardo?'

'We had an excellent ride. He is such a brave little boy, he has quite taken my heart.'

Isabel glanced at him with a passing look of sadness. 'I hope you are not forgetting our son. It still feels like yesterday to me.'

'My dearest Isabel, I will never forget Agustin. He is with me every moment of the day. Every breath I take I am reminded of him, but God has chosen to bring Leonardo into our lives and he is the one who needs us now.'

For the first time since Agustin had died, Carlos was unwilling to return to Seville.

'I have to resume my duties at the bank,' he said reluctantly, when Valeria clung to him.

'But Papa, you can't leave, it will soon be Christmas.'

'It's eight weeks until Christmas, Valeria.'

'But I will miss you and Leonardo will miss you too, won't you, Leonardo?'

The boy, who was watching from a distance, stared at the ground.

'Leonardo,' Carlos called.

'*Si, Don Carlos.*' Leonardo shuffled forward.

Carlos put his arm around Leonardo's slim shoulders and the boy relaxed. When he drew backwards, the child's eyes were filled with disappointment. He patted the top of his head. 'Remember what I said, you are the bravest boy in the world. Look after Doña Isabel and Valeria for me until I get back.'

'With my life, señor.' He smiled through his tears.

Valeria plonked herself down on one of the suitcases that

littered the hall and refused to move. 'I am keeping you a prisoner, Papa,' she stated, with a big pout.

'Really?' He picked her up and hugged her.

She wound her arms around his neck. 'If you love me, why are you going?' she asked.

'Because some of us have to work to keep their little girls in nice dresses. Or pantaloons, in your case.'

Valeria giggled and hung on tighter.

Carlos put her down and tweaked her pigtails. 'Behave for Mama and take care of your new friend.'

'Leonardo is good for our family, is he not, Papa?'

'You are right, as usual, *mi corazon*.'

Dios Mío, he thought, as he walked to the waiting car, there was something about the boy. How could this small ragamuffin have brought so much joy to the family? He had noticed over the last few days that even Isabel had started to laugh again.

As the Rolls Royce Silver Ghost drew away in a cloud of dust, he watched his little family recede into the distance with a heavy heart.

Chapter Thirteen

With new branches of the bank in Madrid and Barcelona, Carlos's days were spent travelling between the two cities and dealing with issues at the head office in Seville. Whatever the political climate, everyone needed money and wanted to make a friend of him. Despite the newly installed phone line that enabled him to keep in touch, he couldn't wait to get home.

On 22 December, his car laden with presents, Carlos arrived back at the hacienda. It was pouring with rain. The butler came out with an umbrella and together they ran towards the house where Valeria was waiting on the step. She offered her wet face to kiss.

'You are soaked through, *pequeña*. Come inside, you are wearing only the flimsiest dress.'

'Papa, come and see the tree. Mama's English cousins said we had to have one and I decorated it with Leonardo. Luna ate the Christmas star, but Bañu made another.'

Words spilled out of her mouth and Carlos laughed. 'So that creature comes into the house?'

'I assume you mean Luna and not Leonardo, Papa?'

'Go and change, you will catch your death of cold,' he exclaimed, planting a kiss on her head.

'Luna doesn't come in all the time, Papa, only when Bañu permits. Sometimes she even makes her sit outside.'

'But the stable quarters are warm, surely?'

'Not as warm as the house, Papa.'

Carlos laughed. His daughter knew she could get around him, and she used every female ruse. 'You are impossible, Valeria! You will be asking me next if Leonardo can spend Christmas Day with us.'

'Oh yes please, Papa. *Es una idea brillante.*'

On Christmas morning after the family had returned from church, Leonardo came inside with Luna. The dog was immediately banished to the boot room by Bañu.

'It's either me or the dog.' Bañu pointed to the room at the end of the passage.

'I know which I would choose,' Carlos leant over and whispered to his wife. Isabel smacked him lightly on the arm.

Carlos had brought presents for everyone, including Leonardo. As the boy pulled the wrapping paper off a cardboard box and opened the lid, his mouth dropped open. Inside was a *vaquera* jacket made from the softest wool. It had five buttons on the front and five on each sleeve.

'Does this make me a proper *caballero*, señor?'

'You are already a *caballero*, Leonardo. Anyone who can ride like you is a knight and a gentleman.'

The boy's face shone and then his eyes clouded. '*Mi madre* called me her *pequeño caballero.*'

Isabel went to the boy and knelt on the floor beside him. 'She would be proud to see you in that beautiful jacket. Shall we put it on?'

She undid the buttons and helped Leonardo into it. 'Look at you now, how very handsome,' she murmured.

Leonardo stood in front of the floor-length hall mirror, turning this way and that, puffing out his small chest.

'It will be the most special thing I have ever owned apart from this.' He touched the half-medallion around his neck.

Carlos stood behind the boy as he gazed into the mirror. 'It must be precious to you.'

'Very precious,' he said with a sigh. 'It is my last present from *mi madre*. She gave the other half to Papa and said we should never take them off, but she is dead now, and my father?' He lifted his hands in a gesture of resignation. 'I don't know where he is and why he hurt Mama. Maybe the *policía* found him and took him away and he is dead too.'

Carlos put his hands on the boy's shoulders. 'You are here now, and we will always care for you. I have been speaking with Doña Isabel, and we think it will be better if you had a bedroom in the house with us, Leonardo. Would you like that?'

Valeria didn't wait for him to reply. She hurtled across the room, throwing herself at her father. 'Papa, thank you. Please say yes, Leonardo. You will be part of our family.'

'I would be honoured, señor.'

'Wonderful, that settles it.' He smiled. 'And before you ask, the bedroom is on the ground floor with access to the garden, particularly appropriate for Luna.'

That night as Leonardo lay in his new bed, his mother's shawl hugged to his chest, he felt her loss so deeply. The señor and the señora had been more than kind, but he longed for Adrianna, ached for her comforting arms, her words as she lulled him to sleep following a bad dream. It was as if a hole had been ripped in his chest, tearing her away from him.

It would have been the first time he hadn't climbed into his mother's bed early on Christmas morning, the first time he hadn't buried his head in her warm neck, waiting in excitement for his Christmas box, hand painted by his mother and filled with treats. He remembered her crafting little gifts in the winter evenings and hiding them behind her back if he peeked. On the Eve of the Epiphany there would be another present, something she had found in the woods, a fossil or a magic stone. Afterwards he would display them on the shelves along with his other treasures, but now there was nothing left. The landlord had taken the livestock in lieu of rent, then he had burnt the contents of the house, every stick of furniture, every memento before they had time to retrieve them. Tears squeezed from his eyes as he remembered the señora breaking the news.

'I am so sorry,' she had said, 'but everything has gone, my child.'

'Have the wild horses been sold?' he had asked, despair gripping him.

'I am afraid so, Leonardo.'

And now even his mother was leaving him. Though she inhabited every corner of his mind, he could no longer smell her. He tried to conjure her voice, but it wouldn't come. He would never again hear her call him her most special boy.

He beat his fist into the pillow. 'Please, Mama, please come back to me,' he sobbed. 'Please let me see your face,' but as hard as he tried, her face was indistinct, floating in the haze of the darkroom.

On the other side of the house, Valeria was leaning out of her bedroom window, gazing at Taurus, her favourite constellation, when she heard Leonardo's sobs. She put on her slippers and ran downstairs and across the central courtyard. She was starting to shiver when she tapped on Leonardo's door.

'Are you all right?' she whispered.

'Go away.'

'Unless you want me to freeze to death, let me in.'

The door opened a crack and she pushed past Leonardo, jumping on the bed beside Luna. The dog thumped her tail.

'You can't be unhappy on Christmas Night. It's not allowed.' She put out her hand and wiped away his tears. 'Please don't be sad, Leonardo.'

Something shifted in Leonardo's heart. When Valeria smiled he felt a lightness in his chest, and he couldn't help but smile back at her.

Chapter Fourteen

1928

As the years flew by, Leonardo grew tall and strong, his dark hair bleached by the sun so that it was tipped with gold. By the time he was twelve, he was not only in charge of breaking the horses, but he was also training them to perform movements they did naturally in the wild. The dressage ménage had been extended and now had a shaded pagoda at one end. Berto, a celebrated trainer from the *Cartuja* stud in Jerez, was commissioned to instruct Leonardo. Carlos and Isabel would watch with their friends.

'Now this is the *passage*,' Isabel would murmur, her eyes fixed on the boy.

As Carlos's most prized stallion performed the highly elevated and powerful collected trot, they would sigh at its beauty and artistry.

'You could become a *rejoneador*,' Carlos suggested to Leonardo after Berto had finished his instruction for the day. 'You would be accepted anywhere in Spain.'

'Surely you wouldn't ask me to risk these beautiful horses in the bullring?' the boy had responded, a frown creasing his forehead as he lifted the saddle from the stallion's back.

'Only if you wanted to.' Carlos put his hand on his shoulder.

'How could I put my horse in peril, just to slay the poor bull with a blade?'

Carlos raised his eyes at Valeria, who was standing at his side.

'Leonardo would never do that, and we would not like him to,' she responded. 'Besides, horses matter to him more than anything in the world.'

Leonardo's face flushed crimson. 'There are some exceptions,' he said.

Valeria continued to blossom in Leonardo's company. The cloud that had descended on her after her brother's death had lifted, and it was as if the boy's arrival had brought back the sun. Only Bañu watched their developing friendship with some misgivings.

'Should you not have friends of your own – different friends?' she asked Valeria one morning, while braiding her hair into a thick plait.

'Who needs them when I have Leonardo?' Valeria had turned her face up to Bañu and her eyes were bright with sincerity.

The old woman could find no suitable answer, but after tying a ribbon around the end of the plait she went to find her mother.

Isabel was having breakfast in the dining room when Bañu entered. She looked up from reading her post.

'Señora, I am concerned,' Bañu announced, with one of her looks that told Isabel she should listen carefully.

'Yes, Bañu?'

'Valeria needs to mix with girls of her own background; she spends her whole time in the stables with Leonardo.' Bañu's words came out in a rush and Isabel folded the letter, giving the old woman her undivided attention.

'I suppose she does.'

'I wonder if you should invite her Italian cousin to stay for a while.'

'You mean Elena? But what about the little ones, Jacobo and Donatella?'

'You could extend the invitation to the whole family. Don Carlos would surely be delighted to see his nieces and nephews,' Bañu declared.

Isabel laughed. Bañu had it all worked out, and it was, of course, a sound idea. When Carlos's younger sister had married the Italian count, Ambrogio Barberini, twenty years her senior, Carlos had worried. But the marriage had proved successful, his sister was devoted to her husband, and Carlos had found a friend in Ambrogio.

'I will write to the Contessa Barberini immediately,' she said with a smile. 'And besides, Jacobo is my godson, it is time he came to visit us here.'

In July the entire Barberini family arrived from Florence with a nanny and a maid. Carlos had taken time off work and was there to greet them.

Elena was the first to jump from the car. Immediately she ran up the steps and put her arm through Valeria's.

'I,' she said slowly in Spanish, pointing to her chest, 'am Elena.' This was followed by peals of laughter. 'I speak fluent Spanish, don't worry!'

Both families treated the visit as a holiday. They went on picnics into the mountains, a donkey carrying their provisions, and they played tennis in the evenings when it was cool. Each morning the two older girls rode with Leonardo and when the horses were untacked, Valeria's old pony would be brought from the field.

'Now it is the little ones' turn,' he would say, picking up Donatella and planting her firmly in the saddle. He had kept a straight face as plump little Donatella bounced around on the pony's back. Then it was Jacobo's turn and Leonardo quickly recognised his natural ability. He became a hero to the children. Within days he had taught them both to sit properly, and he had shown them how to effectively use the aids.

On Jacobo's saint's day, Leonardo gave the children their own special performance. As the stallion floated across the diagonal in half-pass, his supple body bent around Leonardo's inside leg, little Donatella's eyes were round with delight. 'He is a prince,' she sighed.

'More like an emperor,' Jacobo declared.

On the first evening, after a formal dinner in the dining room, Carlos and Ambrogio took their port to the terrace outside. In the distance a fox barked and nearer at hand, the strident clatter of the cicadas filled the air.

'Thank God we can get rid of this nonsense,' Carlos said, discarding his jacket and bow tie.

'At last,' Ambrogio agreed, wiping the sweat from his brow.

They sat down on the garden wall and Carlos passed his brother-in-law a box of cigars. After cutting the tip, he lit up his own.

'Do you worry, Ambrogio?' he asked, puffing out the smoke.

'Always,' the older man chuckled, 'but it depends on what you are talking about.'

'The world. Politics. Everything is changing so fast. You would have thought we would have learnt from the Great War.'

Ambrogio shook his head. 'In Italy we lost over six hundred thousand men, another million were wounded, but I don't think we have learnt anything. And now we have Mussolini. Though I always despised the man, to many he represented change, but then he introduced constitutional acts that gave him complete control and, before we knew it, we had become a Fascist state. He is a clever bastard, I will give him that.' He knocked the ash from his cigar onto the flower bed below. 'That is how a dictatorship starts, a charismatic leader who promises everything to those who have nothing.'

Both men were silent as they gazed up at the night sky.

'And your Primo de Rivera in Spain?' Ambrogio continued. 'He is a dictator, albeit a mild one. I follow the newspapers and it seems he is trying to instigate reforms, but they are constantly blocked by, dare I say it, the upper members of your society. It is a situation ripe for unrest.'

Carlos gave a dry laugh. 'You are right, and change is needed here, Ambrogio, there is such disparity between rich and poor. I would put money on it that in the not-too-distant future there will be war.'

'God help us all,' Ambrogio replied.

Whatever the men's concerns about the political future of Europe, they didn't let it get in the way of the holiday. There were tennis parties and football in the garden, there was an expedition to a bull fight in Seville. The day Valeria would always remember, however, was the ride in the cart to the *parque natural.* On this occasion Leonardo accompanied them.

'You have brought your swimming costumes?' Carlos queried, as the children piled into the cart.

'*Sì, Tío Carlos*,' they chanted.

'Well, then, off we go.' While Carlos drove the cart, gently flicking the whip at the strong grey gelding, Leonardo rode beside them on a sensible bay. As the little procession continued along the trail, Leonardo pointed out the abundant wildlife that inhabited the park.

'Look, there is a Bonelli's eagle,' he exclaimed, identifying a majestic bird that circled above them. 'You can tell from the short, rounded wings and long tail.' Donatella spotted a fawn, and cried out with excitement, sending the shy creature scooting back into the undergrowth. As the vegetation grew denser, the trees blotting out the sunlight, Carlos told the children stories of fairies and elves who inhabited the forest, and they were all spell-bound, even the older girls, who believed themselves too old for such things.

It was late morning when they arrived at their destination, a lake in a forest clearing, with a formation of limestone rocks on one side.

'Who will be first in the water?' Leonardo challenged, and with much giggling the children changed behind their respective trees. While they hovered at the edge, deciding who was going to go in first, Leonardo sprinted to the other side of the lake. He looked back and waved and as the children watched transfixed, he scrambled up the high rock face and stood on the ledge at the top.

'He is not going to dive, is he, Valeria?' whispered Elena in awe.

'I imagine he is,' she replied, her eyes fixed on him.

As he sprang into the air, his arms opening, it was as if he was flying. The younger children gasped with admiration and Valeria sighed.

'Él *es extraordinario no es verdad?*' Carlos exclaimed proudly.

'I don't care about extraordinary,' Elena whispered to Valeria. 'He is the most handsome boy in the world.'

Carlos called them out of the water for lunch. They all ran shivering to get their towels but were soon warmed up when Carlos set the lunch basket down in front of them.

Bañu had excelled herself, and a feast was laid out by Valeria. There were bread rolls filled with tomatoes and cured ham, little cakes, tarts filled with wild strawberries and plenty of homemade lemonade. Valeria believed nothing had tasted so good before.

Elena did not draw breath for the entire two weeks she was in Valeria's company and as Bañu had hoped, the two became the best of friends.

'Now you must learn Italian,' she announced to Valeria. 'Papa says that a person of refinement should speak at least four languages, and you only speak one.' She giggled. 'It also means when adults tell secrets in French, like my parents, you can actually understand what they are saying.'

The two girls were lying on their beds one afternoon, having been told to take a siesta by Bañu, when Elena put down her book.

'You like him, don't you?' She rolled onto her side, so that she was facing Valeria.

'Who?' Valeria asked, knowing exactly who Elena meant.

'Leonardo, silly.'

'Of course I do.'

'No, I mean, *really* like him.'

'Elena, he's younger than me.'

'Only just – so what! Young lovers, it's so romantic.'

Valeria hit her with a pillow, but her face was flushed.

When the family departed two days later, their luggage piled high on the top of the car, there were tears from the girls and promises of undying friendship.

'I'll come and visit you,' Valeria said, sniffing into her handkerchief.

'I'll come to Firenze very soon.'

Chapter Fifteen

In September, the local priest, Padre Alvaro, was summoned to the house by Carlos.

'My wife, Doña Isabel, and I would like you to teach this young man everything a gentleman should know. Italian, English, the classics, mathematics.'

'What about me?' Valeria demanded, her hands on her hips, glaring at her father. 'I may not be a boy, but I would like to be treated like one. I want to have proper lessons too, not just be taught by Mama. And I would like to include French. Elena says that an educated person should speak at least four languages.'

Carlos laughed. 'Well, then, my fiery little lady, if Elena says that, who am I to disagree? If that is your wish, you shall be taught with Leonardo.'

Every weekday, when Padre Alvaro wasn't celebrating Mass or performing other church duties, he came to the house. As the younger son of a landowner, he was well educated and well read. He was also filled with a desire to impart his knowledge to enquiring minds. In the summer months their lessons were taken in the shade of the internal courtyard, but in the winter, they were held in the schoolroom upstairs. Gradually, the paintings on the walls were replaced with mathematical equations and classical texts.

The three of them rode together, they walked together, and Padre Alvaro taught them to open their eyes and look around them, to recognise the simplest plants and flowers.

'It is my belief,' he instructed, 'that God is in this tiny flower; it must not be neglected.'

For her birthday in August, Padre Alvaro gave Valeria a small leather-bound translation of *Romeo and Juliet*. 'I know you will love this.'

He was right; she read it from cover to cover and then wanted more. Soon she had read *The Merchant of Venice*, followed by the *Taming of the Shrew*. When Leonardo suggested there were several comparable Spanish authors, she had a ready reply.

'But there is only one Shakespeare.'

Both children grew increasingly fond of the padre, but when he offered fencing lessons exclusively to Leonardo, Valeria's eyes flashed.

'You are happy to instruct Leonardo upon one of God's little flowers, and yet, when it comes to fencing, you hesitate, Padre Alvaro. You may think I am a mere girl, but I will not be left out,' she proclaimed. Valeria was tall for her age, but her body was changing. Soft curves were replacing her angular, childish limbs. She was also growing into a confident young woman.

'So, Padre,' she said, facing him. 'I think you could call that checkmate!'

'On such a protest, how could I possibly disagree,' he replied with a smile.

Padre Alvaro produced epées, masks and protective clothing and as Valeria faced Leonardo at the end of the internal courtyard it was difficult to distinguish one from the other.

'It seems that in height you two young people are perfectly matched,' Padre Alvaro declared.

Valeria smirked at Leonardo. 'And we will be perfectly matched in combat too, so don't get any ideas.'

Leonardo grimaced, and his teeth were chattering, he would have preferred to fight anyone rather than Valeria.

'First, you will learn the essential rules of the art that originated in Spain,' the priest instructed. 'You will learn about posture and footwork, you will learn how to hold the épée. All hits will be made with the tip and not the sides of the blade.'

During their lessons, the padre watched, instructed and fenced with Leonardo and Valeria. One morning, as he leant against a pillar, observing his pupils dancing around each other, their bodies lithe and athletic, the sunlight glinting on their steel blades, he was almost moved to tears.

Valeria was competitive and though Leonardo's presence was essential for her wellbeing, she couldn't bear to be beaten by him. If they were playing chess it was a battle to the end, and in their lessons, she tried to gain better marks.

Padre Alvaro laughed about it to Carlos and Isabel.

'The presence of Leonardo is so good for your daughter. If there is a text she finds difficult, she will labour over it for hours, determined not to be left behind.'

'She gets the competitive streak from her mother,' Carlos had said, with a laugh, and Isabel had tapped him on the arm.

If Leonardo could do something well, Valeria tried to do it better, but there was one arena in which she could never compete.

They were riding through the woods one morning, when they came across a massive oak that had fallen across the path in a storm.

'We will have to go around it,' Leonardo declared.

'Why?' she said, her eyes challenging Leonardo. 'We can jump the tree.'

'No, Valeria, Balada is too small.'

'Nonsense,' she said with a laugh and before he could stop her, she had cantered back up the path, turned, and was charging at the obstacle.

When the pony clipped the top with his front legs, he stumbled, and Valeria was thrown over his head, crashing to the ground. Balada cantered off, startled, but Valeria lay still as a corpse. Leonardo jumped from his horse, and sped towards her, a million thoughts going through his head.

'Not again, please not again,' he whispered, throwing himself to his knees beside her. Time stopped for Leonardo as he looked at her pale face and her closed eyes. He felt her neck for a pulse and was relieved to feel a flutter beneath his fingers. He could hear the birds singing in the trees, the leaves rustling, but Valeria was silent. He frantically rubbed her hands, but there was no movement. He was about to jump back on to his horse and return to the hacienda for help, when her eyes flickered open.

'Leonardo,' was all she said.

Leonardo could feel the emotion swell in his chest, the tears spring to his eyes. 'You idiot,' he whispered. 'You could have been killed.'

Gradually, the colour returned to her cheeks and Leonardo held her while she sat up. When she was ready, he helped her to her feet. For a moment she swayed in his arms.

'I feel a little wobbly,' she admitted.

'I'm not surprised,' he murmured. 'You probably have concussion. Lean against the tree while I catch Balada, and if you can walk, we will lead the horses back home.'

They had reached the studded oak doors leading to the stable yard when Valeria stopped, her face crumpling.

'Please don't tell my parents, they would be so cross with me.'

'As long as you promise never to do that again.'

'Balada could have been hurt. I could have killed my beautiful pony,' she whispered.

'It was a dangerous thing to do. You put your pony at risk; you should have known better, Valeria.'

Valeria bit her lip. 'For once I wanted to ride like you,' she mumbled.

'But you're better than me at everything else, can't you allow me to have this one thing?'

'I'm sorry, I am completely horrible. You must hate me.'

Leonardo wiped the tear from her cheek. 'I could never hate you, Valeria.'

Chapter Sixteen

Leonardo was nearly fifteen when Carlos took him to Seville. The boy had never been to the city before. Wearing a new suit – in fact, his only suit – their first stop was the bank.

As Leonardo stepped from the car, he moved closer to Carlos. Traffic weaved through the streets bumper to bumper, the occupants hooting at each other aggressively. Trams sped up the hill laden with passengers, there were people everywhere. Even the air was different.

'The family's main revenue comes from within these walls,' Carlos informed Leonardo, taking his arm and guiding him to the door. 'I know it's all a little overwhelming, so I'll show you the city later. Why don't you follow the footmen inside?'

As Leonardo walked through the marble hallway, to the inner sanctum of the bank, it seemed like another world. Rows of tellers sat behind mahogany counters, and in the cool interior, an air of sophistication prevailed.

'Do you have to be frightfully rich to come inside?' Leonardo asked.

Carlos leant over and whispered in his ear. 'Though many of our acquaintances have pretensions of wealth, most of it is borrowed from here.'

Leonardo giggled. 'Can anyone borrow money, señor?'

'You need assets to prove that you can pay it back,' Carlos pointed out. 'So don't get any ideas.'

Leonardo was introduced to the tellers, the managers, the finance director. When his head was spinning, Carlos took him down to the vaults.

'I have saved the best for last,' he said with a smile.

Señor Gil, the slightly rotund but jovial bank manager, joined them. 'So, young man, would you like to see where we keep our reserves?'

Leonardo nodded, and the man indicated a huge circular door.

'In preparation of your arrival, it is set to open at ten,' he explained. 'Do you wish to put in one of the combinations now?'

'Me?' Leonardo stuttered.

'I can't see why not,' Señor Gil replied.

After completing the task, the manager took over and they entered the vaults. Leonardo was silent as they filed through the cavernous chamber towards a barred area at the end. Suddenly he stopped, his eyes round, and looked up at Carlos.

'*Son estos lingotes de oro?*' he gasped.

'I believe the bars are gold, we'd better confirm it with Señor Gil,' Carlos chuckled.

'If I was a burglar, I would love it down here!'

'I am rather hoping you're not, young man!'

They had lunch in the dining room of the new Hotel Alfonso XIII, where Carlos ordered for Leonardo. As the boy gazed around him, Carlos patted his shoulder.

'So, what do you think?'

'I have never been anywhere like this before.'

'I think you will enjoy the food, but between you and me, I find the Moorish grandeur a little over the top.' He winked at

Leonardo. 'But the steak is the best in the city, and there's some pretty good ice cream too.'

When Leonardo had finished the last drop of ice cream in the bowl, and Carlos had paid the bill, they wandered the streets and avenues of central Seville. In *Calle Sierpes*, Carlos headed straight for *Papeleria Ferrer* and bought Leonardo a *Montegrappa* pen and writing paper. The shop was more of an institution, filled with glorious paper, inks, pens and writing accessories. It was where his own grandfather had bought him his first pen as a child.

'For me?' Leonardo gasped, when he handed him the box.

'For you, Leonardo. A gentleman should never be without a fine pen,' Carlos explained.

While Carlos watched amused, Leonardo pressed his nose against the windows of the clothing shops, his comments not always favourable.

'That dress costs the price of an entire house,' he declared. 'And it's not even nice.'

'Quite shocking, I agree. And you are right; Isabel would never wear such a thing. *Viene conmigo*, let's leave this frivolous nonsense and we will climb the Giralda Tower. You will have the finest view of the city up there.'

Thirty-five floors later, Carlos was panting. 'This part of the cathedral was once a Moorish minaret,' he explained, clutching on to the parapet. '*Querido* Leonardo, it seems I am too old for such things.'

'Look at the man over there,' Leonardo protested.

Carlos glanced at the portly figure, who was gasping in the corner and winked at Leonardo. 'So there is life in me yet?'

'I would say so, señor.'

Next, they went inside the cathedral. 'I am told this is the largest Gothic cathedral in existence,' Carlos said with pride. 'What do you think, Leonardo?'

'I believe Padre Alvaro would call it ostentatious.'

Carlos laughed. 'And if he did, he would probably be right. When construction began in the fifteenth century, the church elders wanted to impress the world.'

Leonardo frowned. 'But señor, would God wish for so much splendour when so many people starve?'

Don Carlos ruffled Leonardo's hair. 'Today is a treat, Leonardo, do not carry the weight of the world on your shoulders; just enjoy things as they are. Come, don't destroy your new shoes, let us look at the tomb of Christopher Columbus.'

The boy brightened. 'Did you know Columbus believed he had discovered China, but he had discovered the Americas instead?'

'I can see my money is wisely spent and the priest has been teaching you well.'

Leonardo grinned. 'He has, señor.'

'And did you also know,' Carlos said with a twinkle in his eye, 'that Columbus was later discredited, his titles taken away?'

'Padre Alvaro must have forgotten to mention that,' the boy replied.

'Well, I can still teach you something.' Carlos put his arm around Leonardo's shoulder and the boy breathed deeply. In his lifetime, no man had ever done that before. Only his mother and occasionally Isabel had taken him in their arms. It made him feel warm and secure. Since his mother's death he had constructed an invisible shield to protect himself, but the pain was still there. Sometimes in nightmares Adrianna would come to him, there was always a man on the ground. He had never tried to find out who the man was. Some things were better left alone.

Carlos smiled down at him. 'So, are you enjoying yourself?' he asked.

Leonardo nodded. 'A fine day, thank you, señor.'

While Carlos talked to an acquaintance outside the cathedral, Leonardo's attention was diverted by the sight of the carriages on the other side of the square. The horses were having a brief respite, chewing on their nosebags before their next customers arrived. The way they hung their heads reminded Leonardo of the sales he had attended with his father many years before. In those days while his father looked over the animals he wished to purchase, Leonardo had made it his duty to check on the horses' welfare before they were sold, often reminding the owners of their obligation to their charges. Though he usually received a cuff around the ear, it was his gift to the animals he loved.

He was at the end of the line of carriages when he saw the horse between the shafts. But it wasn't really a horse, more a bag of bones. He was about to berate the owner when the horse raised his head and looked him in the eye. There was a vestige of dignity in the animal's expression, the remnants of pride.

'*Dios mío*,' Leonardo whispered. 'My beautiful colt.' Tears sprang to his eyes. 'What have they done to you?' he whispered, touching the matted grey coat, noticing the scabs beneath the harness and the sores on his nose.

He walked up to the owner, a tired-looking man with a thin face. '*Tu eres una bestia*,' he hissed. 'How could you treat an animal in this way?'

The man curled his lip. 'How dare you tell me what I should or shouldn't do,' he snarled. 'You come here with your fancy clothes and your wealth. Now run to your papa and be away with you.'

'How much?' Leonardo pulled his wallet from his pocket.

'What do you mean? This horse is my livelihood, he is not for sale.'

'I mean, how much?'

The man looked at him for a moment, assessing him. 'Three hundred pesetas.'

Leonardo gasped, the amount would buy six horses and it would take all of his savings. He thought of the camera he had wanted to buy Valeria, the silk scarf for the señora, but this was a matter of life and death for the horse. He couldn't walk away.

He squared his shoulders and looked the man in the face.

'I will give the money you ask, but trust me, I'll be watching you. If I find you working a horse in this condition again, I will beat you myself.'

'Ha,' the man laughed, showing the gaps in his filthy teeth. 'A puny lad like you?'

'I will use any influence that I have to make sure you will never be allowed in this place again.'

He handed over the money and with shaking hands released the horse from the shafts, ran his hand lightly down the scrawny neck and led him away.

Carlos was crossing the piazza to join Leonardo when he stopped for a moment and stared. The boy was coming towards him in his smart new clothes, leading an emaciated horse. He shook his head, bemused.

'So, Leonardo, who is this?' he asked.

'Saturno, señor.'

'Like the planet?'

Leonardo nodded.

'I assume you have rescued the horse, but did you have the money?'

'I used my savings, señor.'

As they returned to the house in the Jewish quarter, Leonardo leading the horse, talking to it occasionally, encouraging it with a whisper or a word, Carlos was filled with admiration. The boy was full of surprises – not only bold but principled and compassionate, as well as extremely bright.

Leonardo took the horse to the mews at the back of the

house and after making up a comfortable bed, he left instructions with the groom.

'I will be out shortly to take care of his feed, but please do not leave him for a moment. As you can see his predicament is dire.'

For the next half hour, Leonardo kept glancing at his watch.

'Go, *querido*,' Carlos advised. 'I understand you need to be with the horse, but ask *el cocinero* to provide you with some supper on the way.'

As the boy left, Carlos smiled. The troubled, unhappy child had come into his life when he was grieving for his own little boy, but Leonardo had caused the light to shine again.

Having sat up with the horse all night, Leonardo excused himself from lunch with Carlos at his club and made his way to the bank.

'Señor Leonardo.' The bank manager he had met the day before was waiting at the door to usher him inside. 'I believe you have a pressing matter to discuss.'

Leonardo smiled. 'You are correct, Señor Gil.'

'Perhaps we should go to my office. Come this way.'

Leonardo followed him into his panelled office and sat down in the proffered chair.

'So, young man, people come to me for one of two reasons, either they wish to invest money, or to borrow it.'

'Sadly, I have nothing to invest, but I have spent the money intended for the purchase of a camera for Valeria. Now I need to borrow some more.'

The bank manager folded his hands in his lap and raised one eyebrow.

'It was a horse. I had to rescue it, I couldn't just stand by,' Leonardo continued, observing the wood shavings attached to his trouser leg. He hurriedly brushed them away.

'Ah, so this was a mission of mercy?' the manager asked, his lips twitching as he remembered the story circulating the bank of a smartly dressed boy marching across the square with a starving beast in tow.

'Indeed it was.' Leonardo drew back his shoulders and the manager smiled.

'Well, then, what are your assets?'

'At this moment a sick horse and Luna my dog. Not much else, I am afraid. But I shall pay you back with interest, as you explained.'

'How much do you need, young man?'

Leonardo drew a rolled-up magazine from his pocket. 'I wish to buy her the Leica Two with a built-in rangefinder. And a case,' the boy added as an afterthought. 'I am aware they are expensive. Do you know where I should find such a camera, señor?'

After a brief explanation of the terms and conditions of the loan, an assistant was dispatched with Leonardo to a shop in *Calle Arroyo*. The camera was purchased, with two rolls of film and a case, and Leonardo returned to the house in the Jewish quarter.

As Carlos waited for Leonardo in the panelled library, he lit a cigar and smiled. It had been cruel misfortune that had brought the boy into their home, but now they couldn't imagine their family without him.

Agustin was dead, Isabel could never carry another child, but Leonardo filled the gap in their lives.

Juan was surprised to see Don Carlos drive into the hacienda that evening with an open trailer attached to the Rolls Royce.

While Leonardo was opening the ramp, Juan hurried across the yard. 'You have a new horse, señor?'

'Leonardo has acquired this poor beast,' Carlos confirmed. 'But I'm afraid it will need all your expertise to keep it alive.'

'I see.' The groom frowned as the horse staggered down the ramp, supported by Leonardo. He clicked his tongue against his teeth in dismay. 'How can anyone abuse an animal in this way?'

'It is shocking, I agree.' Carlos drew in his breath. 'That is why Leonardo rescued him.'

At that moment Valeria came running from the house.

'*Dios mío, el pobre animal,*' she cried, running her fingers along the wasted neck, the jutting hip bones, the scarred cheek. 'What suffering you have endured,' she whispered. 'But if anyone can save you, Leonardo will.'

While Juan emptied sacks of wood shavings into a stable, Leonardo encouraged the horse to drink.

'You are the horse I have seen in my dreams,' he murmured. 'I promise that one day we will fly together, Saturno.'

That night, while Valeria remained in the stable with Leonardo, Luna positioned herself outside.

'You should come in for supper, both of you,' Bañu scolded, but they took no notice. 'I suppose you expect me to bring you something out here?'

Valeria crept to the stable door and hugged her. 'Only if you are offering, Bañu.'

Bañu tutted and stalked off, returning a short while later with a tray of food and a bowl of scraps for the dog. She took a pot of ointment from the pocket in her skirt. 'Put this on the horse's wounds, Leonardo, it's my mother's remedy. I used it on your leg the day you turned up as a waif and stray!'

'So that makes two strays,' Leonardo suggested with a smile.

As the hours ticked by, they encouraged the horse to eat small quantities of sweet, leafy alfafa, and they talked to each other as they never had before. Leonardo had finished redressing the horse's wounds, and was sitting in the shavings next to Valeria, when her head dropped onto his shoulder.

'What do you want to be when you are older, Leonardo?' she murmured.

He glanced at Saturno, who was standing with his neck hanging to the floor, his eyes half closed. 'I imagine I will work with horses, I am not sure that I am cut out for anything else.'

'But you could do anything, be anyone. You can turn your hand to whatever you wish. Anyway, I think Papa has plans for you in the bank.'

Leonardo smiled. 'Don't tell your father, but I am not interested in the city, even though I was intrigued by the bullion bars!'

'And don't you tell him that I have no intention of marrying some rich neighbour's son and producing several spoilt children. I want to do proper work, Leonardo, that is my dream.'

'Everyone should have a dream.'

'I want to make a difference, and I refuse to be told what to do by men!'

Leonardo put his arm around her shoulder and she leant into him. 'Is there any surprise in that?'

'I am not going to bed either,' she said, jutting out her chin. 'I will stay in the stable with you and Saturno tonight.'

And so it was that Bañu found them curled up together in the stable the following morning.

'Valeria, your mother is calling you, and Leonardo, you need some rest. That lazy lout Juan will take over.'

'I heard that,' Juan appeared behind her with a small bowl of alfalfa. 'Let me assure you, old hag, I wanted to do the night shift, but Leonardo wouldn't let me.'

Leonardo and Valeria rose to their feet, and after Leonardo had conferred with the older man, he reluctantly left the horse in his care.

Valeria found her mother on the terrace, a letter in her hand. Isabel beckoned her daughter over with a smile. 'Your father and I have been invited to the de Mendoza summer residence at Tossa del Mar for the whole of August, my darling – I want you to come with us.'

'Please, Mama, I have to stay with Saturno.'

'You want to stay with the boy, more like,' Bañu muttered to herself, standing in the background.

'It's time you had other friends, Valeria,' Isabel said, putting her signature to her acceptance letter. 'A change of scene will do you good.'

'I don't need other friends – I have Leonardo.'

'That's exactly what I mean,' Isabel replied.

The morning before their departure, Leonardo was brushing the yard when Valeria arrived in the stables, her clothes thrown on, her hair in disarray.

'You're early,' he observed, leaning the brush against the tack-room door.

'Couldn't sleep,' she admitted.

'Neither could I.'

For a moment they stared at each other until Leonardo broke the silence.

'Don't move, Valeria. I have something for you. I've been waiting for the right moment to give it to you since we returned from Seville.' He dashed into the tack room and emerged carrying a box.

'For me?'

Leonardo grinned and peered around him. 'Well, yes, you are the only person here.'

Valeria blushed and as she took the box from him, their hands touched. Leonardo's gaze was glued to her as she pulled off the paper.

'A camera,' she breathed. 'No, not just a camera, a Leica.'

'Do you like it? I mean, if you don't, I can change it, I just thought—'

Valeria shut off his words with a kiss. She drew back suddenly and blushed. Leonardo touched his lips.

'If it is not what you want—'

'Want it, Leonardo? Of course I do. I have longed to own a Leica, it is—'

'You have?' he interrupted.

'*Por supuesto*, it's possibly the best camera in the world.'

Leonardo's face lit up.

'But I cannot imagine what I have done to deserve it?' she teased.

Leonardo looked down at his feet but did not reply.

'This is ridiculously generous.' Valeria grinned suddenly. 'I hope you didn't steal the money from the bank?'

'Not quite,' Leonardo said, with a smile.

With the family away, the days seemed endless to Leonardo. He worked with the horses and continued to nurse Saturno back to health, but life felt different without Valeria.

'There's no need to mope, boy. Valeria needs to meet other people of her own class; she can't be with you always. One day she will marry, and she will be gone entirely,' Bañu scolded.

'Thank you for reminding me.'

The old woman touched his cheek where a fuzz of down was growing.

'They haven't gone because of me? I haven't offended them?' he asked.

'You haven't offended anyone, Leonardo.'

That night, when the house was silent and Bañu had retired to bed, Leonardo called Luna from her basket and he went outside. He climbed beneath the railings that led into a small paddock and whistled softly.

Immediately, slow, uneven hoof beats thudded on the dry turf, and a silver apparition moved towards him in the darkness. The horse stopped in front of him and pushed him with his nose.

Leonardo ran his hands down the animal's flanks. The skin was no longer draped over his bones like a rug, and his coat was beginning to shine. He drew the tin of salve from his pocket and ran his fingers lightly over the wounds.

'You feel safe now, don't you?' he whispered, putting his arms around the horse's neck. 'And believe me, Saturno, one day you will be the strongest horse in the world.'

Part Three

Chapter Seventeen

May 2000, Andalucía

The balmy evening was still and the moonflowers had opened their large white petals, flooding the air with their fragrance when Gracia picked up the tin from the wrought-iron table and closed the lid. Almost on cue, Dante's lurcher, Estrella, gave a ghostly howl.

'So this is your grandfather's, Leonardo's story,' Gracia said at last.

'I had always believed he was a Palamera de Santos by birth.' I swallowed hard.

'The family treated him like a son. He inherited the house, the estate, everything when Carlos died.' Gracia was looking at me with an expression of uncertainty. 'I hope I have done the right thing telling you.'

'Of course you have,' I whispered, tears welling in my eyes as I thought of the eight-year-old child running over the hill, stumbling, then picking himself up. I could imagine the terror in his heart. 'That poor little boy,' I uttered. 'In one act of brutality his world totally disintegrated. His mother, his home, everything gone, all at the hand of his own father.'

'It is a dreadful tale,' Gracia agreed.

'Perhaps that's why Papa Leo was so understanding when my father, Ashley, was killed. He never expected me to talk about my feelings, he was just there for me.'

Gracia patted my hand. '*Lo siento*, I'm sorry, *Mia*.'

'My mother was completely traumatised after identifying my father's body. She still loved him though they had been divorced for years.' I filled up my aunt's glass of sherry and took a gulp of my own. 'She tried so hard to support me, but it was only here with my grandfather that I found peace. It all makes sense now.'

My great-aunt sighed. 'In spite of his early tragedy, I believe he has had a good life, Mia.'

'He has had a wonderful life; it seems to have worked out in the end.'

'And you, child. What a consolation you have been.'

I helped Tía Gracia to her feet. 'Has my mother any idea of his past?' I blurted out.

'I don't believe so, Mia.'

I digested this information, but there was something else I needed to know. I paused, wondering if I was straying into forbidden territory.

'Why have I never heard about Valeria? What happened to her?' I asked, holding my breath as I waited for an answer.

She looked at me then, and slowly shook her head. 'It was never mentioned.'

Night was heavy around me, but I couldn't sleep. What I had learnt put my own identity into question. I was not the person I thought myself to be, and neither was my grandfather. It was hard to reconcile that his life and his background were a tissue of lies. If my great-grandfather was a murderer, where did that leave me? I thumped my pillow, realising I was being selfish. It could never change the man Papa Leo had always been to me.

But however hard I tried, these troubling thoughts continued to go around in my mind, until eventually I fell into an exhausted sleep.

The following morning, feeling groggy and unsettled, I accompanied Tía Gracia back to her apartment.

'Will you join me at the hacienda this weekend?' I asked.

'If you would truly like me to?' she responded, her eyes lighting up.

I squeezed her hand. 'It would mean a lot to me.'

Walking into the hospital had a completely different meaning now that I knew my grandfather's history. As I sat at his bedside, looking into his still face, I gently picked up his hand.

'Why didn't you tell me?' I whispered. 'Were you afraid that I would think less of you? Because you are wrong, it actually makes me love you more.' I was really talking to him now and it was as if we were in a room on our own without the tubes, the whooshing of the ventilator and the nurses coming and going. It was just my grandfather and me talking as we always had in the past. I smiled at him. 'I need you to wake up because I have so much to ask you. You must come back to us, Papa Leonardo.'

Dr Canovas encouraged my daily visits to my grandfather.

'I believe you being here makes a real difference,' he told me. 'His vital signs continue to improve.'

And so my regular updates commenced. I would start by telling my grandfather what was going on in the house, always trying to find an amusing anecdote about Manuela. I described walking around the garden and the flowers that were in bloom and, finally, I gave him Dante's detailed report on the horses. On one occasion, I put the tile fragment into his hand, and the fossil of a snail. Every day I finished by asking him what had happened to Valeria. She would have been like a sister to him.

They had grown up together and she had obviously meant so much to him, but he had never spoken of her. It was as if her life was walled in silence and I wanted to know why.

Hoping to find some answers, I left the hospital one sultry late spring afternoon, and made my way to the *Archivo Histórico* in the *Apodace* district of Seville. It was only a short walk from the bus stop in *Calle Almirante,* but I was grateful to get out of the heat into the air-conditioned interior.

The man at the desk was wearing an orange shirt with shocking-pink trousers, which made him immediately approachable. 'I have an appointment. Mia Ferris,' I said.

He opened his diary. 'Yes, here you are.' He tapped the entry with a pen.

'I'm looking for the newspaper section.'

He gave me a friendly grin. 'We have all the latest technology here, you can search the database now. But what period are you after?'

'The 1930s?'

'Ah, so you are finding a lost relative,' this time it wasn't a question. He came out from behind the desk and led me to a bank of computers. 'Just put the name in the search engine and hopefully it will come up.'

I thanked him and settled down in a chair but, half an hour later, having trawled through the archives, the name Valeria Palamera de Santos came up only as the daughter of Carlos and Isabel. There was little of any relevance, only a date of birth, but not of her death. I scrolled down again, disappointment blooming in my chest. Santonja, Santoro, Santovena! There was nothing above or below her name of any interest. The nearest I came to her was a Val Saint, but she was not the woman I was looking for.

I shut down the screen and, after signing out, I left with no more information than I had when I had started.

*

That evening, I returned to my grandfather's study. Valeria must have left something behind!

I was taking another look in his desk when I noticed the corner of a photograph protruding beneath the heavy paper of his leather blotter. I peeled it back to find a tiny image of a girl with blond hair. She was sitting at a desk and staring into the camera. I picked up a magnifying glass and held it to the light. I could make out her features quite clearly, even the flowers on her dress. The desk was unusual with ormolu eagle heads on the corner of each leg. It was hard to contain my excitement; this was surely Valeria.

Afterwards I rang Poppy, but for the first time in my life I found I wasn't completely honest with my sister.

She was burning with curiosity. 'So, has Gracia told you about the mysterious tin?'

I hesitated. 'She didn't know very much, only that the silver medallion belonged to Papa Leo and the card was obviously from Valeria.'

'Well, at least that's a start,' she volunteered. 'Keep hunting, Mia, don't give up.'

As I put the phone down I felt terrible, I hated keeping this from her, but I couldn't tell her everything, not yet.

It would be a few days before I noticed the first imperceptible movement in my grandfather. I was in the middle of singing 'Super Trouper' in my best Abba voice when it happened.

'Did you see that?' I gasped to Nurse Angelina, who was in charge of watching the monitor. 'His eyebrow, it moved, I am absolutely sure of it.' Unfortunately, by the time she came around the bed, his face was completely still. I must have looked despondent because she gave me a hug.

'It happens sometimes; only a muscular reaction, I'm afraid.'

I didn't believe her, so I spent hours scrutinising his face and squeezing his hand, looking out for the tiniest reflex.

I was reading, cross-legged in the armchair, during one of Andalucía's famous thunderstorms, when my grandfather opened his eyes.

'*Santo Dios*,' I shouted, making the on-duty nurse jump out of her skin.

'It's happened. Look, he is awake.'

This time there was no doubt, his eyes moved in my direction and the fingers on one hand flickered, but as quickly as it had happened he had gone.

'He is now in that minimally conscious state I mentioned before,' Dr Canovas later explained, after a thorough examination. 'We can safely say this will improve, but his awareness will come and go. Now is the time for patience, señorita.'

But patience is not my greatest virtue. I wanted my grandfather to know me, to talk to me and, if I am honest, I wanted a Lazarus moment where he would get up from his bed and walk. It took a few days to wean him off the ventilator, and the tube was only removed when Dr Canovas had established he could breathe adequately on his own. This massive step was a matter for much celebration. And then he said his first words. 'Is that you, Rafaela?'

I leant over his bed, so that I was looking into his eyes. 'No, it's me, Papa Leo. It's Mia.'

'Who?'

This wasn't quite the reaction I had expected but I was thrilled that he had spoken at all. It soon became a cause for elation, not only for my mother back in England and everyone at the hacienda, but also for all the staff on the ward. To honour the occasion, Ramon brought in a case of champagne from my grandfather's cellar.

'To be enjoyed at home,' I said, giving a bottle to each of the nurses and doctors involved in his care.

*

'This is such a positive outcome,' Dr Canovas confirmed on one of my daily visits. 'We couldn't have asked for more.' He looked down at my grandfather. 'Could it be the result of all those Abba songs, perhaps?'

I blushed a deep red, realising my recent singing efforts must have been heard well beyond the confines of his room.

'I am so glad for your family, Mia, if I may call you that. Extraordinary, really, for someone of his age. Now I imagine you would like to know when you can take him home?'

'Tomorrow?' I joked.

'I think perhaps you are getting a little ahead of yourself,' he replied with a smile. 'We still need to monitor him for a few more days. He needs to be fully awake before he is discharged from hospital.' His face became serious. 'You do understand he will need full-time nursing, Mia? This will give you the time to meet his staffing requirements. There are several good nursing agencies in Seville who will arrange suitable long-term care.'

He was at the door when he turned back. 'And there is something else you should be aware of; brain injuries can result in a vast array of psychological changes, leaving some patients anxious and depressed. You may have to deal with irrational behaviour and mood swings. I feel I ought to warn you.'

'I am prepared for that,' I said optimistically.

But when Papa Leo returned home a week later, I wasn't so sure.

The entire household were assembled in the hall when the ambulance came up the drive, including my mother, who'd arrived from England the day before. Ramon shot forward to supervise the ramp.

'It is a momentous occasion, Señorita Mia, is it not?' he said, straightening his jacket.

'It certainly is, Ramon,' I replied.

My mother chose to wait by the door, while I went outside with Lucia, the nurse we had engaged to care for my grandfather.

His only words as he was lifted from the ambulance were directed with a glower at Lucia.

'Who the hell are you?' he rasped.

As he was wheeled through the hall, he looked at each of us in turn. 'Quite a reception,' he grumbled. 'I don't like parties.'

'A lovely room has been prepared for you downstairs, Papa,' my mother said rather too brightly, bending down to kiss him.

'What is wrong with my old room?' he croaked.

She looked at me over his head, her eyebrows raised.

The first week was challenging for everyone as my grandfather settled into his new routine, but despite his irascible behaviour, I was extremely glad to have him home.

Amongst the difficult moments, his inappropriate comments did offer some light relief. Walking in one morning when Lucia was brushing his teeth, I overheard their conversation.

'Stop fussing, go to the stables and tack up my horse,' he instructed, obviously convinced she was his groom.

'Tack him up yourself,' she muttered as she walked away.

I am not sure how my mother managed to restrain herself when my grandfather decided to pick on Ashley. Despite the fact that my father had been dead for fourteen years, he was obviously still very much alive to my grandfather.

'I hope that useless rock singer of a husband isn't drinking all my brandy,' he said with a scowl.

There were also days when he stared into the distance saying nothing at all. Ramon seemed to be the only person who could make him smile. Sadly, Aunt Gracia bore the brunt of his frustration. Following one of her visits he croaked to Lucia, 'If that old woman comes near me again, I will cut my throat.'

If Gracia took these comments in her stride, they offended me.

'Papa Leo,' I scolded him after he had alluded to her size for the second time that day, 'it's not like you to be mean.'

He had glowered at me. 'Bugger off, Constanza.'

'My name is Mia. And who's this mysterious Constanza woman, anyway?'

'Your grandfather doesn't mean to be unkind, Mia, my dear,' Gracia had reassured me when I stalked from his room. 'He was so vital, and now, look at him, poor man. It is so hard to be dependent on others. Even that hoist, standing in the corner, must be a constant reminder of all he has lost.'

'But how do you put up with his rudeness?' I asked.

'I am indebted to him, Mia. He was utterly devoted to your grandmother Paloma and so kind to her when she was sick.' She put her warm fingers over mine. 'She was my only sister and I never had the blessing of children, so being with you and your mother means everything to me.'

Later, as I climbed the staircase, I could see Aunt Gracia through the open door of my grandfather's bedroom. The side light was on and she was reading to him. As I listened to her gentle voice, I understood that helping to look after my cantankerous grandfather had given her a new purpose in life, which was far better than being in her small apartment full of memories.

I curled up on the window seat overlooking the garden, remembering my grandfather's patience throughout the various stages of my childhood. There was my ballerina phase when he had optimistically called me a young Margot Fonteyn in the making, and the gothic stage when, at twelve, I had adopted black lipstick and Doc Marten boots. I smiled, recalling an earlier occasion when I had been sent home from school and my mother had packed me off to Spain.

'Shall we take out the cart?' he had asked on the evening I arrived. I was eight at the time and the prospect of an evening escapade had lifted my mood.

'With a horse, Papa Leonardo?'

'Of course with a horse; you don't expect us to pull it ourselves?' After putting the horse between the shafts, he had lifted me onto the seat and had given me the reins.

'Now then, off we go.'

I had looked at him in amazement. 'You want me to drive, Papa Leonardo?'

'Well, who else?' he had said with a grin.

I was about to plunge into my new novel, when my mother came into my bedroom and sat on the window seat beside me.

'I am so proud of you, Mia. Giving up your job, devoting your time to Papa Leo, but don't feel you have to remain here too long. He would never expect you to put your life on hold.'

'I want to be here,' I assured her. 'He has done so much for me, it is my turn now.'

She brushed a strand of hair from my face. 'You are not running away from your own problems, *querida*?'

I exhaled. 'Being in Spain has given me the time I needed to reflect on my life and Matt.'

She threw open the window and we leant out, breathing in the night air.

'Somehow the stars are nearer here, brighter,' she observed. 'You will find clarity at the hacienda, *querida*.'

'Everything is clearer here,' I agreed.

'This has always been your spiritual home. It was for me too until I ran away with your father.' She looked at me and sighed. 'You can't imagine what it was like when I first arrived in England. I felt so homesick and I hardly understood the language.' She laughed softly and I put my head on her shoulder.

'But now you speak English perfectly, and you are still living there.'

'I suppose I am,' she acknowledged.

'What went wrong with my father?' I asked, and a reflective expression came into her eyes.

'Everything. He was hopeless, any income we had came from his family. He would often leave me for days, going off to a gig with the band, returning with no money, having spent everything he earned on…'

'Drugs,' I finished for her.

She smiled. 'In the end I needed to forge a life of my own, so I had to leave him.'

'Why didn't you come back to Spain?'

'What a lot of questions,' she said with a smile. 'But I came to talk about you, not about me. My life is boring.'

'Hardly.' I looked up at her and asked the question that had been on my mind.

'Are you happy, I mean truly happy, with Peter?'

'Why do you ask?' Her eyes widened.

'He doesn't seem to make you laugh anymore, and he patronises you; sometimes I wonder if your marriage is enough for you, Mama?'

My mother bit her lip. 'If I had my time again maybe it would be different, but I am a divorced Catholic, Mia. In the eyes of God that is a sin. Once is enough.'

As soon as my grandfather's mind began to clear, his recovery progressed steadily, and I was surprised at how many glimpses I had of his former vitality. He quickly remembered who I was and seemed delighted to have my mother in Spain. Apart from the occasional lapse he was keen to know what was going on around him. It actually took his wisdom to finally convince me that I should delay the wedding. We had finished lunch and he was resting in the loggia, when I looked up from my mobile phone.

'Matt keeps pressing me to set a date,' I told him.

My grandfather opened his eyes. 'Surely that is normal if you are engaged?'

'But the thing is, Papa Leonardo …' I trailed off.

He looked at me. 'Yes?'

'I'm not sure if it feels right anymore.'

'If it doesn't feel right, you don't marry him, Mia. Never settle for second best when you could be with anyone in the world.'

While my grandfather slept, I remembered the evening Matt had arrived on my doorstep for our first date. He was carrying a huge bunch of roses, the old-fashioned kind with big heads and a delicious scent. I'd been a little bowled over: he was handsome and self-assured, very different from the impoverished students I had been out with before. I thought I had fallen in love with him but when he had asked me to marry him, I hadn't felt the heady emotion I expected. My grandfather and mother were right, I couldn't be with someone I didn't love completely, I wanted to reach for the stars.

Taking a last lingering look at my beautiful diamond ring, I went upstairs to my bedroom, took it off and put it in the bedside drawer.

Chapter Eighteen

June 2000

The days went by and I still hadn't mustered up the courage to call off my engagement.

Despite my personal problems, a routine was established at the house. Manuela made numerous dishes still tempting in their pureed form, while my mother and I made it our job to entertain my grandfather. Lucia did the nursing, excepting her days off when it was a combined effort between us. In her quiet, professional way she took no nonsense from my grandfather. I marvelled at her patience as she settled him into his routine, encouraging him to eat and to do his exercises. If Leonardo was irascible, Lucia was one step ahead, always kind but firm. She would get my grandfather out of bed using the hoist and bathe him in the hastily prepared wet room downstairs. Afterwards, she would dress him and manoeuvre him into the brand-new wheelchair. The first time I entered his room and witnessed him being winched from his bed to a chair he was furious. I will never forget the look on his ravaged face as he stared at me, the humiliation in his eyes.

'Get out,' he hissed. 'Get out.'

'I'm sorry.' I stumbled from the room and ran into the garden.

At once I understood what it was like to be my grandfather. He was now totally dependent on others when only a few months before, he had been fit, active and filled with energy.

Gradually, he accepted my help and I was able to take over from Lucia on her day off. I embraced these occasions, feeding my grandfather, washing his face and hands, and before too long he didn't mind me changing his catheter bag. I soon got the hang of winching him from his bed to the wheelchair so we could enjoy our walks outside. I stopped feeling sorry for him; it was part of his new life and we had to get on with it.

As the summer heat increased, I tended to ride at dawn or dusk, followed by Estrella, who would bound away after a rabbit or hare. In this vast familiar landscape, my whole life in London seemed further and further away.

When we had time, Manuela and I would sneak away for an evening drink in Cazalla de la Sierra. She drove at about one hundred and twenty kilometres an hour, whether we were on a white road or a motorway and each time I stepped from the car, I vowed I would never put my life in jeopardy again. This would be forgotten as soon as we joined her friends. There was Matias, who worked in the newsagent's and had a crush on Manuela, and Alejandro, who owned the second-hand bookshop in the square. Alejandro had dark, soulful eyes and he would read us poetry by Frederico García Lorca and sigh at the poet's tragic end.

'They murdered him,' he said to me, banging down his glass. 'Franco's nationalists drove him into the countryside outside Granada and shot him for his sexuality and his republican views.' As I looked around the table at my new friends, I realised that the anger was still near to the surface, the war still festered after all these years.

One evening, when a squall of rain forced us inside, it seemed the entire population of Cazalla de la Sierra was crammed into the smoky bar for a football match between Barcelona and Real Madrid. As the men and women cheered and groaned, their eyes glued to the screen, I was reminded of Matt's group of friends and their addiction to football. But the more I watched the more I realised that here in the small Andalusian town, the atmosphere was different. It was charged with aggression and excitement. I realised how much allegiances still mattered in Spain. This wasn't just football; it was a battle to the end.

I had just got back from my ride when my mother came to the stables. She poked her head over the door.

'*Querida*, we have a problem, and I am not sure how it is going to be resolved.'

I put away my tack and followed her into the office where she sat down at the desk. Paper covered every inch of the surface: bills, letters, my grandfather's ledgers were open in front of her.

'This came from the bank in Seville this morning.' She thrust a letter in my hand.

I scanned the paper, my heart sinking at the possible ramifications.

'It seems he has been robbing . . .' She stopped. 'What is that very English expression Peter finds amusing?'

'Robbing Peter to pay Paul,' I said helpfully.

She shook a handful of bills. 'The manager failed to warn me that he has borrowed thousands, sometimes for the roof or a new tractor, but this one.' She thrust a bill of sale into my hands. 'Guess what, he borrowed five hundred thousand pesetas to buy a foal!'

'I am not sure how much that is,' I said, trying to do a quick calculation in my head.

'We are in euros now,' my mother said with a frown. 'But in sterling that is nearly two thousand pounds!'

For a moment laughter bubbled in my throat. It was awful, of course it was, but it was so like my grandfather.

'We have to pay for his nursing, running this house, Manuela and Ramon. Oh God, if only Peter were here.'

If I am honest, the last bit annoyed me. 'We will find a solution, Mama, I am sure of it. And we don't need Peter.'

She looked up at me for a moment. 'I was going to go home. He needs me, Mia—'

'Go, Mama, I can manage.'

'But we may have to sell the house, put your grandfather in a home.' She looked as if she was going to cry. 'Papa needs to see out his days here. But how can we pay Lucia?'

I realised for the first time in my adult life that my mother was floundering, and I needed to take charge.

'There are a thousand things we can do,' I said, wracking my brains for any possible solutions. I remembered Peter's pronouncement on the Fabergé egg. 'There are things we could sell.'

She looked hopeful for a moment, then her face fell.

'Don't worry,' I said, reading her dismay. 'You go home, I promise I can manage. If I can sort out Dale, I can certainly deal with the bank.'

'But I can't leave you in charge of all this.'

'Yes, you can. Don't forget there is a team of people to look after grandfather, including Aunt Gracia, who desperately wants to help. We will be absolutely fine.'

After my mother's departure, I had to prove to the bank and to myself that the problems were not insurmountable. With a short-term loan in place, probably due as much to the remaining family connections with the bank as to my persuasive personality, and with the contact details of the most respected auctioneers in the area, I made an appointment with the firm *Ortega e Hijo* from Seville. When the auctioneer arrived, he was forty minutes late. He held out his hand.

'So sorry, Señorita Palamera de Santos. The rain brought the traffic to a standstill and I was detained getting out of Seville.'

He didn't look remotely sorry and I was tempted to ask him why he hadn't left his office earlier. So far his only redeeming quality was his name for me: Mia Palamera de Santos had a certain ring to it.

'It's actually Mia Ferris, as I believe I informed you when we spoke.'

'Excuse me, señorita, it is your grandfather's name…'

I didn't like being patronised but I held my tongue. 'I'll show you around the house, but you will have to do the valuation without me, I'm afraid. I have a meeting at four.'

He glanced at my jodhpurs and I felt the heat rise in my face. He clearly wasn't fooled.

'We will start with the drawing room,' I said, summoning the last vestiges of my dignity. At this moment I felt Felipe Ortega was an arrogant young man and I would not be the subject of his amusement.

For the next twenty minutes he inspected the rooms with the air of someone who is used to larger, more important houses, containing objects of far greater value. I was convinced the Fabergé egg would give him something to think about. Keeping it until last, I went to the safe and took out the very precious object. He turned it over and after taking out his glass and inspecting the enamelled surface and the jewelled clasp, he returned it to me.

'This is a very good copy, but in my opinion, it is not by the hand of Carl Fabergé.'

'Don't you think you should get a second opinion?' I pushed him.

'I would hang my hat on it,' he replied.

I was not in a good mood. I disliked Felipe Ortega and now I discovered that the Russian countess had conned my ancestor.

'If you will excuse me,' I said at last, 'I really have to go. I will, of course, be getting other valuations.'

'Of course,' he said. 'I would expect you to. I hope you have a good ride.' This time I detected a grin and I stalked off in the direction of the stables. He was insufferable.

Chapter Nineteen

After a particularly frustrating morning when my grandfather had refused to eat, and Lucia had threatened to leave, the valuation from Felipe Ortega arrived. I skimmed through it, while drinking a coffee in the kitchen with Manuela.

'You are thinking about that auctioneer,' Manuela stated.

'Hardly surprising, since I am reading through his papers.'

'You are tapping your toe in a way that suggests he has annoyed you. Either that, or you find him attractive.'

I flushed a deep red. 'Felipe Ortega? I can assure you I never thought of him like that. He was arrogant, rude and not my type at all. Anyway, Manuela, in case you had forgotten, I am engaged.'

She grinned back. 'Just an observation,' she said.

To prove my detachment, I took the valuation into Leonardo's study and read it carefully. It was well prepared and comprehensive, and, despite my misgivings, Felipe Ortega obviously had a good eye. He had done the valuation in euros with the equivalent in pounds. I wondered whether this last detail was a requisite of the firm, or his reminder that I was a foreigner. By the time I had finished I realised Ortega was the right company to choose. Now came the unpleasant task of deciding which items to sell.

Surprisingly, a small eighteenth-century chest that I had

never even noticed in the boot room was valued at five thousand pounds. The same estimate was given to *Lady with a Fan*, from the school of Goya. These would be the first to go. As I ticked them off on the list, I accepted it was like putting a sticking plaster over a very large wound. Somehow money needed to be raised and nothing was coming in. Unless we came up with a radical plan, the house would have to be sold.

Manuela found me in the salon taking the painting off the wall. 'So you sell my favourite picture, eh?'

I turned around, clutching the painting to my chest. 'I have to, I'm afraid, I love it too, Manuela, but you know how it is, the bills, the house… Everything is on a large scale. And now we have to pay Lucia.'

'I suppose I am also a burden.'

'Don't be ridiculous,' I replied, seeing the truth in her words. 'That is not what I meant at all.'

Manuela managed a smile.

'But how my grandfather managed to keep this all going, I have no idea.'

'*Voló por el asiento de sus pantalones.* In England, I think you say, he flew by the seat of his pants.'

'Did he teach you that?' I grinned.

'He taught me many expressions, some of them I couldn't repeat.'

We laughed, but it was obvious Manuela was near to tears.

'If you come across a Ming dynasty vase when you are dusting, it would be extremely helpful,' I said, trying to cheer her.

'If I find a Ming dynasty vase, I'm running off with it.'

Manuela's humour was restored.

On an unusually overcast afternoon, Felipe Ortega returned. This time he was early. As he put his briefcase on the hall chair, I found myself glancing in his direction. There was an attractive quality about him. Heavy lids, straight nose, strong jaw with the usual designer stubble on his chin, but his attitude was condescending and arrogant. That was enough to put anybody off.

I put out my hand in what I considered to be a sophisticated gesture. 'Señor Ortega, you are on time. Congratulations.'

'Señorita Ferris, I want to thank you for commissioning my family's company. I am sure it will be a most happy union.'

I raised my eyebrows. 'Your valuation was extremely professional.'

'Well, then, I am a satisfied man.'

I looked at him for a moment. Was he mocking me, I wondered, or was it his English? I really wasn't sure.

When he had declined my offer of coffee, I took him to the drawing room. First, I led him to a small oil on canvas of a waterfall gushing into a pool. The colours were gentle, and the artist had perfectly captured the sunlight flickering through the trees. It had always been one of my favourites, but Felipe had failed to put it in the valuation. I hadn't known whether to be glad or offended.

'Why didn't you include this?' I asked. 'Isn't it good enough?'

'Manuela told me you loved the painting, so I omitted it. The value wasn't going to change your life.' He gave a boyish smile.

As Felipe was leaving, he gestured to the picture hanging over the hall fireplace. The canvas was in a dark wood frame and was lit from above.

'I am assuming this is not for sale?' he queried.

I looked across at the painting. 'This isn't for sale and never will be.'

'It is as if the horse is alive,' he murmured. 'Do you see his eyes follow you?' His voice had changed and for the first time I believed he was genuine.

'What an exquisite animal. Do you know about it, Mia?'

He had dropped the señorita and for a second, I had forgotten that he was the annoying auctioneer. Instead, I noticed that he was unusually tall for a Spaniard, and he had long, elegant hands.

'It is my grandfather's stallion Saturno, the horse he rescued and that later carried him through the Civil War. I am told that he was heartbroken when he died.'

'Horses give you their lives, if you honour them.'

Perhaps there was another side to Felipe Ortega.

'You like horses?' I asked, noticing his jaw soften as he smiled.

'*Amo los caballos*,' he replied.

Felipe called me early the following week.

'I have been thinking about the egg,' he said, a little apprehensively.

'You have?' I queried. 'Are you telling me that you are doubting your judgement, Señor Ortega?' I was beginning to enjoy myself.

'No, but on this occasion, I thought it would be appropriate to have a second opinion. I would not like to be the person who gets on the wrong side of Señorita Ferris.'

I grinned. 'You are frightened of me?'

'Terrified,' he jested.

By the time he put down the phone I was laughing and, if I was honest, I was looking forward to his visit on Friday.

He arrived with Señora Maneiro, a studious-looking woman of a certain age, and after I had shown them into the drawing room, Manuela brought a tray of coffee, while I collected the egg from the safe.

Donning a pair of white gloves she took out her magnifying glass and carefully picked up the egg. At least she was treating it with due deference, I thought.

'Do you have a provenance?' she asked, turning it over.

'Only that a Russian countess gave it to the family in the early 1900s.'

'Well, the date fits,' she said with a smile.

I was definitely warming to the expert. 'What are you looking for?' I asked, my interest growing.

'All pre-revolutionary pieces have a stock number and if you can prove it was on the Fabergé inventory, then your egg is worth a fortune, but I can also tell from the quality of the piece.'

My face must have shown my excitement.

'Sadly, there are very few of them. I am sure you know that Carl Fabergé was court jeweller to the Russian tsar.'

I didn't, but I shrugged my shoulders in what I hoped was an affirmative way.

'Each of his eggs tells a story of the lives and loves of the Imperial Romanoff family, so you can understand why they are priceless.'

'And ours?' I queried.

After further scrutiny she pressed a jewel in the side and the top lifted up, to reveal an exquisite foal inside. I exhaled. I had never known this existed. After several moments she replaced the lid and handed it back to me.

'I am so sorry, but though completely exquisite, yours is not made by the hand of Fabergé, but one of his work masters. If I am not mistaken, it was made by Andrei Adler in St Petersburg in around 1900.' My face must have fallen because her smile was sympathetic.

'But it will still fetch a good price at auction because the enamel and guilloche are particularly fine. Señor Ortega is correct, it is a truly beautiful piece, and yours has the added attraction of the charming little foal.'

I looked up at Felipe and our eyes met.

'But I didn't find the opening mechanism,' he apologised.

'They are well hidden,' she explained.

I stepped forward to shake her hand. 'Thank you so much, Señora Maneiro. I am of course disappointed that it is not by the hand of the master himself, but your visit has been really enjoyable and informative; I just hope you don't feel it has been a waste of your time.'

'Far from it; there were about seventy eggs made, but only fifty have been found, so the tiniest possibility that this could have been one of them made my visit more than worthwhile. This has been such an agreeable morning, thank you, Señorita Palamera de Santos.'

I smiled at the use of Papa Leonardo's name, but on this occasion, I had no desire to correct her. As the car drove away, I returned to the drawing room for another look at the egg with the little foal inside.

On the morning of the furniture auction, I found Manuela in the kitchen puréeing vegetables for my grandfather's supper.

'Where are you going?' she asked, putting the mixture in the fridge.

I smiled. 'Would you like a trip to Seville? The furniture is being sold at approximately eleven today.'

'I see.' Manuela had that smug look on her face.

'What do you mean, I see?'

'I'm assuming Señor Ortega will be there, and you are wearing your Balenciaga miniskirt.'

'So what?'

'And do you wear that every day?'

Sometimes Manuela went too far. 'I shall go and find Ramon,' I said, turning on my rather delicate heels. 'At least he drives properly.'

'No, Mia, I am coming. Give me ten minutes to change.'

*

With Lucia at home to care for my grandfather, we skidded down the drive at eighty kilometres an hour and arrived at the auctioneers off *Plaza de Jesus de la Pasion* in Seville with twenty minutes to spare. We were directed to the sale room and sat down in the plush blue chairs.

'Lot eighty-one, a pair of charming eighteenth-century gilded rococo armchairs, in their original covers. Will anyone start the bid – shall we say one thousand euros?' I recognised Felipe's voice immediately and as I looked up at the podium there was a strange feeling in my stomach.

Manuela nudged me. 'The gold is flaking, it is a crazy price,' she whispered loudly. The hammer was brought down at fifteen hundred euros. 'And with those tatty old covers!'

The nearer it got to the *Lady with a Fan*, the more anxious I became. Though I hated selling the painting, the bidding made my heart beat faster.

'There is something rather fascinating about the process, don't you think?' I said to Manuela between bids.

'Are you sure it is not the auctioneer who is fascinating you?' she replied with a grin.

Manuela was relentless in her teasing, and I chose to ignore her.

The *Lady with a Fan* went for double the estimate, so we would be safe for a while.

We were heading into the foyer when Felipe bounded over.

'I am sorry that I couldn't give you better news on the egg, but I hope you are pleased with today's result?'

'I'm relieved,' I admitted.

There was an almost boyish enthusiasm about him that I found very charming.

'I suppose—' He shook his head. 'You are probably extremely busy, but I would be delighted to show you both around the auction rooms, if you were interested. We have an exciting sale coming up of Spanish twentieth-century art. We have a Miró, not a Picasso, I am afraid, but what do you think?'

'I'd like that,' I blurted out, unable to disguise my enthusiasm.

He looked at Manuela.

'I make my apologies, señor,' she responded. 'But I would love this opportunity to go to my favourite fabric shop in *Calle Don Alonso el Sabio*. It is so rare that I get into town.'

When Manuela had left, Felipe and I wandered through the auction rooms. Future sale items were being catalogued and paintings were being hung on the walls.

'This is what we call an interior designer's sale,' he said, opening the doors of a large room filled with mirrors, decorative items, furniture and even stone garden ornaments and statues. 'Nothing incredibly valuable,' he explained with a smile, 'but we do well from those sales.' Next came a sale of rare books, and lastly, he came to the room in question. 'It is pretty unusual for us to have works of this quality,' he confessed.

As he showed me around, I could see the pride he took in his family business, and I had to admit to myself, I was warming to Felipe Ortega.

We stopped in front of the Miró.

'Do you like Surrealist paintings?' he asked. 'Look at the fantastical landscape, it is extraordinary, wouldn't you agree?'

I gazed at the painting. 'I did an essay on the Surrealists as part of my degree. The strange beauty, the exploration of the human psyche ...'

From that moment we didn't stop talking and without me noticing, an hour soon slipped by. I was disappointed when Manuela turned up to collect me.

'Thank you so much for showing me around,' I said to Felipe, feeling Manuela's eyes upon me.

'The pleasure was mine,' he replied.

*

That night Aunt Gracia joined our outing to Cazalla de la Sierra. After parking the car in *Calle de Chichorra* we made slow progress down *Calle Cipres* towards our favourite bar.

'In the old days the baker was on that corner, and Señor Forjador, the blacksmith, lived in the forge right here.' She had stopped suddenly and peered down one of the side streets. She tapped her forehead. 'That wasn't his real name, of course, but when you are children ...'

'You lived in Cazalla de la Sierra,' I interrupted. '*Abuela Paloma* too?'

Gracia smiled. 'Yes, the entire family. Before the civil war. Sometimes you want to forget these things,' she said with a sigh.

'Will you show us your house, Tía?' I asked, digesting this new information. This was just one more undisclosed fact that added to the mounting reservoir. I had always assumed my grandmother came from Seville.

She hesitated and gave a tentative smile. 'Of course, Mia.'

She led us down a small side street into *Plaza Manuel Nosea* and stopped in front of a large white house that faced the square. She leant on her stick and I could tell she was back in the past.

'It was very different then,' she murmured. 'We were children and knew nothing of political grievances or strife.' She turned her head and looked at me, her shoulders sagging. 'We left before the troubles came, before the world went mad.' When finally she straightened, she tapped her stick on the cobbles. 'No one can understand what it was like, Mia, unless you have lived through such times. It was a period of terrible shame.'

I could feel the weight of her hand on my arm transmitting the depth of her sorrow.

'I am so sorry, Tía, I shouldn't have asked.'

Gracia patted my hand. 'Thank God your generation seem kinder to each other. Come, let us enjoy the evening.'

We stopped at our usual bar in *Plaza Mayor* and our friends joined us. Matias squeezed himself beside Manuela and spent most of the evening gazing into her eyes.

'You are too young for me, Matias,' she insisted.

'I am twenty-two and you are twenty-five, so what is the problem?' He shrugged his shoulders and we all laughed.

Alejandro, my lugubrious bookshop friend, was sitting next to my aunt, with me on his other side.

'Do you know this poem?' he asked her. 'Written by one of the greatest men of your generation. It is scorched into my brain, Gracia, if I may call you that.'

I realised that he was about to recite one of Lorca's poems, and it was too late to stop him.

He finished 'City That Does Not Sleep' with a melancholy bow and gave his undivided attention to my aunt.

'Do you agree, Gracia, it is most profound?' He took a sip of beer, leaving a blob of froth on his lip.

'Oh my dear young man,' she said, taking a clean hanky from her bag and wiping his lip. 'It is truly beautiful.'

Alejandro perked up after that. Tajo, the bar owner, offered me a job towards the end of our evening, possibly because Manuela had told him I was very handy with a bottle of wine.

We were about a kilometre from the town when Gracia wound down the car window.

'Manuela, could you reverse a little, I would like to go to the cemetery; it has been such a long time.'

Manuela weaved backwards down the lane and lurched to a halt.

Instead of going through the small iron gate to the cemetery, my great-aunt remained outside the wall. From the tremor in her shoulders, I knew she was weeping.

'Manuela, why is Tía Gracia so upset?' I cried, wanting to

go after her. Manuela's face was grim. She crossed herself and pointed to the pitted holes embedded in the cemetery wall.

'In the summer of 1936, Franco's nationalists came. It was a massacre. Anyone they believed to have republican sympathies was shot. My grandmother was amongst them. It is said that there is a mass grave somewhere along this wall.'

'*Santa Madre de Dios*, Holy Mother of God,' I exclaimed.

'And now there is an amnesty and Fascist crimes have been forgiven. We have no justice for our loved ones, no help to give them a proper burial. Someday these crimes will have to be acknowledged, Mia. They have to be paid for.'

'But my grandfather was a nationalist,' I uttered, a heavy feeling in my stomach.

'So was Ramon.' Her eyes were unfathomable as she looked at me. 'Those were hideous times.'

The following morning, still troubled by my aunt's weeping and Manuela's face the night before, I grabbed a coffee and went outside. For my entire life I had considered myself half Spanish but suddenly I didn't feel Spanish at all. There were secrets and half-truths, there were a million questions that needed answers, and I knew that I had to find them.

I was having breakfast when I brought up the subject with my grandfather.

'Papa Leonardo.'

He peered at me over his glasses in a knowing sort of way.

'The thing is—'

'What, Mia?'

'Last night we stopped outside the cemetery in Cazalla de la Sierra.'

He was alert now, focussed entirely on me.

'Manuela told me her grandmother was shot and buried in a mass grave outside the cemetery wall.'

There was a long silence. 'And I suppose you want me to tell you what happened there?'

I nodded, focussing on a fly that had landed on my plate. 'Gracia told me the beginning of your story, but I need to know everything.'

His shoulders slumped. 'Then I will continue, but I must warn you, the Civil War was horrific, Mia. Any story from that time will be harrowing; are you sure you want to hear?'

I nodded. 'I have to know, Papa Leonardo, the good and the bad.'

'Well, then, I will start in the summer of 1934. If I remember correctly, I was tacking up Saturno …'

Part Four

Chapter Twenty

June 1934, Andalucía

Leonardo was tacking up Saturno, when Valeria opened the stable door. 'May I come in?'

'Since when have you asked me, Valeria?' he murmured.

'Oh I don't know, perhaps since today.' She looked up at him and their eyes met, but she glanced away.

'Are you coming for a ride?' he asked at last.

'Mama has arranged for me to play tennis with Alberto de la Cueva. I don't want to, but you know how it is.'

Leonardo knew only too well. Every week there were suitors at the house, aristocratic young men from Seville, or sons of the local landowners. Though they were polite to him, occasionally engaging him in conversation, he felt awkward, gauche; in his head he didn't fit in. Despite the name now attached to him, he would never feel good enough.

'Off you go to your boyfriend,' he said.

She bit her lip and her cheeks flushed red. 'Well, then, I shall.'

Leonardo watched her run across the courtyard, the outline of her long legs visible through her muslin dress. The Palamera de Santos family had given him everything when they took him in as their own, but Valeria had always held his heart.

Leonardo tightened the girth on Saturno's saddle and led him outside. Today there would be no schooling, they would gallop over the rough turf and be free.

As they went from the shade into the light, Leonardo felt a moment of pride. Saturno's coat glistened in the sunlight and his body was muscled and strong. The horse's recuperation hadn't happened overnight, it had been a delicate process. Grain and grazing had been introduced slowly, with meticulous care. Several times they had nearly lost him to colic, and Leonardo had dragged him around the yard, willing him to stay on his feet and keep moving. If he went down, they would never get him up again.

Now, five years after the starved creature had arrived at the hacienda, Saturno understood every nuance of Leonardo's voice, the lightest touch of his hand, every aid. In return for rescuing him from his misery, Saturno had given him his soul.

Leonardo vaulted onto Saturno's back, called Luna, and, very soon, they were trotting down the lane.

The following morning, Valeria was down at the yard before Leonardo.

'I couldn't bear to see you downhearted, so today we will spend the entire morning together, you and I.'

'I might be busy.'

Valeria laughed. 'Padre Alvaro isn't coming today, so there is no excuse, Leonardo.'

'If you think I was downhearted because of you, then you are too opinionated, Valeria.'

She pouted. 'Oh well, then, I'll leave.'

'No,' Leonardo said with a laugh, catching her arm, 'I accede, I was a little sad.'

Half an hour later, with water bottles in their saddle-bags and two large slices of Bañu's almond cake, they set off for the deserted Cartuja monastery in the heart of the Sierra Norte Natural Park.

'My mother took me,' Leonardo informed Valeria. 'It was our last adventure together, we had lunch amongst the ruins.'

'And now you are taking me. I am honoured, Leonardo.'

'As long as you don't mind ghosts,' Leonardo said with a grin.

'What do you mean, ghosts?'

'If you listen carefully, you can still hear the monks chanting. They were thrown out early last century, during the dissolution of the Spanish monasteries. A few of them refused to leave and—'

'No, no, I don't wish to hear any more, you are being ridiculous.'

Leonardo lowered his voice. 'Wait and see.'

As they walked their horses along the river bank that wound through the wooded valley, they chatted about their hopes and dreams. Leonardo believed it was just like old times.

'Do you like this Alberto de la Cueva?' he asked as they came out of the shade and into the bright sunlight.

'Depends what you mean by like, Leonardo. He's nice, but that is all.'

'I thought—' They were now riding up a steep track with olive orchards either side.

Valeria flicked away a fly with her whip. 'Do you really believe I would marry someone whose only ambition in life is to do as little as possible? You should know that is not for me.'

'What is for you, Valeria?'

Valeria turned to him, her eyes shadowed by her wide-brimmed sombrero. 'Thanks to you, I know where my future lies.'

'You do?'

There was a pause as she looked at him.

'I shall be a professional photographer. It came to me the moment I held the beautiful Leica in my hands. It seems you have determined my destiny, Leonardo.'

*

When they came to the top of the track, they jumped down and gazed at the group of buildings shimmering in the sunlight ahead of them.

'The Cartuja monastery,' Leonardo murmured. 'But like so many things in Spain, its early history belonged to the moors. When I came here with Mama, we discovered the remains of an eighth-century mosque. I remember my excitement when I unearthed a fragment of tile amongst the ruins. The glaze was still a perfect blue.' He pulled the small corner from his pocket and showed it to Valeria. 'I have kept it with me since that day.'

He slipped it back in his trousers, a distant look in his eyes.

Valeria smiled softly. 'You should be an archaeologist; that could be your destiny, Leonardo.'

They had tethered the horses and were stepping through the crumbling gatehouse to the monastery beyond, when Valeria drew in her breath. The atmosphere had changed, the warm air replaced with the smell of damp and decay. Bats' droppings littered the ground.

Leonardo took hold of Valeria's hand.

'I don't need looking after,' Valeria complained, but she did not draw away.

They stole through the central cloisters, moving from room to room, stepping over broken roof timbers and rotten floors. But Leonardo had saved the best till last. He led her across a patch of scrubland towards an ancient church. Reaching the heavy oak door, he told her to close her eyes and guided her over the threshold.

'Now you may open them and look up,' he instructed, and as Valeria gazed above her she was silent.

The dome was partially open to the sky, but the structure remained. Prisms of light filtered onto the stone floor.

'It is utterly beautiful,' she whispered.

'I knew you would appreciate it,' he replied, showing her the ancient frescoes that remained on the flaking pink walls. 'My mother loved it, and I wanted you to be part of that memory.'

They were leaving to return to their horses when Valeria grabbed Leonardo's arms.

'Chanting,' she whispered. 'I can hear it, Leonardo.'

'I told you,' he said with a smile.

Chapter Twenty-one

July 1934

Leonardo drew up outside the *casa del párroco*, in Aliana, the tiny village near Cazalla de la Sierra, where Padre Alvaro lived, and the priest climbed out of the car. 'Same time tomorrow, Padre?'

'Same time.'

'Are you sure you won't come for a drink? I'm driving into town.'

'I have vespers in half an hour and however much I would like to, I cannot, my friend.'

'It wouldn't do for the priest to be drunk in charge,' Leonardo said with a grin.

'Get on with you, young man.' The priest doffed his black biretta and winked at Leonardo. 'Now I shall have to pray for you.'

As Leonardo started the engine, he glanced back to see the tall, elegant priest climbing up the steps of his house. How he valued his friendship. It had been Padre Alvaro who had inspired him mentally and physically, who had opened his mind.

'You have a sound intelligence, Leonardo,' he had said after his first lesson, 'but more importantly, you wish to learn. It will be an honour to teach you.' And he had kept his word.

The lessons had become the highlight of Leonardo's day, and when Valeria chose to be with her friends rather than in the schoolroom, they had eased his disappointment. It was Padre Alvaro who had helped him to grieve for his mother.

'You cannot run away from your grief, Leonardo, embrace it and you will emerge on the other side.' Finally, Leonardo had revealed the circumstances of her death.

'So you see, my father is a murderer,' he finished. 'Do you still like me now?'

'Like you, Leonardo? Do you think this has changed anything? The Lord God is compassionate and gracious. I am merely one of his humble servants. He loves you, my son, and so do I.'

This morning they had ridden the horses before the sun came up, Leonardo on Saturno, and Padre Alvaro on the Mad One, now renamed Dulce, at Carlos's request. But there was still nothing sweet about the horse. While the priest expertly handled the challenging stallion, he had briefed Leonardo on the state of politics in Europe and Spain. They discussed the effects of the Wall Street Crash and the worrying emergence of a man called Adolf Hitler in a decimated Germany. This was followed by a healthy debate on the socialist and republican democracy that had swept to power in Spain two years before, ending years of dictatorship under Primo de Rivera. With a brief respite for a gallop along the top of the hill, they had walked home continuing their discussion. Breakfast was taken at nine, with Isabel, who was a devotee of the intelligent and sensitive priest.

'So, Priest,' she always called him that, 'is my adopted son doing well?'

'Extremely well, señora; his grasp of mathematics is improving daily, and his interest in politics is sincere. It seems he wants to improve the lot of the common man.'

Isabel looked at Leonardo for a moment, a small frown

appearing on her forehead. 'You are not a communist, I hope, Leonardo?'

'Not a communist, Mama—' Isabel had begged him to call her that – 'but I admit to leanings. At this moment I believe in democracy because at last the workers have a voice and, please God, there will be change.'

Isabel's delicate eyebrows raised as Valeria entered the dining room and flung herself into a chair.

'Mama, have you any idea what is going on around us? Peasants are beaten constantly. Wages are appalling, starvation is endemic.'

'We do our best to look after our workers here,' Isabel replied, drawing in her breath. 'Papa makes sure that everyone is properly housed and has plentiful food.'

'Papa is a good employer, but we are in the minority.' Valeria glanced at Leonardo. 'While other landowners block reforms, nothing improves. Papa needs to use his voice to bring about change.'

'Valeria is right, we are unusual,' Leonardo confirmed. 'On other estates, despite our so-called democracy, conditions are still inhumane. Peasants are actually killed for the smallest transgression. Can you believe that on an estate not far from here, a man was shot for stealing acorns?'

'It's time we did something, don't you see, Mama?' Valeria was leaning forward, her elbows on the table, her eyes shining with passion. She glanced up at Leonardo and he nodded in agreement.

'Everything you say shocks me to the core, but you are not ganging up on me, are you?' Isabel looked a little aggrieved.

Padre Alvaro, who had remained silent throughout, now spoke. 'I don't believe they are, señora, but you must be so proud of the way you have brought them up. They are fighting for justice for the common man.'

Isabel glanced at the priest. 'Thank you, Padre Alvaro, I am certainly proud, but now I can see I must do something.' She wiped her mouth on her linen napkin and stood up. 'Well, then, my children, it is high time I saw this brutality for myself. I suggest we make a few surprise visits to our neighbours and friends.'

Chapter Twenty-two

Leonardo and Valeria had rarely quarrelled in the past, but when Valeria missed her scheduled ride with Leonardo for the second time in a week, his frustration boiled over.

'These days you can't even keep an appointment,' he snapped at her.

She had been about to apologise, but instead she faced up to him. 'I was hardly aware that a ride with you was an appointment.'

Leonardo shook his head as he continued to untack Saturno.

'I am sorry; I overslept.'

Leonardo took off the saddle and hung it over the door. 'Why do you mix with those people?'

'What people?'

'You are still with that Alberto de la Cueva – you said yourself he is a spineless fool living off his father's money.'

Valeria rounded on him. 'That is not what I said, and that is beneath you, Leonardo.'

'Ha, beneath me? It is not only Alberto who is a fool. I thought better of you, Valeria.'

Valeria stormed from the stable and ran to the house, slamming the back door behind her.

'What on earth is wrong with you?' Bañu asked. 'You have a face like thunder.'

'Leonardo,' she cried. 'That is what is wrong with me.'

Bañu shook her head in exasperation and continued sweeping the floor.

Slightly perplexed by her daughter's unwillingness to be social, Isabel encouraged her to hold a party.

'You never see the local girls, *querida*, I think you should mix more.'

'You mean mix with the local gentry, Mama.'

'Would that be so bad?'

Despite her misgivings, Valeria finally agreed but Leonardo declined to attend.

'I promised to take Padre Alvaro into town, I can't let him down.'

'That's an excuse and you know it,' Valeria challenged.

He laughed harshly. 'You are right, it is an excuse, but come on, Valeria, you know what I think, so I don't know why you bothered to ask me.'

'I won't make the same mistake again.'

The evening arrived, and as the girls wafted through the gardens in their gossamer silk dresses, and the boys made polite conversation in the central courtyard, Valeria wondered why she had agreed.

At precisely nine she clapped her hands.

'You had better sit down or cook's soufflés will collapse,' she directed, 'and I wouldn't be in any of our shoes.' Laughter rippled through the guests and as they took their places at the long table, Valeria felt a pang of regret. It had taken her all day to decorate the courtyard, arranging the flowers in the slim vases, positioning the lanterns on the terracotta floor, but the only person she wished to see the magical world she had created wasn't there.

'You are so accomplished, *mi hermosa Valera*,' Alberto murmured, leaning towards her, and Valeria winced, knowing it was time to tell him she would never be his beautiful Valeria.

The last plate had been taken away and the girls had retreated to the edge of the garden pool, when Valeria accepted that she was no longer part of their world. Throughout dinner she had observed her childhood friends, and had listened to their idle chatter about parties and dresses, who was in their set, who was out, and she had longed to get away. More importantly, she had wanted to see Leonardo. Quarrelling with him was stupid and painful to both of them. She would make it up with him immediately.

She was running past the terrace where the boys had taken up residence with a bottle of brandy, when she heard their languid voices drifting through the night air. She stopped, her body still as she listened to their words.

'You know they adopted him, what were they thinking of?'

'Leonardo is a decent chap,' Diego de Mendoza countered.

'Apparently, his father is a murderer, there is bad blood there,' Alberto argued.

He was backed up by another of her so-called friends. 'Don Carlos had a lapse of judgement taking him into their home.'

Valeria couldn't stand it any longer. What was she doing with these rich and indolent fools, with nothing better to do than gossip at other people's expense?

She walked onto the terrace and the conversation stopped.

'You are talking about my brother,' she said quietly, but her voice was deadly. 'Having accepted our hospitality, you have the ill manners to be vile about Leonardo. But I am not fooled, you are jealous because he is better-looking than you, his riding outshines you all, and he has a far superior brain. I think it is time that you left, all except Diego, who had the courage to stand up for him.'

Alberto went towards her. '*Disculpas, mi belleza*, you were not meant to hear.'

'Well, I did.' She turned on him. 'And I am not your beauty, so get out now.'

News of the dinner party sped around locally but Valeria didn't care. It had taught her a valuable lesson, one she would never forget.

Chapter Twenty-three

Leonardo was watching Carlos play tennis with Diego de Mendoza, when Valeria handed him a glass of lemonade and dropped down in the grass at his side.

'What do you think of him?' she asked. 'Do you approve this time?'

'Who?'

'You know exactly who,' Valeria prodded him.

'I assume you are talking about the golden boy playing tennis with your father.'

'That's mean,' Valeria retorted with a smile. 'Are you ever going to like anyone I go out with?'

'Probably not,' he replied with a grimace. Leonardo looked at her over his glass. 'But it is not about me. Do you like him, Valeria? He certainly seems better than the last one, Alberto . . .?'

'Alberto de la Cueva,' she said, leaning against him. 'And yes, Diego is nice.' She took his glass and sipped at the lemonade. 'And he is good-looking, which is helpful.' She scrunched up her nose. 'I have known him for years, so that makes it easy, and Papa and Mama approve.'

'Valeria, this is not about whether Papa and Mama approve, it is whether you could love him.'

Valeria handed back the glass and put her arms around her

knees. 'I am not sure what that kind of love is. I know what sibling love is, because I would die for you and die again, Leonardo.'

'You can only die once,' Leonardo prompted.

'You know what I mean.'

Leonardo put his arm around her shoulder. 'I know exactly what you mean. But I want you to promise me that you will make sure that the man you marry is kind. Kindness is everything, Valeria.'

Valeria twisted a strand of hair in her fingers and turned to look at him. 'When you fall for someone, I will probably kill them, Leonardo. I don't think I can share you with anyone.'

Leonardo started to say something, but the moment was lost when Carlos threw his tennis racket in the air.

'Game set and match, and to think an old man can still beat a stripling like you, Diego.'

'You are a better man than me in every way, Don Carlos,' the young man said with a smile.

The sun was dipping in the sky when Carlos and Leonardo took their evening stroll.

'I can see that you have grown to love this estate,' he murmured, looking beyond him, to the olive groves and woods, the golden wheat and tobacco fields.

'*Por supuesto.* It is the most beautiful place in the world.'

'That is why you shall inherit. When I am gone, it will be yours.'

'Though I am honoured, señor, I could not deny Valeria her birthright.'

'I have discussed it with Valeria and we both agree that it is better this way. Soon she will marry, probably Diego de Mendoza, and he has large estates of his own. Leonardo, one day it will be yours and my lawyers are dealing with the inheritance side. I have instructed Thiago Gallego to prepare you on every detail of estate management. The steward will teach you book keeping, the wage structure, crop management, the business of cultivating soil. And, most importantly, you will learn how to run an estate properly and fairly. It is what I have spent my life trying to achieve. Are you in agreement, my son?'

Leonardo had tears in his eyes as he looked at Carlos. He had never called him that before.

Chapter Twenty-four

On a fine Monday evening, Leonardo drove into Cazalla de la Sierra to complete some errands for Bañu and Juan.

First stop was the confectioner on the corner of *Calle de San Francisco*, to purchase sweets for Bañu; second stop, the tobacconist, to buy cigarettes for Juan. With his purchases completed, he strolled down *Calle Parras* to his usual bar. He had no sooner ordered a beer, when one of the girls from the next-door table leant over.

'So you are Leonardo, the horseman?'

'You could say so, I suppose, but forgive me, I don't believe I know your name.'

The girl laughed and Leonardo noticed her wide mouth and elongated eyes. Her thick black hair hung down her back in a glossy sheet.

'That will be because you are the son of Don Palamera de Santos and I am only Constanza Baptista, the daughter of our local school teacher.'

Leonardo found himself laughing. 'It seems you are determined to put me at a disadvantage, but I do know of your father, he is well respected and well liked.'

'Well, are you going to ask me for a drink?' she said, with a cheeky smile.

Leonardo was taken aback; this girl was unusually forthright. He smiled inwardly; he would definitely have a drink with her.

'Yes, I would like that.' He stood up and pulled out a chair, only too aware of her giggling and inquisitive friends.

When the waiter had taken their order, he offered her one of Juan's cigarettes and took one himself.

Moments later he was coughing and spluttering, and the girl laughed. Leonardo noticed her small white teeth.

'So, Leonardo, you are not used to cigarettes, which tells me one of two things: you are a nice boy and you have bought them for someone else, or you believe smoking to be sophisticated and you are trying to impress me.'

'If it is the latter, I have failed miserably,' Leonardo said with a laugh. 'Actually, I'll be honest. I bought them for Juan, who I work with, and he will be cross because I have opened his packet, so I lose out on both counts.'

The girl looked at him suggestively. 'Not on all counts, Leonardo.'

'So, Constanza, daughter of the school teacher, do you have ten brothers and sisters who drive your poor mama mad?' he asked, pouring her a *Cruzcampo* beer.

'Sadly, not, there is just me and my sister Mariana, who is nanny to a grand family in the north of Spain. I hardly ever see her because she never comes home.'

'I'm sorry, that appears to be a cause of sadness.'

Constanza laughed. 'Life is too short to be miserable. Anyway, my mother is noisy enough for one household. She is the town dressmaker and the local gossip. The fact that I am having a drink with you tonight will be known by the entire population of Cazalla de la Sierra by this time tomorrow.'

'Should I be scared of her?'

'Definitely, but she makes great clothes. This year the whole town is in polka dots.' Constanza raised her eyebrows.

'Men and women?' Leonardo asked with a grin.

'You're a funny boy, Leonardo.'

Leonardo took Constanza home and arranged to meet her the following night.

'Shall we go for a walk?' Leonardo asked as dusk was drawing in.

'Are you a romantic, Leonardo?'

'Nobody has ever called me that before.'

'But you must have had lots of girlfriends, a handsome boy like you.'

Leonardo shrugged his shoulders and Constanza laughed. 'Well, then, I shall be your first girlfriend.'

Leonardo nodded in assent. Constanza was gorgeous and he longed to kiss her.

The following night they sat on the front steps of her house.

'One day I shall fly far from this place.' She waved her hand with a dismissive flip. 'Times are changing, Leonardo.'

'Where will you go?'

'Somewhere, anywhere but Cazalla de la Sierra.' She looked at him then, her dark eyes challenging. 'At last women have the vote and, trust me, soon we will fight with the men.'

'Who said anything about fighting?'

'Ha,' she tossed her head, 'fighting will come.'

Before she could say any more, Leonardo took her in his arms and kissed her, delighting in the taste of her mouth, her hot, darting tongue.

She drew back at last. 'I was about to tell you—' Leonardo silenced her again and put his fingers on her lips. 'Tomorrow you can tell me your political aspirations and views, but tonight I just want to kiss you.'

'That sounds perfectly fair to me,' she said with a small grin.

*

Soon, as predicted, the whole town knew of his budding relationship with Constanza. Shop vendors talked about it, even the barber knew about it.

'So how is that pretty Constanza?' he asked, as Leonardo arrived for a haircut.

Leonardo grinned. 'Is nobody's business private?'

'Not in this town, it isn't.'

Two weeks after they had first met, they were walking down the lane outside the small town, when Constanza dragged him towards the cemetery wall.

'Kiss me,' she demanded, unbuttoning his shirt.

'Are you sure the cemetery is appropriate? All the dead will be watching us,' he murmured, kissing her neck.

'It will stop them being bored,' she giggled. 'They won't have had such fun in years.'

As Leonardo unbuttoned her blouse and buried his head in her soft flesh, he no longer cared.

Leonardo excused himself from supper the following night and Valeria rolled her eyes.

'He has a girlfriend, Mama,' she announced, stabbing a potato with her fork.

Isabel looked at Leonardo and smiled. 'Run along, then, *querido*, you should never keep a young lady waiting.'

As Leonardo drove into town, the full moon shining through the windscreen, he was filled with anticipation. Constanza's suggestive comments had made it quite clear that she wanted to sleep with him.

He met her in the old olive orchard at the edge of the town. Taking her hand, he led her down the hill, until they were away from the eyes of the world, and he laid a rug on the ground.

One by one he undid the buttons on her blouse, then he unzipped her skirt.

As he ran his hands down her body, Constanza arched towards him and Leonardo was lost in her soft skin and her slim, supple limbs.

Constanza introduced Leonardo to her intimate circle of friends and he immediately felt at home. Daniela, her best friend, had auburn curls and a happy smile.

'So you are the boy I hear so much about,' she said. 'You had better look after her, Leonardo.'

There were students training to be teachers or lawyers, young people going into the family business having just left school. The boys liked him for his quick wit and ready jokes, the girls admired him for his natural good looks and athletic physique, but also for his talent with horses. He began to feel a new sensation, a lightness, which he recognised as contentment.

When Leonardo first brought Constanza to the house, Bañu seemed relieved.

'A nice girl,' she said to him afterwards. 'Most suitable.'

Leonardo knew what suitable meant. Valeria's reaction was different. He noticed a change in her mood every time Constanza came to the house. Valeria laughed too brightly and talked too much. One evening before he went into town, Valeria came to the stables where he was brushing Saturno. She leant over the stable door.

'So, you like this girlfriend of yours?'

Leonardo put down the brush. 'Pass me the hoof pick, will you, Valeria?'

Valeria took the hoof pick from the hook outside the stable and passed it to him.

'I do like her, she is opinionated.' He gave a sideways glance at Valeria. 'But I'm used to opinionated women. And she's very attractive.'

Valeria grimaced. 'She's not as pretty as she thinks she is; her nose is too tilted, and her teeth are a little crooked.'

'I hadn't noticed.'

Valeria rolled her eyes. 'I suppose you were too busy noticing other parts of her body.'

'And Diego? How is your boyfriend?' The words were out before he could stop them.

'He is splendid, actually.'

Leonardo put down Saturno's hoof. How he hated Diego. Though Valeria's boyfriend was charming to him, complimenting him on his riding, his fencing skills, he made Leonardo feel ashamed of his background, ashamed of who he was. He knew he should be glad for Valeria but he was alarmed by his constant desire to sabotage her happiness.

When Diego wished to go for a ride a few days later, Leonardo put him on Dulce. They had not gone a kilometre before the horse bucked him off. His small victory was ruined when Valeria marched to the stables and threw open the door.

'How could you put him on Dulce?' she shouted, her blue eyes cold. 'Not only was that unkind, it was also dangerous. Why are you behaving like this, Leonardo?'

'Don't yell, you'll frighten the horses,' he admonished, refusing to look at her. 'Anyway, I can't help it if Diego can't sit a buck.'

'Agh.' Valeria dithered for a moment, then she stormed out, closing the stable door behind her. As Leonardo undid the girth strap and removed the saddle, he was filled with shame. From now on, he would make a major attempt to behave.

His contrition did not last long, however. When he came across Diego reading to Valeria in the garden, his head in her lap, he redoubled his efforts to make her jealous.

Constanza became a constant feature at the house, playing

lawn tennis with Leonardo, walking with him arm in arm. It was as if Constanza sensed it, because she was always even more demonstrative when Valeria was around.

Finally, Valeria came to him. 'Diego's mother has asked me to stay, and I'm going.'

'Where?' he spluttered.

'To their town house in Seville, and I shall stay with Papa afterwards. You are acting like a child and I can't bear to be around you.'

Leonardo reeled backwards as if he had been hit. 'I see. Well, if that is what you think of me, I won't stand in your way.' He turned on his heel and strode across the yard.

Valeria had been away only five days when Leonardo took out his pen and wrote to her.

Dearest Valeria,

Forgive me, I am ashamed of my behaviour. You are right, I did wish to embarrass Diego and it was childish and unkind. If I am honest, I am finding it hard letting you go. You said once you didn't want to share me with anyone. I am finding the same. You have always been my best friend, and though of course I want your happiness more than anything, no one will ever be good enough for you, querida.

There is another thing and I have to say this in a letter because I am probably not brave enough to say it to your face: Don't marry Diego just because you think you will be making him, or indeed our parents happy, only marry him if he makes you happy, Valeria, only if you truly love him. I know you so well and you don't appear to be madly in love, but of course I may be wrong. Please, I beg of you, only marry him if you are sure.

If this letter annoys you, tear it up, but know it comes from a good place in my heart.

Now I shall go because there are horses to ride and work to be done. Padre Alvaro sends all his love and he is missing you too.

Leonardo saw Constanza most evenings and though he found her extremely attractive, something was always holding him back.

'Sometimes I think your mind is elsewhere,' Constanza complained as they walked home from a gathering of their friends in the local bar.

'Nonsense,' he said putting his arm around her shoulder. 'Where else would I want to be, but in your delicious arms.'

Constanza leant against him. 'I hope that is true, my beautiful Leonardo; when I have so readily given you my body, I would quite like some sort of commitment in return.'

As she said the words, Leonardo drew back. In that instant he knew Constanza was not his future.

'I thought you were the girl who was going to fly far from this place,' he reminded her.

'I was hoping you might come with me,' she replied.

When Valeria returned home six weeks later, she rushed into Leonardo's arms. 'I'm sorry I was so awful. I missed you, Leonardo.'

He held her tight. 'Me too. Truce? I won't be beastly about Diego and you'll be kind about Constanza.'

'Definitely truce.'

Isabel found them lying on the library floor playing chess, the weak evening light slanting across their prone bodies. She watched them, their heads close together, absorbed in their game, absorbed in each other.

Valeria looked up at last. 'Hello, Mama.'

'Hello, my child.'

Isabel sighed and left them together. She hoped her daughter would be happy with Diego de Mendoza.

Chapter Twenty-five

A New Year's Eve party was planned at the hacienda to celebrate the dawn of 1935. For weeks there was a flurry of preparation at the house. Isabel had engaged Señora Devera, a well-known chef from Seville, to plan and cater for the evening, persuading a reluctant Bañu to relinquish her kitchen.

'She has no idea,' Bañu complained to Isabel. 'She may work for the nobility, but have you seen the table napkins shaped like swans? *Ridículo*.'

Alfonso joined in the criticism, putting his foot down.

'If she thinks she can tell me how to pour wine in *my* house, she is mistaken. Nor will she go near *my* cellar. I will instruct the waiters on how it should be done.'

Though tensions were running high, it was obvious Señora Devera was an expert in her field. On the morning of the party, the smell of cinnamon and cloves wafted through the house as fruit compotes were prepared. Haunches of venison were brought in from the cold room, and the kitchen bustled with activity. Bañu was intrigued by the fish quenelles, Señora Devera obviously had a penchant for French cuisine. It would be a sumptuous feast for the fifty guests.

There was one person who was less than enthusiastic, and that was Leonardo.

'Why all this absurd expense?' he grumbled to Bañu.

She looked at him closely and then patted his hand. 'You need to accept the inevitable, Leonardo.'

Leonardo shook his head and walked off, his stomach in knots. He knew that tonight Diego would announce his engagement to Valeria. The moment he had been dreading had arrived.

Leonardo found Valeria in Saturno's stable, her face buried in the horse's mane.

'Shouldn't you be getting ready for *your* party?' he murmured.

'It's Mama's party,' she replied, turning around to face him so that her back was against the horse. 'Oh Leonardo, why is it that we have our best moments when we are with the horses?'

'Not always,' Leonardo reminded her. 'It wasn't long ago that you mentioned you couldn't bear to be near me.'

'Did I say that?' Valeria looked up at him and Leonardo noticed her blue eyes were sparkling with unshed tears. 'That was mean of me.'

'I deserved it,' Leonardo commented.

'*Qué lástima* I should be excited, but I am full of nerves. Supposing Diego proposes tonight? I am not sure that I am ready to make that decision.'

Leonardo walked towards her. 'You are right, it is a pity, *querida.*' He was about to draw her close, when Isabel's voice rang through the yard.

'Valeria, you are needed in your room, the hairdresser has arrived.'

Valeria patted Saturno's neck and went towards the door.

Leonardo stood in her way. 'Don't marry him,' he whispered.

Valeria drew in her breath, her eyes fixed on him. 'Give me one good reason why I shouldn't?'

Leonardo's gaze shifted away. 'It's just that—' He paused, unable to go on.

'Just what, Leonardo?' A look of irritation crossed her face. 'Why do you put these doubts in my mind?'

'He is not good enough for you.'

'Just leave me alone; you have done enough damage already.' She pushed past him and ran across the courtyard leaving Leonardo staring after her.

When Valeria came down the stairs in a green velvet gown with a low neckline, and Isabel's diamond necklace nestling against her pale skin, Leonardo had to stop himself from gasping.

She paused at the bottom and smiled at him, but it was a distant smile, and Leonardo's heart cracked.

'You look nice,' he uttered.

'Thank you, Leonardo, you do too.' She fiddled with a strand of loose hair, then glided past him to Diego.

Dinner passed slowly, one course led into the next, but Leonardo hardly tasted the food; all he could think of was Valeria opposite him, and all he could see was Diego leaning towards her in conversation.

After dinner, Diego put his arm around Valeria's waist and addressed the assembled company.

'Thank you, Don Carlos, and Doña Isabel, for allowing me to join your family this evening. I feel sure there will be many more years and many more celebrations together. May I raise a toast to my beautiful Valeria.'

Leonardo was looking at Valeria as Diego spoke. He could see the effort behind her smile and his heart turned over. He realised that for the first time he was more concerned for Valeria than for his own feelings. But on this occasion he couldn't interfere; she had made that abundantly clear.

The music started and Leonardo led Constanza onto the

dance floor to join the dazzling group of guests. At just before midnight he put his arm around her slim waist. 'You look beautiful,' he whispered. 'Let us find a glass of champagne.'

But as everyone raised their glasses to toast in the New Year, Leonardo's eyes searched the room for Valeria.

The first of January was ushered in by a gale that ripped tiles from the roof tops and sent an ancient oak crashing to the ground. Every man was on hand trying to secure a barn that was in danger of blowing away. It wasn't until early evening that Valeria saw Leonardo striding up the hill towards the olive groves with his ancient dog, Luna. Pulling a shawl from the rack, she ran after him.

'I've been looking for you for hours. Please talk to me, Leonardo,' she panted, arriving at his side.

'You must have noticed it's been a busy day, Valeria.'

'Don't patronise me, I've been helping Juan with the horses.'

Leonardo brushed his hand across his eyes. 'I apologise, but I am not in the mood for an argument.'

'I am not here to argue, but you have to tell me, why do you dislike Diego so much?'

Leonardo could feel the anger building inside him.

'Last night, he treated you as if he owned you. And what about his family? You know his father's reputation with his workers? If you marry Diego, your name could be tarnished. Doesn't that worry you, Valeria?'

'I will make them change,' she declared.

'Come on, Valeria, don't be naïve, you are a woman. It's hardly likely they will take any notice.'

'So it matters that I am a woman! And I thought you were different.'

Leonardo threw up his hands. 'You know what I am trying to say. We live in a society dominated by men.'

Valeria's chin jutted forward as she glared at him. 'Well, it's high time it changed. Anyway, it's unfair to judge Diego by his father's standards, he is completely different.'

'I very much doubt it, Valeria.'

'To hell with you, Leonardo. Can't you be happy for me?'

As Valeria ran back down the hill, she knew Leonardo was right, that she was betraying herself by being with Diego. She reached the house, charged into the study and threw herself into her mother's arms.

'I can't marry him,' she exploded in tears. 'It feels wrong, I can't do it, Mama.'

Isabel held her daughter away from her. 'Where has this all come from? You seemed so happy.'

'It's too quick and I don't know—'

Isabel stroked Valeria's hair.

'Well, then, you need time away to reflect on what you really want, *querida*. What about a trip to Florence to visit your cousins?'

'Really?'

'*Por supuesto.*'

Valeria hugged her. 'Thank you for understanding.'

'Your happiness is more important to me than anything, hopefully a break away will make everything clear.'

Bañu supported Isabel's suggestion. 'Go, *mi vida*, my life, your mother is correct, it is the best idea. Elena will certainly keep you occupied, if, of course, you don't go deaf first with her babbling.'

Valeria buried her head in Bañu's bony shoulder.

'Leonardo was right. He said you have to love someone with your entire being if you are going to marry them, and now we will part on such bad terms.'

Bañu kissed her cheek. 'Leonardo will be here when you return. Everything will be all right, you'll see.'

Chapter Twenty-six

January 1935, Florence

Valeria arrived at Santa Novella station to find her cousin waiting for her.

Elena flew towards her. 'Valeria, we are so excited to see you. Mama didn't come to the station, she has a cold. Is this your luggage?'

'*Questo è il mio bagalio*,' Valeria announced with a triumphant smile.

Elena clapped her hands. 'So you now speak Italian, *brava*, Valeria.'

Her two younger siblings emerged from the crowd.

'Jacobo, Donatella, you must keep up, I could lose you in this madness.'

Before they had time to say hello, Elena had summoned a porter who hurried down the platform towards them.

When the suitcases had been piled onto the trolley, they followed the porter back across the marble concourse to the car.

'We have a small errand for Mama to do on the way. Are you happy, Valeria?'

Valeria wasn't given a chance to breathe, let alone reply, but she was more than happy. She hadn't seen Elena for years and she was just the antidote she needed. She hadn't stopped talking the entire week they had spent together in Seville, and it seemed nothing had changed.

The car stopped outside the *Farmacia di Santa Maria Novella* and everyone piled out.

'Mama needs some bath oils and something for her cough,' Elena announced, pushing open the door. 'You will love this incredible establishment, Valeria, it is not really a shop, more like a—' she paused for a moment, trying to think of a name, shook her head and went on. 'The monks have run it for centuries and it is my favourite place in all of Florence.' She ushered them inside and as Valeria wandered from one exquisite room to the next, she could quite understand why. There were coffered ceilings with ornate plasterwork, vaulted and frescoed ceilings, intricately patterned marble floors. The glazed walnut cabinets were filled to the brim with coloured-glass bottles and jars, each with an intriguing Latin inscription. There were pastes with ingredients promising soft skin, creams to cure eczema, lip balms – and the monks had made them all. But it was the smell that delighted her most. Every flower she could think of had perfumed the air with its delicate scent. She was drawn to the counter where a monk was serving.

'I can see that you wish to purchase one of our beautiful scents,' he observed.

'There are so many to choose from,' Valeria responded, running her fingertips over the glass counter.

'Well, then, let me advise you.' The monk took the stopper from six bottles and put a small cardboard strip into each.

'First, I suggest that you close your eyes and hold this blotter beneath your nose, like so.' He demonstrated the technique, inhaling slowly through his nose. He opened his eyes again and beamed at Valeria. 'If you inhale slowly, you will experience the top, middle and base notes of the scent. Don't rush, *signorina*, this may be one of the most important meetings of your life.'

Valeria took the first blotter.

'Now this is *Acqua di Santa Maria Novella*, our oldest fragrance. Caterina de Medici commissioned our Dominican monks in 1533. What do you smell?'

Valeria bit her lip as she concentrated. 'I think – I think citrus?'

The monk clapped his plump hands. 'You are right, signorina, it is a bouquet of citrus notes with a base of bergamot.'

Valeria shook her head. 'I love it but—'

'Your senses will tell you if you have found your fragrance, let us continue.'

For the next few minutes they tried scents with floral notes, woody notes, sweet, oriental notes.

Valeria was quickly absorbed in the process, but it was the last bottle that brought tears to her eyes. She breathed deeply, letting the top note work its magic until it had diffused, and the other notes pervaded.

'What is it?' she whispered. 'What can make me feel this way?'

The monk smiled, his round face crinkling into a thousand lines. '*Melograno*, *signorina*, the pomegranate. This bouquet of sweet, floral notes, with a hint of the orient, appears to have chosen you.'

'Thank you, Father,' she breathed. 'This is definitely the one.'

'I can see that,' he said with a smile.

Valeria had just taken possession of her little bag when Elena arrived, her arms laden.

'Has she selected well, Father?'

'Of course,' he replied with a smile, 'and it will now be her perfume for life, so she will return to our beautiful pharmacy in Firenze each year.'

Before returning to the Palazzo Barberini, the driver took a circuitous route through the city.

'So what do you think?' Elena asked. 'A little different to Seville, no? We are less inhibited here.'

Valeria had to admit that Florence was different to anywhere she had been before. The palazzos were severe, but glorious statues and sculptures occupied the squares and colonnades, giving a feeling of lightness to the city.

'I shall take you everywhere,' Elena promised. 'We shall go to Fiesole, to the Boboli gardens; it is so good to have you here.'

With promises of days filled with culture interspersed with light-hearted fun, Valeria knew it was just the diversion she needed. She had left Spain because it had become quite clear to her that she couldn't marry Diego, but she didn't know how to disentangle herself. It had been much easier just to run away.

A week after arriving in Florence, she wrote to her parents:

I do hope you will forgive me my dearest parents for making such a mess of things. I like Diego, of course I do, and I am sure he would make the perfect husband, but not for me. His speech at New Year surprised and baffled me, it was as if we were already engaged. I felt trapped.

When I return, I will find the courage to tell him to his face. He will probably despise me, but I realise we could never make each other happy.

In the meantime, I am enjoying my time here with Elena. Florence is definitely the place to be distracted. I am behaving like a tourist and it is so liberating. Elena takes me from one magnificent palace to the next, and I have used five rolls of film, which means that I have taken one hundred and eighty images. If you ever had time to put three more in the post, they would be gratefully received.

I have seen more scantily clad statues that would make many a Spanish maiden blush, but the funny thing is, here no one blushes. These beautiful nudes are part of their life.

I have been to the opera, the theatre, to a hundred gardens, and I have walked until my feet are sore. I have already been introduced to several suitable young men. Could it be that you have encouraged Aunt Bernadita, Papa?

She has been the most generous hostess. Yesterday, she guided me down Via Montebello and into a leather shop owned by a Signor Bruscoli, where she bought me a stunning red bag. It arrived at the palazzo three hours later, initialled and embossed with our crest. I am now the smartest signorina in Florence.

There are drawbacks to this beautiful city, however. Fascist militia march through the streets with an energy that seems almost brutal. They terrorise anyone with differing opinions; you would hate that, Papa. Yesterday, we took the train to Rome and watched Mussolini speak from a balcony above the Piazza Venezia. I admit he is a brilliant orator, but his speech filled me with a strange paralysis. I know that all is not well at home in Spain, but I hope we can hold on to the freedoms we have.

Please keep so well and miss me a little, but not too much.

Valeria

Xx

PS It has been raining all day and we couldn't go out. Aunt Bernadita was convinced the banks of the Arno would burst and her favourite bridge, the Ponte Santa Trinita, would be swept away. Fortunately, her predictions were unfounded, and the rain has finally stopped! How awful to think of this beautiful city flooded.

Shortly after posting the letter, Valeria was standing at the top of the hill in Fiesole with Elena, looking out over the terracotta rooftops and spires of Florence, just ten kilometres away. Any sign of the rain had gone, and it was a bright January day.

'Do you see the Duomo, Valeria?' Elena pointed to the cupola of Florence's famous cathedral. 'The project was started by Arnolfo di Cambio in 1296, and the building with the incredible tower is the Palazzo Vecchio, where I took you yesterday. You must remember the Statue of David?'

She nudged her cousin in the ribs and Valeria giggled.

'It's good to hear you laugh, cousin; you have seemed a little preoccupied of late.'

Valeria sighed. 'I cannot marry Diego, and I don't understand what is wrong with me. He is thoughtful, kind, everything Leonardo said I should look for in a man.'

Elena studied her for a long moment. 'Perhaps your heart is with someone else, Valeria.'

'But there's no one else.'

'Are you sure?'

'Yes, well. No one I could possibly dream of being with.'

Elena put her arm through Valeria's. 'Well, if it is not him, there will be a thousand others. Look at me, I am plain. I make up for it by being talkative, the life and soul of the party, but even so – the man I love doesn't even know I exist.'

'But you're wonderful,' Valeria reassured her.

'Wonderful maybe, but I have crooked teeth, mousey hair and I am most ordinary.'

'Anyone who knows you, Elena, would love you completely.'

'They would have to know me pretty well first,' Elena retorted, her voice flat.

Valeria squeezed her hand, her heart going out to her. 'Tell me, dearest cousin, who is the man in question? He would need to be special to deserve you.'

Elena smiled, her face lighting up as she spoke. 'He is the impossibly handsome, charming young man you met at lunch yesterday, Conte Farinata da Montone. But he is pursued by every girl in Florence and it seems by every aspiring mother, so there is absolutely no hope for me.'

As they drove back to Florence, Valeria stared from the window. Elena's revelation had touched her to the core. She had been selfish, inconsiderate. She had never considered her own looks to be anything special, and she certainly didn't consider her cousin plain, but perhaps she hadn't thought and that was the problem. She had been so wrapped up in her own misery, so self-centred. She would make it up to her, she vowed.

The following morning, Valeria rose early and made her way to a jeweller she had seen on the *Ponte Vecchio*. With all that was left of her allowance, she bought Elena a charming gold and enamel butterfly brooch.

'This is for you,' she said at breakfast, handing her the box.

'For me?' Elena's eyes were wide.

'For my beautiful cousin and friend.'

On Valeria's penultimate day in Italy, there was a party at the Palazzo Barberini. It seemed the whole of Florentine society had been invited. While Elena had chosen a dress of pale-blue taffeta with the butterfly brooch pinned to her shoulder, Valeria wore a slip dress of pale grey silk with a pink shawl draped over her arm. Her blonde hair was caught up in a diamond clip. As the two girls hovered at the entrance to the enormous ballroom, Elena took her hand.

'Come on,' she encouraged, and they swept inside, past the liveried footmen holding trays of champagne, past the men and women who flitted through the room like jewelled birds with flashes of diamonds and silk. It was a spectacle of glamour and wealth and Valeria had never seen anything like it before.

'It seems everyone is looking at you,' Elena murmured.

'And you,' Valeria replied.

Grabbing a glass of champagne from a passing silver tray, Valeria caught sight of herself in one of the gilded mirrors.

'This dress, it's so revealing. Maybe it's too—'

'Gorgeous,' Elena finished for her and dragged her further into the melée. Valeria was introduced to one guest after another, she smiled until her cheeks ached, but when her feet could stand no more, she looked around for a chair.

'Over here.' An old lady was beckoning to her and Valeria advanced towards her. There was something vulnerable about the slight, silver-haired figure, sitting on her own amongst the throng of chatting, vibrant people.

'Come and join me.' The old woman indicated the gilt chair at her side. 'It has been empty all evening.'

Valeria sank down with a sigh. 'I am exhausted, so many people asking me questions—'

'So many young men,' the woman interrupted, with a knowing smile. She held out her hand to shake, '*Signora Durante, e tu*?'

'Valeria Palamera de Santos.'

'Forgive an inquisitive old lady, but I have been watching you. May I know your age? It is considered rude to ask anyone over thirty, but not to ask someone as young and as charming as you.'

'Twenty,' Valeria laughed. 'I will soon be twenty-one and, according to my parents, definitely of marriageable age.'

'Ah, parents! They try to force their will upon their children.'

'They would never try to force me, but I still feel the pressure. I want to make them happy.'

'Don't. It is your life and you must follow your heart. I once had a beautiful daughter, but she was lost to me decades ago. Maria was your age when I disapproved of her marriage to an impoverished Englishman. I have regretted it ever since. I lost not only my daughter, but also my granddaughter, Alessandra.'

'You can still make it up to her,' Valeria replied, surprised at the intimacy of the conversation. 'It is not too late.'

'My daughter is dead.'

'I see,' Valeria felt the shock of this unknown woman's death deeply, 'I'm so sorry.'

'But my granddaughter, Alessandra, survives.'

'You must write to her.' Valeria had found herself being pulled into the conversation and becoming part of the woman's story. 'Promise me?'

The old woman smiled. 'You are an earnest young woman, but I give you my word.' She stood up and leant on her cane. 'I don't say this often, but it has been a pleasure to meet you. Should you ever need anything in Florence, here is my card.'

'It has been a pleasure for me too, Signora Durante.'

Valeria escorted the old woman down the wide stone staircase to the waiting car.

When she was ensconced in the back seat, and the chauffeur had placed a rug over her knees, she leant forward and grasped Valeria's hand. 'Good night, Valeria, and remember my words.'

Valeria nodded. '*Buonanotte, Signora Durante.*'

Valeria watched the car pull away and as the lights faded into the distance, she pulled her wrap close. She would probably never see the old woman again, but the chance encounter had affected her. She would do as she had said. She would follow her heart and be damned with the consequences.

Dearest Leonardo, she wrote on a postcard of the Duomo.

You are my best friend. It is you that I have thought of most while I have been away. I have missed you and I have many things to tell you.

Please be at home when I return.

With all my love,

Valeria

Chapter Twenty-seven

Leonardo was having a last ride with Padre Alvaro before he left for his apprenticeship at the bank in Seville. They had enjoyed a gallop along the top of the hill and steam was rising from the horses as they began the long walk home.

'My days will be a little empty when you are gone,' the padre volunteered, letting out the rein so that Dulce lowered and stretched his neck. 'You will be my last and finest pupil, Leonardo.'

'I am sure that can't be true.'

Padre Alvaro smiled, ignoring Leonardo's interjection. 'And it has been an honour to teach you.'

'Without you I would be nothing,' Leonardo said with feeling and glanced across at the priest.

Padre Alvaro chuckled, 'Now that is nonsense. I have helped you a little, perhaps, but you were always going to be special, Leonardo. You have fire and spirit, but you also have compassion.'

Leonardo patted Saturno's neck. 'I take that as the greatest compliment.'

'And so you should. You are a fine young man, and if there is one piece of advice I can give you, it is this: be proud of who you are, what you have achieved. It is no mean feat, Leonardo, but never be ashamed of your roots.'

Leonardo glanced at the priest, who now wore an open-neck shirt beneath his jumper with no outward sign of his priesthood. How well the priest understood him; he knew the chinks in his armour better than anyone. He may have reinvented himself from the rough boy who had arrived on the doorstep all those years before, but inside his head, the son of Esteban the horse breaker remained. Whatever happened in life, he could never run away from his past.

'I will do my best, Father.'

'Now, Leonardo, I have one more question for you: when will you ask Constanza to be your wife? It is clear she loves you deeply, so what are you waiting for?'

Leonardo looked up and the padre could see the anguish in his eyes.

'It is complicated,' he replied.

It was six o'clock when Leonardo pulled the car up outside the *casa parroquial*.

'Are you sure I can't persuade you to have a drink?' he asked.

Padre Alvaro shook his head. 'Notwithstanding the decree that church bells must be silent, I still have a congregation.'

'Of course you do,' Leonardo replied. 'God still exists in the countryside.'

The priest sighed. 'I would like to think so, but our foolish government is trying to rid Spain of its religious heart. Last week a priest was killed by a mob of angry workers only twenty kilometres away from here, and last month two more. The violence is escalating. Monasteries burnt without any intervention from the Government, Church education banned. It is bringing about an attitude of hatred towards the clergy. I agree with democracy, my son, and with socialism. I had great hopes for this new government, but not at the expense of the Church.'

Leonardo frowned. 'I'm worried about how deeply divided society is becoming. Trouble is on its way, and I am not sure where my loyalties lie. My new friends are encouraging me to join the communist party, but my father supports the right and the generals.' He kicked at the bottom step. 'But it distresses me deeply that the Church is being threatened. It is at the heart of all our communities.'

Padre Alvaro smiled sadly. 'The Church has been guilty of greed and of siding with the rich to the detriment of the poor.' He stripped a flake of peeling paint from the door and chuckled. 'I think it is clear that money and power has never been my motivation.'

'Everyone knows you have given your life to the people. You will be safe here, Padre, and if anyone tried to hurt you, I would kill them first.'

The priest's finely boned face broke into a gentle smile. 'Well, then, it is a good job I taught you to fence.'

'I have learnt from the best,' Leonardo countered with a grin.

'But would rapiers serve us well amongst the angry hordes?'

'Promise me one thing, Padre, if ever you are in danger, ring the church bells and I will come.'

'I promise, my son.'

Leonardo was finishing his beer when Constanza came across the piazza towards him and pushed open the bar door. There was something about her walk that always drew attention, perhaps it was the sway of her hips or the swell of her breasts, but every man in the bar was looking at her. This evening she looked particularly striking, in a turquoise wool skirt and a white blouse, pulled together with a wide belt.

She kissed him on the lips and slipped into the chair beside him.

'Have you had a good day?' she asked, pushing her long dark hair from her face.

He nodded. 'Beer?'

'*Cruzcampo, por favor.*'

She fiddled with the mat. 'So,' she asked, 'are you going to ask about my day?' She was looking at him with a hint of defiance in her dark eyes.

'Of course, but I thought—'

'Sometimes you don't think, Leonardo.'

Leonardo was about to retaliate when he stopped himself. He was going to tell Constanza their relationship was over; it would be far better to end it as friends.

He put his hand over her slim fingers. 'I have a feeling you know what I am going to say—' he began.

Constanza's eyes were wary suddenly. 'What do you mean?'

'The thing is, we've been bickering, I think perhaps it's better—' He hesitated; this was not how he had meant to start the conversation.

'I see.' Constanza scraped back her chair and jumped to her feet. 'You are dumping me?' All the men who had watched her earlier were now alert and waiting for his reply.

'Yes – no. I'm so sorry, but I have to be honest with you.' He glared at the fascinated onlookers, who quickly returned to their beers. 'Don't you see, Constanza, I am leaving for Seville, and you are going to be a teacher in Madrid. We are both moving on.'

'But you will come home.'

'Think about it, Constanza. You want freedom, you don't want to be tied to me.'

'Don't tell me what I want.' Constanza was shouting now, her lip trembling.

'We have had a wonderful time, or at least I have,' Leonardo responded.

'I thought we would be married. Everyone did, Leonardo.'

She hurried away from him and after slamming the bar door, she fled across the square. Leonardo followed but was stopped in his stride as she whirled back to face him.

'Leonardo, I have always known that I would have to share you. But I thought you understood you can't have her. I even allowed myself to believe you loved me. How foolish I have been.'

As Leonardo drove home, Constanza's last words rang in his head. He was ashamed and felt suddenly exposed. But he couldn't have married her. She should be with a man who loved her completely, not one who dreamed of somebody else.

At the house, Bañu tried to waylay him but he avoided her, desperate to be alone. 'Leonardo,' she started, 'Valeria is—'

She got no further because Leonardo gave her a distracted smile. 'Sorry, Bañu, can you tell me in the morning?' He left her standing in the hall, and retreated to his ground-floor room on the other side of the internal courtyard.

'Valeria is arriving at about five in the morning,' Bañu finished, speaking to the air. 'I thought you would like to know.'

Leonardo pulled off his clothes, and leaving them in a heap on the floor, went to the shower. As the water ran down his skin, he sighed, a great weariness settling over him. Constanza was right, his heart had been given away long ago. Putting a towel around his waist, he opened the French doors and stepped barefoot onto the lawn. As he gazed up at the stars, brilliant in the night sky, he breathed deeply, accepting at last that there would never be anyone but Valeria. For years he had denied the truth, but it was no longer possible. *You are my best friend*, she had said in the letter. What did that mean? he wondered. Could it give him cause to hope?

Well, she would be home soon, and he would ask her. He might never have another opportunity. Perhaps the stars were aligned in his favour at last.

When Luna scratched on the bedroom door, he returned inside and let her in, burying his head in her rough coat.

'Have I done wrong, old girl?' he asked. 'Have I misled Constanza?'

The dog looked at him with wise eyes and Leonardo gave a wry smile. 'Don't you start, you mangy hound, or I'll put you back where you came from.'

The dog lifted her paw.

As the shadows lengthened, Leonardo paced the room, finally stopping in front of the mirror.

His body was now a man's body, his chest muscled and strong. The half-medallion his mother had given him gleamed against his skin. He unhooked it from his neck, placing it in an old tobacco tin for safe keeping. It signified the past, not the life he led now.

It was four o'clock when Luna emitted a low growl from her blanket on the floor. Leonardo stirred. He thought he could hear the French doors open, but all was silent again. In his dream a warm body stirred beside him, caressed him. He woke with a start.

'Constanza, what are you doing? You shouldn't be here,' he exclaimed, his tone sharp.

'I was mean,' she purred. 'I wanted to make it up to you.'

'No, Constanza, you must leave now.'

'I am sorry, I should never have said those things.'

'But I meant what I said, Constanza,' he declared, wide awake now.

Constanza jumped out of bed. '*Bastardo*,' she yelled, reaching for her clothes. 'I will never forgive you, and when you come crawling back for me I won't be waiting for you, I will be gone, Leonardo.'

Leonardo watched as Constanza ran across the grass. She was nearing the end of the garden, when she froze, caught in the headlights of a car. The car slowed down as it passed and Leonardo groaned with despair. Valeria was home.

Part Five

Chapter Twenty-eight

June 2000, Andalucía

Leonardo's voice was beginning to lose its strength, and his eyes were closing.

'That is enough for now, Mia. Could you find Lucia?'

Raking up the past had obviously exhausted him, so I kissed his forehead and was on my way to the door when his quavering voice stopped me.

'Yes, Papa Leonardo?'

'So now you know the truth; do you still like me?' he whispered.

'Those were the exact words you said to the priest, Papa Leonardo.'

'So I did.'

'And my answer is the same,' I replied.

When my grandfather was rested, Lucia hoisted him into the chair, and I joined him for the exercises the physiotherapist had devised.

'Can't you see, it is useless,' he shouted at us. 'I hate this ridiculous nonsense; we all know I am never going to walk again.'

'We have to stop your muscles wasting,' Lucia retorted. 'And anyway, look how the mobility in your arms has improved.'

He gave up arguing and did as he was told. Afterwards, I wheeled him into the loggia where a ragout of mashed beans, ricotta and courgettes was waiting for him. I tried to feed him but he turned his face away.

'I can't stomach this baby food any longer; can't you cook me something decent?' He glared at Manuela.

'*Sí, señor*, tomorrow I will give you steak, and you can choke on it,' she retorted. 'I prepare nutritious things and all you do is complain.'

My grandfather looked suitably contrite. Manuela was the only person able to achieve this reaction.

'*Lo siento*, Manuela.'

'I will give you sorry when I leave for good.'

At this, my grandfather's cheeks visibly sagged. 'Please don't go away, Manuela.'

She went around the table and wagged her finger at him, but she was smiling. 'Then you will have to behave.'

After lunch, while I read a book, my grandfather sat in his favourite spot overlooking the garden.

'I was completely lost back then, Mia,' he said, breaking the silence. 'The longing was all consuming.' He turned his head a little, to see if I was listening.

'I can imagine,' I replied, wondering how it would be to love someone so completely. 'But what about Grandma Paloma, surely you loved her too?'

'Of course I did, but it was different.'

I thought of my grandmother. Whilst Tía Gracia was plump and outspoken, her sister had been slender and reserved. I remembered her making me clothes that I had never wanted to wear. God, how I had hated the smocked dresses, but I put up with them, knowing the hours of work that had gone into them.

'She was a wonderful grandmother, Papa Leonardo, and so kind.'

'She was indeed.' He gazed into the distance, his thoughts obviously drifting back to the past.

I was in the middle of the chapter when Leonardo interrupted me again. I put down the book, one of my mother's all-time favourites, *The Thorn Birds*. A highly improbable story, but a totally addictive novel about a priest and his love for a beautiful young woman.

'Do you still take photographs, Mia? I haven't seen you with a camera for years.'

'Not since Ashley died,' I replied, feeling the usual stab of pain when I mentioned my father. The best present, indeed one of the rare presents he had given me, was a polaroid camera for my eighth birthday. It was still at my mother's house, where it had remained since his death.

Leonardo looked as if he wanted to say something, but he refrained. He had loathed my father, rightly so, for being a hopeless husband and an equally bad father. I remembered the first time my father had instructed me to call him Ashley.

'Forget the "Daddy" bit, Mia, it makes me feel old,' he had said, 'but I'd like to be your friend.' He wasn't much of a friend, but I still called him Ashley.

Leonardo patted the arm of my chair, pulling my attention back to him.

'What would you say if I gave you Valeria's camera? You know the Leica I bought for her?'

At once I was gripped with excitement. The camera was a link to Valeria and a connection to everything that had happened before.

'Are you sure?' I gasped.

'Completely sure. It's in the bottom drawer of the linen

cupboard in my bedroom, it should be easy to find.' He watched me dithering. 'Go and get it now.'

I charged upstairs. Papa Leonardo's bedroom was another place I had never explored.

His room was tidy, there were fresh flowers in the window, his riding trousers were hanging over the back of a chair. The small Pooh Bear my father had given me and I had discarded in anger after his death, was tucked behind a cushion.

I found the camera case beneath the sheets at the bottom of the drawer and took it back to my grandfather. He held it for a moment, his eyes closed.

'For you, Mia,' he said at last, as if waking up from a distant dream. 'Perhaps you will take up where Valeria left off. She loved that camera, using it throughout the war as a photo journalist. She was very well respected, I believe.'

It was difficult to thank him adequately, as the storm of emotions swirled through me, so I just squeezed his hand.

Unscrewing the lens cap, I looked through the view finder. The camera had seen so much, it had witnessed a country at war.

'What became of her?' I asked, holding my breath.

He looked up at me for a moment, his eyes dark with pain.

'Oh Mia, it breaks my heart.'

My grandfather was asleep when I left him, the lines on his forehead relaxed. Putting my beautiful camera on the hall table, I went to see Lyra. As I rested my face against her gleaming coat, I felt the past and present collide. My grandfather had found the resolve to leave Constanza, knowing that his affection for her was not enough. By telling me his story, he had highlighted the failings in my own relationship, giving me the strength to set myself free.

With Lyra nuzzling my arm, I took out my phone. Matt answered immediately, and I drew in my breath.

'Matt, the thing is…'

'I am assuming this is important, sweetheart,' he interrupted, 'because I have a meeting at three.'

'It is,' I paused before taking the plunge. 'I am so sorry, but I really can't marry you.'

'What are you talking about? Have you gone mad, Mia?'

I swallowed, imagining the shock on his handsome face. 'No, Matt, I am not mad, it's just that I am not the girl you met three years ago. I can see now we want different things.'

'I prefer that girl, Mia, not the woman you seem to have become. Are you telling me you would rather look after an invalid on some estate in the back of beyond, than take the life I could give you?'

'Matt, that is entirely uncalled for.'

'Uncalled for? Hardly, Mia. I offered you everything, I—' His voice broke and for a moment I wanted to reassure him.

'It will be for the best, Matt; you will meet someone else who shares your interests.'

His voice hardened. 'Well, your biological clock is ticking, so good luck, Mia.' With that he slammed down the phone.

Chapter Twenty-nine

With the dreaded phone call finally made, it was time to tell my family. None of them were particularly surprised.

'*Ah querida*,' my mother said. 'However difficult, you have made the right decision. If you need me, I am here.' Having reassured her that I was fine, I dialled Poppy's number next.

'Golly, you did it, are you OK?' she asked. 'Just look on the bright side, Mia, think of all those dreamy Andalusians who are no longer out of bounds.'

Typical Poppy, I thought, putting down the phone. The situation was put completely into perspective when I walked into the kitchen.

'You gave up a man who loves football, how could you?' Manuela wailed. 'And he was rich!' she exclaimed, throwing her hands in the air. 'My mother says you should always hang on to a good man.'

'Thanks for that, Manuela,' I said but she had not finished.

'It is not easy to find a suitor, especially at your age, Mia.' She looked at me appraisingly. '*Sí*, you are pretty, if a little undeveloped in certain departments. Maybe someone in an auction house will find you attractive.'

Delighted by her faith in me, I went to see my grandfather.

'It's done, Papa Leonardo, I am no longer engaged.'

'You know the old saying, Mia – when you are thrown off a horse, you get straight back into the saddle. Now you can get on with your life, what a gift that is.' He smiled at me for a moment, his face brightening. 'Why don't you take Valeria's camera into Seville to get it looked at. There is a photography shop in *Calle Arroyo* that has been in the same family for the last hundred years, I am sure they will stock the right film.'

Later that afternoon, while Ramon manoeuvred the car through the heavy traffic, I mentioned my break-up with Matt.

'I am not very knowledgeable in these situations,' he said, looking in his rear-view mirror. 'But if I have learnt one thing, it is this: if something is wrong in your life, you need to change it – more importantly, you should always follow your heart.'

Moved by this taciturn man's observation, I thanked him, lapsing into silence until he had found a place to park.

'Can I ask you a question, Ramon?'

'It depends on what it is,' he said, with a wry smile.

'Why you don't call my grandfather by his Christian name when you are such close friends?'

'Because he is my employer,' he responded. 'And he was also my senior officer in the army during the Civil War.'

That was something I was not expecting. I clutched the camera, realising that, bit by bit, I was unpicking the past.

Peering through the shop window, I studied the girl behind the counter. She had a ponytail and glasses and seemed to be immersed in a manual that she continued to read. The shop had one of those bells above the door that clanged loudly even though the interior was tiny and I was the only customer.

'*Buenas tardes.*' I smiled at her and she nodded, returning to the manual. Though not the friendliest welcome, it gave me time to look around.

Every inch of space was filled with cameras, both modern and old. There were digital Olympus, Pentax and a Hasselblad, all crammed onto the shelves. Tripods, wide-angled lenses, flash units, every possible piece of equipment and accessory, was piled into the other half of the small shop.

'Do you sell film?' I asked.

She glanced at the shelf behind her, stacked with films, started to say something, obviously impolite, and then changed her mind. Her attitude transformed, however, when she saw my camera.

'Ah, I see, for this.' She took it from me and stroked the surface. 'Beautiful,' she whispered as if talking to a lover.

I nodded. 'I'm going to use it again.'

Her chin jutted forward. 'If you don't, it would be a crime.'

I began to realise I was in the company of a camera nerd and I would have to watch my words.

She selected a roll of film from the shelf. 'Cameras like these are fashionable again. Thank God not everyone is digital. Did you know that, unlike the Leica Two, this exquisite Leica Three includes an extended range of slow-shutter speeds?'

I didn't, but agreed that it was a remarkable camera.

'The shutter speed on this is one five hundredth to one twentieth of a second. Amazing, no? Sorry, once I get started on the subject, I can't stop. I will load it for you now.'

She opened the back and was about to pull out the spool when she stopped and closed it again. '*Dios Mío*, there is film still inside.'

'What? But I don't think it has been used since the 1930s.'

'It would be better if you leave this with me. My father will probably be able to retrieve it intact.'

'You mean it could be developed? Over sixty years later?' I repeated in surprise.

'Possibly,' she said, turning the camera over with reverence.

'But it will have to be sent off to an expert. You wouldn't want it to be compromised.'

I couldn't bear to be parted from the Leica, but I left the shop with a white slip of paper and the promise that she would send me a card as soon as she had any further information.

Ramon didn't share my excitement when I relayed the news. 'You need to tell your grandfather first,' he said, looking at me sternly as he closed the car door.

'I will, Ramon,' I assured him. 'Let me find the right time.'

That night, I tiptoed down the stairs and into the garden. It was cool at last, and a soft breeze fanned my face. I lay down on the lawn and remembered when I used to lie on the grass with my grandfather, looking up at the moon.

'You can make a wish when it is full,' he had said to me once. 'A big wish.' And I had scrunched my eyes tight.

'How big?' I had opened them again.

'This kind of big.' Papa Leonardo had stretched his arms so wide that the wish was half the size of the whole world, or so I had thought at the time.

'Should I say it out loud?'

'If you want to, Mia,' he encouraged.

'Then I wish that Ashley was different. I don't mind him being in a band, Papa Leo, but I would also like him to do normal things like the fathers of my friends.'

There was silence and my grandfather had given a small cough. 'I am not sure that is the best wish, Mia, because there are some things we cannot change.'

'I understand,' I had said, but I didn't really. I believed if I wanted something badly enough it might come true. It hadn't, because, six years later, Ashley's motorbike had collided with a lorry on the way to the recording studio.

As the heavy scent of flowers drifted through the garden, I

thought about Matt. He had been my safety net: predictable and straightforward, so very different from my father. But he would never have lain on the grass with me making wishes to the moon, nor would he have galloped through the meadows at night trying to catch the fireflies.

As I looked up at the yellow lozenge in the sky I wondered what my future would bring.

Chapter Thirty

July 2000

I was examining a letter from the bank when Gracia knocked on the office door. I had no idea why she felt the need to knock, but she always did.

'Do you want a coffee, *querida*?'

'No, thank you.' I looked up from the pile of bills and there must have been a scowl on my face because Gracia put a hand on my shoulder.

'If you ever need any help, dear, with the accounts, that is …'

I gave a big sigh. '*Tía*, thank you, that is so kind, but I can manage.'

'The thing is, I am quite good with numbers. I have done a little accounting before.'

'You have?' A feeling of relief began to flood through me.

'After the war I worked in the accounts department of a shop in *Calle Velazquez*. I would love to help.'

I looked at the sea of chaos in front of me, pushed back my chair and hugged her. 'I am a little out of my depth,' I admitted, enveloped in a waft of lavender talcum powder. 'I thought I could do it, but it's such a mess.'

'Well, then it is settled.' Great-Aunt Gracia had an efficient look on her face and I smiled.

From that moment she took over in the office. Actually, it wasn't really an office, more of a library. Dark wood bookshelves filled the walls and an old globe stood in the corner. I believe my grandfather had removed some of the bookshelves from the library in Seville when the house had been sold.

There were suddenly in-trays and out-trays, and my grandfather's chaos, which I had tried to reorganise, miraculously disappeared from the desk. Unfortunately, I still needed to keep on top of the funds.

I came into the office early one morning to find Gracia at work, her head bent over a sheaf of papers.

'Coffee?' I asked, smiling at how the tables had turned.

She shook her head, and pushed her glasses, a scaled-down version of Dame Edna's retro pink spectacles, back on her nose.

'I assume we are solvent?' I jested.

She looked down at her neat rows of figures and cleared her throat. 'Not exactly, Mia. The Ortega sale helped, but as you know there were so many outstanding debts. I hate to suggest this but…'

'You mean,' I said, feeling a heaviness in the pit of my stomach, 'is there anything else we can sell?'

'Five thousand euros would get us through the next few months.'

I forced a smile to my face. 'I'll see what I can find.'

I knew immediately the item that had to go. The egg was now back on the drawing-room table. I picked it up and pressed my finger against the jewelled clasp. At first it didn't open, but I tried again with a lighter touch, and the top lifted to reveal the beautiful little foal. Carl Fabergé or not, it was still a wonderful piece and the workmanship was exquisite. I took out the tiny golden object and held it in my hand, marvelling at the miniature limbs, the delicate head. I couldn't bear to sell it, but as my eyes swept the room, I realised there was no other piece likely to fetch the money we needed.

After gaining my grandfather's permission, I wrapped it in tissue paper, and before I could change my mind, I went to look for Ramon. An hour later I was back at the front desk of the Ortega salerooms in Seville. It was there that Felipe found me.

'It's you,' he teased, emerging from one of the auction rooms. 'It seems you can't keep away from us.'

I could feel my face turning pink. 'I have to sell the Fabergé foal,' I blurted, 'I mean the egg.'

'But it is precious to you.'

'There is no other way, we—'

'Forgive me, Señorita Ferris, that was thoughtless. There must be many expenses with your grandfather. Please sit down for a moment while I go to my office.' He reappeared ten minutes later, and leant over the front desk.

'Move my last appointment, will you, Livia,' he instructed, before turning back to me. 'This is not the action of a professional auctioneer,' he admitted, 'but I have arranged to take you to a friend of mine who is a jeweller in *Calle Tetuán*. He specialises in Fabergé and I am sure he will offer a good price.'

'But…?'

'Then you won't have to pay our exorbitant commission,' he explained with a boyish grin.

'Ramon is waiting outside for me.'

'Tell the charming Ramon that I will drive you back home afterwards.'

'That's extremely kind, but why are you doing all this?'

He smiled a slightly lopsided smile. 'To be honest, Mia, I have absolutely no idea.'

*

Felipe was as good as his word; the jeweller was more than fair. As I held the Fabergé foal for the last time, I knew there was no other choice, but it was still difficult to let it go.

'*Venga*,' Felipe encouraged as we left the shop. 'I can see you need a diversion, please allow me to take you to the *Museo de Bellas Artes*. The Picasso exhibition finishes next week.'

Over the next hour we discovered a shared love for Picasso's work.

'My favourite period,' Felipe murmured, standing in front of a canvas of a seated woman huddled in a blue cloak, her head drooping, a solitary glass on the table in front of her. 'She was probably one of the inmates from the St Lazare woman's prison, but somehow her cloak elevates her from a tragic destitute to a representation of the Virgin Mary. Extraordinary, don't you agree?'

'The Blue period,' I whispered, my gaze moving from the painting to Felipe, aware suddenly of the passion in his eyes and the way his brow furrowed when he concentrated.

His voice was now soft. 'His great friend Carlos Casagemas shot himself during this time. Apparently, it was *at* a farewell dinner at the *Café de l'Hippodrome* in Paris. It was only a few years after the death of Picasso's seven-year-old sister. You can see the grief in his canvases, Mia.'

I had never thought of it in this way but suddenly all of Picasso's struggles, his vulnerabilities, were in the images in front of me. I could see his poverty, even his emotional frailty, and I was moved.

When we stood in front of the enormous copy of the famous *Guernica* there were no words.

'That is what war looks like,' Felipe said eventually, his face grim. 'But *Guernica* was more than just war, it was a bloody massacre.'

I swallowed, looking at the raw emotion in the black-and-white canvas. The artist's anger and outrage over the Nazi bombing of the Basque city in northern Spain was expressed so powerfully, it brought tears to my eyes. It had become a symbol of the genocide committed not only during the Civil War, but in wartime generally, and it provoked a deep sadness within me. I shook my head, 'Will people never learn,' I said with a sigh.

Afterwards, perched on stools in a tapas bar, the image of *Guernica* still fresh in our minds. Felipe put down his glass.

'Even now, old loyalties divide communities, anger and hatred bubble beneath the surface.' He looked at me and I could see his hesitation. 'My grandfather was a colonel in the republican army and I am aware that Señor Palamera de Santos was on the nationalist side. I hope that doesn't make us enemies.'

I toyed with the olive in my drink and looked across at him. 'Hmmm, difficult,' I said with a slight grin. 'But I think we can still be friends.'

Chapter Thirty-one

The following morning, I rose early and walked up my usual track. Each day my roots in Andalucía were deepening. England seemed more remote and unfamiliar, and I wasn't sure that I ever wanted to go back.

I remembered the car journey home with Felipe. Pink Floyd was playing in the background and the windows were open.

'It meant a lot, sharing the exhibition with you, Mia,' he had murmured.

'So many incredible paintings,' I volunteered, 'but the *Guernica* affected me most. I realise I know so little about the Civil War; my grandfather rarely mentions it.'

'I think you will find it is a common thread with many of that generation.' Felipe was strumming his fingers on the steering wheel in time to the music, his face lit by the dashboard.

'I'd like to learn more,' I said, aware of the emotion in my voice. 'Not just from books, but from people who fought in the war. There is little time left, they are all old men.'

'And women,' Felipe qualified. 'Yes, you are right, we shouldn't let the truth die.' He smiled suddenly, his jaw softening. 'And I might know someone who would be willing to talk to you.'

*

I reached the top of the hill and paused to catch my breath, a wave of guilt washing over me. I had broken off my engagement to Matt and now, only a short while later, I was falling for someone else.

What was I thinking of? Felipe's firm was involved with my family on a professional basis. I shouldn't mistake his kindness and generosity for anything else. Any romantic ideas that I might feel were highly inappropriate.

My thoughts were interrupted by the shrill ringing of my mobile phone.

'Mia?'

I recognised his voice immediately and my stomach lurched.

'Thank you for yesterday,' I said, my voice unsteady.

'I have been reflecting on what you said. My grandfather, the colonel, still comes into the auction rooms two afternoons a week. He would be delighted to meet you and you can question him on the Civil War. For ninety-three, his memory is formidable.'

It seemed that my excitement at meeting Felipe's grandfather overtook any feelings of remorse, because on Thursday I was back in Seville. Señor Ortega stood up when I entered his office. Despite his age, his bearing was erect, his figure slim. Immediately, I noticed the glint of humour in his eyes.

'You want to quiz me, apparently?' he said with a warm smile. 'Please sit down. My grandson tells me you are interested in *la Guerra Civil*. Felipe, can you arrange for some coffee.'

Over the next half-hour I learnt of the challenges he faced as a colonel in the republican army. When he spoke, it was as if the war had finished only weeks before.

'I am afraid the Non-Intervention Agreement badly let us down,' he admitted with no outward rancour.

I must have looked puzzled, because he sighed.

'Of course you don't know, why should you, but in brief, your English Prime Minister, Stanley Baldwin, called for the European powers to abstain from intervening in Spain.'

'For what reason?'

'I think they feared the spread of Communism from the Soviet Union to the rest of Europe. Twenty-seven countries signed the agreement in September '36. No arms or munitions were to be shipped to Spain, can you imagine that? How can you fight a war without them?'

My face fell. 'I am so sorry.'

'Germany, Italy and the USSR subsequently ignored it, but what a catastrophe!'

I looked down at my hands, unsure what to say.

'You see, Señorita Ferris, if we had received the expected aircraft and armaments from France and Britain, our position would have been very different. The French government was persuaded that if they assisted us, Mussolini and Hitler would aid the nationalists. They did anyway, of course, so we had little chance of competing with the small number and ineffectual aircraft the Russians gave us. It was a miracle that we managed to hold out for three years, but in the end, we were overcome.'

When Señor Ortega stood up, he looked drained and I realised this signalled the end of our conversation. It was only when he accompanied me to the door that I became aware of his limp. He noticed my look and patted his leg.

'A legacy from the Battle of Alfambra,' he said, with a grimace. 'It continues to give me pain all these years later. Half the men in my unit were massacred. Cut down by swords, trampled beneath iron-clad hooves. It was the stuff of nightmares seeing those horses thundering across the ground towards us.' He drew in his breath. 'It was horrifying being on the other end of a cavalry charge. I survived, but many didn't. I apologise for mentioning this now, but the battleground is forever in my mind.'

He bent over my hand. 'It has been a pleasure to meet you, Señorita Ferris, and thank you for listening to the ramblings of an old man.' He straightened, and a mischievous grin crossed his face. 'Here is something to think about, young lady. However much I despised Franco, I have to admit his perverse machinations did keep us out of the Second World War!'

Chapter Thirty-two

In late July, I decided to take up Tajo's offer of a job in the bar in *Plaza Mayor*. Although the wages were basic, he assured me I would more than make up for it in tips. It was a good way to keep up with my friends and provide a small contribution towards the cost of Leonardo's care.

The church, *Iglesia de Nuestra Señora de la Consolación*, was at one end of the square and the appropriately named Tajo's was at the other. Following the Sunday service, worshippers would pile out of church and go straight to the bar. In summer the chairs and tables spilled off the pavement and onto the cobbled road, but no one seemed to care.

Tourism was a big industry in Andalucía, but it seemed that this particular July they had all made their way to Cazalla de la Sierra. Matias was always guaranteed to lift my spirits when I was flagging

'Sit down, *querida*,' he said one evening as I rushed past.

'But I can't, Matias, I am working.'

He smiled and shrugged his shoulders.

'If I wasn't in love with Manuela, I would marry you and give you lots of babies, so you wouldn't have to work at all.'

It wasn't exactly what I had planned for my life, but I grinned, feeling immediately better.

Alejandro was also a constant at the bar; if he wasn't with Matias, he would be on his favourite stool inside. Whether I was carrying a tray of drinks or preparing an order, he would distract me with a poem that he would put into the pocket of my apron.

'Learn this, Mia, and you will understand Spain.' I believed it would take a lot more than a poem on a scruffy piece of paper to understand the complexities of the Spanish race, but I appreciated the thought and read them at home.

There were also new friends I met through my work at the bar. Anna from the *farmacia* painted each of her fingernails a different colour and had bosoms that turned heads. Tomás was an architect from Seville who returned to his parents' house most weekends. Then there was Ruiz Belmonte, a local electrician who offered me free safety checks at the hacienda if I would have a drink with him after work. I think it had something to do with the length of my skirts rather than the quality of our beer. On one shift, when I wore a floaty dress that reached halfway down my calves, he was obviously disappointed.

'Ah, Mia, you have ruined my day. You are hiding the best legs in Andalucía.'

Even though I was delighted with his compliment I didn't believe a word of it, but I was still humming half an hour later.

I was inside collecting my salary and tips from Tajo, when there was the roar of a Harley-Davidson outside. I knew its distinctive sound immediately.

I looked up but all I could see of the helmeted rider were long denim jeans, a white linen shirt and tanned hands.

I was grumbling to Alejandro as I cleared a table, but when Felipe Ortega took off his helmet and shook out his long wavy hair, I have to admit, there was a flutter in my chest.

'I had to persuade Manuela to tell me where to find you,' he told me with a grin.

'Have you just found out the Fabergé egg is by the master himself, and it is worth a fortune?' I teased.

'Actually, this has nothing to do with work. I came to take you to the beach.'

I could see Ruiz bristling as he glared at Felipe.

Felipe suddenly looked apprehensive. 'Forgive me, I didn't mean to sound presumptuous.'

I pushed a strand of hair behind my ear. 'But it would take an hour to get there.'

He raised an eyebrow. 'Not on that.' He gestured through the window and a shiver went down my spine. There was something intimidating about the motorbike, and exciting, but since my father's death, it was definitely not allowed.

'I can't,' I muttered, knowing I had given my mother my word.

'Please, Mia, I would love you to come.' The expression on his face was appealing and I found it hard to resist.

'But I shouldn't…' It wasn't the moment to tell him about Ashley.

'There is something I want to show you.' He could see I was wavering. 'Please?'

I laughed. 'I give in, but first I must get my things.'

Rushing to the cloakroom, I applied a dab of lipstick and brushed my hair. My logic told me it was a bad idea, but my heart said otherwise.

As I walked across the square, I could feel all eyes upon me. I knew this signalled an end to any complimentary checks from Ruiz.

Felipe passed me his spare helmet, and I couldn't help wondering who had worn it before. I hitched up my long skirt, put my arms around his waist and we roared over the cobbles.

'We are not actually going to the coast,' he shouted as we headed inland.

'If you're trying to kidnap me, I promise I'm not really worth the trouble.'

Felipe laughed at this. 'Kidnapping was not exactly what I had in mind. If you want a beach there is one on the river nearby, but where I am taking you is actually a little more . . . picturesque. It is also one of my favourite places in the world.'

For the next half-hour we drove at speed in the direction of *San Nicolás del Puerto*. There was something exhilarating about being on the powerful machine, but also something intimate, the proximity of our bodies, my face pressed into his back. As the road climbed upwards and the trees shut out the sun, I leant closer.

We parked by the sign and leaving our helmets on the handlebars, we scrambled down one of the many mountain paths. There were fallen branches to negotiate and tangled vegetation. Occasionally, Felipe took the wrong trail and we had to double back. We had just clambered over a boulder when, without any warning, the trees petered out and we entered a large clearing. Encircled by limestone cliffs was a crystal-clear pool. Cascades of frothy water tumbled over the rocks and gushed into the water below.

I held my breath because I recognised the spot, it was familiar and calming, even the stream gurgling down the rill was known to me. I had imagined it so many times.

'It's utterly beautiful,' I murmured.

'The Huéznar cascades. It's the view in your favourite painting,' Felipe replied.

That night I couldn't sleep, my mind still full of the glittering water and of the scent of Felipe's back as I pressed against him. He knew about my love for the painting, and he had taken me there. No man had ever done anything like that for me before.

Chapter Thirty-three

August 2000

I had just returned from my lunchtime shift at the bar when I found the official card waiting for me. The camera was ready for collection. This time, Manuela offered to take me and once again I put my life in her hands. As we hurtled through the streets of Seville, I remembered the first time I had seen Manuela's tiny Fiat 500 screech to a halt outside the kitchen door.

'Don't worry, she cooks better than she drives,' my grandfather had promised, already beguiled by Manuela. And I recalled the Christmas party she had taken me to, or rather the Christmas party I had missed because we had ended up in a ditch. I had been wearing my vintage Balenciaga black-and-white mini-dress, but the only man who saw it that night was the mechanic who had driven the recovery truck.

In a way Manuela reminded me of Poppy. Not in her looks, of course – where Poppy was lean like a racehorse, Manuela was short and curvaceous – but in her attitude to life. Both were irreverent and confident, they seemed to grab life with both hands.

At last we screeched to a halt outside the camera shop, and while Manuela waited in the car, I staggered in, my legs shaking.

The girl looked up. 'You are obviously impatient to get your camera, but there are speeding fines on this road,' she said with a grin.

Immediately I liked her better and knew we would end up friends.

She took the camera from a locked drawer and handed it to me. 'And before you ask, no film. It is still with the experts in Madrid.'

'When will you know?' The question popped out before I could help myself.

She looked at me over the top of her glasses and shrugged her shoulders. 'It has been in the camera for seventy years, so what is a few more weeks? *Paciencia, señora.*'

I grinned at the reprimand. It was quite obvious you should never pose a question like that to a camera fanatic.

I paid what seemed to be a very reasonable amount for six rolls of film and a smart new camera case and was going out through the door when she called after me.

'I have a message from my grandfather. He remembers selling the camera to a young boy over seventy years ago.'

'That boy was my grandfather and he is still alive,' I said with growing excitement. 'They should meet again.'

'They would have much to talk about.' She held out her hand. 'My name is Rosa, by the way,' she said with a smile.

My grandfather was sitting in a high-backed chair in the study when I returned. The windows were open, a warm breeze ruffling the curtains.

Lucia had placed his legs on a stool with a soft sheepskin beneath his feet, but when he turned to greet me, he grimaced with pain.

'Your legs?'

He nodded and I sat down on the stool and began to massage them.

'I hate you having to do this,' he admitted, his face relaxing.

'I would rather I didn't have to, but only because I wish you were walking, and your muscles weren't so stiff, not because I mind.' And it was true, I really didn't mind these days. My grandfather was a human being in pain and I would do anything for him. I discovered that my capacity for love transcended any squeamishness, and I realised there were things I actually liked about myself. This was a revelation because there hadn't been much before.

'Do you know what I miss most, Mia?' His words broke into my thoughts. 'I would love to sit on a horse again, however impossible it sounds.'

His eyes had a faraway look and I could see he was dredging up memories of flying over the turf on his beloved Saturno.

'I would risk it all again, Mia, just to feel a horse beneath me and have the wind in my face.'

'I am so sorry.'

'Don't be, that's life.'

At that moment the unique aroma of horse sweat and stables wafted through the open window.

'The stables have come to us,' my grandfather said with a sigh.

We were listening to my grandfather's favourite piece of music, a classical guitar duet by Enrique Granados, when I told him I had collected the camera.

'Do you want to see it in its new case, Papa Leonardo?'

He nodded. 'I am so happy you are going to use it.'

I retrieved the camera from the hall and put it on the table beside him.

'Oh Mia, so many memories,' he responded, drawing in his breath.

I was about to mention the undeveloped film, but something held me back. I didn't wish to raise his hopes if it was damaged. At that moment he looked peaceful, the rich guitar music reverberating around the room, Valeria's camera close to him, it seemed a pity to interrupt the mood.

The following day, I started taking photographs. It was as if the camera belonged in my hand. There were photographs of the horses, the house, even Dante's dog, anything that came into my range. The only person who escaped the shutter was Leonardo. He was a proud man and would never wish to be remembered in this way.

I took it with me to work and when my shift had finished, I photographed ordinary Spaniards going about their business or relaxing in the square. I wished to capture their expressions, the lines on their faces, the knowledge in their eyes. I had just taken a shot of a group of old men playing dominoes, when Felipe appeared in the centre of my lens.

I stepped back, feeling like a child caught in the act of doing something wrong.

'So you ride horses and you take photographs?' he asked.

'I actually have a lot of talents,' I replied with a grin, hoping that my cool exterior did not betray my confusion.

'Well, let me show you something worthy of your camera. Have you been to the old Carthusian monastery?'

I shook my head, shamed that in all these years I had neglected to go there.

'I will take you now. We can go on my motorbike or we can walk, it is your choice, either way it won't take long.'

Four kilometres later we were still walking. 'This better be worth it,' I puffed, as we neared the crest of a hill.

'It will be,' he replied. 'It is now a hotel, but the atmosphere hasn't changed.'

Sure enough, perched on a plateau looking out over the hills and olive groves of the *Sierra Norte*, an ancient monastery glowed in the late-afternoon light. The fusion of architectural design was breathtaking. The pointed windows of the early Gothic style were in contrast to the almost Renaissance simplicity of a small chapel. It was definitely worth the walk.

We continued up a steep track bordered by olive trees leading to the Cartuja gatehouse.

'So now you have brought me all this way, you need to tell me the story,' I said with a smile.

Felipe passed me a bottle of water and we sat down on a wall in the old cloister and he told me about its past.

'The monastery was built when Andalucía was still Al Andalus. Will that do for a start?' he said with a grin.

I nodded, encouraging him to go on.

'Before the Carthusian monks consecrated this site in the Middle Ages, Celts, Romans and Moors came to sample the natural springs ...' As Felipe's deep, but gentle voice washed over me, we stood up and wandered through the ancient buildings absorbing the atmosphere. He described how a retired Spitfire pilot had bought the crumbling monastery in the 1970s, living there with his young mistress, who, tiring of the isolation and her elderly lover, had finally left. We strolled into the church where the belfry and dome had been restored, but their decaying splendour remained. Felipe explained how the monastery's rescue was due entirely to the determination and creativity of Carmen, a property developer, who had made it her life's work to save the monastery for future generations to enjoy.

As we went from one ancient building to the next, I was drawn not only by Carmen's romantic name but also her vision.

The sun began to set and Felipe bought us wine in the hotel bar. We took it onto the terrace and soaked up the tranquillity of our astonishing surroundings. I was gazing over the hills and valleys of the *Sierra Norte* when my attention returned to Felipe. He was looking at an eagle soaring in the sky above us, his profile towards me. I surreptitiously took out my camera, thinking how noble he looked. He reminded me of the wild and romantic country that was Spain.

On our long walk back to the village, with the dusk gathering around us, I was quiet, my conscience once again getting the better of me. I'd only just broken off my engagement – I should be taking a break from men, finding out who I was, not taking romantic walks to exquisite monasteries, listening to Felipe's mesmerising voice.

Chapter Thirty-four

A week after our visit to the monastery, I asked Felipe to return to the hacienda to look through the contents of an old dressing-up chest in the attic. I had forgotten all about it until Papa Leonardo had sent me up there in search of his father's silver-topped cane.

'Now that I have the use of one hand, I need it to attract your attention,' he had said with a gleam in his eye. I was not convinced this was a sound idea.

Felipe was due at two, but throughout lunch I found myself looking out for him, glancing through the window every time I heard a noise. My ears picked up the thrum of the motorbike engine long before he knocked on the door.

My grandfather was not in the best of moods.

'I'll not have a stranger snooping around my house,' he bellowed. 'I've kept my privacy for fifty years and I don't want anyone interfering now. Get rid of him, Mia.'

'Do you want to keep the hacienda or not?' I retorted.

When Great-Aunt Gracia arrived on the veranda with a pot of coffee, she tried to intervene, but he shouted at her too. 'Keep your nose out of it, woman.' He was in that frame of mind.

'What if I introduced him to you, Papa Leonardo?' I asked, hoping to pacify him.

'Why would you wish to do that, Mia? Do you like him?'

'Of course not,' I replied.

He gave me a strange look, as if he could see right through me. '*Santo dios,* Mia, let the poor man do what he came for, and afterwards you had better bring him here.'

An hour later I climbed the staircase to the attic only to find Felipe surrounded by the contents of the chest. In his arms were a pair of moccasins and a Native American beaded dress. On his head was my grandfather's feathered headdress that I used to wear as a child. I stared at him for a moment and he had the grace to look extremely embarrassed.

'Couldn't help myself,' he explained.

I started to laugh, 'Minnehaha I presume?'

'Memories of childhood were too strong,' he apologised.

I giggled. 'My grandfather would like to meet you, but I suggest you take the feathers off first.'

I had no sooner introduced them than they were talking non-stop and I could see I was surplus to requirements. While Felipe drew up a stool next to the wheelchair, I went to pick some beans for Manuela. When I returned, they were still talking. My grandfather was actually laughing; this was a first.

'You didn't tell me the boy loves horses, Mia,' he said, pointing his cane at me – I was right, the cane was a bad idea.

'You didn't ask, Papa Leonardo.'

'Take him out for a ride now and show him the old tobacco plantations. He can borrow my boots. Ask Dante to saddle up Seferino.'

'Seferino?' I queried. 'Are you joking?'

'Are you telling me I can't judge a horseman?'

'Of course not, but I am reluctant to kill our auctioneer.'

Felipe laughed. 'I am happy to ride the stallion, Mia, if you don't mind.'

I found my grandfather's spare pair of boots in the gun room – his best pair having been cut off him in hospital – and handed them to Felipe.

'These should fit you,' I said, running off to get changed.

When we arrived at the stables, Dante was hovering nearby.

'Are you sure this is a good idea, Señorita Mia?' he whispered.

'Not at all,' I replied.

I made another attempt with Felipe. 'Seferino is extremely strong; you could always take the bay.'

He laughed. 'Have faith in me, Mia, I will be fine.'

He was more than fine. As soon as he took the reins and sprang into the saddle, I realised my doubts were unfounded. Felipe rode as if he had been born in the saddle, his seat was deep, his contact with the horse's mouth elastic.

The heat had gone from the sun and we trotted down the lane towards the redundant tobacco fields. We were on the top of a rise looking out over the fields below, when he reined in the stallion.

'Can I ask you a question, Mia?'

'You're clearly going to,' I replied.

He looked at me and grinned. 'Why is the land fallow? You could make it work for you, rather than selling the contents of the house.'

'I admit I have thought about it. But everything takes money, which, as you know, is in fairly short supply.'

Felipe tapped his whip against his boot and Seferino leapt sideways. 'Steady, old boy,' he laughed, patting the horse's neck and Seferino calmed immediately.

'There are grants for this sort of thing, Mia. We both know the bottom has fallen out of the tobacco market, so what about planting olive trees? I can see it now, acres of olives – better for the environment and it would be profitable, of that I am sure.'

'Once upon a time this was an ancient olive grove,' I informed him.

'Well, then, replant, Mia. How many hectares do you have?'

'Approximately five hundred, more or less,' I said.

He whistled. 'A good amount.'

I smiled. 'In my great-grandfather's day there was much more, but Papa Leonardo gave it to the farm labourers at the end of the Civil War. There was no money to help them get back on their feet, but he gifted them the land they deserved.'

'He is clearly a good man,' Felipe murmured. 'Think about it, the olive oil industry is booming. There are agricultural grants. I am not talking about intensive farming, but in the old way.' Felipe's eyes were shining with excitement, and I laughed.

'You look as if you would like to be an olive farmer.'

'I believe we, the young, should protect all this, Mia.' He lifted a hand from the reins and swept it over the landscape. 'We need to sustain the rural environment and the communities, something your grandfather was obviously trying to do, but it might also enable you to hang on to your beautiful home.'

Part of me hoped he was about to say he wanted to hang on to me.

On the way home, we let out the reins and let the horses stretch their necks. To my surprise I revealed more about myself to Felipe than I had to anyone in a long time. I told him about my aspirations to be a writer or an editor on a national newspaper. I revealed how I longed to do something good, to achieve something memorable. I mentioned Dale and the way she had constantly undermined my work, I even told him about the camera. But I wasn't yet ready to tell him about Matt.

I learnt that Felipe had three sisters, which, according to him, gave him a good understanding of women.

I laughed at this and he seemed perplexed.

'Felipe, you can't say that. Many women would kill you for less.'

'Are you going to kill me, Mia?' He looked at me, one eyebrow raised, his face a little flushed beneath his tan and I may have wished for some things, but his death was not one of them.

The more I learnt about Felipe, the more I admired him. His parents' separation had caused consternation in his conservative Catholic family and had obviously affected him.

'Families at war,' he said, frowning, and I wondered if he was just talking about his family or the Civil War that had torn so many Spanish families apart.

'It hasn't been easy,' he admitted. 'My mother was devastated when my father left to live with his mistress.'

'That must have been difficult.'

'It was, for all of us. My mother relied on me and treated me like her confidante when I was only thirteen.'

We were silent for a moment and I realised that Felipe had his own issues. I longed to reach out my hand and reassure him.

'Sorry, I have said too much.' He cleared his throat and I could tell the subject was closed.

Over the next half-hour I learnt other things about Felipe. Apart from riding, which had been a passion his entire life, he was also a keen philatelist.

'Stamps can teach you so much,' he said, earnestly. 'Not very sexy, but I find them fascinating.'

He told me he had been to Madrid university where he had studied art history, before joining the family business.

'To me it's not a job, Mia, every morning I am excited to go to work. How many people can say that? I love anything with a history. Furniture, paintings, stamps – in fact, anything with a bit of age about it.'

'Like your Harley-Davidson?' I asked innocently.

He laughed. 'There are, of course, a few exceptions.' He looked at me and my heart gave a little lurch.

When a partridge flew up, causing Lyra to shy, Seferino for once behaved like a lamb.

As the sun was setting behind the distant rocky peaks, we had a drink on the terrace. Tonight Andalucía was doing her best for me and the sky was a glorious mixture of cerise, purple and blue.

When I was a child, my grandfather had told me the beautiful colours were painted by the fairies – if there was no sunset they were in a bad mood. I had believed every word and for years I had imagined they were sloshing paint onto the sky with their fairy brushes.

As the sky became darker, the final rays, slipping behind the hills, Felipe touched my hand. 'A penny for your thoughts,' he said gently. 'Isn't that what you say in England?'

I laughed. 'Are you sure you want to know?'

He nodded, and I told him about sunsets and fairies, about my childish dreams. When I'd finished I was concerned that he would laugh at me, but instead he looked at me thoughtfully, his head to one side.

'When I first met you, I only saw the beautiful but tetchy girl on the surface, not the girl inside. Now I feel I have had a glimpse of the real you.'

'And do you like the real me?' I asked a little shyly.

'*Por supuesto*, of course. Mia, I like you a lot,' he whispered, lifting my hand to his lips and kissing my fingers.

As we finished our wine, I watched the shadows fall across his face, highlighting the cleft in his chin. I listened to the inflections in his voice and observed the way he used his hands to express himself. My feelings for Felipe Ortega were definitely growing.

Chapter Thirty-five

I came into the office one morning to find my great-aunt huddled over her adding machine, a frown furrowing her brow, and I knew immediately we must be running short of funds.

'Don't look so glum,' I jested, trying to reassure her, 'you usually manage to pull the rabbit out of the hat.'

'I can't seem to find the rabbit,' she clarified, her expression gloomy as she looked up at me.

'Well, thank goodness the auction is coming up at Ortega on September fifth. I'm sure we will manage until then. On this occasion not only was I correct, but the lots far exceeded our expectations. It seemed the New York dealers had come over in force and the Hiawatha outfit more than saved the day.

With the exception of the headdress, which Papa Leonardo insisted on keeping, the rest had gone into the sale. The beaded dress turned out to be eighteenth-century Sioux Native American, and if I hadn't been prancing around the flowerbeds in it for most of my childhood, the price would have been higher still. The moccasins proved to be an early pair of Eastern Great Lakes in quilted hide, fetching the princely sum of thirty thousand pounds. None of us could believe the dress came under the hammer for five times more!

When I told my grandfather he roared with laughter. 'That

old stuff. I bought the outfit for your mother from the market in Santa Fe for her twelfth birthday. I paid twenty dollars for the lot.'

When I asked him about the headdress, his expression changed. 'That came from a toy shop in Seville, Valeria bought it for me. If it was worth a million, it would never be sold.'

With the enormous amount of money achieved in the auction, I arranged a meeting with the bank manager in Seville. Over coffee and a glass of sherry we discussed my wish to pay off some of the loans and our exciting new plans to plant olive trees.

I believe he looked at me with a new respect.

'I am delighted the name of Palamera de Santos is on the ascendency once more,' he said, shaking my hand as I left.

With funds in the kitty, Tía Gracia turned her hand to applying for the relevant grants and there was a happy smile on her face as she hummed her way through the day.

Life was definitely getting easier. Without the constant worry about money we could actually find ways to make the estate work. Every day I reported back to my grandfather, and I could see the growing interest in his eyes. It was as if the sale of the American Indian costume had injected him with enthusiasm. His old spark was returning.

'Bring the boy to see me,' he instructed me one afternoon. 'I want to congratulate him myself.'

At thirty-three, Felipe was hardly a boy, but he seemed delighted by the summons. He duly arrived at the house armed with the latest Sotheby's catalogue on the sale of American Indian art and I left them pouring over the photographs, discussing the comparative prices. I could hear their animated voices from the study next door.

'You were so clever, señor, to buy these things and at the price you paid. Your vision has saved this house.'

'If it hadn't been for you, they would still be rotting away in the attic and we would still be broke!' My grandfather guffawed at his joke which brought a smile to my face.

'I am delighted to say we achieved better prices than the famous auction house, Sotheby's, *ciertamente* that is quite a coup.' Felipe's words reached my ears and I grinned.

My part in the sale didn't come into it, but at this stage I really didn't mind.

As the days passed, I allowed myself to think more about Felipe. He was on my mind constantly and I would wake up at night with a terrible longing. When I caught him looking at me, I wanted to throw caution to the wind and hurl myself into his arms.

Chapter Thirty-six

It was one of those Andalusian September afternoons when the heat was still fierce with not a breath of wind. My grandfather was taking a nap and the house was silent, except for the fans whirring overhead. My attempt to read was distracted by a mosquito nearby. It was a happy relief when the telephone rang and it was Felipe suggesting a trip to the Huéznar cascades.

'You could bring your swimming costume,' he said.

I flung on a gauzy dress I had bought recently in the *Mercado del Jueves* in Seville, laced up my pink trainers and ran downstairs.

Manuela smirked, of course, when I told her where I was going, and Lucia raised her eyebrows in a gesture I had become accustomed to. I ignored both of them and went to wait on the step, my bright orange costume in a canvas bag.

When Felipe skidded to a halt in the drive, he looked at me for a moment.

'Will I do?' I asked.

'You certainly will,' he replied, and his voice was different, softer. When I climbed on the motorbike, he took my hand and placing it around his waist, we set off down the dusty lanes. I could feel the hot wind in my face, the thrum of the engine. All my fears and promises to my mother blew away as we sped across the ground. Forty minutes later we picked our way through the undergrowth, towards the cascades. When I stumbled, Felipe helped me to my feet, and brushed the dust from my dress, holding me longer than was necessary. Our eyes met and any thoughts of Matt disappeared.

We continued down the narrow path in silence. I could hear the birds singing, each separate note flawless in my ears, the dry twigs snapping beneath my feet. I could smell the wild oregano in the scrub.

When we reached the pool, I peeled off my dress, conscious of Felipe's unwavering gaze. I stood there in my pants and bra, feeling the sun flickering on my skin, touching my cheeks.

Then it was my turn to watch as Felipe unbuttoned his shirt, revealing his muscled chest. He took off his jeans, moving closer to me.

'Are you going to put on your swimming costume?' he murmured.

'No swimming costume,' I replied.

He raised an eyebrow and my stomach did a flip. He took my face in his hands and kissed me slowly, his lips touching my eyelids, my neck until our mouths found each other. Our kiss became deeper and I believed I would drown before my feet had touched the water. He unclipped my bra and ran his hands over my body. 'I brought you here to swim,' he said, his voice husky. 'Perhaps we should get in the water.'

When I had slipped down my pants, he picked me up and carried me into the pool. The water was surprisingly cool and the shock made me giggle. Felipe entwined me in his arms and we floated in the water, the sun blazing down on us. I wrapped my legs around him and we drifted towards the shallows, the waves lapping against our bodies as we came to rest on the shore.

He ran his hands down my body until I arched towards him, longing for him.

'Are you sure this is what you want, *querida*?' he murmured.

'Quite sure,' I whispered, pulling his face to mine.

Making love with Felipe was a revelation. For the first time in my life I really understood the meaning of the phrase. Felipe was thoughtful and tender, exploring every part of my body, caressing my breasts my stomach, creating sensations that I didn't know existed. I was giving myself to a man that I was falling for so deeply and I had never met these emotions before.

We dried our bodies in the sun and settled on a towel.

I leant my head on his chest and he played with my hair. 'I remember the first time we met, you didn't like me at all.'

'I admit I thought you were arrogant and—'

'And now, Mia?'

I didn't have time to reply because his lips were on mine.

Much later, I found my watch in the canvas bag and leapt to my feet.

'It's six o'clock,' I gasped, the normal world returning fast. 'I promised my grandfather I would take him around the garden before Aunt Gracia joined us for drinks.'

'Then, *querida*, I shall take you home.'

We scrambled back up the hill, put on our helmets, climbed on the Harley-Davidson and set off down the road.

Felipe parked the motorbike at the end of the drive and waited while I jumped down.

'You go on,' he instructed, caressing my neck. 'There is a rattle in the engine I need to investigate. I'll follow in a moment.'

I giggled, unable to think of a suitably inappropriate reply and wandered up the drive, memories of our recent tryst playing through my mind. Perhaps it was my dream-like state that made me forget to remove the helmet or notice the three people waiting on the steps until it was too late.

As I fumbled with the helmet strap, Matt leapt down the

steps and the next moment I was enfolded in his embrace. I could see my mother's withering glance over his shoulder and Poppy standing next to her.

'Mia,' he breathed in my ear, 'I've missed you so much. I want you back.'

I could see Poppy raise her eyebrows at this and shrug. I tried to pull away but Matt held onto me.

'I can understand your grandfather's accident confused you, but I am hoping that you have had time to realise how special we are together—' He stopped suddenly, looking over my shoulder, his hands dropping to his sides.

I turned from Matt to Felipe, who had walked up behind me, and felt the earth opening up beneath me.

'And are you going to introduce us, Mia?' Felipe asked softly, but I could see his eyes blazing.

'Yes, yes, of course.' My voice was trembling as I fidgeted with the helmet. I flung out my arm. 'Felipe, this is my mother, Rafaela, and my stepsister Poppy. And Matt.'

'And who's this?' Matt interrupted, glaring at Felipe.

'Just the auctioneer.' The three words were out before I could stop myself. 'He works for Papa Leonardo,' I finished lamely.

'If you will excuse me—' Felipe nodded at my mother and Poppy, and reached out to grab the helmet. He glared at me for a moment and shook his head in disbelief. 'I have an urgent appointment in Seville. As your daughter has told you, señora, I am a very busy auctioneer.' He turned on his heel and walked away down the drive.

There was a rumble of the engine as he disappeared through the gates, scattering the gravel.

My mother whirled round, her face white with anger. 'Have you been riding around on that thing? I'm so disappointed in you, Mia.' Without another word she went inside. I tried to say something, but the words wouldn't come. Poppy looked as if she would follow, but I shook my head.

'Please don't go,' I begged.

Matt's jaw was tight and a vein stood out in his neck.

'So this is what you have been doing while looking after your grandfather. I thought better of you, Mia.' He was clenching and unclenching his fists. 'Well, you certainly didn't waste any time getting to know the local talent.'

I flinched, unable to defend myself and kept my eyes fixed to the gravel.

'Jesus, I come halfway across the world to see you, and I find you with some bloody Spaniard.'

This time I answered him. 'First, I am half Spanish, Matt, and second, Spain isn't halfway across the world.'

Matt kicked at the step and cursed wildly as his foot met the unrelenting stone. 'You are behaving like a slut.' He was shouting now. 'We were engaged to be married and—'

'I didn't ask you to come! And you might recall the engagement is over. This is your fault, not mine,' I snapped back.

'What? My fault that you are screwing around. My fault that—'

'Matt, stop. That is enough.'

Matt's shoulders slumped. 'Were you having an affair during us?' he asked at last.

'Of course not. You should know me better than that.'

'I don't think I know you at all.' He stomped back up the steps but at the top he turned. 'Don't worry, Mia, you won't be hearing from me again.' He slammed the oak door behind him.

The only person remaining was Poppy.

'Well, that was interesting,' she said, trying to make light of it, but her face was white with shock.

When I burst into tears, she sat on the front step beside me.

I buried my head on her shoulder. 'You could have warned me he was coming?'

'You know what Matt is like, Mia. He had convinced himself the break-up was a temporary aberration on your part. He really believed he could win you back. I told him it wasn't a very good idea, but he was determined, and I suppose we went along with it.'

I raised my eyebrows and gave her a look.

'Anyway, it was meant to be a surprise visit for Papa Leonardo's birthday,' she concluded.

'Not a very good surprise. Oh God, Poppy, Mama will never forgive me. I had given her my word never to ride on a motorbike, she has every right to be furious with me.' I put my head in my hands. 'Matt knew it was over, what on earth was he thinking of?'

Poppy shrugged. 'I'm so sorry.'

'I thought he was going to have a heart attack,' I spluttered. 'I can't imagine he will hang around now.'

'I expect he is already haranguing BA to get him on the next plane home,' Poppy said, some of her old humour returning. 'Golly, Mia, you kept me in the dark about this one. Who is the gorgeous man?'

'Felipe, and I have just blown my chances with him. I didn't expect you all to just turn up out of the blue.'

Poppy gave a small chuckle. 'Not brilliant timing. It might have helped if you had confided in your sister.'

'It was all so soon after Matt; I thought you might be cross with me.'

Poppy guffawed at this. 'You are speaking to the girl who is always getting in a muddle, but if I am honest, this appears to be rather a spectacular muddle.'

I sniffed loudly. 'Oh Lord, what is Felipe going to think of me, how am I ever going to explain this?'

Poppy took my arm. 'Let us think about that later, first we have to face the music inside.'

Chapter Thirty-seven

The day after Matt's rapid departure we had a birthday party for my grandfather. It was a sorry affair. Manuela gave me that *I told you so* look and Poppy talked at a hundred miles an hour. My mother sat on my grandfather's right, ignoring me. Gracia chattered on as normal, unaware of the undercurrents circulating in the room.

'You're a happy bunch,' my grandfather complained. 'What the hell is wrong with you? You have come all the way from England to give me a party and your faces are like pokers.' When no one answered, he ate his cake and grumbled to Gracia.

He beckoned to me afterwards. 'Well, are you going to tell me, Mia?' he demanded.

I wheeled him into his bedroom and shut the door. 'Are you sure you want to hear? It's not good, Papa Leonardo.'

'*Santo Dios*, Mia, what are you talking about?'

I pulled up a chair and sat down beside him. 'You will probably think I have behaved appallingly, Mama certainly does.'

'I rather doubt that.' I could see my grandfather was beginning to enjoy himself, so I told him everything, or almost everything. When I had finished he patted my hand, something he did a lot at the moment.

'*Qué lástima*,' he pronounced.

'What do you mean, Papa Leonardo, *what a pity*? Is that all you can say? It is not a pity, it is a catastrophe.'

He shook his head. 'Not in the scheme of things, Mia. The world isn't going to tip on its axis. You could say the timing was unfortunate, Matt was a fool to just turn up, but actually your mother shouldn't have allowed him to come. Surprises like that are not welcome.'

I nodded my head in agreement.

'But I had given Mama my word never to ride a motorbike.'

'A little more difficult, but then she shouldn't project her fears onto you.' My grandfather had a soft smile on his face and I stood up and hugged him.

'And Felipe?'

'I would say your words were not entirely tactful, that might take a little longer to resolve.'

I groaned. 'I have made such a mess of things, Papa Leonardo.'

He smiled. 'It will turn out all right in the end, *mi preciosa nieta*, my precious grandchild.'

One consolation in the whole miserable debacle was Poppy. We walked together, talked all night and I even managed to get her on a horse. I was able to show her where the olive trees would be planted and she was there to celebrate the confirmation of our grant.

After thanking Tía Gracia for her efforts with the olive oil co-operative, we opened a bottle of champagne.

Occasionally Poppy joined me for my shifts at the bar and while the customers vied for her attention, Alejandro and I looked over the books he had brought from his shop.

'What is your opinion?' I asked, opening yet another manual on the management of olive groves. 'How many trees should we plant, and should they be young or mature?'

Alejandro scrolled down the page. 'My cousin has an olive

farm and I am fairly sure the land once belonged to your family. In the past, it was approximately two hundred and eighty planted per hectare, but with modern farming it seems to be five times more.' He smiled apologetically. 'Even if you start with twenty-five hectares, that is still a lot of trees.'

I reassured him with a *Cruzcampo* beer on the house, and we finally settled on four hundred olives per hectare, using three-year-old trees.

As I placed the order with the nursery, for delivery in February, my apprehension was overtaken by a sense of purpose. This was the only way to secure the future of the estate.

'I have a horrible feeling I am going to lose you to Andalucía,' my stepsister lamented afterwards.

'Oh, Poppy, would you hate it so much if I didn't come home?'

'Of course I would. The new girl in the flat leaves her dirty mugs in the sink and it drives me mad.'

'Is that the only reason?' I asked, pretending to look hurt.

'I miss you terribly, but I can see you're happy here – despite the current situation. You were treading water in England, Mia, so I must now be a grown up and let my stepsister go.'

'This will always be your home too, Poppy.'

'I know,' she said with a resigned smile.

My mother's continued anger was strange and unsettling. We had never really fallen out before.

When I heard raised voices coming from my grandfather's bedroom, I stopped in the corridor outside. I normally drew the line at snooping, but under the circumstances I believed that adding a further felony to my list of misdemeanours didn't count.

'You are being too hard on her, Rafaela,' my grandfather insisted.

'She gave me her word, Papa.'

'You gave me your word, Rafaela. But you broke it and ran

away with that no good, dead beat. And now you can't even forgive your daughter.'

'But I loved him at the time, he swept me off my feet. Now I can see I was rather impetuous.'

'Rather? That is an understatement. I begged you to listen to reason, but you were strong headed, just like Mia.'

My mother's tone softened. 'Did I really hurt you, Papa?'

'Of course you did. I shut myself away for months when you left, but that's what happens when you love someone too much.'

I could hear my mother's voice crack. 'I'm so sorry, I didn't realise.'

'Well, I forgave you a long time ago. Now be grown up, Rafaela, and make it up with your daughter. Don't add to her confusion. She is young, and whether you like it or not, she is in love. Matt was totally wrong for her and particularly stupid to turn up like that, and may I tell you this young man Felipe apparently rides like a dream.'

Suddenly there were peals of laughter. 'Papa, you are appalling, anyone who can handle a horse is perfect in your eyes.'

'Not true,' he said. 'But it helps.'

I could feel a huge lump forming in my throat and hot tears slipped down my cheeks. I wasn't sure whether I was crying because of everything that happened in the last few days or from happiness. I had always known there had been a rift between my mother and Papa Leonardo, and now they were talking again, truly talking. I knocked on the door and went in. My mother was sitting on the edge of the bed and she was holding Papa Leonardo's hand. I hadn't seen her looking so happy in years.

Leonardo gave her a nudge.

'Go and talk to Mia,' he said.

*

We went out to the terrace and my mother opened her arms.

'I am sorry,' she murmured into my hair.

'I am sorry too,' I replied.

She held me away from her a moment. 'I was so frightened, Mia, when I heard the motorbike and then you appeared; all I could think about was that I could lose you. Don't you see, Mia, I love you more than anything in the world.' Her words caught in her throat.

'I love you too,' I confessed, trying not to cry.

My mother pulled a handkerchief from her pocket and wiped my eyes. 'But I was wrong ...' Her voice trailed off.

'I was wrong too. I broke my word and it was unforgiveable. And I have hurt Matt again, and he doesn't deserve it.'

'Well, he did bring this on himself.' She smiled and there was a wicked glint in her eye. 'He will find someone else and, if I am honest, I found him a little boring. From Gatwick to Seville he talked incessantly about his job, his football and himself. Not an ideal combination for my gorgeous girl.'

She giggled suddenly. I started to laugh and soon we were helpless with laughter. Poppy found us holding our sides.

'Am I missing something?' she said.

To my delight Poppy agreed to stay on until the beginning of the new academic year, but my mother kept to her original plan.

'I had better get back,' she said a little reluctantly. 'Peter can't even work the washing machine let alone iron his clothes.'

On the morning of her flight we walked up the hill. My mother was wearing a pink floaty dress and with her dark hair hanging loose, she looked liberated, more like the mother I once used to know.

We were watching a young man from the village preparing the ground for the trees, when she put her hands either side of my face. 'If I haven't told you recently, you are an amazing young woman. This place was in dire straits, and it seems you are turning it around. You are making a real difference to people's lives.' She smiled suddenly, her face lighting up. 'And to think our Hiawatha outfit raised over one hundred and fifty thousand pounds!'

She put her arms around me, holding me tight, and I thought I would cry all over again.

When we reached the house she stroked my cheek. 'Don't come to the airport, *querida*, I hate goodbyes. Remember, I'll be back very soon.'

Chapter Thirty-eight

Every other September, the greatest Flamenco festival in the world, the *Bienal de Flamenco*, came to Seville. For nearly a month, singers, flamenco dancers and musicians flocked to the various stages all over the town. Of course I had to take Poppy. At my grandfather's suggestion, I booked us into a hotel in the Jewish quarter that had once been home to our family.

'Consider it your treat,' he had said, waving his good hand in a benevolent sweep.

Our bedroom was at the end of a passage with double doors that led onto a large balcony. The room was furnished with two single beds, an armoire, a chest with a swing mirror on top and a desk. Paintings filled the walls and a Turkish rug covered the floor.

On our first night my mind wouldn't rest. I was in a strange room in a city still thrumming with noise and activity, yet somehow the room seemed familiar to me. At dawn, a hush fell over the city and finally I closed my eyes. As I drifted in and out of sleep, I imagined the room as Valeria's. I could picture her brushing her hair in the mirror, writing her letters at the desk. Feeling a whisper of breeze on my face I sensed her presence. As light began to filter through the muslin curtains, I remembered the black-and-white photograph that I had found in my grandfather's study, the close-up of Valeria sitting at a writing desk, a pen in her hand. She was staring into the camera and she was laughing, but it was the detail of the desk that I recalled, the faded leather top, the eagles' heads at the corner of each leg. While Poppy slept, her quiet breathing comforting my racing heart, I tiptoed across the room and ran my fingers over the desk. Sure enough, the eagles were there, the ormolu cold beneath my touch. As a spider's fragile web shimmered in the emerging light, I was filled with wonder. Valeria had seen many of her young hopes crushed and promises fulfilled within these four walls, and now she lived in my head. Tears pricked at my eyes. 'I have found you, Valeria,' I said.

After a late breakfast, Poppy and I spent a leisurely morning wandering the packed streets of Seville. We had drinks in the tapas bars, crepes in the cobbled plazas and we went from one location to the next. However fanciful it might seem, I imagined Valeria beside us. I could almost see her running down the streets, her blond hair a halo amongst a sea of dark heads. When we listened to the flamenco guitarist Paco Peña, my heart ached at the music and the stories it told.

The beautiful gypsy Joaquín Cortés, gave us a glimpse of his fusion of classical ballet and flamenco, as well as his bare chest. We were spellbound, our bodies flowing along with the exotic rhythms of sex, power and sweat. It was then that I caught Poppy's hand.

'She's here,' I said, my hips swaying as I stamped my feet in time to the music.

'Who?' Poppy asked, spinning in front of me, her red hair flaming around her.

'Valeria.'

Poppy didn't laugh at me. She smiled, her cheeks flushed pink, and flung her arms around me.

'Of course,' was all she said.

I was so caught up in the performance, that I didn't notice Poppy nudging me.

She prodded me again. 'Isn't that…?' she stopped.

'What?' I whispered, my feet suddenly quiet.

'Nothing,' she assured me, but I knew her too well. I looked around and my eyes alighted on Felipe. His arm was draped over a young woman's shoulders and they were both laughing. My euphoria evaporated instantly, and I grabbed Poppy's arm. 'Let's get out of here,' I urged. 'I want to leave, Poppy. Now.'

As we pushed our way through the crowds, it seemed the music was louder suddenly, harsh in my ears. I needed to escape from the crush. We reached the edge of the square and the crowd dissipated. It was like standing on the moon looking down at the world, we were suddenly apart from it all. As my heartbeat returned to normal, I saw him again. I would recognise him anywhere. He half turned and looked back across the square, and for a fleeting moment our eyes met, before he disappeared in the crowd.

Chapter Thirty-nine

October was one of my favourite months at the hacienda. It was the season of abundance, of ripe fruit and harvest.

There were mists in Andalucía, but not like those in England. Ours were hazy morning mists that floated over the olive trees, putting a spell on the landscape. They were the promise of the day to come when the heat had gone from the sun, but still retained its warmth. October was the time for gathering the oranges and late pomegranates. As a child I used to long for the autumn half-term when I would visit my grandfather. On one occasion we invented an extreme bout of flu, so that I could stay on another week. My mother had yet another reprimand from the school and the following year we were forced to behave.

In those days Papa Leonardo, Ramon and I would take our baskets and ladders and we would collect the fruit. Leonardo would bring his big straw hat and my favourite game was to climb the ladder and shake the top branches, letting him catch the oranges in his hat. He was a master of the sport and would cheer in his rich gravelly voice. Ramon would give a suggestion of a smile. Now it was Manuela, Ramon and me. Ramon was a little creakier, so his job was to pick the ripe fruits with Manuela, and to carry the baskets afterwards. I resumed my usual place on the ladder.

You always knew when the pomegranates were ready because the perfect spheres changed shape and the skin lost its shine. This year we parked Papa Leonardo in the shade where he spent many happy hours shouting instructions with the help of his cane. Ramon was very good at cutting the fruit, one snip of the shears and they were off.

The last pomegranate was in the basket and Manuela was hauling a load to the kitchen to juice it for the celebratory drink, when Papa Leonardo cleared his throat.

'Valeria wore it, you know,' he murmured.

'Wore what, Papa Leonardo?'

'*Acqua di Colonia Melograno*, I can almost smell it now.' His face was bleak as he continued. 'I found it amongst her things when she died. I kept it to remind myself…' His voice broke. 'Will you get it for me, Mia. It's in my bedroom chest.'

I found the bottle at the back of the drawer with a tiny quantity of brown liquid inside. As I held it to the light, I could still make out the faded gold lettering on the front: *Farmacia di Santa Maria Novella*. Even the name sounded romantic.

'Will you remove the stopper, *querida*,' my grandfather instructed, his voice soft, but his reaction was not the one I expected.

He wrinkled his nose in disgust and pushed my hand away. 'This is not the scent of long ago.'

As his face sagged I squeezed his shoulder. 'One day I shall go to Florence, Papa Leonardo, and if the shop is still there, I shall buy some more.'

I had returned from my evening ride with Dante and was putting Lyra away when I noticed the old cart had been removed from the barn and was standing at the back of the yard. The coachwork was chipped, and the wheels scratched, but it had memories of picnics and expeditions with Papa Leonardo. It was the cart I had loved as a child.

'I haven't seen this in years,' I remarked.

Dante looked shifty. 'I need to oil the wheels, Señorita Mia.'

'Are you going to use it?' I asked.

'No, at least I don't think so.' Dante was looking uncomfortable. Perhaps he had a girlfriend and he was going to take her out for a drive, but none of the horses were trained to go between the shafts.

'I can see you're not going to tell me, so I'll have to find out another way,' I teased.

When I came home from my shift in the bar a week later, a pot of fuchsia paint was on the tack-room floor and two planks of wood. It was all increasingly strange.

'Are you painting the stable doors?' I asked, an innocent look on my face.

Dante's eyes shifted away. 'They are in need of restoration, Señorita Mia.'

I peered at the doors; they looked perfectly fine to me. 'So they are going to be pink?' I enquired.

When he didn't say any more, I was justifiably intrigued. Things were very odd around here. It would be several weeks before I came near to the truth.

If Andalucía can do good sunsets it can also do spectacular storms. For most of that night I had watched lightning flash across the sky and I had listened to the thunder rolling around the hills, delivering shockwaves that boomed and crackled. As I paced my room, I imagined Lyra in her stable, jumping out of her skin. At 3 a.m., I ran through the rain to the stables and let myself inside. Lyra immediately relaxed, pushing me with her nose. What I did next would not be recommended in any manual of horsemanship, but I sat down in the straw, and before long, I had closed my eyes. I woke at 6 a.m. to a clear sky and, more importantly, a fresh morning. Papa Leonardo had once assured me it was the ions that had cleared the air, by removing particles, and I had imagined a million bugs chomping up the storm – the reality was a little technical for me.

I was preparing the morning feeds, when a red Seat Toledo drew into the yard and out stepped Felipe.

We looked at each other for a moment and I felt the heat rise in my face.

'What are you doing here?' he spoke first.

'I might say the same about you. In case you hadn't noticed, this is our yard.'

He didn't look the least bit perturbed. 'True, but isn't it early for you to be around?'

I pulled a piece of straw from my hair, painfully aware that I was not looking my best. 'I'm always up at this time,' I lied.

'I have to come now. If you remember, I work in Seville,' he explained patiently, as if to a child.

'But what are you doing here at all?' I quizzed.

Felipe grinned. 'I am helping Dante. There are horses to be schooled, and I admit riding Seferino before I go to work is the best part of my day. If that is all right with you, Mia.' His voice oozed sarcasm.

'Do what you like,' I replied.

Early the following morning as I came into the yard, Felipe was leading Marte, my grandfather's sedate and sensible bay, to the dressage ménage. He had a pair of long reins in his hand.

When I passed them a short while later, he was turning Marte across the diagonal, halting him, going in a circle and doing a figure of eight. Even from this distance I could tell Felipe was a natural. He looked so patient and calm; he certainly had the gift with horses.

He was there again the following day.

'Why are you long-reining Marte?' I asked. 'When there are younger, more promising horses in the yard.'

'I am teaching the horse to be straight; it is a lot easier without me on board.'

I wasn't aware that there was a problem with Marte, but for once I didn't comment.

'I would offer to show you the technique... but maybe not.'

I must have looked crestfallen because his voice softened. 'Why not come to the arena now.'

Despite my misgivings I entered the dressage ménage that had been used extensively by my grandfather over the years.

'Long-reining is teaching the horse to go forward and to listen to your voice,' he explained, stroking Marte's neck. 'It is a process of building up trust between you and the horse.' He slipped on the bridle and fastened a roller behind the withers. 'It also builds his confidence. Marte is not young, but as with anything, it is never too late to learn.' He glanced across at me and I wondered whether he meant me or the horse.

As I watched his hands, I wondered if I was there because I wished to learn, or because I wanted to be close to Felipe. But as so often happens with horses, the moment he described the purposes of the different tack, showing me how to pass the reins through the roller to the bit, I had forgotten our differences and was absorbed in the harmony between man and his equine friend. When I moved into position behind Marte, I could swear Felipe's hand touched my arm, but his face was impassive. It was as if that day at the Huéznar cascades had never happened at all. I put those thoughts aside and with one gentle slap of the rein, the horse strolled forward, and Felipe climbed through the rails into the small pavilion, leaving me working Marte alone. Twenty minutes later the lesson was over, and Felipe had left for Seville.

*

It was another three weeks before I found out what was really going on. It was Saturday morning and I was having a coffee with Manuela when Dante came to the kitchen door.

'Señor Ortega requests that you bring your grandfather to the yard, Señorita Mia.' His words tumbled out and he was obviously excited.

'And perhaps you should bring your great-aunt and the nurse – and you must come, of course, Manuela.'

'What on earth is going on, Mia?' my grandfather asked as I wheeled him outside. 'I am not in the mood for nonsense.'

'I really have no idea,' I said truthfully.

'If this is one of those ridiculous surprises…'

Seconds later it all became clear. As we turned the corner into the yard, I drew in my breath.

Felipe was waiting for us and my heart tipped over. There was a boyish look on his face, slightly unsure, as if he needed our approbation. Behind him Marte stood between the shafts of the ancient cart. But this would be a misrepresentation, for now the paintwork gleamed and the wheels were a glorious pink.

Dante was holding Marte's bridle and the horse looked pleased as punch, his coat shining with good health. On cue he turned his head and looked at my grandfather.

'What the hell…?' My grandfather was lost for words after that.

'So that was what the long reining was for,' I exclaimed.

The cart was transformed. The padded seats were higher at the back and deeper at the front. I suspected they had been specially made. I studied every inch of the interior, the rings on the back seats where a harness would hold my grandfather in place, and the harness itself. Nothing had been left to chance.

I wanted to congratulate Felipe, thank him for his extraordinary kindness. 'It is incredible,' was all I managed to say.

I went to Dante. 'Now I understand the pink paint,' I said with a smile.

He grinned. '*Lo siento, Señorita Mia.*'

'No apology needed, I am overwhelmed. Thank you, Dante,' I replied.

Last I went to Marte. 'You are a devious horse,' I whispered, and he nuzzled me with his nose.

'Señor, your carriage awaits,' Felipe announced, his face glowing with pride. Then came the next part where we had to get my grandfather into the cart, but Felipe had thought of everything.

A ceiling hoist was now attached to a track on the beam. My grandfather was put in his usual harness and at a flick of a switch he was lifted up and then lowered into the seat. When he was secured into position, Felipe jumped onto the cart beside him and Dante brought them from the barn.

It was as simple as that, except that it was hard not to cry. As we stood in the yard watching the cart trot away from us, I heard Felipe's words as he turned to my grandfather.

'No, you take the reins, señor, you have one good hand.'

We were waiting for them when they returned an hour later. My grandfather looked jubilant.

'Next week?' he called to Felipe, as Lucia wheeled him away.

Felipe bowed. 'Most definitely next week, Don Leonardo.'

When everyone had gone inside, and Dante was fetching the horses from the field, I loitered behind.

'Thank you, Felipe, that was an extraordinary gesture.'

'Your grandfather can't sit on a horse, but he can still drive a cart.'

'We all appreciate your kindness.'

Felipe was picking out Marte's hooves. He looked up at me. 'As long as you understand that I am only here for your grandfather. He is a fine man.'

There it was, out in the open. He didn't care for me.

'Of course,' I stuttered. Felipe Ortega couldn't have made it clearer if he had tried.

The driving became a weekly affair. Felipe came to the house on Saturdays while I disappeared for my shift at the bar. On the occasion he invited me to join them, I declined. To my amazement I thought I noticed a fleeting look of disappointment in his eyes.

After that it was just a nod of his head as we passed on the drive, so it was a surprise when, one Saturday in November, he screeched to a halt and came around to my car door.

'We need to talk.'

I looked up at him through my open window. 'I am not sure that there is anything to say; you have made your feelings abundantly clear.'

'*Disculpe*, Mia, I have made *my* feelings abundantly clear? We had made love for the first time, and I find your fiancé at your house. Then you dismiss me as a nobody. I think I have reason to be confused and a little angry, wouldn't you agree?'

'Ex-fiancé,' I qualified. 'But it doesn't look great.'

'On that you are correct. I am sorry that I am neither rich enough, nor grand enough.'

'What?' I gasped.

'*Just the auctioneer* – really, Mia. I thought you were different.'

'But that's not what I meant, Felipe. Those words were said in panic. Yes, they were stupid, and trust me I have regretted them, but to say you are not grand enough is ridiculous.'

'Ridiculous? I would say to the contrary…'

'And to make matters worse we arrived on your motorbike.'

Felipe's jaw softened momentarily. 'Your grandfather explained about that, I am sorry. You should have told me. But it still doesn't defend—' Felipe was obviously working himself up again.

In the end, he threw up his hands and glared at me. 'What is the point?'

A tear slipped unwittingly down my cheek and I brushed it angrily away. 'I'll be late for work,' I said, winding up my window and driving away.

The following week I was able to avoid Felipe after volunteering for an earlier shift. It was quite apparent that he was my grandfather's friend, but no longer mine. I wished it could have been different, but my words had hurt him deeply and I deserved his contempt.

I had just finished a Sunday afternoon game of Scrabble, having been severely trounced by my grandfather, and was putting the pieces away, when he removed his glasses.

'It seems, Mia, either your mind is elsewhere or the knock on the head has only improved my ability to beat you.'

'I don't know what you are suggesting,' I observed.

'You are are thinking about Felipe, and quite rightly so. I was rather hoping something would happen between the two of you.'

'You are talking nonsense, Papa Leo.'

'It's a shame really, Felipe has all the qualities I would expect in a—

'Enough,' I exclaimed.

My grandfather looked unrepentant.

'If you go to my bureau, you will find a letter from him. I would like you to read it to me.'

I was about to ask him why he couldn't read it himself, when my curiosity got the better of me. I fetched the letter in what I believed was a nonchalant way and took it out of the envelope.

Señor,

First may I say it has given me such pleasure to help you in some small way and I greatly enjoy our weekly outings. I understand your wish to reimburse me for the restoration of the cart but please accept this as a gesture of thanks for commissioning my firm. The Hiawatha outfit exceeded all our expectations! Allow me the honour of doing this for a man I truly admire.

Yours,

Felipe Ortega

I folded the letter and looked at my grandfather.

'It's nice,' I agreed. 'And his generosity was never in doubt, but I don't see what this has to do with me.'

'You obviously still care for him.' My grandfather gave me a piercing look.

'My feelings haven't changed.' I shrugged my shoulders. 'But men are different, they just move on.'

He chuckled at this. 'I think women are often stronger than men, but we are proud. Once slighted it can be hard to forgive.'

'There is no point speculating. He has someone else. Poppy and I saw him with a girl at the Flamenco Fiesta.'

'Ah, Mia, appearances can be deceptive. Perhaps it needs a little more investigation,' he suggested, a twinkle in his eye.

'It's too late,' I shot back. 'And Papa Leo, don't you get any ideas.'

My grandfather obviously wasn't listening.

'In this world everything can change in an instant. Trust me, Mia, I have a feeling this will all work out in the end.'

Chapter Forty

I was sitting in the office with Gracia, signing cheques, when the telephone rang. I'd discovered there was something rather satisfying about wielding your pen on a chequebook and signing away your debt. It was Rosa from the camera shop, telling me that the film had been successfully developed and could she deliver it with her grandfather this very afternoon. When I put down the phone, I gave a whoop of delight.

'Are you all right, Mia?' my great-aunt queried, looking perplexed.

'If you excuse me, Tía Gracia, there is something I need to tell Papa Leonardo and I can't put it off any longer.'

I walked onto the terrace where he was reading a battered copy of poems by Lorca.

'Papa Leonardo, I have something to say.'

He looked up at me.

I hesitated, gathering my courage. 'You know you gave me the Leica?'

'Yes?'

'You see—' I paused. 'There was a roll of film still inside.' I gave him a moment to let my words sink in.

'A roll of film,' he said at last, his lip quivering. 'What is on it?'

'It was developed by specialists in Madrid, so I have no idea.

The man who sold you the camera seventy years ago is coming to deliver the photographs with his granddaughter this very afternoon.'

At three o'clock, as the first drops of rain plopped onto the gravel, I opened the door to Rosa and her grandfather, Señor Galacia. Though bent double with arthritis, he peered up at me, his eyes twinkling.

'I am so looking forward to meeting Don Leonardo. It has been a very long time.'

'A few years,' I agreed.

I led them to the loggia where my grandfather was waiting.

'I wish I could stand to greet you,' he said, 'but as you see I am unfortunately confined to this thing.' He tapped the side of the chair impatiently.

'I am not sure which is worse,' Señor Galacia replied with a wry smile, 'to shuffle like me, or not to walk at all.'

He sat down near to my grandfather. 'I am not sure that I recognise you,' he jested. 'But I do remember the day you came into the shop with an employee from the bank. You wanted the most expensive camera.'

My grandfather chuckled. 'You were wearing a striped red shirt with a white collar, and I thought how very dapper you were. Funny how we can remember these things, but not what happened in the last half-hour.'

While the rain thrummed on the loggia roof, the two old men reminisced about the past. My grandfather dismissed my suggestion that we should return inside.

'Don't treat me like an invalid, Mia,' he said with a wave of his hand.

Manuela brought in some tea and some recently baked pastries, followed by Gracia.

'I could smell the pastries from the office,' she said, shaking Rosa's and the old man's hands.

'Of course you could,' my grandfather muttered, and I silenced him with a glare.

After we had finished tea, Rosa took a large envelope from her bag. It had been sealed with tape.

'Inside are the negatives and your developed film. As you can see, the seal is unbroken, but the company in Madrid would love to speak to you, if you ever have the time.'

Papa Leonardo took the envelope and set it on the table beside him. Every so often he glanced at it.

When it was time for them to leave, Ramon brought an umbrella round and helped the old man into the car. I stood beside him as they disappeared down the drive.

'So, you have the developed film?' Ramon asked.

'We have the film,' I said.

He gave me one of his long looks. 'Be gentle with your grandfather, Señorita Mia.'

When I returned, my grandfather was hunched in his chair, at once a frail old man.

I wrapped a rug around his shoulders and was about to wheel him inside when he opened his eyes.

'Sit down, Mia.' I glanced at the water-logged lawn.

'Stop fussing,' he insisted. 'I am absolutely fine.' He cast me a look. 'If I don't tell you now, Mia, I'll change my mind. So many years of hiding the truth, so many lies. I hope in time you will understand.'

I could feel the butterflies in my stomach as his voice went soft. 'Are you ready?' he asked.

I nodded.

'Very well,' he said with a sigh. 'It was 1937 when I returned to this house from the city. I know this because at that time, we were already one year into the Civil War...'

Part Six

Chapter Forty-one

15 July 1937

Leonardo had returned from the city to the Hacienda de los Santos. While many of his contemporaries at the bank had joined the army and were fighting with Franco's nationalists, he had declined. It was the only quarrel he had ever had with his adopted father.

'I cannot,' he had said to Carlos. 'Don't expect me to fight for a cause I don't believe in. If I joined up, I'm afraid it would be for the other side.'

'A republican, after everything we have done for you?' Carlos had yelled, his face turning red. 'Have we taught you no values, Leonardo?'

'In my heart I am a republican; I am sorry, I have to be true to myself.'

While his father had been made a *coronel provisional* in the army and was fighting somewhere in the north of Spain, Leonardo had returned to Cazalla de la Sierra to oversee the estate.

On a blistering July day, as heat shimmered on the ground and the birds were too hot to sing, Leonardo and his workforce of women and old men were harvesting the tobacco crop. He looked up as Bañu came through the field towards them, dragging their ancient donkey.

'*Burro estúpido y vago*,' Bañu cursed, tethering the animal to a tree. She unpacked the paniers and in an instant the workers were hovering nearby.

'Get your thieving hands off.' Bañu slapped the arm of one old man who had grabbed a hunk of bread and cheese. 'You'll be sacked if you don't behave.'

When his brow puckered, she relented, for Bañu realised this work was his salvation, for it was a good job with fair pay. How well she understood what it was like to labour sixteen hours a day and live in a hovel for a deplorable wage, with no protection over rights and pay. She had watched her own mother die of starvation, leaving seven mouths to feed and had seen four of her siblings go the same way. But she had been one of the lucky ones, taken in by Isabel's grandmother fifty years before, she had given the family a life of service in return.

While the lunch break continued, Leonardo rested in the shade of an oak tree with his ancient dog, Luna, panting at his side. Letting his eyes close, he let his mind drift back over the last three years. Most of it had been a disaster.

The so-called elected democracy had tried and failed to unite the country. The government had become increasingly divided between the socialists of the left and the pro-monarchists of the right. The refusal of the left to concede victory to a coalition of the right in two successive elections provided the excuse for the intervention of the military. The consequence for the Popular Front was the unleashing of the Civil War. What many had believed would be a quick victory for the nationalists, had turned into a brutal and cruel struggle. The nationalists, a stronger, more disciplined fighting force, were being supplied with arms by Mussolini in Italy and by Nazi Germany. Franco, a ruthless and efficient army general who had honed his military skills in Morocco, was now head of the nationalist government. The Republican Popular Army, on the other hand, was short of arms and ammunition and their problems were compounded by different factions fighting amongst themselves. In desperation, the republicans had turned to the Soviet Union.

But what the republicans lacked in military expertise, they made up for in passion and commitment. They refused to give up their freedom, encouraging idealists from all over the world to take up their cause. An Englishman, whom Leonardo had met in Seville, had become the only employee at the bank to join the International Brigades. William Augustus Montcrieffe had died only the week before.

Leonardo's shoulders slumped as he remembered his friend. He had met William during his first months in Seville. They had quickly moved into an apartment, the five decaying rooms, once the servants' quarters of a grand palace. Though the boiler rarely worked, and damp seeped through the walls, it didn't stop the two young men from partying till dawn. Perhaps it was the storm clouds gathering overhead that had inspired their carefree behaviour, but in July 1936 it all came to an end. As the Civil War burst into life around them, they had watched from their balcony as Seville had been overrun by nationalists. They had listened to the gunfire coming from the other side of the river and had learnt of the massacre of republicans in the Macarena district.

'I cannot stand by,' William had cried. 'I will not, Leonardo.'

'It is not your fight,' Leonardo had pleaded. 'Go home, William,' but his friend wasn't listening.

'I am joining the International Brigades, I have to fight this injustice, Leonardo. God has to be on our side.' He had been so sure of himself, that Leonardo had believed him, but it seemed God wasn't on his side. Now only a year later, the young idealist was lying dead in an unknown grave, apparently shot by nationalist soldiers, his arms tied behind his back with no cover for his eyes.

As Leonardo poured some water into a bowl for Luna, he remembered his last letter from his friend written only five days before. He had described in detail their move towards the heavily defended village of Villanueva de la Cañada, which, as yet, republican forces had been unable to secure. He had portrayed the heat and the horrible thirst the soldiers had to endure. As Leonardo remembered the optimism in his dear friend's words, he wept.

Under constant bombardment from the air, the International Brigade had been unable to move with the speed they needed to capture the unoccupied heights. The nationalists were able to mow them down. Of the three hundred and thirty-one volunteers, Leonardo was able to ascertain that only forty-two still remained alive.

As he stood up, he took a letter from Valeria from the pocket of his shirt. Though eighteen months old, in times of sadness, it gave him the will to go on.

Dearest Leonardo,
While the whole world is crumbling around me, I am at the point of exploding. I have to do something, and when war comes it is not going to be knitting socks. I need a vocation that makes a difference and I think I know what it is. Would you approve if I worked for a newspaper, took photographs for a living with my beautiful Leica? I remember telling you years ago the camera would be part of my future, and now I am sure.

If you have a moment to tear yourself away from your apartment and your new friend Will, and all those girls I keep hearing about, then I would love to meet you for a glass of wine.

When you go back to the hacienda, please be sure to give my love to the horses and Saturno, but most of all, keep my heart for yourself.

Valeria xxxxxx

Chapter Forty-two

22 July 1937

When Leonardo fell into bed at night, he had little time to sleep before he was up again at dawn. It was a relentless slog, working all hours with the labourers, picking the tobacco leaves from the bottom of the plant to the top, stacking them onto carts and dragging them to the curing barn. If that was backbreaking toil, the next process was harder still. Each man had to take it in turns in the stifling heat to keep the firebox stoked, gradually increasing the temperature to dry out the tobacco. But one thing was for sure, the workers would get a bonus. Trade with the government graders and tobacco buyers was brisk, cigarettes were needed as a diversion in the war.

Leonardo was returning to the house from the curing barn, his mind focussed on a bath and a long glass of beer, when he heard a sound that made him stop in his tracks. He glanced at his watch. The church bells were ringing, and it was not time for vespers. His stomach churned for it was an ominous clang, not the usual welcoming peal. Despite the heat, a chill ran down his spine as he remembered his words to the padre: *'If ever you are in danger, ring the church bells.'* It was their warning signal. He turned and ran to the yard.

Juan, who was sitting cross-legged outside the stables, his gun across his knees, jumped to his feet when he saw him.

'*Patrón?*'

'I need Saturno, now, no time for a saddle, grab the mare and follow me with the gun.'

In less than a minute, Leonardo had vaulted onto Saturno's back and was galloping down the lane, veering off to the left to take a short cut through the scrub.

He was halfway to Aliana when the bells stopped. Leonardo's heart lurched, there wasn't a moment to lose. He spurred Saturno on and the horse gathered momentum.

He reached the village. The children's playground was empty, the shutters were down, not even a dog was barking. He prayed he wasn't too late. Only Fanuco, the simpleton, dribbled a ball down the street.

'The padre, where is he?' he yelled.

Fanuco picked up the ball, his eyes watering.

'Men with guns came,' he pointed to the church, but Leonardo had gone.

What Leonardo found in the church would haunt him for the rest of his life. Padre Alvaro was strung up by the neck, his head dropped forward, his feet dangling beneath his black robe.

Leonardo ran to him roaring with pain. He supported his body while he cut the noose with his knife. As they both collapsed to the floor he tried desperately to revive his mentor, putting his mouth over the priest's, then pressing down on his chest in the vain hope that he could save him, that there was still a spark of life. He was pumping at the priest's chest when Juan ran in, removing his hat at the door.

'*Dios Mío,*' he cried, crossing himself. 'What evil has been done here?'

Leonardo did not look up and continued the sequence of resuscitation. When, ten minutes later, there was no response, Juan tried to pull him away.

'Leave him now, *Patrón*, he has returned to his maker. Let him rest in peace.'

Leonardo shook him off. 'He will live, he will...'

Lowering his head onto the priest's chest, he wept, cradling the lifeless body on the marble floor. His beloved friend and teacher had been murdered using the rope from his own church bells.

Leonardo came into the sunlight, gently carrying the body of his friend. 'So this is your priest,' he yelled. 'The man who gave his life to you, married you, gave wise council.'

The villagers gradually gathered in the square around him. They were whispering to each other; an old woman was crying. Children hid behind their mothers' skirts. Leonardo shouted at the baker who was hovering nearby, his grief-stricken voice echoing around the square.

'Arlo, who did this?'

'I don't know, señor,' he responded, not meeting his eye.

'He was your friend, your priest,' Leonardo accused him. 'How could you stand by?'

The baker wiped his hands on his apron and looked at the ground. 'There were three of them, señor.'

'You are cowards, *cobardes*, the lot of you,' he spat. 'And you, Pedro,' he snarled. 'He christened your baby only a few weeks ago.' Pedro shuffled his feet and said nothing. 'And Gael? He listened to your confession every week, and you didn't even try to help him.'

A young woman came up to him and kissed the priest's hand. 'What could we do against their guns, señor? We had to protect our children. What good would it be if we were dead too?'

When Constanza's best friend, Daniela, approached him, she touched Leonardo's arm.

'You know he would have given his life to save us. You go after them, Leonardo, while we prepare our padre to meet his blessed Father.'

Leonardo returned Padre Alvaro to the cool of the church interior and sent Juan to fetch the horses.

They followed the tracks into the hills and picked their way through the rocky outcrop, but finally the hoof prints scattered in different directions. The horsemen had gone their separate ways.

'*Bastardos*,' Juan muttered. 'What do we do now the sun is going down?'

Leonardo reined in Saturno and looked down over the rocky landscape below.

'If Luna were younger, it would have been different; she would have scented their trail. But it is pointless carrying on, they are already several kilometres away.'

When they returned to the village, candles had been lit in the plaza and the lamps in the church were glowing. Old ladies had brought the last of their garden flowers and the children had woven a cross made of straw. A coffin had been hastily made by the carpenter and a priest had arrived from a nearby village to preside over the vigil that was about to begin.

While Juan returned to the hacienda with his horses, Leonardo stayed with his friend. The padre was buried the following morning in the churchyard where he had served the congregation faithfully for more than twenty years.

The priest's death marked a turning point for Leonardo. He travelled immediately to Seville for a meeting with his father, who was home on leave.

'Papa,' he said coming into the dining room where Carlos was eating breakfast.

Carlos stood up and put his arm around Leonardo's shoulders. 'Many of the churches in Cazalla de la Sierra, gone, and now our own Padre in Aliana. I am so sorry, Leonardo.'

'Padre Alvaro was gentle, wise, he served the community. He gave his life to them.'

'That is one of the main reasons we are fighting. The republicans have created this atmosphere of hatred towards the Church. I lay this atrocity at their feet.'

Leonardo slumped into a chair and put his head in his hands. 'If you had seen his face when I cut him down...' His voice broke and Carlos coughed, keeping his own emotion in check. He had seen too many atrocities committed on both sides.

'The hacienda is well served having you there, but of course it would serve the country better if you were to fight by my side.'

Leonardo looked up at Carlos, his face grim. 'Take me to your headquarters,' he said.

Chapter Forty-three

23 July 1937

Valeria was leaning against her desk gulping a quick *carajillo* when a tall man with a broken nose and a mop of curly hair, kicked open the door with his foot. He was clutching a stack of photographs.

'On the brandy again?' he joked, glancing at the open bottle, as he dumped the photographs on her desk.

Valeria grimaced. It had taken her weeks to even try the rough brandy that many of her journalist acquaintances tipped into their coffee, but after a while she got used to it and it helped calm her nerves.

'Good work, Valeria, I have just developed your negatives and we already have several newspapers interested.'

Valeria ran her hand through her cropped hair without even glancing at the photographs.

'So they should, because we nearly got killed taking them.'

'I can see you're in a good mood,' he said with a wry smile.

'Sorry, I am tired, that's all.'

He kissed her forehead. 'Take a peek, girl, while I fetch some chemicals for the darkroom.'

A moment later his head reappeared around the door. 'And if

you are going to Seville to see your mama, it needs to be now!' He sauntered off, whistling a tune.

Valeria picked up a photograph and as she looked at the grainy image, her exhaustion disappeared. This was her life now, exposing war in all its ugliness, and she wouldn't change it for the world. But it wouldn't have been possible without her business partner Walter Mayhew, or Walt, as he was known. The twenty-eight-year-old from the East End of London had arrived in Spain ten months before, intending to fight for the republicans in the International Brigades. He had quickly realised he would be better at recording events than fighting in them.

'Convergence insufficiency,' he had admitted to Valeria when he first caught her attention at an underground meeting in Seville. When Valeria had looked confused he had grinned. 'I am unable to see three-D, not great for shooting a gun, but I can still take bloody good pictures.' Following the meeting, he had pestered her for days, cajoling her to go freelance and join him at the Front.

'Let's do it, Valeria, you need to be brave and get out there. You need to record this atrocious war.'

Without his bullying she would never have known what she was capable of and the skills she would acquire while risking her life in the pursuit of capturing the war in all its desperation. Without his sense of humour, and his extraordinary sense of being in the right place at the right time, none of it would have happened at all.

Together they had taken some iconic images that they hoped would one day be published all over the world.

Valeria remembered when it had all started eighteen months before. She was having breakfast with her mother in the dining room in Seville.

'Mama, there is something I wish to discuss,' she had said, clearing her throat.

Her mother had put down the newspaper. 'Obviously something important.'

'I am going to get a job.'

'Really, Valeria? Are you sure? Papa might not like it.'

'Well, Papa will have to get used to it. I will not be like every other rich girl in Seville.'

'*Querida*, that is unfair, we have never stopped you doing anything.'

'I won't be one of those subjugated women, Mama.'

Isabel started to laugh. She stood up and went to her daughter. 'My dear girl, in a minute you will be chaining yourself to the railings, like that woman in England, what was her name?'

'Emily Pankhurst. But now I have the vote and I can get divorced if I wish.'

'Shouldn't you get married first?' her mother said, still chuckling.

'Mama, you know what I mean, and I intend to work.'

Isabel stroked her daughter's cheek. 'I am not making fun of you and I do understand. Now don't look so cross, your father needs a secretary. It would save him having an outsider; that really is a good idea.'

'I won't be working for Papa or any of his friends, nor will I work at the bank.'

'What do you intend to do, my love?'

'I have an idea. I just need to apply.'

She was leaving the room when her mother caught her hand.

'Have you spoken to Leonardo?' she asked. 'He would advise you, *querida*.'

Valeria had fingered the letter in her pocket.

'I have, actually, Mama, and he says the world is changing and girls should do as they please.'

'Well, if your brother says that, who am I to disagree,' she had said with a smile.

Afterwards, Valeria had escaped to her room to read the letter again.

My Dearest Valeria,

If I had known you wished to see me, I would have come to every one of the dinners at home. I believed your calendar was filled with engagements with the most eligible men in Seville.

I admit I am missing you more than I can say. Our rides, our discussions, even our arguments (not the bad ones, obviously), are important to me, and without them I am bereft.

If I am entirely honest, I am glad Diego no longer features in your life. However nice, he was not good enough for you, Valeria.

With regards to work, you know I support you entirely. The world is changing, and women are part of that change. I am also delighted that the Leica will come with you in your new career. I am praying it will keep you safe.

I can see your views are becoming more republican daily, but I beg of you, keep them to yourself. It is a brutal world, Valeria, war is coming, and nothing is secure.

Again, I say to you, when the battle commences, please keep safe for me.

The following week, Valeria had approached the subject of work with her mother again. She had been lingering in Isabel's bedroom while her mother got dressed.

'Have you thought about what I said?'

Isabel had pulled on a light summer dress over her slip. 'Will you do me up, Valeria?'

She had done up the buttons at the back and had watched her mother in the mirror.

'Quite a lot, actually,' Isabel had smiled at her daughter, 'and I agree with you entirely. If you wish to get a job, I will support you, but we may have to keep the details from your father.'

Valeria had hugged her. 'You are wonderful, thank you, Mama. I want to do something useful. I need to make a difference.'

'Difference?' Isabel's eyebrows were raised. 'I am not sure that is what I had in mind.'

'You had a strong will; that is where I have got it from. I cannot ignore what is going on in the world. Elena has found a worthwhile job; she is now nursing in Florence.'

'So where will you find this work, *querida*?' Isabel had pushed a strand of auburn hair into the large hair comb with little success.

'Here, let me,' Valeria had taken out the comb and expertly piled her mother's hair into a chignon. 'I am a good photographer, you said so yourself. I have already contacted the editor at ABC and he is giving me an interview tomorrow.'

'The newspaper?'

'Yes, Mama, the newspaper in Seville.' She had kissed her mother's cheek and had left the room, a smile playing around her lips.

For the first few months at the newspaper she had taken photographs of religious festivals and commemorations, occasions that required a certain amount of skill but no imagination, until one day she arrived back at the office with a photograph and had placed it on the picture editor's desk.

He had picked it up and studied it carefully, looking first at the photograph and then at Valeria. From his rapid blinking, Valeria could tell he wasn't pleased.

'Who took this?'

'I did.'

'You have taken a photo of the Civil Guard opening fire on striking mill workers.' He tapped his pen on the desk. 'Of course we could spin it our way, the republican government initiated this disaster; it might even be good for our cause.'

The photograph was published but Valeria was dissatisfied. The editor's words had shocked and disgusted her. She had photographed a massacre perpetrated by their own Civil Guard and yet her editor was talking about political spin.

As her views leant more and more towards the left, she knew she could no longer work for the right-wing newspaper. The war was six months old when she had moved to Madrid and become a freelance photographer, renting a flat, mixing with journalists and photographers from all over the world. She had frequented the bars and hotels where they drank and had become part of their community. It was her first taste of independence and she loved it. Her mother had begged her to come home in a telephone call, taken at a hotel in Madrid.

'*Querida*, your father is mad with worry. He says it is too dangerous and you must leave immediately. Madrid will fall and who knows what will happen.'

Her response was firm. 'Mama, I am fine. I am a personal assistant to the editor at the ABC. I am doing a good job and I wish to stay. And as to Madrid falling, I think he is being hasty. Whatever bombs fall on this city, whatever carnage is inflicted on an innocent people, they will not give up.'

'Please, Valeria,' she had begged, her voice shaking. 'Papa says he will come and drag you out personally.'

'Remember we are under siege by the very rebels he is fighting for. Do you believe republican Madrid would allow a nationalist colonel to walk right in and collect his little daughter? I think not, Mama. Whatever you or Papa say, I will not change my mind.'

Afterwards, she had written to Leonardo. Because of the censors it was brief, giving nothing away:

Dearest Leonardo,
Mama is trying to make me come home but perhaps you can reassure her and beg her to leave me alone.

PS my camera is a huge source of comfort to me because it brings you closer.

That had been months ago, before Walter had come into her life.

Now Walt Mayhew and Val Saint, as she had come to be known, were freelance photographers with newspapers and agencies all over the world bidding for their work. Their office in *Calle de Tetuán* in Madrid had become a hub for journalists, writers and poets, and for the first time in her life, Valeria felt she was doing something worthwhile.

As Valeria contemplated the black-and-white image, she held her breath and her eyes stung with tears. How had she managed to record the event, she wondered, how had she managed to remain calm while an adolescent boy had been gunned down no more than thirty metres away? But in the height of the moment, her professionalism had taken over. If she hadn't taken the shot, the world would never see the fear on the boy's face, they would never know the atrocities committed every day. And this is what she did; she recorded war in all its gritty destructiveness.

Chapter Forty-four

29 July 1937, Seville

Bañu found Valeria pacing back and forth in her bedroom. 'I thought the floor would collapse. What is it, *querida*?'

Valeria threw herself down on the bed. 'Oh Bañu, there is so much I would like to tell you, but I can't.'

Bañu sat down beside her and rubbed her back as she had when Valeria had been a child. 'You think I don't know what you have been doing, that I am unaware of the photographer, Val Saint? You may have kept your identity from your father and mother, but you can never fool me. When I saw the pictures in your father's American newspaper, I knew immediately.'

Valeria groaned. 'Papa would never understand. The things I have seen, watched. Last week I photographed—' She stopped and buried her face in the pillow.

'Tell me, my love, it will help.' Bañu waited patiently. Valeria would tell her in her own time.

'I watched a youth being shot by the nationalists, and I stood by.'

'I know little of your new world, but I am aware that journalists and photographers are meant to record events, not take part in them,' Bañu said softly.

'But I will never forget the look on his face, the moment of death. He was no more than fourteen, just a child. His arms were up in surrender, but they still shot him. I wanted to yell and scream, but I took my picture and got away.'

'I am so sorry, child. I had hoped for change, but not like this.' The old woman raised her hands and dropped them to her sides. 'Atrocious things are happening. Every day I read of more tragedy, more innocent children dying, but it is you I worry about, Valeria. You take these terrible risks but will enough people care when your story reaches them?'

'I hope so, Bañu, I can only do my best.'

Bañu continued to massage her back and when the tension had left her shoulders, she cleared her throat. 'I am so sorry, but there is something else you need to know. Not good, I'm afraid.'

Valeria rolled over and looked at her.

'Padre Alvaro is dead.'

Valeria sat up, her hand flying to her mouth, tears springing to her eyes. '*Dios Santo*, what happened?'

'He was murdered, Valeria. Our poor priest was hung from his own church bells. That is why I returned to Seville with Leonardo.'

'Not the republicans?' Valeria whispered, already knowing the answer. War had created monsters of men.

'They came on horseback, the padre wasn't the only victim, Señor Herrero's estate steward was decapitated, it is a mercy the old man was away. The killing seems to be indiscriminate; one day it is a republican atrocity, the next it is the turn of the nationalists.' Bañu stood up and went to the window.

'Leonardo followed their tracks but was unable to find them. Now, of course, he wishes for revenge.'

'So he is going to fight with the nationalists?' Valeria accepted a hanky from Bañu and wiped her eyes.

'He went to see your father at the barracks, and yes, that was the outcome of his talks.'

Valeria swung her legs over the side of the bed and put her head in her hands. She felt dirty, soiled. War had created this vile society where brother was killing brother, friend was denouncing friend. But to kill their priest. And now Leonardo was going to fight for the side she opposed.

'I must see him,' she whispered.

'By that I assume you mean Leonardo. He dropped the dog in only yesterday.'

For the first time Valeria noticed Luna curled up by her bed. 'I thought you didn't like her.'

Bañu shrugged. 'The dog is fifteen, I have put up with her for all these years – in fact, I have grown rather fond of her.'

Valeria went to the old woman and buried her head in her bony chest. 'Oh Bañu.'

'I know, my love.'

When Bañu had returned downstairs with Luna, Valeria went to her desk. She took a piece of paper from the drawer and started to write, then she tore it up and started again.

Despite the passage of time, she finally admitted to herself that she loved Leonardo, and she couldn't let him go to the front without telling him her true feelings.

Dearest Leonardo,

Bañu told me you were the one to find our dear Padre Alvaro. I can only imagine the depth of your despair. Know that I am crying with you, Leonardo, that your pain is shared. Every moment of the day you are in my thoughts and my prayers. Life has the cruellest way of taking away those who you love.

I have also heard that you are going to fight for the

nationalists and I am scared. In the past you have shown a blatant disregard for your own safety and you are going to war with anger in your heart.

Please meet me, Leonardo, there is much I want to say. I will be at the house in Seville for the next few days.

Always,

Valeria

She put the letter in an envelope, changed, retrieved her hat from the cupboard and went downstairs.

Half an hour later, wearing her most feminine dress, she approached the military headquarters in Seville.

'Excuse me, capitán,' she said to an officer as he came through the gate.

'*Sí, señorita, puedo ayudarla?* Is there anything I can do to help?'

'Oh please,' she simpered, peering up at him from beneath the brim of her hat. 'I would be so very grateful if you could deliver a letter to Capitán Palamera de Santos, I believe he is billeted here.'

The officer bowed.

'And what is he to you, young lady?'

'He is my brother, señor.'

It was easy after that, the officer assured her he would carry out the task even if he had to die for it, and Valeria smiled prettily in response.

On her way back to the house she pulled off her hat, exposing her short hair, and grinned. It seemed she still had a certain allure.

Valeria didn't have to wait long to receive a reply. The following morning, it was delivered by Leonardo.

After holding her close for the briefest moment, he put a letter in the pocket of her dress. 'Read this later when Mama is not around,' he whispered.

'Padre Alvaro, his death,' she drew back, her voice choked with tears. 'I am so very sorry.'

Leonardo cleared his throat. 'Senseless, brutal—'

Valeria put her hand on his arm. 'It broke my heart that I wasn't there to support you.'

'I thank God that you were not.'

They were interrupted by Isabel. 'Leonardo, my son.' She put her hands around his face. 'And now you have joined the cavalry and I will be worried about you every moment of the day.'

Leonardo took Isabel's hands. 'Your prayers will protect me and so will Saturno. He will bring me back to you, Mama.'

'He had better; you are a son to me.'

At that moment Luna padded slowly down the passage towards them. She peered at Leonardo, a film over her once-bright eyes.

'You and I go back a very long way,' Leonardo whispered, kissing her shaggy head. 'Keep well, my friend.' He then looked at Isabel. 'Look after her for me, Mama.'

Isabel smiled, a little too brightly. 'You know I will, and when this beastly war is over, you shall live with us again?'

Leonardo glanced over Isabel's head at Valeria, a question in his eyes.

'He knows his home is here, Mama.'

Isabel hung on to Leonardo's arm. 'Can you stay for lunch?'

Leonardo hugged his adoptive mother. 'I have to return to the barracks, but I will come again before we leave.'

Isabel's eyes were bright with tears. 'You know we love you – don't we, Valeria?'

'We do,' Valeria replied.

After Leonardo had gone, Valeria ran down the maze of winding passages to the internal courtyard. Hiding behind one of the terracotta pots, she tore open the envelope.

You always wanted to go to the summer palace of the Nasrid rulers in Granada, so meet me at the train station on Monday morning at ten, and I will take you there.
Always,
Leonardo

Clutching the letter, she returned to her room and threw herself on her bed. 'Leonardo has remembered,' she whispered, every sense in her body alive.

On 2 August, Valeria chose a pale-blue muslin dress that fell beyond her knees and a cream straw hat. It was suitably demure, she decided, a smile lighting her face, but her thoughts were not. She sprayed scent from the *Farmacia di Santa Maria Novella* on her neck and arms, packed her rucksack with her work clothes and slung her camera round her neck.

'Goodbye, Mama,' she slipped into the dining room where her mother was eating breakfast.

'You are obviously not returning to the office wearing that pretty dress,' her mother observed, putting down her newspaper.

'After meeting a girlfriend in Granada, I'll go straight back to Madrid.'

Isabel's gaze was stern when she looked at her daughter. 'Something has been troubling me, Valeria. When I spoke to the offices of the ABC in Madrid to tell you about Padre Alvaro, they did not seem to have you on record as working there.'

Valeria put her arms around her mother's neck. 'Please don't ask me, Mama.'

Isabel took off her glasses and stood up. 'Just be safe, *querida*, and whatever it is that you are doing in Madrid, please be careful.'

'*Por supuesto*, Mama.'

'You say "of course", but I am not sure that I believe you. I worry so much about the bombs; the city is besieged, and you are in the thick of it.' She rubbed at her glasses. 'I suppose nothing I say will change your mind?'

'Nothing, Mama. I promise, I'll be careful, but I can't sit around here waiting for the war to end. Remember I love you more than anything.'

Isabel pulled a handkerchief from her sleeve. 'Go, Valeria, you know that I hate goodbyes.'

Valeria went next to the kitchen where Bañu was baking bread. The old woman stopped kneading the dough, looked her up and down and sniffed the air.

'I see.'

'What do you see?' Valeria asked, her face flushing.

'You are courting danger, Valeria.'

'Bañu, I have to see him, you know that.'

'I have been dreading this day since he first came to our house.' Bañu shrugged her shoulders in a gesture of resignation and looked at Valeria. 'You know this will only end in tears.'

Chapter Forty-five

Leonardo was waiting on the packed platform when Valeria first saw him, his pale shirt a contrast to his suntanned skin. She stood for a moment watching him, committing to memory the expression on his face, the look of anticipation in his eyes, then taking the lens cap off her Leica, she focussed on Leonardo. There was something exquisite about his beauty, his bearing, relaxed and unafraid. After releasing the shutter button, she replaced the lens cap and walked down the platform to meet him.

'You came,' he said. 'I thought you would change your mind.'

'Why would I do that?' she asked.

He shrugged his shoulders and grinned. 'Your letter was too good to be true.'

'But I said little,' she teased.

'It is what you didn't say,' he replied.

They waited an hour for the train, and after a stampede for the seats, they found places at opposite ends of the packed carriage. As the train rumbled slowly through Andalucía, pulling into the loop occasionally to let the troop trains pass, Leonardo's head lolled forward. Despite his joy at being with Valeria, the brutal death of his friends, coupled with his induction into the rebel army, had left him emotionally and physically exhausted. But Valeria couldn't sleep. For her entire adult life she had longed for this moment and she was not going to miss a second of it. They were approaching Antequera when she pulled her thumbed copy of Federico García Lorca's poems from her rucksack and started to read.

Hot southern sands
Yearning for white camellias.
Weeps arrow without target

As the scorched landscape flashed past, Lorca's poignant memories of his homeland, Andalucía, touched her deeply. Who knew what sadness the future would bring, but for this one day she was with Leonardo.

Four hours after leaving Seville, the train pulled into Granada station and Valeria joined Leonardo.

'We could wait for the bus,' Leonardo suggested, as they pushed through the crowds and emerged in the street outside.

'Bus?' Valeria responded with a laugh, her eyes challenging him. 'What is wrong with walking?'

An hour later they were still walking. At Valeria's request they made a detour and stopped outside her mother's childhood home in *Gran Via*.

'This is where—' she paused for a moment to consider her words – 'Isabel and Carlos met.'

Leonardo gazed at the impressive house, a myriad of emotions building in his chest. His voice was soft when he spoke. 'Imagine, Valeria, without their meeting, you wouldn't be here.'

'And you wouldn't know me,' she whispered in reply.

They found a restaurant close by, and while Leonardo ordered salted cod, Valeria chose *frisuelos*.

'I don't suppose you are going to tell me where you are really working in Madrid?' Leonardo murmured, putting his hand over Valeria's. 'We both know it is not the ABC.'

Valeria looked at him over her glass of wine. Of course she wanted to tell him, longed to reveal her work, but it was safer for both of them if he didn't know everything. She would give him a version of the truth. She took a deep breath.

'Let us say it involves the republican news agency in Madrid.'

Leonardo raised an eyebrow and spoke softly. 'It's strange that I should be the nationalist and you the republican. I always thought it would be the other way around.'

'Then you don't know me very well.'

'Perhaps better than most, but even I am surprised you haven't bowed to parental pressure.'

Valeria smiled. 'Since when have I done anything I was told?'

Leonardo speared a piece of fish. 'And I suppose you think I am not being true to myself?'

'I know your choice was made when Padre Alvaro died.'

Leonardo grimaced. 'You didn't see him hanging at the end of a rope. It changed everything for me, and now I am fighting for the nationalists when I don't even believe in this war.'

'I don't believe in any war, Leonardo.' Valeria ran her hand up his arm, felt the muscles beneath his skin.

'There has been enough violence in my life,' he continued. 'My great friend, William Montcrieffe, gave up his life fighting for the International Brigades, a cause he believed in, and me –' he shrugged, his mouth twisting in pain – 'he would have been ashamed to have known me, Valeria.'

'He would have understood that your decision was made in the heat of the moment.'

Leonardo pushed his plate aside, his face bleak. 'And now my orders are to bring Saturno. If he is hurt, God help me I will—'

'He has to keep you safe, Leonardo, so you will come through this together. He has to bring you back to me.'

When Valeria had finished her pancakes, Leonardo stroked her cheek.

'You always had a sweet tooth,' he murmured. 'They probably don't taste the same without sugar.'

'I'm getting used to it,' she said with a sigh.

Leonardo paid and they wandered through the narrow, hilly streets of the Albaicín quarter of Granada where, only recently, there had been a 'cleansing' of republicans. Valeria ran her fingers over the bullet holes that peppered the bougainvillea-clad wall, her expression grim.

'This is our day, Leonardo, and yet everywhere we look we are reminded of the hell we are living through. There is no escape, not even for a second.'

Leonardo took her hands.

'From this moment we will not think about the war, we will not talk about it. We mustn't waste our precious time together. Today there are no nationalists or republicans; it is only you and me. *Promesa*, Valeria?'

'*Promesa*,' she replied.

In the cobbled *Plaza Mirador San Nicolás*, with the view of the Alhambra on the opposite hilltop as a backdrop, Valeria loaded another roll of film into her camera and Leonardo smiled into the lens.

While she continued to click away, he adopted different poses, each one more exuberant than the last.

When he vaulted onto the parapet and lurched precariously over the gorge beneath, she squealed.

'You get down this minute, Leonardo.'

From there it was shopping in the bazaars at the bottom of the hill. When Leonardo spotted a blue shawl that matched the colour of Valeria's eyes, he paid for it and dragged her into a tiny alleyway.

'Captivating,' he whispered, draping it around her neck.

'Me or the scarf?' Valeria giggled.

'Definitely the scarf.' He took off her hat and brushed his lips against her forehead. 'Did you know I took out a loan to buy the camera? It took years to pay it back.'

Valeria shook her head, unable to speak.

He drew his finger down her cheek. 'You know I love you, Valeria.'

'For a while I thought that you despised me,' she whispered.

'I could never despise you. I would die for you.' He pulled her closer, the camera coming between them, and lowered his head.

'I hated Constanza, I wanted to kill her,' Valeria murmured until his lips silenced her.

When at last they parted, Leonardo laughed softly. He ran his hands through her cropped hair.

'And what about Diego and the stream of other men that passed through our doors?'

'I wanted to make you jealous.'

'Well, you succeeded,' he replied.

'Shouldn't we go to the Summer Palace?' she asked. 'It is getting late.'

'I said I would take you there, but I didn't say when. I will take you there by moonlight, Valeria.'

They were wandering up the hill towards the *Plaza Arquitecto* when an ambulance sped past, screeching to a halt at the entrance of the Alhambra Palace Hotel. As two porters rushed outside, Valeria buried her face in Leonardo's shoulder. He lifted her chin. 'Look away, Valeria. You made me a promise, remember?'

'My parents used to come here for celebrations, now it is a military hospital filled with the dying.'

'Everything was different then,' Leonardo affirmed, taking her hand.

The sky was darkening when they skirted the ancient fortress and the original Alhambra Palace.

'*Extraordinario*,' Valeria said in a hushed tone.

'The Nasrid dynasty were great builders,' Leonardo explained. 'The interiors of this palace are considered some of the finest in the world, but in my opinion, the most romantic part is yet to come.'

Following the fence line, they found a small gap and went through. From there they ran through the woods following the contours of the hill, until they met up with a path that led to the Summer Palace.

'*Generalife*,' Leonardo murmured, when at last they had come into the open and the palace shimmered in the moonlight below them. 'Which to the Nasrid rulers meant garden of the architect.'

Valeria looked up at him. All her life she had heard stories of the summer palace belonging to the Muslim caliphates, surrounded by one of the oldest Moorish gardens in the world. Now she would see it in all its monochrome beauty with Leonardo.

Slipping through the gardens, they reached the first courtyard where the rulers and their entourage had once dismounted their horses, and went into the second. From there they negotiated the winding stairs that led into a water garden framed by flowerbeds, cloisters and pavilions.

'The *Patio de la Acequia*,' Leonardo clarified, watching her gasp in surprise.

'It's more beautiful than I could ever have imagined,' Valeria whispered. And as Leonardo watched her reflection shift in the long pool, a lump formed in his throat. The palace was beautiful, of course, but to him it paled in comparison to Valeria.

He caught her hand and led her down a colonnade bordering one side of the garden, until they came to a small pavilion that looked out over the landscape below. Delicate lattice-work windows were set low in the walls. The only sound disturbing the silence was an owl hooting in the woods nearby. Leonardo put his arm around Valeria's shoulders.

'From here, the Nasrid rulers could look out over the city and the valleys of the rivers Genil and Darro,' he murmured into her hair.

Valeria pulled away from him and leant back against the wall. She put her fingers to his lips. 'I know why you brought me here, Leonardo.'

Leonardo lifted her chin, his eyes searching her face.

'Perhaps we are wrong, this is wrong. In the eyes of the world you are my sister.'

'But we are not blood, you are not my brother. You lost your mother and came to live with us, so there is nothing standing in our way. Fate has brought us together, Leonardo.' Valeria wound her arms around Leonardo's neck and drew him towards her.

'I have wanted you for years,' she whispered, her voice catching, and as Leonardo buried his head in her neck, breathing in the sweet scent of pomegranate, he was lost completely.

As Valeria undid the buttons of his shirt, he pulled up her dress and caressed the soft flesh of her thighs. Valeria groaned and pushed herself towards him.

Kissing her deeply, Leonardo knew it was too late for restraint. His past had gone, the future was with the woman in his arms.

*

When some time later they lay together on the ground, the speckled moonlight filtering through the latticework, casting patterns on Valeria's pale skin, Leonardo ran his hand over the contours of her back.

'*Gracias, mi amada Valeria*,' he breathed, his voice soft with love, and she rested her head on his chest and looked up at him.

'Whatever happens in this life we have had this,' she said, running her fingers down his body until they came to rest.

'We will have this and more, my love,' he murmured. 'We will have forever.'

Chapter Forty-six

August, 1937

Constanza was lying belly down in the ditch, the barrel of her Mauser bolt-action rifle over the edge, as the nationalist detachment approached. The sun was relentless and for two hours she had sweated profusely, unable to move, powerless to halt the column of ants that had made their continual march across her body. For the entire time she had dreamt of a long, cool beer and she had longed for the shade. But her discomfort was nothing if her detachment could prevent reinforcements getting through to Belchite, supporting their overall aim of recapturing Zaragoza only a few kilometres behind enemy lines. The retaking of the Aragon capital would be a great boost to their flagging morale. She glanced at her watch, tension building in her chest as a message from the commander went down the line. 'No firing until I give the order, let them come closer.'

Constanza looked through the sight and drew in her breath. It wasn't the killing that concerned her, it was the build-up, the interminable waiting. She would never forget the first man she had shot and the look of surprise on his face as he fell backwards, the second she had found difficult, but after that she had felt nothing at all. It was simple really, life and then death. From the moment the war had started she knew she would fight.

'Become a nurse,' her mother had begged as they ate supper at the kitchen table. 'The soldiering is for men.'

'Leave her be.' Her father, a mild man, had looked up from his rabbit stew.

'But a soldier, Victor, you realise your daughter will carry a gun, she will be required to—' she had paused, unable to say the word.

Victor winked at Constanza. 'Whatever you say, Amparo, your daughter will do as she pleases. She is strong and brave like her magnificent mother.'

Amparo had simpered, puffing out her ample chest. 'But Victor—'

'No buts, Amparo Batista. No buts at all.'

As a member of a communist paramilitary group, Constanza was one of the increasing number of women fighters. At last women had a role and they were participating in the struggle to free Spain from the tyranny of the nationalists.

There was no doubt atrocities had taken place in the republican name. Churches had been burned, monasteries sacked, priests, nuns and landowners killed. In fact, anyone who they believed to be a threat to the republican cause was at risk. Women, it seemed, could be just as ruthless as men. There was one village, she couldn't even remember its name, where the militia had built a bonfire using the mayor's furniture and books as firewood, before tying the terrified man to a stake.

'Don't shoot him first,' a woman soldier had yelled. 'Light the match and let him feel the pain of his sins.' Constanza had walked away, the act too brutal to witness, but in reality, she had been guilty too.

Constanza's thoughts were interrupted when the word came

down the line. They were coming. As the infantry marched past, on the commander's instructions they opened fire, and an ear-splitting fusillade of guns and grenade explosions rocked the nationalists. The surprise element was in their favour, and only two of their own men were lost. They killed twelve of the enemy that day, preventing the nationalist company from reaching Belchite.

Constanza was eating her rations later that evening when the adjutant came to find her.

'Please come to the captain's tent,' he instructed.

Wondering if she was about to be congratulated on a successful day's work, she followed him through the wooded clearing to the largest of the tents.

The captain didn't acknowledge her presence at first, but finally he looked up, the light from the oil lamp casting shadows on his face.

'Forgive me, too much work.' He rubbed his hand over his unshaven chin.

'I have some news.' His glance shifted away from her and Constanza was suddenly afraid.

'Capitán, is something wrong?' she asked.

'I am afraid so.' His eyes returned to her face, and Constanza was at once aware of the telegram in his hands. 'There is no easy way to say this, but your village has been attacked. Anyone with republican sympathies has been shot. I am afraid your father was amongst them.'

'Cazalla de la Sierra is miles from the front. It was taken by the nationalists at the beginning of the war. There is no reason, no—'

'Your father is Victor Batista?'

Constanza nodded, gritting her teeth to prevent herself from crying.

'But he is a school teacher,' she said at last. 'He just wants this war to be over.' But then she realised with a jolt that she was his connection to the republicans. She had been the cause of her father's death.

'And my mother,' she whispered.

'It was only the men and boys. There were the usual brutalities.' He didn't say the word, but his meaning was clear. Constanza drew in her breath.

'Was my mother raped?' she asked finally.

The captain fiddled with his pen. 'I don't have the details, I'm afraid. I suggest you take some leave and go home. Go and care for your mother but then come back to us. We need you more than ever before.'

As Constanza travelled home, taking lifts wherever she could, from army vehicles, trucks, even a tank, she was filled with rage. She would kill a hundred nationalists; they would pay for what they had done.

Moving in and out of nationalist territory, she changed into her only dress and continued to take whatever transport was available, her pistol never far from her hand.

On the last leg of her journey, when a nationalist officer offered her a lift, she took it, her smile pleasant, but there was hatred in her heart. Could she shoot him, she wondered, take the pistol from her bag, steal the vehicle and go? But what good would that do, they would come for the rest of her village, kill more innocent victims.

'*Gracias, capitán.*' She smiled provocatively and walked from the car, her hips swaying. 'I'll kill you one of these days,' she whispered.

Constanza found her mother in the kitchen of their house. She was sewing.

'Is that you, Victor?' she asked, without looking up.

'No, Mama, it is me.'

'Your father is late, he said he'd be home for lunch—'

Constanza could see the plates on the side. 'But Mama, Papa is—' She stopped, her breath catching, was there a chance the intelligence was incorrect? Could her father still be alive? 'Is he at the school, Mama?'

'If I know your father, he will be late for his own wedding; it is too much, Constanza.'

'What are you talking about?'

'Look, the dress is finished and I have to collect the flowers.' Suddenly Amparo's face crumpled. Constanza took her in her arms.

'It's all right, Mama,' she soothed.

'They took them to the cemetery. So many men and boys. Little boys, *querida*. Then they lined them up outside the cemetery wall and shot them. Thank God you and Mariana weren't here.'

Constanza flinched, the image clear in her mind. Her beloved father whom she loved more than anyone, was dead. The man who had made her believe that anything was possible, had been murdered outside the cemetery wall.

'Where is he now, Mama?'

Amparo slipped to her knees on the floor. 'The bodies were piled high, but they didn't give them the dignity of a burial, they left them for the flies. They had other things on their minds.' She pulled up her dress and Constanza could see the welts on her thighs. 'I'm fifty years of age, Constanza, an old woman, and yet they still used me.'

Constanza knelt on the floor beside her and put her arms around her.

Amparo looked at her again, her eyes vague. 'Come now, Constanza. I must get ready for my wedding. It wouldn't do for both your father and I to be late.'

*

Constanza put her mother to bed, cleaned the plates, and went in search of her friend.

But Daniela wasn't in the house, in fact, she was nowhere to be found.

She learnt later that Daniela had taken her own life when the nationalists had finished with her.

Chapter Forty-seven

Valeria woke as the soft morning light filtered through the latticework onto her sleeping lover's back. She kissed his shoulder, woke him gently and they dressed in silence, knowing that very soon they would part.

They had reached the station and were approaching the platforms, when Valeria drew Leonardo into the shadows.

'The train to Madrid is already here. Kiss me and we will go our separate ways. It is better like this.'

Leonardo held her face in his hands, drinking in the image of her lips, her eyes, as if he could reach into her very soul. 'We belong to each other, Valeria, I am yours entirely. You are more precious to me than anything in the world, so please be careful, *mi hermosa amada.*'

Valeria smiled, but her lips were trembling. 'I have been waiting my entire life for this moment, even if I didn't know it. And now that I have found you—'

Leonardo took her hands and kissed them. 'Leave now, or I will never let you go.'

Valeria ran from him; she did not look back.

Throughout the long day and night Valeria endured the journey back to Madrid. She ignored the lewd comments of the soldiers sharing the carriages with her, the filth and the smell. She accepted the four changes without complaint, climbing wearily over the damaged tracks. Even the fighter planes screaming overhead hardly affected her, for though she dropped to her knees with the rest of them, in her mind she was still in the *Generalife* with Leonardo. She could feel his hands on her body, his breath on her face. She remembered every nuance of his speech, and every word that he said.

When the train finally pulled into Atocha Station, Valeria hurried along the platform and went straight to the office, disturbing Walt, who was asleep in his chair.

'So you are back,' he cried, jumping to his feet as she dropped her rucksack to the floor. 'But dearest, you look terrible.'

'Well, isn't that a nice welcome!' Valeria smiled weakly.

Walt peered at her, his head on one side. 'And if I am not mistaken there is something different about you.'

'I admit I am a little tired,' she uttered, sinking down on the top of her desk.

'Oh God, not a man – not *the* man?'

Valeria blushed.

'I can see I've hit upon the truth. You are a cruel, heartless woman for spurning me.'

Despite her exhaustion Valeria began to laugh. 'I would never spurn you, Walt.'

Walt struck up a pose. 'Me mam said you could never trust a foreigner.'

Valeria shook her head. How she loved Walt. She had never had a good male friend and Walt filled that gap. He was thoughtful, funny and, she suspected, a little in love with her.

'Leave me alone, Walt, I beg of you, let me have just two hours' sleep.'

*

For the next few weeks, Valeria concentrated on a series of photographs capturing ordinary civilians caught up in the war. There was a photograph of a child amputee hopping through the rubble supported by his crutch, his dusty face turned towards the camera, another of an old man sitting on a chimney pot, a haunting expression of bewilderment in his eyes. She had captured a mother's agony as she held her dead infant in her arms. When she developed a photograph of a toddler with fair curls lying amongst the ruins of a house, a teddy bear at her side, she took the image to her desk and put her head in her hands. 'How could this be?' she whispered, remembering the moment she had come across the little body. 'She was just a baby, a tiny child.'

They were working in the darkroom, developing their latest batch of photographs, the last in the series, when Valeria suddenly retched into the sink. The smell of the chemicals had never bothered her before, but she'd started to feel nauseous of late. Walt cleared his throat and coughed.

'Please don't say anything, Walt,' she groaned.

Walt ploughed on despite her protests. 'I've noticed a few things about you recently, Valeria. Have you thought – is there a chance you might be pregnant?'

'Enough, Walt, I don't know what you're talking about,' Valeria snapped, nearly dropping the roll of film in the developing fluid.

'Just an observation, that's all.'

Valeria said nothing, and she was biting her lip as she worked. She had missed her period and the sickness confirmed her suspicions.

'Come on, you can tell me, love,' Walt said at last. 'You won't be able to hide it for long.'

Valeria checked on the exposure and took the prints out of

the water while Walt pinned them on the line that was strung across the darkroom.

'Not ideal timing, Walt,' she admitted at last. 'I am sorry.'

'I assume the child was conceived in Granada?'

Valeria ignored the question. 'But I will go on working for as long as I can.'

'You could always say the baby is mine.'

'What are you suggesting?' she asked in surprise.

'A lifeline, I think.'

She reached out towards him. 'You would do that for me?'

'I'd do anything for you.'

Valeria ran her finger across his cheek. 'I do love you, Walt.'

'Of course you do,' he quipped. 'That being the case, we might as well make good use of me. I take it your parents would be horrified if they found out the truth?'

Valeria peered at Walter in the darkness. 'My father would never speak to me again.'

Walt cleared his throat. 'Well, then, it's settled. You can wear my ring and you can pretend we are married. After the war is over, you can run away, leaving me entirely heartbroken, and go to England with your lover. I have a flat in London you can use. Now that has to be the best deal in the world.' He took a silver ring off his finger and found her hand in the dark.

'See, it fits perfectly. That has to mean something.'

'It means that you are too thin,' Valeria said with a giggle.

'I wish it were for real,' Walt sighed, so quietly that Valeria wondered if she had imagined it.

When Valeria was three months pregnant, she wrote to Leonardo. If he knew her so well, would he understand the workings of her mind? she wondered. Would he know she wanted to tell him something, longed to reveal the truth? After three attempts she sealed the envelope and took it to the post. Hopefully, this would get past the censors and find its way to Leonardo.

My dearest Leonardo,
I am sending this letter to Bañu. Put an obstacle in her path and she will find a way around it. I feel sure she will get this to you, wherever you are.
Just know that I am missing you more than you can imagine. There is so much I want to say, so many thoughts I want to share, but for now they will have to stay in my mind.
Loving you always,
Valeria

On a cold December afternoon when Walt was shivering at his desk, Valeria put a steaming mug of acorn coffee in his hand, laced with the usual brandy.

'It's not looking good for us, Valeria.' He grimaced. 'The nationalists gain more ground every day; I think the end is in sight.'

'Don't be so pessimistic, Walt, it is not over yet.'

'But I do have a plan—' He looked at Valeria for a moment, then he shook his head. 'I just can't put you in danger!'

'I am pregnant, not sick, so tell me what this is all about.' Valeria put her arm around Walt's shoulders, feeling the bones jutting through his jumper.

He stood up and grabbed his leather jacket. 'Come on, I'll tell you in the bar. Walls have ears.'

As they picked their way through the broken streets to the bar in *Calle de Echegaray*, the signs of the devastation were everywhere. Notices warning of unexploded bombs were positioned amongst the rubble. Twisted and tangled metal was yet another hazard in the chaos.

'If it hadn't been for the International Brigades, the city would have been overrun by nationalists,' Walt muttered, bypassing a road block.

Valeria accepted Walt's hand as she climbed over a collapsed wall. She brushed the dust off her dress and looked around her in disgust. 'And they are German bombs; look what they did at Guernica.'

'Spain is just an experiment.' Walt's face was unusually grim. 'They are playing war games with us, before they try it out for real on the rest of Europe. Unfortunately, the Russian fighters don't seem to be able to stop them.'

They walked on in silence until they reached their destination. The dull green sign above the entrance gave no indication of the lively atmosphere inside. As usual *La Venencia* was heaving with customers and while Valeria dived for a table as a couple were leaving, Walt pushed his way to the bar. The corner table was the perfect place to talk and keep an eye on the other customers. You never knew who was watching these days. It seemed to be the usual crowd: locals, soldiers on leave and hacks. Valeria waved to a journalist and he sauntered over.

'Anything good going down?' he asked, his soft American drawl unmistakable.

'Not at the moment, Felix, we will let you know.'

'Thanks, Val.' He winked at Valeria and sauntered off, his leather jacket slung over his shoulder.

Walt returned with two beers. After several minutes of casual conversation, he leant towards Valeria, his voice low. 'So now the news I have been waiting to tell you. Last week our republican contact got hold of me.'

'Yes?' Valeria waited impatiently.

'He wants us to do something pretty dangerous.'

'Everything we do is dangerous, Walt,' she retaliated in a low whisper.

Walt put down his drink and leant towards her.

'OK, so he wants some photographs of an airfield, but it must be full of German aircraft. The republicans are desperate for the world to know how much support Germany is giving to the nationalists.'

Valeria's eyes widened. 'Interesting.'

'They need them as soon as possible. But that's not all. Last week I also had a conversation with a London journalist, Jeremy Page from *The Times*. I'd seen him before, hanging around this bar, hoping to sniff out a story.' Walt took a quick glance around and leant closer still. 'This time, he had deliberately sought me out. We got into conversation; two English blokes.' He grinned briefly. 'He's posh, though, Cambridge and all that, not an East End Jew like me.'

Valeria smiled. 'Well, if you are sure this is genuine, and it's not a set-up.'

'I was dubious at first, but not by the end of the conversation.' Walt sipped his beer. 'Jeremy said he'd seen some of our photographs and was impressed. He wanted to use them, but here is the coincidence, Valeria. He asked if we had any examples of German aircraft stationed in Spain. Apparently, they could be used alongside an article he was preparing.'

'So in a matter of two weeks, we have been approached by two different organisations to photograph the same subject. Don't you think that is a little strange?' Valeria strummed her fingers on the table.

'I knew you would ask that, but we definitely know our republican contact is genuine, and I've looked this Page bloke up. He's well respected and Felix says he's kosher.'

'Kosher?' Valeria questioned.

Walt grinned. 'It means he's legit.'

She still looked puzzled and he kissed her nose. 'Anyway, Jeremy says he can get us some documentation that would allow us into the nationalist zone. I didn't ask how, but naturally an airfield is part of the equation.'

Valeria looked unconvinced. 'You expect us to walk in and find an airfield filled with German planes, just like that. Are you joking, Walt?'

Walt drained his beer, and smirked. 'I've found one already: Villa del Prado, fifty kilometres south-west of Madrid. I know it's taking a chance, but if we get the right shots, they will be syndicated right across Europe and America. It'll help the republican cause no end.' He grinned sheepishly. 'It will do us no harm either. So what do you think?'

'You say it's taking a chance. This is more than dangerous, this is mad.' Then with a grin, Valeria added, 'Yes, of course.'

Chapter Forty-eight

Three days later they met up with Jeremy Page, at the same bar. Documents were passed beneath the table, and Walt gave him the date of their travel.

'What's the name of the airfield?' Jeremy asked.

Valeria fixed her blue eyes on him. 'That's our business. You'll have the name when you get the photographs and we get the cash.'

When they were alone, Valeria put her head on one side and looked at Walt.

'There's something odd about him,' she mused. 'Are you sure he's *kosher*?'

Walt laughed. 'I'll make a good Jewish girl out of you yet.' He ruffled her hair. 'I reckon half the people in this bar are not what they profess to be, and that includes us. But you still want to go through with it?'

Valeria nodded. 'Let's do it two days later than planned. If it's a trap, then we will not fall into it.'

'We will tell our republican contact that we've put the operation back by two days,' Walt said, putting the documents in his jacket pocket. 'That will help him anyway, give him more time to get the transport ready, and the petrol. He knows people that can help us cross into the opposition's area. And, more importantly, to get us back.'

*

On the morning of the operation, Valeria put on a black dress beneath her coat and Walt a dark suit, suitable for their cover story. They were now siblings returning home for the burial of their sister, killed by a Russian shell.

Halfway to Villa del Prado they left their contact's van and Valeria took the wheel of a small black car. Each time they passed a group of nationalist soldiers, or they were stopped at a roadblock, Valeria smiled coquettishly at the guards, repeated their story, and they somehow got through.

After just over an hour, they reached the airfield and drove around the perimeter fence, looking for somewhere to park. Eventually, they came across a wooded area and Valeria dived into the trees to change.

She came back in a dark boiler suit and sank onto the grass.

'Jesus, Walt. Next time, can we photograph a wedding?'

He grinned at her. 'And you'd like that so much?'

After taking a couple of gulps of red wine and eating some hard bread and cheese, they agreed on a plan.

'About fifty metres from here, on the other side of the chain-link fence, there is a wooden hut,' Walt explained, getting out his pad. 'If we work right behind it, we will have cover while we cut an opening in the fence.' He drew a small diagram and showed it to Valeria. 'The hut appears to be unoccupied, and if we are lucky, no one will be there during the night. We'll go around midnight, then, when dawn breaks, we will get our shots as quickly as we can and return to the car. I will stand by the hut and swing the camera in an arc to cover as many aircraft as possible, while you, Valeria, creep amongst the aircraft to obtain the close-ups you need.' His glance lowered to her stomach.

'Perhaps this time I should go out in the open and you stay here,' he murmured. 'It is safer.'

'No, Walt, this is what we agreed.'

'You're sure?'

Valeria nodded, pushing down the feeling of dread that had been with her all day. 'But I admit I will be happy when it is over.'

Walt squeezed her hand. 'You are a consummate professional, but remember, we'll meet back at the hut afterwards, fifteen minutes at the most, Valeria. I know the risks you take, but on this occasion be satisfied with a small number of shots. Promise me?'

'I promise,' Valeria agreed.

During the night everything went according to plan. They cut the gap in the fence, keeping a constant watch for sentries, and were now waiting for dawn.

Both slept intermittently, until dawn came up. With their equipment packed, they set off, easing themselves through the wire. Slipping along the fence line, they reached the end of the hut. They were now exposed and in the open, the real danger in front of them. They crouched down, waiting for a challenge, but none came.

'OK, here I go.' Valeria pointed to a large bomber. She darted towards it and concealed herself beneath the wing.

While Walt started taking pictures of the overall airfield, trying to get as many aircraft in each photo frame, Valeria took off the lens cap of her Leica.

First, she took a photograph of a Heinkel 111, then its engines, cockpit and nose, lastly, the machine guns. Crouching down, she ran towards the Dornier 17 and repeated the procedure. The small fighter plane, a Messerschmitt 109, stood some distance away. For a split second she hesitated. If she left now, they would certainly get away with it. But it was a beautiful shot. She sprinted towards the plane.

She was about to leave when she noticed the cockpit canopy

had been left open. A picture of a cockpit interior would certainly be a scoop. With shaking hands she loaded a new film. She could do it if she was quick. Before she could change her mind, she hauled herself onto the wing and scrambled along the slippery surface to the cockpit. Glancing at her watch she could see her fifteen minutes was up, but she was now committed. Breathing deeply to calm herself, she steadied herself with her left hand, thrust her right hand and camera into the cockpit and pressed the shutter release button. She had done it. All she needed now was to make her escape.

She was turning around when her feet slid from beneath her and she slipped off the wing, crashing on her side to the ground, her ankle bent beneath her. Momentarily stunned, she waited for the inevitable.

'*Wer ist da?* Who is there?' It was a German voice. 'Make yourself known.'

Valeria knew she had one chance to get out of there. She picked herself up, grabbed her equipment and made a run for it, zigzagging all the way back to Walt.

Walt was shouting now, careless of his own safety. 'You can make it, girl, you are nearly there.'

Valeria was running, though the pain in her ankle was excruciating. Cracks of rifle fire rang out.

'Quick, Valeria.' Walt's arms were outstretched, there was only a short way to go.

The gunfire had intensified, shattering the windows of the building, splitting its wooden cladding. Suddenly she saw Walt staggering towards her, clutching his stomach, his eyes filled with surprise.

'Sorry,' he gasped, collapsing to the ground. 'I'm afraid you're on your own, love.' His voice was fading. 'Take my camera and the pistol. Remember, just point the gun and pull the trigger. You have to pull the trigger, Val.' His eyes emptied.

Valeria picked up the pistol, numb with shock. She would grieve later, there was no time to lose.

At the clump of German boots she cocked the pistol and waited. The German soldier was only metres away. He froze when he saw the gun.

Valeria's hand was shaking and as their eyes met she hesitated, believing she couldn't do it, but then she thought of Walt.

She pulled the trigger twice and the soldier fell backwards, hitting the floor with a thud. Gathering up the cameras and pistol, she stuffed them into her rucksack and ran. Diving through the fence she looked for the car. As she limped across the grass she prayed it would still be there.

Valeria would never forget hurtling towards Madrid, car tyres screeching, conscious a German unit could be only a short distance behind. Each time she glanced in the mirror her heart turned over, but she had to get the photographs out, she had to do it for Walt and for Spain. When she reached the crossing point where she had met her republican contacts with Walt the day before, they were waiting for her. She switched off the ignition, threw over the keys and climbed into the back of the van, collapsing in pain.

Valeria woke up in her tiny flat ten hours later. As her mind cleared, she turned her cheek to the pillow and wept. Her best friend was dead, and she was responsible. He had said fifteen minutes but she had wanted that extra shot.

She dragged herself to the sink and doused herself with water. In the mirror her blotched face stared back at her. Somehow it was different. This was the face of a woman who had just killed a man.

Taking her camera bag and Walt's Contax, she unlocked the door to their office and climbed the narrow stairs. Walt's desk was just as he had left it, but he would never return. She could hear his voice making fun of her, his infectious laughter. She took a gulp of brandy straight from the bottle and went into the darkroom. Removing the rolls of film from her camera bag, she remembered the last time she had been there with Walt. But there was no time to cry. Walt would want her to finish the job. She developed Walt's films first. The results were excellent and as she scanned one photograph then the next, she had goosebumps on her arms. It was as though she was looking through his eyes at the exact moment he had pressed the camera button.

'Thank you, Walt,' she whispered. 'I'll make sure these photographs make a difference.' Then it was the turn of her films. Considering the urgency, the results were first-rate. She was about to extract the last unfinished film from her Leica, when she put the camera aside. She should never have taken the pictures of the cockpit interior, they had got Walt killed.

She put a set of photographs in two envelopes. One for her republican contact, and the other for the Englishman. Now, she had to make arrangements to deliver them.

The following evening, she dropped the first envelope into a secure dead letter box and continued to *La Venencia*, where she would meet Jeremy Page. She arrived at 7 p.m. and chose a corner away from the bar. Placing an ABC newspaper on the table with the photographs concealed inside, she scanned the room, but the journalist wasn't there. When, ten minutes later, he had still not arrived, she glanced at her watch, and was about to put the incriminating photographs back in her bag, when he sauntered into the room.

'If you have finished with the paper, could I have it, señorita?'

She drained her brandy in a gulp and pushed the newspaper towards him. 'You are right, I no longer need it. Consider it yours, señor.'

He handed her a small envelope and leant down as if adjusting his shoe lace.

'Villa del Prado,' she whispered.

'Thank you and goodnight.' He straightened and walked away as if they hadn't met at all.

Valeria left the bar and went straight to her flat. Leaning back against the door she opened the envelope. Inside there were several hundred American dollar bills together with a note; it was short and direct.

I'm sorry to hear about your colleague, but be assured your work will help Spain and be of great importance to Britain and other countries elsewhere.

She wouldn't keep the money, of course; it would go into a fund for the republic, a cause that had meant so much to her dear friend.

Chapter Forty-nine

February 1938

Leonardo was in the cavalry regiment under the command of General Monasterio, and they were on their way to Alfambra, as part of the battle to reoccupy Teruel. The town in the Aragon region of eastern Spain was a nerve centre for communications, its roads and railways reaching several important cities. It was also a link to the mines.

The cavalry was not, as some believed, a relic from a past era, unable to compete with a modern mechanised infantry. In the mountainous regions of Spain, it was still a vital part of the manoeuvres. It increased mobility as horses could go where tanks could not. But there was also the psychological advantage, charging horses encroaching into occupied territory put the fear of God into the enemy's hearts.

As Leonardo's division rode through the bleak landscape, traces of the war were everywhere. They passed burnt-out armoured cars, dead mules, frozen body parts emerging through the snow. Troops, their backs hunched against the wind, trudged towards their destinations, prisoners shuffled along in the freezing cold.

Saturno was better equipped than most. Leonardo made

sure that he had thick saddle blankets to warm his back, and sheepskin-lined boots to protect his legs. At night he was the warmest horse in the lines.

On 5 February, the instructions came through that the attack would be launched with a massive cavalry charge. Leonardo knew that the day would bring death and misery, whichever side you were on. As he waited for the command, the horses either side of him fidgeting and snorting nervously, he glanced down the line. How many of the magnificent creatures would return, he wondered, how many of them would be killed or maimed?

The signal came and with his heart pounding in his chest, he patted Saturno's neck and gave him the lightest nudge with his leg. The horse sprang forward, and they were thundering across the flat plain.

It was a formidable spectacle, the horses spread out in a line, bearing down on the enemy. As they approached the opposing forces, Leonardo raised his sword, one of several hundred cavalry against the men on the ground. While the din of gunshot and the screams of men and horses continued, the stench of gunpowder and blood increased. Quickly the enemy were surrounded. Many were trampled underfoot as they fled in disarray.

Scavenging birds had begun to circle overhead when the cavalry division made their weary departure from the battlefield. Leonardo surveyed the carnage and was filled with despair. It had been a travesty. Republican defence was weak, with a new regiment that had never seen combat before. These were young men with little training and poor munitions; they were his countrymen. As Saturno picked his way through the detritus of dead and dying men, Leonardo was ashamed. Where were his ideals of long ago? His sword, now back in its scabbard, was chipped and coloured red. He shuddered, thinking of the men who had stained the cutting edge with their blood.

His thoughts turned to Padre Alvaro. He would never have condoned this slaughter. And how could he explain it to Valeria? She was a republican working in Madrid, a city that had been besieged by nationalist forces for the last sixteen months.

In the camp, Leonardo dismounted and checked Saturno for wounds. Miraculously, under the dried lather and dust, apart from superficial scrapes the horse was unharmed. Whilst others had stumbled and fallen, Saturno had carried his master to the end. When his groom approached, flinging a sweat rug over the horse's back, they went together to the picquet post.

'His feed is ready, Alférez de Santos, but I shall lead him round first.'

'Thank you, Ramon.' Leonardo gave him an exhausted smile.

Ramon took the reins from Leonardo. 'You did well, you have brought him back unscathed.'

While Leonardo went to wash and change, Ramon led Saturno down a leafy track, all the while running his hands over the horse's shoulder, talking softly to him, encouraging him.

'*Eres un caballo milagroso*,' he whispered. 'A miracle horse indeed.'

Later, as he brushed the dried sweat from Saturno's coat, he reflected on the path that had led him to the second lieutenant. Imprisoned and awaiting execution when the nationalists took Seville, his salvation actually came from the rebels he despised.

'You will join the nationalist army or face the firing squad,' he was told. 'The choice is yours.'

Assigned to the cavalry division, he quickly found he had a way with horses. They seemed to respond to his quiet manner and gentle touch. Scorned by his fellow soldiers, he had kept to himself, his world revolving around the animals in his care. They had been given no choice, so it was his duty to protect them.

His world had changed again when Alférez de Santos arrived.

He would never forget the moment Leonardo had found him in the lines.

'Are you the man they call Ramon?' the young officer had asked.

Ramon had looked up from the horse's leg, where he was treating a wound, believing another insult was coming his way.

'*Si, señor.*'

'I've bribed the senior officer considerably to have you as my groom – they say you're the best. If you can keep my horse safe, you will have my undying support.'

Leonardo had kept his word and a bond had quickly formed between them. Now Ramon would gladly die for Alférez de Santos, and he did everything in his power to make sure the horse survived.

Chapter Fifty

Though brandy had dulled his senses, images of the wounded soldiers and horses consumed Leonardo. It was nearing midnight when he put on his greatcoat, unfastened the tent flap and went outside. Making his way across the frozen ground to the picquet post, he found his beloved Saturno.

'Please forgive me,' he whispered, feeding Saturno a bucket of stolen oats. 'How could you possibly understand?'

When the horse had gently taken his food, he turned his head to look at Leonardo.

'While I am of sound body and mind, I will never let you down,' Leonardo promised.

Much later he returned to the tent and by the light of the small oil lamp he pulled Valeria's letter from the pocket of his coat and read it again.

There is so much I want to say, so many thoughts I need to share, but for now they will have to stay in my mind.

What was she trying to tell him, he conjectured, sinking into the narrow camp bed. God knows when he would see her again, but he prayed it would be soon.

*

In the morning, the cavalry was in action again, riding on ahead of the nationalist squadrons, causing the republican forces to retreat. The insurgents were now in control of the mountains that rose to the west of the valley and had reoccupied several villages below.

So the slaughter went on, the cavalry occupying village after village until the infantry arrived.

On 23 March, Leonardo was among several cavalry squadrons instructed to cross the Ebro river and block the road from Zaragoza, to prevent the republicans getting through. While some divisions rode ahead of the marching columns, others were sent to seize the small town of Pina. It was here that Leonardo's luck ran out.

It was a fine spring morning, and as the five young cavalry officers who had recently trained and fought together entered the town via the *Avenida Zaragoza*, they believed nothing could go wrong. The streets were empty, the houses shuttered and closed. They had reached the deserted *Plaza de Espana*, when Leonardo drew Saturno to a halt. Not a sound broke the silence, not a bird.

'It's too quiet,' Leonardo murmured to his friend, who was riding a skittish bay gelding beside him.

'My horse seems to agree with you,' Jorge observed.

Leonardo scanned the whitewashed houses, the closed shops. A tall bell tower dominated the square. He glanced upwards; it appeared to be empty, but it would be the perfect place for a sniper to take aim.

'I have a bad feeling about this,' he reiterated, his instinct telling him something was wrong.

The officer to his left, Capitán Gurtabay, chuckled. 'You are too cautious, Santos.'

Those were the last words he spoke. A bullet caught him

in the chest, killing him instantly. The next bullet just missed Leonardo. Seconds later he felt pressure in his shoulder then a strange feeling of lightness in his head. He put his hand to his jacket and it was sticky with blood. Flight was his only option, if he wanted to survive.

'Let's get the hell out of here,' he whispered, leaning forward over Saturno's neck.

It was as if the horse had wings. As the pain increased Leonardo was entirely reliant on Saturno. The horse galloped back to the bridge, then down the same road they had come.

Jorge galloped beside him. 'Come on, Santos, you can do it. Hang on.'

With every vestige of remaining strength Leonardo centred his body over the saddle. If he fell, it would be over. Whatever happened, he had to stay on. When finally they met up with the infantry, Leonardo slipped to the ground.

When Leonardo opened his eyes, Jorge de la Cueva was standing at the end of his hospital bed.

'Where's Saturno?' were the first words he said.

Jorge looked down on his friend and grinned. 'I get you to the field hospital, rescue you from an almost-certain death, and your first words are not "Thank you, Jorge", but "Where is my bloody horse?"' He stopped for a moment, seeing Leonardo's distress. 'It's all right, my friend. I found your beloved Saturno in the regimental stables, but he is now living in the lap of luxury with my cousin, the Conde de la Cueva, only fifteen kilometres from here. When it was suggested the horse be passed to another officer, I protested mightily, saying the animal was a brute with anyone else on board.'

'What can I do to repay you?' Leonardo asked, with a weak smile.

Jorge put his hand on his heart. 'An introduction to that beautiful sister of yours will suffice.'

Leonardo laughed and then winced as pain tore through his shoulder.

'In all seriousness,' Jorge said, 'you are lucky to be alive.'

Carlos visited him later that week.

'I have heard glowing reports about your progress, and indeed your capabilities on the battlefield. You are a fine soldier, my son.'

Leonardo looked up at his adoptive father, his eyes filled with misery. 'Please may I go home with Saturno, Father?' was all that he said.

Carlos walked to the window and stared outside. In the courtyard lines of the dead were waiting for burial, poor, broken young men. Leonardo could have been one of them. Carlos winced, unable to contemplate the possibility and turned back to Leonardo. He had covered himself in glory on the battlefield, he had been brave beyond the limits of ordinary men, and yet he was fighting for a cause Carlos knew he didn't believe in. He would use whatever influence he had to try to get him discharged. But he knew it would be a fruitless exercise. Provisional officers like Leonardo were few and far between, the army would be foolish to let him go.

He rested his hand on Leonardo's head, his voice gruff. 'I will see what I can do,' he said.

He was nearly at the door when Leonardo called after him.

'And Valeria, do you know where she is?'

'Unhappily, the foolish girl is still in Madrid. I just wish she would give up whatever she is doing and return to Seville.'

When Carlos had gone Leonardo stared at the ceiling, grimacing in pain. 'Please let me see her,' he whispered. 'I have to see Valeria.'

Chapter Fifty-one

6 August 1938, Seville

The early morning sun was slanting through the muslin curtains onto the pretty painted cot when Isabel put her head round the door.

'May I come in, *querida*?'

Valeria smiled at her mother. 'And if I said no?'

'Then I would disobey. I can't bear to be away from Rafaela for a moment. I could swear she recognises me, Valeria.'

'She's only just three months old, Mama.'

Isabel's face fell, and Valeria laughed.

'Of course she does. In fact, you spend so much time looking at her, you will be the first person she remembers.'

Isabel gave her warm, tinkling laugh. She kissed Valeria and advanced to the cot.

'She changes every day, she is so beautiful, her features straight, and look at her dark hair. She is a true Spaniard, Valeria.'

'Except that Walter was English, Mama.'

Isabel frowned. 'I'm sorry, that was tactless. It must be terribly hard for you.'

Valeria bit her lip. She missed Walt so much that it made the lie easy. 'It has been very difficult,' she admitted. 'He was a good man, Mama, you would have loved him.'

Isabel picked up the now gurgling baby and passed her to Valeria.

'Don't you think it's time we told Papa about her? He will fall in love with her as you have!'

Isabel kissed her daughter's forehead. 'I believe it is wiser to wait until he is here in Seville, Valeria. Questions will be asked in his regiment. These days you can never be too careful; walls have ears. He is coming home soon, let him find out then.'

When Isabel had gone, Valeria nursed her baby, kissing the chubby hands, the dark fluff of hair, running her fingers down the tiny nose. What a falsehood it had been, but she couldn't tell anyone, not yet.

Por supuesto, Bañu had guessed.

'All very convenient,' she had commented only the week before.

'What do you mean, Bañu?'

'I find it strange that this infant bears a striking resemblance to—'

'Bañu,' Valeria cut her off. 'The child is so young, it's impossible to tell anything at this stage.'

'I have seen a lot in my life, Valeria.'

Tears had sprung to Valeria's eyes and the old woman had sat down on the bed beside her, putting her wrinkled hand over Valeria's.

'*Disculpe*. You're right, of course, Bañu.'

'What do you intend to do?'

'When this war is over, we will go away, somewhere far from here where no one will judge us. America, perhaps, England, who knows.'

Bañu's face had dropped and Valeria had hugged her.

'You will come with us, I couldn't live without you, Bañu.'

'Well, I suppose I should be pleased about that.' Bañu had given her a look and had left, quietly closing the door.

As Valeria lay with the child in her arms, she thought about Walt. How she missed his laughter, his quirky face, his optimism. If there was a problem, Walt would find a way out of it. 'Forgive me, Walt,' she whispered, her tears falling onto Rafaela's head.

Valeria was in the kitchen when the postman arrived with a letter forwarded from her office in Madrid. There was something amateurish about the typing that made her heart beat faster. She retreated to the internal courtyard and ripped open the envelope.

My dearest Valeria,
For obvious reasons, I feel it is better to send this anonymously. First, may I reassure you that I am well, but after a confrontation with a sniper some months ago, I will finally return to the barracks in Seville. I have been given a few days' leave and if there is the smallest chance of seeing you, then the mishap will have been worthwhile. I miss you and I think of you every minute. Each nationalist bomb that falls on Madrid, every attack on the capital, fills me with horror and shame.

Querididísima *Valeria, I long to run away from all of this. When the war is over, I beg you, come with me. Let us spend the rest of our lives in a country where there is no enmity between brothers, no hatred.*

I often think of the death scene from Romeo and Juliet, *Padre Alvaro reading to us in the shade of the tulip tree. Your face as you turned to me. Star-crossed lovers, you whispered. But this is true no longer, we have a chance to be free.*

I will always love you,
Leonardo

PS The one thing that has kept me going through these dark days is the thought of returning to the hacienda with you. If this is at all possible, meet me outside the church in Calle Dos de Mayo on 12 August at 10 a.m.

I will use any influence I have to beg, borrow or steal a car and some petrol.

Valeria was concealed behind the screen of blue Turkish pots when her mother found her. She stuffed the letter in the pocket of her dress.

'There you are, Valeria. I have wonderful news, I have heard from Leonardo and he is returning to Seville in a few days' time.' Isabel's words came out in a rush and her face was flushed.

'There is something else, *querida*. I kept it to myself because of the baby, but he was wounded in March – only a small wound, and I thank the Lord, he is now fully recovered.'

Valeria kept her face composed as she hugged her mother. 'You should have told me about his injury, Mama, but you are right, we can thank God that he is well, and we shall see him very soon.'

Valeria found her Bañu in the kitchen ironing the pillowcases with her new electric iron.

'What is it?' the old woman asked, propping the iron on the edge of the board. 'Your face tells me you want something.'

'I am going to meet Leonardo at the hacienda. I can finally tell him about our child.' Valeria threw her arms around her and hugged her.

'Careful,' Bañu scolded her, pulling out the plug. 'You'll get your fingers burnt, and it won't be with the iron.'

'But don't you see, when the war is over, we can spend the rest of our lives together with Rafaela.' Her eyes were shining as she looked at the old woman.

'And who do you expect to cover for you when you go to the hacienda? Who is going to tell more lies?'

'Please, Bañu, please will you help us?'

The old woman put her hands on her hips. 'You always were trouble; I said to your mother the moment you were born that you'd be trouble.'

'Please, Bañu.'

'Agh!' Bañu raised her hands and flapped them at Valeria. 'Get away with you.'

Bañu crossed her arms across her bony chest. 'You will tell your mother you have to deal with some of Walt's papers in Madrid, but you will be back the next day. I can't cover for you beyond that.'

Valeria kissed her. 'Thank you, Bañu.'

Chapter Fifty-two

9 August 1938

Constanza was whimpering in the corner of the packed cell.

'Shut up, *puta*.' A woman took off her shoe and threw it, hitting Constanza in the head, but she couldn't stop. The pain was incessant. For three days she had been used by the nationalist soldiers, passed around like a package. And when she thought it was over, they had started again. She was too tired to rebuke the woman, too terrified to sleep. It was only the pain.

She had arrived in Corbera two weeks before, as part of the republican advancement. As a soldier in V Corps, she had been tasked to cross the River Ebro in order to take the town. When the nationalists had resisted the assault, V Corps came under attack. After days of relentless shelling and German bombing, with little food or water, they had finally been captured in the remains of the school. Emerging from the dust and debris, their arms up in surrender, they had been marched through the streets, then pushed against the church wall. One by one she had watched her comrades shot, she had seen the blood blossoming on their shirts, the life go from their eyes, and then it was her turn.

'We have a woman,' a nationalist soldier had caught her by

the hair and pulled her head backwards. 'Very soon, pretty scum, you will wish you were dead.'

He was right, the soldier. She wished beyond anything that she had been shot with her comrades, that God had put an end to her misery, but God was making her pay for defiling his work, burning his churches, so she couldn't look to him now.

She rocked back and forth on the foul-smelling straw.

'God forgive me,' she whispered. 'Please forgive me, for I have sinned.'

Suddenly she was back in her childhood, chastised by the priest for stealing pesetas from the offertory collection. How humiliated she had felt, how wicked she believed herself to be. Now she was truly paying for her sins. All the people she had killed, all the damage she had done. She deserved her end.

When a guard unlocked the door, and dragged her from the room, she caught hold of his sleeve.

'Please no torture,' she whispered. 'I can't take any more.'

But for Constanza this was not to be the end. For two hours the nationalist captain shone a light in her eyes.

'If you give us something useful, we will shoot you now and that will be an end to it. If you do not, it will be an unimaginable death.'

Another man came into the room, she was aware of him watching her. He was tall, slim, with long polished boots, a cold, detached face.

'Tell us something, Constanza.' It was the new man with a voice like silk. He was calling her by her name.

'Please, I don't know anything.'

'But I think you do, Constanza. My name is Colonel de Rosa, and if you give us information, you will be treated well.'

Constanza shook her head, tears slipping down her cheeks. She had nothing to tell them, she knew nothing. And then it came to her. Val Saint the photographer, the darling of the republicans, was Valeria Palamera de Santos. She was an enemy to the nationalists, she exposed their brutality, she exposed their bloody war. If she revealed her identity, told them where to find her, she would be spared. But she was also on her side.

She ran her tongue over her cracked lips, she couldn't do it, wouldn't do it.

The captain produced a poker from the corner of the room. 'This is what we do to whores like you.'

Constanza lifted her head and with dull eyes gazed at the poker.

'Please,' she whispered. 'Not that.'

'Give us something and you will be spared the ordeal,' the colonel said.

Constanza stared at his boots, her mind racing. If she told them to go to the hacienda in Cazalla de la Sierra, their search would be fruitless. Valeria worked in Madrid, she never went home. She would be out of their reach.

'I know something,' she said.

Teniente Coronel de Rosa was part of the elite unit known as the Spanish Foreign Legion. He had trained in Morocco and lived by their battle cry, *Viva la Muerte*, Long Live Death. In the Legion, where brutality and success went hand in hand, his blood-thirsty appetites were indulged.

Endowed with a strong sense of self, he believed that his swift rise through the ranks was due, not to the high mortality rate, but to his own exceptional ability. This confidence was coupled with an enjoyment of power, particularly when it came to the decisions of life over death. In his case it was usually the latter.

On this particular day, he was in an especially good mood. Like the great man Hitler himself, Colonel de Rosa believed in omens – it was well known that after a performance of Wagner's *Siegfried*, a sign had led Hitler to provide twenty Junkers bombers when Franco had only requested ten. This morning, a white feather – a message from the angels – had fallen at de Rosa's feet. Shortly afterwards, the girl had given him information that would help him get his revenge.

He thought back to his humiliation of fifteen years before. As the young steward on an estate near Cazalla de la Sierra, he worked with the theory that physical punishment was the only way to keep the peasants in line. His views, however, were contrary to those of his employer. He would never forget Don Carlos's cutting words: 'I will not have my workers treated with cruelty and blatant disregard for their welfare. You will leave now.'

'You would sack me?' he had stuttered. 'Put me below the worthless peasants?'

'The fact that you call them worthless is exactly why your employment is terminated. These men have toiled night and day on wages I would never have countenanced, and it has all been done in my name. You have also stolen from me. You think I am unaware of the money that has lined your pockets. I am not a fool, so do not treat me as such. You will leave the estate, and if you ever show your face in these parts again, I will be forced to expose you as a liar and a thief.'

De Rosa grimaced; the words stung him even now. But old scores would be settled, fate had played into his hand.

He strode back to the interrogation room with new purpose. The whore Val Saint would get what she deserved and Constanza would be saved.

The girl was slumped over the table when he closed the door. 'Please, I've told you what I know,' she whispered, her head in her hands.

He fiddled with his moustache, a habit he had when he was thinking.

'What would you say if you were told you would not die

today?' He turned the wooden chair so Constanza was facing him.

Constanza lifted her head. 'I would say it was another of your games.'

The colonel winced. He enjoyed toying with his victims, but the girl would not respond.

'I have decided to spare you.'

Constanza said nothing.

'Surely there is something you would do for me?' he questioned her, eyeing the tear in her dress. Though she had been passed around the regiment, she still had a fierce beauty, a raw sensual quality that would satisfy his appetite. And there was no doubt of her bravery, a quality he admired. With a few good meals inside her she would be a credit to her sex. He would, of course, have her checked out for any nasty disease.

'I am offering you a lifeline.'

Constanza raised her head. 'What are you saying?'

'I am tired of using the prostitutes here. You will be my mistress,' he declared.

It had come to this, Constanza thought, scratching a scab on her arm. She would be mistress of the murdering nationalist filth. The idea was abhorrent, but the only other option was death. As life became a possibility, she realised she didn't want to die. She would accept his offer, take his protection and for the first time in weeks she would be clean. The lice that crawled over her body night and day would be gone. She looked up at the colonel. Yes, she would become his mistress, but one day she would kill him.

Two days after Constanza's interrogation, Colonel de Rosa called for his most reliable officer. When the captain entered the room, he raised his arm in salute.

'You wanted me, colonel?'

'There is a matter that needs careful handling and you are the man I trust to carry it through, Capitán Reyes.'

The captain drew back his shoulders. 'That is an honour indeed.'

'You have heard of *our* Acting Colonel Palamera de Santos.'

'Of course, he is well respected and well liked.'

'But you may not be aware that his daughter Val Saint is the whore photographer, much loved by the republicans. I want her dead, but you must make it look like a *republican error*; let them be blamed. Her father must never find out the truth.'

The captain ran his hand over his trimmed beard. 'So if I have this right, you are asking me to kill the republican daughter of a famous nationalist soldier, but I have to make it look as if she was killed by her own side?'

'That is correct.'

'You are sure about this, colonel? If this act against his daughter becomes known, the consequences could be dire for us.'

'But it will not become known, will it, Reyes?'

The captain looked uncomfortable. 'Do you have any idea where we can find her, Colonel de Rosa?'

'I have learnt from Intelligence, that her colleague, Walter Mayhew, was killed at Villa del Prado airfield, whilst photographing our German aircraft, but the girl remains at large. Her offices in Madrid are at present closed, so she may have returned to their house in the country. I suggest you try the family hacienda at Cazalla de la Sierra. But any mistakes and you alone will be held responsible.'

'I understand, colonel.'

'I am sure that you do.'

Chapter Fifty-Three

12 August 1938

On the morning of Valeria's reunion with Leonardo, she fed Rafaela at one and again at five, but instead of going back to sleep, she returned to bed with her daughter in her arms.

'You are going to have the best of everything,' she whispered. 'You will have the most devoted Mama and Papa, you will have all the love in the world.' As she looked down into the tiny face she was filled with joy. This is what it meant to love your child, she realised. It was an intensity of feeling that meant she would protect Rafaela to her last breath. 'You will have a good life, the best.' She kissed her soft forehead, stroked the downy hair. 'And I will be with you, always and forever, my beautiful little girl.'

When Rafaela was back in her cot, Valeria made up ten bottles of milk, and went to find Bañu.

'There is enough formula in the refrigerator until I get back,' she said, 'but I have another request.'

'And what is it this time?'

'Oh Bañu, always grumpy, always scolding me, but you love me, don't you?' She skipped away from her. 'There is something you need to be aware of, and it is in my room. Could you come upstairs?'

Bañu followed her up the winding stairs and along the corridor to her bedroom at the end. The terrace doors were open, the muslin curtains fluttering in the breeze. Valeria went to the armoire and rummaged inside. Seconds later she pulled out a large wooden box.

'If anything should happen to me, please will you give this to Leonardo.'

'Do not talk like that, Valeria, you have to keep safe, you are a mother now,' Bañu protested, slumping onto the bed.

'I intend to, but we both know we need to think of these things.'

Valeria sat down beside Bañu and put her arm around her shoulders. 'Nothing is going to happen, but just in case.' She tapped the lid. 'I will show you the contents when I get back, my photographs will assuredly make you weep, but I am proud of them, Bañu.'

'You have a lot to be proud of,' Bañu protested, her mouth quivering.

'In time, the suffering may be forgotten, life will go on. But these photographs tell the truth.'

'You say all this as if you shall not be here. I am an old woman, Valeria, you will outlive me by years.'

Valeria returned the box to the cupboard and placed the key in the drawer of the desk with the eagle mounts, then she put on her white muslin dress. 'Do I look presentable?' she asked, spinning in front of Bañu.

'If you are asking me, do you look as if you have just had a baby, then the answer is no,' Bañu grumbled.

Valeria ran her hand over her stomach. 'I am going to tell him, Bañu, but I want to do it in person and my way.' She looked down at Rafaela one last time. 'Look after my perfect baby?' she murmured.

'You know I will,' Bañu replied.

*

When Valeria entered her mother's room she was sleeping, the first rays of sunshine slanting across her bed. She was still a beautiful woman, she reflected, studying her flawless skin, the auburn curls that tumbled across the pillow. She was also gentle and wise. For a moment her eyes filled with tears.

'I love you, Mama,' she whispered.

Isabel opened her eyes. 'Do you think you should be travelling to Madrid? It could be dangerous, *pequeña*.'

Valeria kissed her forehead. 'My papers are in order and I've done the journey a thousand times. Don't worry, I'll be fine.'

Isabel shook her head. 'Remember, you have Rafaela to think about now, Valeria.'

Valeria smiled. 'That is just what Bañu said. I will see you the day after tomorrow, Mama.'

Chapter Fifty-four

Valeria turned into *Calle Dos de Mayo* and hurried towards the church, checking her watch. It was still well before ten. From her work as a photographer she was used to keeping in the shadows, avoiding watchful eyes. She slipped into the church porch, lifted the muslin veil from her hat and shook out her hair. When she saw the small car approaching with Leonardo at the wheel, her heart turned over.

'I thought my letter wouldn't reach you, that you wouldn't come,' Leonardo uttered, as she climbed in, putting her camera and small suitcase in the back.

'Well, you can see that I'm here.' She smiled and kissed him on the lips. 'You must know that I would travel the world to find you.'

'I had hoped, but—' Leonardo hesitated.

'But what, you foolish man? Nothing would keep me away from you.'

'There is the small matter of the war,' he murmured with a smile.

'For once the gods were on our side, Leonardo. I was at home when your letter was forwarded from Madrid.'

As they passed the bullfighting stadium in *Plaza de Toros*, Valeria drew in her breath. 'Do you remember…?'

Leonardo broke in. 'Of course I do, every word. Your father suggested I should become a *rejoneador*.'

'And you said,' Valeria laughed, '"How could I put my horse in peril, just to slay the poor bull with a blade?" And you never did. But now you are in the cavalry and you and Saturno are both at risk.' The light had left her voice and her expression had changed.

She gazed back at the huge baroque bullring, remembering the time they had been there with her parents for the biggest festival of the year. It was meant to be a treat, but it had been torment for the ten-year-old boy. She recalled the roar of the crowds reverberating around the packed stadium as the matador had plunged the final *espada* into the base of the bull's neck. Seeing the anguish on Leonardo's stricken face, she had taken his hand and they had crept from their seats. She had never enjoyed it again.

They were silent as they drove out through the city. They had been through so much since the last time they had met.

'I've thought about you constantly,' Valeria murmured at last.

'It was remembering your beautiful face that kept me sane,' Leonardo admitted.

They had passed the village of Parapanda and were nearing Antequera, when she put her hand on his sleeve.

'There is something I need to tell you, *mi vida*… It's Luna, I'm afraid.'

Leonardo pulled the car into the side, 'I had a feeling I would never see her again,' he whispered.

'It was so peaceful, she died in my arms.' As Valeria described holding Luna for the last time, she remembered the wisdom and tenderness in her clouded eyes.

'It was a good death, Leonardo. She was asking me to let her go.'

'I should have been with her.' Leonardo lowered his head

onto the steering wheel. 'She was my dog, and I didn't even do that for her.'

'You couldn't have been with her, however much you wanted to.'

Leonardo looked at her, his face creased with pain. 'Because I am fighting in a war that I despise.'

As the main roads turned to country roads, Valeria tried to distract him with anecdotes of life in Seville, avoiding the horror stories. She told him of Bañu's imaginative cooking now the staff had left, and Isabel's first attempt at ironing.

'It's strange being away from Madrid,' she confirmed. 'I really needed this break at home, but I will have to return to the office at some point, Leonardo, even if it is only to clear it out.'

As Leonardo listened to her voice, he glanced across at her. Her hair had grown again so that it hung to her shoulders, but there was a softness about her, she was rounder, every bit as beautiful but different. She seemed more vulnerable somehow. He sighed, his eyes returning to the road ahead. He certainly didn't deserve her, not now, not after everything he had done.

Leonardo stopped the car outside the hacienda gates.

'Valeria, I have to tell you—' He turned towards her, the words sticking in his throat. Valeria would be disgusted, she would hate him and walk away.

'I am not the person you once knew,' he disclosed at last.

Valeria exhaled. 'Neither am I, neither are any of us, Leonardo.'

Leonardo shook his head. 'I have killed men, Valeria, I can't keep this from you.'

She didn't respond.

'I despise myself for what I have done.' He stared at his hands, remembering the blood they had drawn, the slaughter he had been part of.

'This war makes us do things we would never believe possible,' Valeria murmured. 'We behave in a way that would be alien in a normal world. But it is not a normal world. I have so much to tell you, *cariño*. But let's go inside, I have been yearning to be at the hacienda, if only for a day.'

Leonardo helped Valeria over the wall, and they walked hand in hand up the drive. 'You are not as agile as you were,' he observed with a smile. 'I can't put my finger on it, but you look different. Perhaps a little—'

'Fatter?'

Leonardo laughed. 'Straight to the point, as always.'

'I admit I have put on weight,' she sighed.

'It suits you,' he reassured her. 'You look more womanly, no longer the skinny little girl I knew.'

'I'm older than you,' she retorted.

Leonardo laughed. 'Oh, Valeria, I've missed you so much.' He kissed her and drew her towards him. 'I would feel it in my heart if anything had happened to you. It is the one thing that kept me going. When the bombs were falling on Madrid, I believed that you would be safe in the shelters. You had to be, because I couldn't go on without you.'

The nearer they came to the hacienda the more they noticed the neglect. Last year's geraniums had shrivelled in their pots and weeds were growing in the paths.

'I will find Juan,' Leonardo suggested. 'I need to bring the car inside.' He kissed her forehead. 'I will be a few moments, *querida*.'

Valeria took a house key from her bag and opened the back door. Dust sheets covered the furniture and the shutters were barred. She threw the drawing-room windows wide.

It was true, she had needed to be here more than anything, and now Leonardo was with her.

She turned when he entered the room. There was a new

sadness in his eyes and a grim set to his jaw. He stood beside her, and as they gazed towards the distant hills, he put his arm around her shoulders.

'I don't think Juan has moved from the stables since I left. He guards our two remaining horses with his life and would shoot anyone who tried to steal them, no matter which side.'

Valeria looked up at him and smiled. 'I remember Papa being cross with him for putting you on the black stallion. You defended Juan even then; he would give his life for you, Leonardo.'

She pulled the dust sheet from the sofa and sat down, patting the cushion beside her. '*Viene, mi amado, siéntate.* There is something you should know.'

Leonardo's brow creased as he looked at her.

Valeria smiled and took his hand. 'Don't look so worried. You mention that I am rounder – it is true, but there is good reason. I have carried a child, our child, Rafaela. We have a beautiful baby girl.'

Leonardo looked at Valeria, his eyes swimming with tears. 'I have loved you my entire life and you have given me the greatest gift of all.'

Valeria retrieved a crumpled photograph from her pocket and gave it to Leonardo. Rafaela was lying in a blanket in her arms, her little face exposed.

'Mama took this on her camera. I thought you would want to see your daughter.'

Leonardo stared at the photograph, then held it to his chest, his shoulders shaking.

'You can say something,' she said at last.

Leonardo grinned. 'Men shouldn't cry, but at this moment I can be forgiven, as you have made me the happiest man in the world.'

'Don't forget I have seen you cry before,' Valeria whispered.

'On that occasion you were sad, but now your tears are for joy.' She was thinking of his first Christmas at the hacienda. He had been a small lonely boy, but she had loved him even then.

He took her hand. 'Isabel, what does she think about this? It must have come as a great shock to her.'

As they sat on the sofa, the sunlight pouring through the windows, she told him about Walt, about her career as a photographer and Walt's idea to pass the baby off as his until the war was over. She spared no details.

'When Walt was killed I continued with the plan. It made sense.'

'I can't believe that I didn't know about the baby—' His brow cleared. 'Now I understand the meaning of your letter.' He kissed Valeria. 'I admit it will be difficult pretending, but at this moment it is for the best. *Por supuesto*, when the war is over, and we have gone to America, everyone shall know that Rafaela is *our* daughter.'

'America?' Valeria raised her eyebrows. 'Were you going to consult me first?' she asked with a smile as Leonardo held her tight.

Later, as they lay in bed, the scent of jasmine drifting through the open windows, a nightingale sang in a tree nearby. It was just as Valeria remembered from her childhood, but now Leonardo was lying at her side. She touched the wound on his shoulder and laid her lips against it. Tonight there was no war, no injustice, there were only the two of them and their love for each other.

'Are you happy?' she whispered, wondering if he was asleep.

'More than I could have believed possible.' Leonardo raised himself onto his elbow and looked at her. 'I have everything, or nearly everything I need in the world right here. And soon I will meet our daughter.' Leonardo ran his hand over her stomach. 'I can't believe Rafaela started life in here.'

Valeria smiled. 'I still find it extraordinary. Such a lot changed at her birth. All I can think of is protecting our daughter. Things I could do before she was born, the danger I put myself in, it has all changed. I am no longer brave, I need to be safe for her.' She laughed, the intoxicating, joyful laugh that Leonardo loved and remembered so well from their youth.

'And all these months you said you worked in an office in Madrid, I should have known you would have been on the front line.' Leonardo lifted her chin and looked into her eyes. 'Journalists are killed every day, I just thank God I didn't know you were one of them. I beg of you now, for the sake of our child, please give this up? You have already done your bit, let someone else take the risk, Valeria.'

Valeria lay her head on his chest. 'You are right,' she murmured. 'I have got too much to lose.'

He pulled her close.

'Whatever happened to Constanza?' Valeria asked, her eyelids heavy with sleep. 'I heard there were nationalist reprisals in Cazalla de la Sierra, I hope she wasn't there.' She sighed, moving closer to Leonardo and he kissed her neck.

'I imagine Constanza will be out there somewhere, fighting in this war.'

At nine o'clock the next morning, Leonardo went to find Juan to unlock the gates. He hovered in the doorway as he left, watching Valeria dry her hair.

'I can't bear to be away from you for a moment,' he admitted.

Valeria threw a towel at him and laughed. 'Don't be ridiculous, I am not a child.'

Leonardo crossed the room and kissed her wet forehead.

Valeria was dressed and stripping the bed when she heard a sound in the hall below.

'Leonardo is that you, *querido*? You were quick.' There was no reply. She called again, but when there was still no answer, unease prickled down her spine. She tiptoed across to the window, her heart thumping in her chest. A man was standing outside the garden wall holding some horses, she counted quickly – there were four of them. For an instant the man looked up and their eyes met. Valeria gasped and stepped backwards. Something was terribly wrong. She had to warn Leonardo. She was running along the landing when she saw three men taking the stairs two at a time, pistols in their hands. She swivelled and turned the way she had come, trying to reach the back stairs.

She could hear their voices now, strident, ugly voices and they were telling her to stop. She kept on running down the passage, her breath coming in short spurts. They were gaining on her and she knew she would never make it outside. She twisted back to Agustin's nursery that looked towards the stables. If she could reach his room and lock the door, there was a chance she could get the window open and jump to the garden below. She was trembling, sweat breaking out on her forehead, her thoughts in chaos. If she went towards the stables, Leonardo and Juan would be in danger. She changed her mind again and darted across the landing towards her father's dressing room at the end of the corridor. It had a much stronger door with a good lock. If the key was in it she would be safe.

'Please God let the key be in it,' she chanted. She reached the room and slammed the door, but there was no key. She ran to the window, her fingers fumbling with the shutters. She could hear running feet along the passage outside. As the three men entered the bedroom, her leg was over the sill. She was pulling herself up when one of them grabbed her by the arm. She started to scream, but he dragged her backwards and hit her across the face.

'What do you want?' she screamed, lurching to her knees.

He pulled her to her feet and thrust her against the wall.

'Please,' she begged, seeing their ragged clothes, their unkempt hair. 'I am one of you.'

They did not reply.

As two bullets smashed into Valeria's chest, she staggered backwards, then she slipped to the floor, blood blooming on her white dress.

Leonardo was filling the car with petrol when he heard the gunshots, short, sharp cracks.

The dry metallic taste of fear was in his mouth as he started to run. 'Please,' he begged. 'Please not Valeria.'

Juan dived after him and grabbed him by the arm. 'Wait, señor, you have to take my gun.'

Leonardo tried to pull away, but Juan held fast. 'Be sensible, señor.'

Juan charged inside the stable where the gun rested against the wall and returned with some cartridges. He thrust them at Leonardo. 'Go to the house, and I will cut them off the other way,' he instructed.

While Leonardo raced to the house, Juan grabbed a piece of chain that was lying in the corner of the yard and sped towards the gates. He was in time to see four men vaulting onto waiting horses and galloping away.

'*No Pasarán*!' one of them yelled. Juan spat in the dust, recognising the republican battle cry. '*Es malo, muy malo*,' he uttered. 'Where is God on this terrible day, those men have only brought death.'

As he returned to the hacienda, he picked two spent Russian cartridges from the flowerbeds. He recognised them immediately from the stamping on them.

'Republican bastards,' he spat.

As Leonardo approached the back of the house, he could feel the blood pumping in his head, his lungs bursting.

'*Santo dios*, help me,' he cried, repeating the long-ago words he had chanted running over the hill, on the day his mother had died. 'Lord, come quickly. Dear God, let Valeria be safe.'

His body was shaking as he bolted up the back stairs. The smell of stale tobacco made his stomach turn over. He ran first to Valeria's bedroom, screaming out her name, but it was empty, then to each room in turn around the large landing. He found her lying on the floor of her father's dressing room, blood seeping through her dress. He grabbed the towel, making it into a ball and pushing it into the point between her ribs where the blood was gushing. Her eyes flickered open and she tried to focus.

'My beloved, I am here,' he said, holding her with his free arm.

'Perhaps I wanted too much,' she whispered. 'We were star-crossed lovers after all.'

'No, no, don't say that, *corazon*. We are made for each other, we belong together, always.'

'Juan,' he yelled, as the groom charged into the bedroom, gasping for breath. 'Get help now.'

'Don't leave me, Leonardo.' Valeria's eyes were glazing over.

'I will never leave you, never.' Leonardo kissed her face. 'Please stay with me,' he begged.

'Look after our little girl,' she whispered.

'Hold on, Valeria.'

Valeria's eyes were closing. They fluttered open again for a moment and then she let out a small sigh, her body relaxing.

'*Santo dios*, no,' Leonardo moaned, clinging on to her, cradling her head in his arms. 'Please no.'

They buried Valeria in the enclosed plot beyond the family chapel. As the sun shone on the gravestones, bleaching the familiar names to a sparkling white, Leonardo wept. It was not Valeria's turn, she was far too young; she was his world, his everything. He had waited most of his life for her, and now, when they had a chance of happiness, she had been taken from him.

He knelt on the ground by the newly dug grave, letting the sprigs of lavender slip from his fingers onto the shrouded body below.

'Why, Juan, why?' he cried, grabbing a handful of soil and flinging it into the gaping void. 'Is this what we have come to?'

Juan grimaced, his dark eyes filled with pain. 'I know not, señor. The war, it is ugly, friend killing friend. This time it was the republicans, the next it will be the nationalists. It makes no sense, I can only assume they were killing the daughter of a famous colonel.' He shook his head sadly, a tear slipping down his leathery cheek. 'But I admit I know nothing anymore.'

Part Seven

Chapter Fifty-five

November 2000, Andalucía

My grandfather was leaning back in his chair, his face grey with exhaustion. He was obviously still in the past.

'*Santo dios*, please not Valeria,' he whispered. He looked up suddenly, his eyes clearing, and wiped away a tear. 'Ah, Mia,' he sighed. 'So now you know it all. You are probably angry and rightly so. I have lied to you, *querida*, so many lies.'

His voice faded and as I looked at the frail man in front of me, I was only confused. How could I be angry with the man who had lost so much? I knelt on the floor beside him, the fog obscuring the landscape beyond the loggia, separating us from the world. 'Papa Leonardo, I am so sorry.'

'That was not the end, Mia, there is more to tell you, but not this evening.' He shook his head. 'I am so tired.'

I held his cold fingers, rubbed them in my own. 'We need to get you inside, please, Papa Leonardo.' I went to push his chair, but he held up his hand.

'She was beautiful and so brave. She had your spirit. You remind me so much of your grandmother.'

It was in the open now. Valeria was my flesh and blood. No

wonder I felt such a connection to her. No wonder she was inside my head.

'Does my mother know?' I said at last.

'I wanted to tell her, but it would have been unfair to Paloma. She brought her up, pretended to the world Rafaela was her daughter. She was a good woman and a truly loving mother. When it was safe to tell Rafaela, it was too late.' My grandfather's shoulders sagged. 'Sometimes you have to lie to those you wish to protect. My love for Valeria had put us outside the law and I needed to safeguard my daughter. It was the only way. Franco and his henchmen would have killed us all for less. You cannot understand what it was like back then; every day people were brutally tortured, murdered, it was a culture of hatred and blame. And that was long after the war had ended, we couldn't take the risk. Carlos never knew, only Bañu, Isabel and, of course, Ramon.'

'And Tía Gracia?'

'Never. She thinks she is family and it would be cruel to take that away from her. You have to understand, even Carlos's reputation wouldn't have saved the daughter of the famous republican photographer. There is an irony, of course, I only went back to fight for the nationalists, thinking the republicans had killed my beloved Valeria, but it was all an elaborate game. Miguel de Rosa, a nationalist, had ordered her death and had made it look like the republicans were responsible. He was a coward who wanted his revenge.'

He sighed, his head falling on his chest.

'And me, Papa Leonardo, you didn't feel you could tell me?'

'I was afraid that you would never forgive me.'

But I realised I could never be angry with my grandfather. He had been through so much, he deserved only my love.

I wheeled my grandfather to his room and went to find Lucia.

'I think the señor should go to bed,' I explained. 'He looks a little flushed.'

She gave me one of her withering looks.

'I tried to bring him inside earlier, but he wouldn't come,' I qualified, my voice trailing off.

Lucia marched in front of me and felt his forehead.

'*Santo Dios*, Mia, he has a fever. Fetch me the electric fan, and a bowl of tepid water.'

She always made me feel as if everything was my fault and, in this instance, it may have been. While I ground up his pills, Lucia bathed his chest and neck in the cool water to bring down his temperature, then she sent me away. I was only allowed back when my grandfather was wearing clean pyjamas and had been hoisted into bed.

'We should have come in earlier,' I murmured, automatically brushing his forehead with my fingers. 'Now both of us are in trouble.'

'Good.' He gave a weak grin. 'I have to have some independence, Mia.'

I was about to leave when he opened his bedside drawer and drew out a tiny crumpled photograph.

'We will go through the envelope later,' he uttered, his voice fading as he placed the tiny image in my hand. 'Your grandmother with Rafaela, don't lose it,' he said with a sigh.

As I looked at the faded black-and-white photograph, a lump formed in my throat. Valeria was smiling into the camera, her arms wrapped around her beautiful baby girl, my mother. There was such love in her eyes, such joy. It must have been taken shortly before she died.

'The photograph is a priceless treasure, Papa Leonardo, I promise I will look after it.'

That night as I lay in bed, water dripped from the eaves onto the ground below. I had once written an editorial on the healing sound of rain, but tonight the pattering on the roof tiles couldn't relax me. My mind was in turmoil. So much tragedy had happened to my family, so much pain, and there was yet more of the story to come.

I wasn't allowed to see my grandfather the following day, nor for two days afterwards.

'You have been coughing,' Lucia accused me. 'You will not go near him.'

'I wasn't going to,' I replied tartly, knowing that Lucia was correct as always, and that she had my grandfather's best interests at heart. I went after her, feeling thoroughly guilty. 'Thank you, Lucia.'

She looked at me suspiciously.

'We are so grateful for everything you do for the señor, and we couldn't manage without you.'

'Really?'

'Truly. My grandfather is not always an easy patient and you handle him with tact and care.'

Suddenly Lucia's stern face softened, and she ran a hand through her bobbed hair. For a moment I thought she would cry, instead she beamed, and it was as if the sun had come out.

'Well, that is the nicest thing anyone has said to me in a very long time.'

Everything changed after that. Lucia often smiled, and I made an effort to include her in the family. On one of my lunch-time shifts Manuela brought her to the bar, leaving Aunt Gracia in charge.

'Are you sure you can manage?' I had asked my great-aunt before I had left.

'Do you mean cope with the responsibility, or your cantankerous grandfather?' she had said with a smile.

Without her uniform and with a touch of lipstick, Lucia looked softer, more approachable. After a glass and a half of wine she was laughing and chatting with our friends.

'I'll relieve Gracia,' I insisted, when my shift was over, and the party was in full swing.

Lucia was about to disagree with me, but I was already at the door. 'I can sort out Papa Leonardo,' I called. 'You have some fun for a change.'

I was crossing the square when I noticed a familiar figure coming towards me. I dithered for a moment, aware that everyone was watching me, then I strode towards my bike. I was in the process of unlocking the chain, when Felipe caught up with me.

'I was hoping I would find you, Mia.'

'I work here, remember,' I retorted, wondering why I always had to have the last word.

'Leave the bike and come for a walk,' he suggested, ignoring my comment.

'Sorry, Felipe, I need to get back.'

'I see.' His face changed.

'I have to look after Papa Leonardo,' I qualified, wishing we were anywhere but in view of the bar.

'Then I shall walk you some of the way.' There was no argument after that, he just took my bicycle from me and I had no option but to fall into step beside him.

We had left the centre of the town and the inquisitive gazes of Tajo and Manuela behind us when he turned to face me. 'We need to sort this, Mia.'

I wasn't sure that there was anything to sort but for once I said nothing.

'I really felt—' he started again. 'I believed you felt something for me. Was I wrong, Mia?'

I looked at the ground.

'It's important for me to know.'

'Of course I did,' I muttered.

'Then why did you treat me like that? Do you normally make love to a man then dismiss him like a fly?'

I glared at him, my anger bubbling. 'Enough, Felipe, I have already told you, and if you have come to give me another lecture—'

He caught my hand. 'I am not sure what it is about you, Mia Ferris, but I can't get you out of my mind.'

'You have a funny way of showing it,' I retorted. 'And besides, you were draped over a girl at the Flamenco Fiesta.'

'That girl was my sister and the moment I saw you, I realised I couldn't be with anybody else.'

'You mean,' I gasped, 'after everything, you still want to be with me?'

'You are infuriating, stubborn, annoyingly attractive, and it seems you have got under my skin.'

'Me, stubborn? I could say the same about you.'

A smile twitched on his lips. 'Let's not argue about that now. If you will excuse me, Mia, I really have to go. I am meant to be having supper with friends in Seville. They already think I am completely mad coming here on the off chance. I will somehow have to prove to them that I am still a man.' He leant across the bike and I lifted my face. There was a moment of indecision but then he brushed my lips with his own. 'To be continued,' he said.

As I bicycled past the cemetery, the sky was a glorious dappled indigo, the moment when day merges into night. Did Felipe really say that? I wondered. Was it possible after everything that had happened? There was a smile on my face and a feeling of lightness in my heart. Maybe Papa Leonardo was right and it would all work out in the end.

I propped my bike against the wall and went straight to my

grandfather's room. Gracia was in a chair on one side of his bed with Ramon on the other. My grandfather was sitting up and he didn't look the least bit tired.

'I see everyone has been having a party, can I join in?' I suggested.

I was obviously a dampener on the gathering, because Ramon made his excuses, leaving the room, and Gracia kissed my grandfather's cheek. For once he didn't complain.

'I have left supper for you both in the warming oven,' she explained. 'There is fruit afterwards. We have had such a nice evening, haven't we, Leonardo?'

My grandfather raised his eyebrows, but I could see it was in jest. 'Exhausting,' he joked.

When she had gone, shutting the door quietly behind her, I moved to the side of the bed.

'You look pleased with yourself, Mia. Could it have something to do with Felipe? He rang here earlier.'

'I think it might, Papa Leonardo.'

After supper, when I regaled my grandfather with every detail, I propped up his pillows and made him more comfortable.

'Could I have one square of chocolate?' he begged.

'As long as you keep this from Lucia,' I warned, giving him a square of his favourite *Clavileño* chocolate.

I was turning on the television when he stopped me. 'Not tonight, Mia.'

I looked back at him, my face still.

'You will find your grandmother's box in my bedroom cupboard. Get it now, *querida*, before I change my mind.'

I entered the room upstairs, and though nothing had altered, for me everything had changed. I drew in my breath, conscious that even with my grandfather's blessing, I was trespassing into the past.

Inside the cupboard, ties drooped from a rack on the back

of the door, and suits I had never seen my grandfather wear, hung on a brass rail. A tiny vaquero jacket was pushed to the end. I ran my fingers over the brittle cloth, the small buttons. Was this the jacket Carlos had given him on his first Christmas at the hacienda? I held it to my face as if some half-forgotten smell would linger on the stiff material. I was putting it back when I found the box hidden behind the clothes. The surface was dusty, and it had the air of being undisturbed for years. Valeria had entrusted this wooden casket to Bañu on the day before she died.

'Leave it on the windowsill, Mia,' my grandfather instructed when I returned to his room. 'We will come to that later, but first sit by me.'

I sat down by his bed and rested my chin in my hands.

'I need to finish my story,' he said.

Part Eight

Chapter Fifty-six

August 1938, Seville

When Leonardo arrived at the house in Seville, Bañu opened the door. He leant against the jam, his body trembling.

'What is it, Leonardo?' Bañu gasped.

'Valeria,' he whispered. 'She's dead, Bañu.'

The old woman knew in that moment her worst fears had been realised, her nightmares had come to pass. She led him to the library, where he collapsed onto the sofa.

'Republican fighters shot her, Bañu. We had made plans for our future, she died in my arms.' He was wailing like an animal, all the pent-up grief spilling from him. Bañu held him as he cried, tears streaking down her wrinkled cheeks.

That was how Isabel found them.

'What is going on?' she asked, her hand flying to her mouth. '*Santo dios,* spare me, not Valeria?' She sank onto the sofa on the other side of Leonardo and rocked to and fro. 'My beautiful girl,' she moaned. 'Please not my beautiful little girl.'

When Isabel had heard every detail, she gazed at Leonardo, uncomprehending.

'All these years and I didn't guess. How stupid I was, how blind. It makes sense now.' She shook her head, trying to assimilate the facts. 'What fools we have been.' She looked then at Bañu. 'But you knew? You understood, Bañu.'

The old woman nodded. 'When he came across the mountain, I saw the way she looked at him. It was instant. I couldn't deny what I saw with my eyes.' The old woman was speaking as if Leonardo wasn't present.

After a while Isabel stood up and went to the mantelpiece. Every shred of colour had left her cheeks and her knuckles were white as she gripped on to the marble. She drew in her breath and held it for a moment, before slowly exhaling.

'Leonardo, you shall meet your daughter, Rafaela. Everything we do from now will be to keep her safe, every lie perpetuated will be for her. Come with me.' She led him up the stairs to the nursery next to Valeria's bedroom and opened the door.

Leonardo hovered on the threshold.

'Go,' Isabel gave him a little shove, her voice trembling, 'she is your daughter, she will be your life.'

Leonardo leant over the cot and his face changed. He looked back at Isabel and Bañu. 'Can I touch her?' he asked, his voice filled with awe.

'She won't break, you may pick her up,' Bañu uttered, her face riven with grief.

The following morning, Isabel found Leonardo watching over the crib. He looked across at her. 'How can I live without her?' he whispered.

She came to stand beside him and put her hand on his arm. 'We must all learn to live without her, Leonardo. So, this is how it will be, remember everything we do from this moment is for your daughter, Rafaela. First you will get married. The girl will come to live at this house and the child will be assumed to be hers.'

'I cannot,' Leonardo cried.

Isabel held up her hand. 'It is the best option, the only option. My daughter was a photographer for the republicans, part of their propaganda machine. When this war is over, and the nationalists have won, the reprisals will be terrible. If you want your daughter to be safe, you have to listen to me and do what I say.' She paused and looked him in the face. 'And Carlos can never learn the truth, it would break him completely and it would put him in danger. There has been enough tragedy in this house.'

Her hand was on her forehead, her head pushed forward as she strode around the room. 'I think I know of someone who will be willing to comply, a nurse without prospects. She works at the charity hospital where I am a patron.' She shook her head. 'No – no, of course that won't do. She can't be known to the hospital.' Words were spilling out of her. She stopped for a moment and her face cleared. 'Yes, I have it. Paloma, the daughter of my old friend Señora Espartero. There is a sister, Gracia, but she is working abroad, so she may not even know of her pregnancy. Don't look like that, Bañu,' she shouted at the old woman. 'Of course there is no pregnancy, but Señor Espartero is dead, they have no money and Paloma has no prospects. She is an attractive girl with a kind heart, she will be the perfect mother to Rafaela. I will go and visit my friend.'

She stopped pacing and thrust a letter at Leonardo. 'Please take this to the *Hospital de la Caridad* in *Calle Temprado.* I have written to say we wish to book the priest for a christening and a marriage service tomorrow at noon.'

'Tomorrow?' Leonardo gasped.

'Yes, tomorrow. There is no time to lose.'

'Suppose she doesn't want to marry me?' he intervened.

'She will,' said Isabel, a look of fierce determination in her eyes.

Chapter Fifty-seven

At noon on 17 August 1938, Rafaela was christened at the chapel of the *Hospital de la Caridad*, Seville. Immediately afterwards, while Bañu held Rafaela, Isabel acted as witness to the marriage of Leonardo and Paloma.

Though the priest may have believed it unusual to follow the service of christening with a marriage, he did not object. Señora Palamera de Santos was a generous patron, and he could afford to overlook details in a time of war.

'Do you take this woman…' Leonardo glanced at his bride. She was slim and dark with a heart-shaped face and pretty eyes, but she was not Valeria. Sweat broke out on his forehead.

'Will you love her, comfort her, honour and care for her?'

He could hear a voice affirm the vows, but how could it be his voice when only a few days before, he had made a promise to Valeria? They came to the final declaration and he cleared his throat, '*I do*,' he whispered, his heart cracking. When Paloma squeezed his hand and looked up at him, smiling shyly, he thought he would weep.

'I may not have your love,' she whispered, 'but I will do my best to make you happy, and I give you my word, I will be a good mother to Rafaela.'

Before Leonardo returned to the Front, Carlos arrived. When

he heard that Valeria was dead, he wept like a child. It was Isabel who comforted him.

'We have to get through this. Valeria would insist that we were strong for Leonardo, Bañu, for all of us.'

'But who is this woman Paloma?'

'We have met her many times, my beloved, you just don't remember. She is the daughter of my good friend, Señora Espartero, and I am so glad that she has married Leonardo.'

'How can I remember anything at this moment, when I can only think about our beloved Valeria?'

'I know, Carlos,' Isabel murmured, enfolding him in her arms. 'All we need to know is that dear Paloma is now part of the family and they have a beautiful baby girl. Rafaela will become our reason to go on, we have to keep her safe.'

Carlos was trying to undo the buttons on his army jacket, when he gave up and sank to his knees. When he was able to speak he looked up at his wife.

'I do have one piece of good news for Leonardo. The boy's horse is returning to Seville. There will be no more cavalry charges for Saturno.'

On the day Leonardo returned to his regiment, Isabel took him aside. 'Keep safe, *querido,* and be strong. If you die, there is little for any of us to cling on to.'

'I will do my best.' He took the tiny photograph from the pocket of his shirt and Isabel winced.

'To think I took that only a few weeks past. She was so happy, Leonardo. She . . .'

Leonardo put his arms around her. 'Look at Valeria's smile, her love. We have to believe it is still surrounding us or none of us could go on.' He put the photograph back in the pocket of his shirt. 'Now I must go and look for my wife.'

*

Paloma was folding linen in her bedroom. She put it down and came towards him.

'Thank you,' he said, trying to keep his voice even. 'I am grateful for your kind words during the marriage service and I will do my best to be a dutiful husband.' He kissed her forehead. '*Adiós*, Paloma, please treasure Rafaela.'

'*Por supuesto* and stay safe,' she whispered in reply.

Next Leonardo went to the library, where Carlos was prostrate on the sofa, a brandy in his hand. 'Goodbye, Father.'

Carlos looked up, his eyes unfocussed. 'She was the most perfect child,' he uttered. 'Perfect in every way.'

Leonardo took the brandy balloon from him and lifted Carlos's legs onto the cushions, covering him with a rug as his eyes fluttered closed.

'Perhaps she was too perfect for this world,' Leonardo murmured, quietly closing the door. He was leaning against the wall when Bañu found him.

'You have to come with me. Valeria left something, a chest containing her photographs. She instructed me to give them to you should anything happen to her.' Her voice quavered. 'She seemed to know, Leonardo.'

Leonardo breathed deeply. 'I hope you are wrong, I pray she saw only a wonderful future ahead of her. I would have done anything for her, Bañu.'

'I am being fanciful, forgive me, but I believe she would want you to see these before you return to the Front.'

Leonardo hesitated.

'Let's look at them together, Leonardo.'

Bañu took the wooden box from the cupboard in Valeria's bedroom and after retrieving the key, she opened the lock. The inside was packed with photographs and papers.

As they sorted through them on her bed, neither said a word. Leonardo's throat constricted, he could hardly breathe. When he came to the grainy image of the boy on the point of death, he cried out in shock, and when he held the photograph of a dead baby in her mother's arms, he sobbed. There were hundreds of them, honest, shocking portrayals of the war and they were all taken on the Leica he had given her.

'These are extraordinary,' he said at last, his voice shaking, 'and heart-breaking.'

Bañu picked out the photograph that Valeria had taken in Granada. Leonardo was standing against the low wall with the view of the Alhambra behind him. It was the day Rafaela was conceived. His shoulders were thrown back and his mouth was wide with laughter. She passed it to him.

'Perhaps I should keep this to remind myself what it is like to be happy,' Leonardo uttered, his face contorted with grief.

'One day,' the old woman said, taking his hand in her own, 'I know you will be happy again.'

Chapter Fifty-eight

November 1938

Leonardo returned to the regiment now based at Zaragoza. Consumed with grief and anger, and as yet unaware he had been double crossed, his only desire was to rid the country of republicans. With little regard for his safety, he requested to be allowed to lead a unit fighting at the front line.

Two days later he was told to report to the Operations Room, where the commanding officer was sitting behind a large desk. Despite the small heater, it was bitterly cold.

'So, Alférez de Santos, here are your orders. It seems you have your wish.' The colonel's uniform jacket was buttoned up to the neck, and a great coat hung over the back of his chair. A staff officer, Leonardo presumed, a desk man, with very little battle exposure – until he noticed the empty sleeve hanging at his side. He too had been a casualty of war. He spoke with a soft, clear voice, his unusually light eyes glancing at a map that was laid out in front of him.

'There are several groups of republicans coming up from the south trying to get to the Pyrenees; if they do, they'll probably make it to France. Before, though, they will have to negotiate the descent down from the Iberian mountains.' He pointed on the map with a ruler. 'Here, do you see?'

Leonardo nodded.

'If they make it, they will push on towards the River Ebro. After crossing the river it's a slog to the Pyrenees. We need you to intercept one of these groups as they are making the mountain descent and stop them from reaching the Ebro.' He paused and looked up at Leonardo. 'It is a challenging trek. The routes are all steep, rocky and forested, with deep gorges, carved out by flowing water and, in this weather,' he shrugged his shoulders, 'they could freeze to death first. My advice is to catch them as they struggle through the water, but you will have to judge the most advantageous place. Whatever happens, they must not cross the River Ebro. Their leader, a devious bastard, has been causing trouble of late and we don't want him to get away. You have something to say?' He paused to let Leonardo speak.

'Crossing fast-running water, with a heavy equipment pack, and a rifle, would certainly be a challenge. I've done it on a horse and it was hard enough, but on foot! They should be an easy target.'

'This man has slipped the net in the past, he's clever, so don't be too sure. We know which of the mountain passes they like to use. The scouts are always on the lookout. Once they have been detected, a scout will find you, and give you their position. Then it's up to you to organise the ambush.' He put down the ruler and stabbed his finger on the map. 'This is where you will make your base camp. If you pitch your tents about fifty metres from the water's edge, you won't be seen from the other side of the river.'

'But we could be there for days,' Leonardo conjectured.

'You could, Alférez de Santos, but you will find ways to amuse yourselves, I am sure. If no one contacts you after seven days, make your own way back.'

'And rations, colonel? There have been occasions when they have been short, and in this weather the men will need to be well fed.'

'Rations?'

Leonardo stood his ground, 'Yes, colonel.'

The officer guffawed at this. 'You question me, sir? You should try the republicans. They are a disorganised rabble. I am told they set off for the Front only to find they had left their supplies behind! You will have rations for seven days, camouflage clothing and tents. I've been there myself – you are right, at this time of year it is unspeakably cold.'

'It is important for my—'

'Santos, you will let me finish before you interrupt again.' He smiled for a moment, his eyes crinkling at the corners. 'Don't worry, the men going with you are used to the mountains, they can look after themselves. Lastly, weapons? What do you need?'

Leonardo believed he was being tested and he wouldn't fall short. 'I need a machine gun and side pistol for every man, and two hand grenades each, just in case. If they spot us first, we'll need every bit of fire power we can get.'

The commanding officer made a note of his requests. 'If you don't have any further questions, I'll let you go. *Buena suerte.* Good luck.'

Leonardo was about to leave the room when the officer called after him. 'Remember, de Santos, the regiment has no facilities for prisoners of war, I am sure you understand.'

Leonardo understood completely. He looked back at the officer and saluted.

Leonardo met the eight soldiers in his team and was amazed to find his old groom Ramon amongst them. 'A sergeant, now, and in the infantry; you must have some powerful friends,' he teased, his mood lifting.

Ramon shrugged his shoulders. 'With everything now mechanised, I asked to be transferred.'

'But here? Is that coincidence, Ramon?'

A fleeting smile crossed Ramon's face. 'It occurred to me that if Saturno no longer needed me, Alférez de Santos, you might!'

Leonardo looked at the stocky, unobtrusive man and a lump formed in his throat. How right Ramon was. He did need him and when the moment was right, he would tell him everything. It was a blessing that he was here.

Early, on a bright but bitterly cold morning, Leonardo and his men were taken south to *La Almunia de Doña Godina*, and dropped at a village at the foothills of the Iberian Mountains. With the loads on their back and machine guns at the ready, they began the long trek up a wide river gorge.

Keeping within the cover of the forest, they stayed as close to the river as possible. Black kites and the occasional golden eagle circled above the canopy of leaves. Higher still where the vegetation had petered out, ibex and wild goats leapt precariously from rock to rock in the now barren landscape. Every so often the howl of a wolf or a brown bear's roar echoed through the canyons.

As they marched, Leonardo's thoughts were of Valeria. Though his ears were attuned to every sound, she was a constant in his mind.

When they had reached their planned base camp and the tents had been pitched, the latrines dug, and a fire made, Leonardo called the men together again.

'Here's the strategy for the ambush, but if any of you have a suggestion, you should voice it now.' He looked at the men, tough veterans of the war, fully capable of the task before them. When no one spoke, he continued. 'We'll divide into three groups. I expect the republicans to cross in a line at a crossing point a kilometre up the river. The waters are running fast, so they will be looking down, trying to avoid any submerged rocks. I'll lead the first group, we will concentrate on those at the front of the line; Alberto's group—' he looked at an unshaven man with a wiry physique – 'you will target the middle section, and your group, Ramon, those at the end.' He paused. 'I'll fire first, then everyone should follow immediately. Don't pick out a single man. Spray your fire in an arc. That way we make sure we hit every one of them.'

'What if they don't cross in a line?' Alberto took a packet of cigarettes from his pocket and passed them around.

'Let those who attempt to cross reach the middle of the river. Alberto, yours and my section will then open fire. You, Ramon, look towards the far bank and target any republican you can see. Finally, I don't need to remind you, we won't be taking prisoners.'

When, two days later, a scout arrived at the camp, the men gathered around him.

'The Reds are about eight hours away; moving slowly down this gorge.' The scout, an undernourished Spaniard with almond eyes and lips blue from cold, pointed to the map. 'There are about twelve of them, all well-armed, but they look exhausted. The trek over the mountains has definitely slowed them down. They're following a pass that will join up with the river, here. It is my guess they will want to get over the river first, and then rest up for a while.'

Leonardo glanced at the map. 'That gives us about four hours. Take some rations and don't forget your weapons!' A titter ran through the men.

After thanking the scout they gathered their kit, and were on the move. As they climbed higher, the landscape changed. Once again, rocks, bush and scrub had taken over from the thick forest. Snow was falling and the wind was sending large white flakes scurrying across the ground. Soon everything was carpeted in a white blanket. The going became more difficult, each step harder than the last. They trudged onwards, their voices muffled by the wind. Eventually, they reached the point where the republicans would cross the river. As Leonardo had predicted, a series of large rocks were embedded in the river bottom. He placed his men twenty-five metres downstream and five metres higher. They had a perfect view of the target.

While some of the unit huddled together trying to rest, Leonardo and Ramon shared the duty of lookout; watching the opposite bank, swapping the binoculars every fifteen minutes, quietly sharing stories to keep themselves awake.

'So, Ramon,' Leonardo whispered, 'there is something I would like to know.'

'*Si,* Alférez de Santos?'

'What crime did you commit to get yourself in gaol?'

'You ask me now, after all this time?'

Leonardo grinned. 'It's as good a time as any, my friend.'

'Shall we say my employer was beating his wife and I couldn't stand by.'

'And what happened to your employer?'

'He received a broken jaw.'

'Quite right,' Leonardo murmured with a smile.

At noon, Ramon nudged Leonardo and passed him the binoculars.

The republican leader was emerging from the scrub on the opposite bank. He stood for a moment, his leonine head tilted as if he was listening, then he strode from the shore, wading into the rapidly flowing river. Water was swirling around his legs, but he pushed on unperturbed. It was beyond his knees when he paused again, testing the depth and strength of the flow, glancing occasionally towards the opposite side of the river.

Leonardo focussed the binoculars. There was something familiar about his strong build and long shaggy hair. The way he wore his heavy jacket with the buttons undone, with total disregard for the icy conditions, and the thick belt studded with silver, struck a chord in his memory, but he couldn't place it. He rebuked himself, it didn't matter who he was. One thing was sure, he was a republican and they had killed Valeria.

When the man reached the middle of the river, he twisted around, and beckoned to the others. At once they began to scramble down the bank in single file. Leonardo counted twelve. The last, smaller and thinner than the rest, had trouble keeping his balance. About a third of the way across he turned to face the flow and side stepped, holding his gun above his head.

The leader was climbing up the bank when Leonardo gave a hand signal and raised his machine gun. The others followed suit, and at once a deafening roar filled the gorge. Birds rose into the air screeching in terror as each gun spat fire and flame.

As the bullets rained down on the republicans, panic ensued. Several tried to turn back, but were swept downstream. Others floundered before they fell, their bodies caught between submerged rocks, their blood turning the water pink. The two in front managed to reach dry land, but were cut down in the snow.

Leonardo raised his arm to stop the firing. The action had lasted less than a minute and apart from the rush of the river, silence returned.

'Let's get down there,' he said at last, 'but keep your eyes open and your pistols ready. Don't be the victim of a dying man.'

They walked towards the river, where the white snow was now spotted red. 'Gather the bodies that you can find,' he instructed. 'Let us at least give them a decent burial. I would hope someone would do the same for me.'

The leader lay by the edge of the river, the water lapping over him. As Leonardo approached, he lifted his hand.

'Finish me,' he whispered. 'We are all Spaniards, finish me now.'

Leonardo raised his pistol and pointed it at the wounded man's head. 'I will do your bidding,' he uttered, adjusting his grip on the gun. His finger was about to flex, when he saw it, the flash of silver at the man's chest. Leaning forward he saw a silver half-medallion lying amongst the tangle of chest hair. Leonardo reached out and turned it over, his breath quickening, but he knew what he would find. The medallion matched his own, for on its back was an engraved letter 'E'. This man, lying half dead before him, was his father, Esteban. His mouth went dry. He had always believed the day would come when they would meet, but not like this, not with his father prostrate beneath him on the ground.

'Do you know who I am?' Leonardo asked, a cold fury settling on him.

'No, but get it done with,' the man urged, his voice cracking in pain.

'My name is Leonardo,' he said, eyes flashing with unspent rage, 'and I am your son.'

The man's lids flickered open, yet he showed no sense of recognition, no sense of remorse or feeling. 'Then in the name of God, I beg of you, if I am your father, do this for me.'

'Why, when you took my mother away from me? Tell me, why should I make it easy?' Leonardo demanded.

A single tear leaked down the man's face and Leonardo noticed the stubble on his unshaven chin, the long scar across his cheek, but still no remorse.

'She betrayed me,' he gasped, forcing the words from his lips. 'She was sleeping with my friend. The shame was too great, Leonardo.' He tried to raise himself up, but he fell backwards, his head hitting the ground with a dull thump.

Leonardo leant down on one knee, so that Esteban could hear him, the freezing water soaking his trousers.

'So you shot her?'

'I have regretted it every single day of my life since then.'

Leonardo pointed the pistol at his father's temple. 'I will never forgive you. You will go to your maker, knowing that your son will never forgive you.' His finger was on the trigger, but his hand was shaking.

Ramon came up beside him. 'This is someone you know?' he asked in a low voice.

Leonardo nodded, unable to speak.

'Walk away,' Ramon said quietly. 'Leave it to me.'

Leonardo left his father with Ramon and walked up the bank. He was in the cover of the trees when a single shot rang out. His father had gone.

Chapter Fifty-nine

The war was drawing to a close, the inexorable force of the nationalists gaining one town, then the next. Leonardo was too weary to notice, too drained to care. As they moved from camp to camp, they passed lorries coming the other way and ambulances returning from the front. Bedraggled groups of refugees shuffled through the snow. Occasionally, they fell, dropping to the ground. There was no noise, no complaint, and the others trudged on. They drove through towns, once dignified and full of life, now reduced to rubble. Death was everywhere.

When Leonardo learnt the International Brigades had been withdrawn and were returning home, he grieved for his friend. If only William had been amongst them, if only he hadn't come to fight at all. So much death, so much hatred and for what? As they moved further east, the snow changed to constant, driving rain.

Having just made camp near Mollerusa, in north-east Spain, Leonardo and Ramon ran through the rain to the squat shack the locals called a tavern. Leonardo shoved the door with his foot and they hurled themselves into the smoke-filled interior. Ramon searched for a table while Leonardo pushed his way to the bar.

'*Dos Cruzcampo, por favor,*' he instructed, his gaze taking in the soldiers guzzling their beer, the prostitutes, pathetic creatures in gaudy clothes and bright lipstick, flattering the men. He was sitting in the corner with Ramon when he noticed the woman slouched over a table, a bottle of wine in front of her. There was something hopeless about her demeanour that Leonardo recognised, an air of defeat that he could well understand. She looked up and for an instant their gaze met.

'Constanza,' Leonardo whispered her name in surprise. For a moment he remembered her youthful optimism of years before, her fiery slanting eyes, her glowing skin. He remembered their friends coming together in Cazalla de la Sierra, calling each other *comrade*, filled with youthful passion. What was she doing in a nationalist-held town?

He went towards her. 'Constanza?' he asked uncertainly.

Her eyes darted around the room. 'Please don't be seen with me,' she begged.

'But what are you doing here?'

As a draft of cold wind blasted into the poorly lit room, a colonel in a thick army greatcoat swept in.

She jerked her head away, 'Go please,' she whispered out of the side of her mouth.

Leonardo returned to his table and sat down.

'A friend?' Ramon queried.

Leonardo nodded. 'I knew her a long time ago, the colonel also.' From their quiet corner he observed the colonel pull off his leather gloves and stretch his long legs beneath the table. He flicked his fingers at the surly innkeeper. Though de Rosa wouldn't recognise him, Leonardo had recognised the colonel. He had been an eight-year-old boy when de Rosa, the estate steward, had been sacked by Carlos. He remembered the fury on his face as he had galloped from the yard, the hatred in his eyes. As Leonardo leant back in the wooden bench, he recalled the night after de Rosa's dismissal, and the festivities organised by Carlos. The *braceros* had brought their tambourines, their guitars and castanets, and the women had put on their finest clothes. Leonardo and Valeria had been allowed to join in, and as the music had reverberated through the cloistered courtyard, they had danced and whirled and stamped their feet with the rest of them. They been so caught up in the music, they hadn't noticed Carlos and Isabel watching from the entrance. They had run towards them laughing and panting from exertion.

'Oh that was good, Papa,' Valeria had cried, flinging herself into her father's arms. 'Did you see it all?'

'We certainly did,' he had replied.

Leonardo's mind was jolted to the present as he scrutinised de Rosa. The hardness in his face had increased over the years, but it was the mean twist of his mouth that set him apart. The cruel streak now legendary in the army had been evident at the hacienda. As he observed Constanza cowering beside de Rosa, Leonardo felt his heart lurch in pity. The beautiful, vibrant girl he had once known seemed to have been crushed by this evil man.

It was ten o'clock when they left the tavern. Ramon had gone ahead to relieve himself in the bush when Leonardo felt a tug on his sleeve. He turned to find Constanza behind him. She was wearing only the lightest dress with a shawl covering her head. Her grubby silk shoes were spattered with rain.

'Can you meet me behind the church tomorrow, Leonardo?' Constanza's words came out in a rush.

He nodded. 'Go back inside, Constanza. And yes, I will meet you tomorrow night at ten.'

As the girl skidded over the wet ground, she glanced back over her shoulder. 'Please be there,' she mouthed.

The following night, Leonardo left the camp and went to the church where Constanza was waiting for him in the porch. Though the shawl was wrapped around her shoulders, she was shivering with cold.

'You are risking a lot to meet me,' he said.

'I had to,' she replied. 'You have to know the truth, I have done terrible things.'

Leonardo raised his eyebrows. 'What are you talking about, Constanza? Tell me it wasn't you who betrayed the padre.'

She shook her head. 'He was my padre too, Leonardo, I would never do that.'

'Well, then, what have you done that can be so bad?'

Constanza looked up at him, her eyes swimming with tears. 'More than you could ever know. I have killed people, Leonardo, young men who didn't deserve to die, old men, but this war makes animals out of us all. I was a republican soldier until they caught me, until he—' She gulped. 'It was life or death, give up a secret or they would torture me. They were going to—' She shook her head and started to sob, and Leonardo took her in his arms.

'It's all right, Constanza,' he soothed.

'But it is not all right, Leonardo, I told them where to find her.'

'Who, what are you talking about?' He stopped, holding her away from him. '*Jesucristo*, you are talking about Valeria.'

Constanza nodded, her voice small and broken. 'Kill me now, Leonardo,' she begged. 'I deserve to die. But I had to tell you first.'

'Why, Constanza?' Grief, anger and horror mingled together as he stared at the woman in front of him.

'Your nationalist soldiers had a burning poker, they were going to use it on me if I didn't tell them something, anything. But I thought she wouldn't be there. That no one would be there. She was brave and a republican. I may have hated her because of you, but I never meant for her to die. It was de Rosa,' she wailed.

Leonardo was shaking. He thought his legs would give way. He breathed deeply, gulping the air into his lungs. He could kill

Constanza now, he could strangle her with his bare hands, but the realisation dawned on him that he didn't hate her. Faced with the prospect of a truly horrible death, she had done the only thing possible to save herself. He vowed it would be de Rosa he would kill. The cruel monster had to pay for what he had done.

'Please believe me, Leonardo,' she whispered.

'I believe you.' He felt drained, emotionless. 'But why are you with de Rosa now?'

'It was part of the deal, I can't get away from him.'

'You must escape, the war will be over soon. Go home.'

'I have no home to go to. My father was murdered by the nationalists, my mother has lost her mind, and my sister Mariana—' she shrugged her bony shoulders – 'I have no idea if she is still alive. But don't you see, I am now a nationalist whore. How would the people of Cazalla de la Sierra take that? De Rosa will kill me if he learns that I have spoken to you. So, you see, it is done. Please give me your gun, let me finish it now,' she begged, reaching forward and stumbling in her eagerness.

Leonardo gripped her arm. 'No, Constanza, I intend to kill de Rosa, but I will need your help.'

She nodded. 'Then you will give me a gun? There is nothing left for me, Leonardo.'

Leonardo sighed, seeing the depth of her despair. 'Then you'll have your gun,' he agreed.

She nodded and gave him a scribbled piece of paper. 'This is where I live, let me know when it shall be.'

Leonardo watched her run away from him. He would kill de Rosa, whatever the risk to himself; he would do it for Valeria. But as his rage dissipated, he realised there was something more important than his anger. He had their daughter, Rafaela to think about. She was the reason he must live.

Chapter Sixty

Ramon listened quietly while Leonardo told him everything.

'Quite a story, Alférez de Santos. Now your real father is dead, and you will end the life of de Rosa.'

It was not a question, just a simple statement of fact and Leonardo nodded. 'He has taken everything from me, robbed me of my chance of happiness with Valeria.'

'Then I will help you.'

'If we are found out, there will be no court martial, we will both be shot. You understand?'

Ramon looked him in the eye. 'I do. The first day I met you I knew that our paths had crossed for a purpose. And now you will have my support when you despatch this man.'

'War has brought us together, Ramon, but you know our friendship will not end here.'

'Throughout my life I have been an outcast, until I met you. You have treated me with respect and as an equal. I will do anything for you, de Santos.'

Leonardo smiled. 'It is an honour to have you as my friend.'

Two days later, the plans were in place, and they were waiting in the forest outside the camp. They didn't have to wait long before they could hear angry voices approaching.

'You little whore, who are you meeting all dressed up like that?'

'Why do you care? It's not as if you are sleeping with me anymore. You have women everywhere, de Rosa.'

'Who do you think pays for your rooms, your fancy clothes?'

'Fancy clothes!' There was a loud laugh. 'I have frozen all winter for lack of them.' There was the sound of running feet and then a loud slap and a woman's gasp.

'Slut, I should have let them finish you,' de Rosa shouted.

'But then you wouldn't have known about Val Saint. I couldn't have told you if I was dead,' Constanza taunted, drawing de Rosa further and further into the forest, towards their designated landmark. Then Leonardo could see them.

When he stepped out from behind a tree holding a gun, de Rosa had his arm around Constanza's neck. 'Let her go.'

'So, she was meeting you, was she . . . ?' De Rosa's eyes were hardened flints, as he took in the figure before him.

'Alférez de Santos,' Leonardo finished for him.

'If she is that valuable to you, you can have her,' he said, his eyes fixed on the barrel of the gun. 'I can assure you she is a useless fuck.'

'It is not the girl I am after,' Leonardo said, his voice quiet.

At that moment Ramon emerged out of the darkness and de Rosa's face changed. Leonardo could see the fear in his eyes.

'What, what is going on? You won't get away with it,' he stuttered. 'Do you know who I am?'

'I know precisely who you are. That's why I am going to kill you.' Leonardo spoke quietly, with no emotion.

De Rosa's eyes widened and Constanza used the opportunity to slip away from him and run to Ramon's side.

'So you are in on this, you dirty whore?'

'My name is Santos,' Leonardo interrupted, drawing de Rosa's attention again. 'We have met before.'

'Where?' De Rosa's face was pale.

'You worked for Don Carlos Palamera de Santos.'

'Palamera de Santos?' he uttered, a tremble in his voice. 'But he didn't have a son, Agustin is dead.'

'I became his adopted son. I was a child then and I remember you. Your cruelty to the workers was infamous, and now you have murdered Valeria.'

Colonel de Rosa opened his mouth. 'It was another officer, Capitán Reyes,' he stuttered. 'He will be shot. I give you my word as an officer and a gentleman.' He was dribbling now, his body shaking. He started to sob. 'Dear God, it wasn't me, I beg of you.'

'Kneel on the floor and take this like a man,' Constanza snapped, walking towards him until she stood in front of him. She spat in his face. 'Kneel, coward.' She stood aside while de Rosa sank to his knees. Leonardo screwed a silencer onto the German revolver, lifted the gun and took aim. Seconds later there was a muffled shot and de Rosa fell forward.

Leonardo and Ramon lifted the body and dumped it into the shallow grave, dug by Ramon that morning. They filled it in with earth and covered the spot with leaves and fallen branches.

When they were satisfied, they stood back. 'We need to get out of here,' Leonardo instructed.

'First, you need to give me that gun.' Constanza came forward and opened her hand.

Leonardo nodded, and emptied the barrel into his pocket. 'You have one bullet, and it is not for a soldier. Enough has been done, Constanza.'

Constanza gave a sad smile, her previous fire and rage snuffed out. The colonel was gone, she had had her revenge, she was ready to face her decision. 'I need only one, Leonardo.'

Leonardo placed his hand on her arm and she flinched, tears springing to her eyes. 'You could still go home,' he suggested, knowing that it was hopeless, but having to try one last time. 'Please go home, Constanza.'

Constanza ignored his words. 'I imagine it would be better for you if it is far from this place. It will be in my room, Leonardo.' She was about to leave when she turned back and ripped a small locket from her neck. 'When all of this is over, would you find my sister and give her this? She will be the only one left to care.'

Leonardo put the locket in his pocket. 'If any of us are alive, I will find her,' he vowed.

She hugged him quickly, then broke away. 'I hope one day you will see it in your heart to forgive me.' Then she turned and started to run. She did not look back.

The regiment were told of Constanza's death the following day and though a brief search was made for de Rosa before the camp moved on, his body was never found.

'Probably an act of revenge,' they said in the barracks. 'Poor bastard, getting entangled with a republican whore.'

Chapter Sixty-one

November 2000

My grandfather closed his eyes and rested his head against the pillow. 'We can continue tomorrow, Papa Leonardo,' I urged.

'No.' The lids flicked open again and there was an urgency in his tone. 'I have to tell you everything.'

'If you're sure.'

'I have never been more convinced.'

After taking a sip of water he resumed his harrowing account.

'Within weeks, Mia, every town and village had fallen to the nationalists. Madrid finally succumbed to the Francoist armies on the twenty-eighth of March. Three days later they controlled all Spanish territory and I was able to return to the hacienda with Paloma, your mother and Ramon.'

His brow furrowed as he relived his memories of the past.

'The atmosphere was so different without Valeria. I would find myself looking for her, going to the stables, expecting to see her, listening for her voice. And, of course, I had lost my dear friend, Padre Alvaro.

'In time, our lives returned to some sort of normality. Papa Carlos and *Abuela* Isabel decided to give up the house in Seville and made their permanent home with us. They adored being near your mother, and Paloma was an exceptional daughter-in-law. She was so thoughtful, Mia, and never obtrusive. She sensibly allowed Bañu to take over the household again. Although she was now in her late seventies, there was no persuading the old woman to slow down. I was grateful, I believe she grew to love Paloma, taking her under her wing, and to everyone's amusement, she even struck up an alliance with Ramon.'

'I wish I had known Bañu,' I interjected. 'She sounds incredible, a force of nature.'

Papa Leonardo chuckled, then his face became serious. 'Indeed she was, we would never have managed without her. She told me once that looking after the family was her reason for living. Carlos, however, had lost his strength and resolve. He never recovered from the shock of losing his beloved Valeria. That and the hideous war had broken him.'

'And Isabel, how did she cope?' I asked.

'She retained her dignity and her sense of style, but she was so fragile, Mia. She put on a brave face, tried hard to disguise her agony, but she couldn't fool me. She had lost her son and her daughter, too much for a mother to bear.' His lip trembled. 'It was little Rafaela who saved us all. She was such a charming child, bringing much-needed joy and laughter to the family. Most evenings we gathered in the library and Rafaela enjoyed entertaining us before she was scooped up by Bañu. Bedtimes were always an object of frustration for your mother; she would have preferred to have stayed downstairs with the grown-ups. She had pigtails that stuck out each side of her head. She enchanted us all, and it was difficult to deny her anything.' Leonardo looked at me then and smiled. 'You were just the same, Mia. *No, Papa Leonardo, one more chapter, one more game.*'

'I do remember that you always gave in,' I said, my voice a little unsteady.

He gazed at the box for a moment, then he took a deep

breath and resumed his story. 'So, life continued. And as for me, Mia, I gained strength from the unity and harmony within my close circle. All around us chaos still reigned as Franco's dictatorship continued their campaign of terror and brutality. Resistance bands lived in the forests and Franco's men hunted them down like wild animals. To those brave men, a quick death was preferable to capture. *Pobres bastardos*, they knew what would happen to them if they were caught.' He brushed his hands across his eyes. 'While the war was raging in the rest of Europe, Franco was waging war on his own people.'

'At least you were safe here,' I interjected.

'You are right, Mia. At the hacienda we had created a small, isolated bubble; it seemed secure, but at any moment it could have changed. Sometimes at night gunshots echoed in the hills, but I could do nothing to help. If I had died, your mother would have had no one to protect her. Ramon, now that is another story. When I noticed the store cupboards and some of our medical supplies were diminishing, it didn't take me long to guess the reason for Ramon's excursions into the hills. On one occasion, I saw him ride off into the night with his saddle bags bulging, I asked no questions, of course, but years later he told me the truth. To this day I can remember him standing in front of me, giving me one of his rare smiles: "I fought for the nationalist side during the *Guerra Civil* because I had no choice, but in the aftermath, I felt it was my duty to support what was left of the republicans. I knew you would not begrudge the food. My only regret was that I didn't kill some of the nationalist scum on the way."'

I imagined Ramon galloping up the rocky mountainside with supplies for the resistance. 'What a remarkable man, Papa Leonardo.'

'He was – indeed he is, Mia. If he had been captured by

Franco's men, he would have died under torture rather than give anyone away.'

He drew in his breath and I could see the effort it was taking to continue.

I put my hand over his. 'Stop, Papa Leonardo.'

He shook it away. 'No, Mia, you must know everything. Poor Carlos had believed he was fighting for right, for the Church and for good Spanish values, but over time I know he had become disillusioned. We kept news of the atrocities from him, it would have killed him, Mia.'

I went to fill the jug with water while Papa Leonardo rested for a while. He looked up at me as I handed him his glass.

'I know that at least fifty thousand were executed. That did not include the numbers of republicans arrested and interned in concentration camps.' He shook his shaggy head. 'Hundreds of thousands, apparently, but who knows. It should have been a time of peace, but I could do nothing, say nothing. I had to protect my family. Only with Ramon, my comrade-in-arms, was I able to discuss these terrible things.'

I squeezed my grandfather's hand. 'You shielded everyone, Papa Leonardo.'

'I tried. It was necessary to live as normal a life as possible. At the beginning of the war, five of our horses had been requisitioned by the army and that was the last we had seen of them. Soon the stables began to fill again. Juan and Ramon worked well together, looking after the young horses that I trained and sold on. We started a breeding programme, Saturno, of course, was the first stallion, and he lives on to this day in Lyra and Seferino.'

'And what about you? You talk about everyone else, but not yourself.'

My grandfather's smile was nostalgic. 'Just like your mother, always wanting to know everything. Well, there were times during those early days, Mia, when I was inconsolable. One evening, Isabel was playing the piano in the drawing room. The light must have played tricks on me because for one, exquisite second, I could see Valeria, running her fingers over the keys. My dream crumbled when it was Isabel who looked up. Her face a mirror image of her daughter's, they seemed indivisible. She came towards me and held me in her arms as we cried together. Over the years it became easier with many happy times: your mother's first ride on a pony, her first flamenco contest in Seville. She won, of course, and made us so proud.'

I sensed that we were nearing the end of the story because Papa Leonardo had a faraway look in his eyes as though he was gathering strength for the final part.

He coughed, and his eyes focussed again. 'And then Carlos died, a true gentleman to the last. He was the first to go on a fine spring morning five years after they returned from Seville. He was taking his usual walk in the orange grove after breakfast when he fell. I heard a cry and got there in time to hold him in my arms.

'"I am so proud of you," he had whispered. "You have been a wonderful son to me and I thank you from the bottom of my heart." I remember kissing his forehead and saying, "And you have been the best father in the world, Papa."

'I didn't know how I could let him go, how I could live with another member of my family leaving me. I remained in the orange grove holding my father's body, until Ramon came to find us. My face told Isabel everything. She was so strong and brave. I loved and admired her more in that moment than I can say.'

For a moment I looked at my grandfather, and all these years later I could see the depth of his pain. He sighed and pressed on.

'Of course, in life there is always death. Bañu went next, at Easter time three years later. She died quietly in her sleep, proving even in death to be as discreet as she had always been in life. I mourned her more than I could have imagined I would. She had been kind to me, a ragged eight-year-old boy who had arrived on the doorstep with an even scruffier dog all those years before. She instinctively understood my shock following my mother's murder, overcoming her initial suspicion to become my staunchest ally and friend. Paloma rose to the occasion, looking after us all. She no longer wanted any help with Rafaela, but I managed to persuade her to employ Magdalena our cook.'

I didn't interrupt my grandfather because I could see the effort it was taking him.

'You can imagine, *Abuela* Isabel went downhill rapidly after losing Carlos and then Bañu. Sadly, she became increasingly frail and just after Christmas succumbed to pneumonia. Every day I missed her grace and beautiful face. She reminded me so much of Valeria and while she had been alive, the link was still there. I sometimes wonder if I would have survived without Ramon.

'The final heartbreak came when it was my beloved Saturno's turn to go. He had carried me through the war, Mia, saved my life on many an occasion. One morning, I found him cast in the stable, he had positioned himself too close to the wall and was unable to get up. I managed to get him to his feet and led him around the yard, but he looked at me with his steadfast eyes and I knew it was time. The biggest gift we can give these beautiful creatures is knowing when to let them go. With Ramon's help I took him into the field and we stopped beneath his favourite tree. To this day, I am not sure how my legs supported me, knowing I was about to end the life of the animal that meant everything to me. I counted to ten, raised my gun and shot Saturno between the eyes. I had to do it, for he was my talisman, the horse I had seen in a dream as an eight-year-old boy. As the shot rang out and Saturno crumpled, I sank to my knees and cried like a child. I couldn't take any more. Ramon had to wrench the gun from my hand. It was at that moment that he gave up being a groom.'

As the tears slipped down my cheeks, I stood up to embrace my grandfather. There were no words to express my sorrow.

When I pulled back, he focussed on me once more. 'So, there you have it, *querida*, my life's story. But I am not alone in this tragedy. Every family lost someone. No one went unscathed.'

'How did you carry on?' I whispered.

'The loss of Valeria was a life sentence, Mia, but I had Rafaela, she became my reason for living, and dear Paloma looked after us until she died.' He gave a lopsided grin. 'And we still have Gracia!'

'And your real father, did you ever forgive him?'

'Never. Though I had dreamt of killing him a thousand times, when I came face to face with him, I couldn't pull the trigger. Perhaps that was weak.'

I touched his cheek. 'Weak? You are the bravest man I know. To walk away from the man who murdered your mother shows the depth of your courage. I always knew your bond with Ramon transcended friendship. I can see you are bound together by loyalty and love.'

'Oh Mia, you have Valeria's honesty and directness, you even have her funny little idiosyncrasies. When you were little, you had this habit of chewing on your lip when you were anxious; Valeria did it too. You also wound your hair around your finger when you were thinking. So many similarities, not only with your real grandmother but also with Isabel.'

The moon was coming up over the horizon and he gazed towards it. 'We buried him, you know – my real father, that is – and the others. Whatever side you are on you have to honour the dead. I often ask myself if he was truly evil, Mia. But after what I have seen I believe there is evil in many of us. We are capable of terrible things.'

His shoulders drooped. 'I think, after all that, I could do with a brandy. Is that allowed?'

'Under the circumstances, Papa Leonardo, you deserve it. I will go and fetch you a glass.'

My grandfather perked up immediately. 'Better still, there is some *Gran Reserva Brandy de Jerez* in the decanter. That is if your Great-Aunt Gracia hasn't drunk it already.'

'Well, there's nothing wrong with your memory,' I said with a smile.

He smirked. 'Perhaps you will join me?'

'Do you know, I think I shall,' I replied.

As we chinked the glasses together, my grandfather glanced at the envelope on his side table.

'Do you want to see the photographs now, Mia, or tomorrow?'

'Tomorrow, Papa Leonardo.'

'You know that for years I have longed to tell you, but I was so afraid. Now, of course, there is the question of your mother.'

I smiled. 'There is, and she needs to know.'

Chapter Sixty-two

I didn't disturb my grandfather until after my lunchtime shift the following day, and when I went into his room he was waiting for me.

'I thought I would rest this morning,' he admitted. 'I was a little tired.'

'I am sure you were, Papa Leonardo. I really struggled at the bar.'

He indicated the box. '*Si estas segura*, we will finish this,' he said.

I fetched the wooden box from the windowsill and put it on his bed. The seconds ticked by while my grandfather stared at it, and I could see his resolve was weakening.

'You open it, Mia,' he said at last. 'You have waited long enough. I will show you the contents of the envelope afterwards.'

I turned the key in the lock and lifted the lid. I could hardly breathe, let alone move. I must have closed my eyes, because my grandfather touched my arm.

'You can look, Mia,' he prompted.

The box was filled to the brim. It was a treasure trove. Valeria's life was spread before my eyes.

My grandfather's face softened. 'I haven't looked at this for years, Mia, but if my memory serves me correctly, we need to start at the bottom. Take everything out and put it on the bed.'

Soon the cover was hidden beneath the piles of photographs and other mementos of Valeria's life. I picked up a small volume of poetry by Federico García Lorca, and a Spanish translation of *Romeo and Juliet*. There was a notebook in a brown cover and some faded cuttings held together with a clip. At my grandfather's request I put the notebook and newspaper cuttings on his bedside table. The volume of poetry fell open at a bookmark as if it had been read the day before.

Hot southern sands
Yearning for white camellias.
Weeps arrow without target

Without thinking, I murmured the words as if drawn by an ancient thread.

'That was one of her favourite poems, Mia,' my grandfather whispered. He picked up the volume of Shakespeare. 'And she loved this too.' He chuckled softly. 'After Padre Alvaro gave it to her, she wouldn't put it down. She always kept it in her camera case. I believe you will find his words at the front.'

I opened the shabby cover and, sure enough, there was a small message from the priest in delicate script.

To Valeria on her fifteenth birthday, may Shakespeare inspire and enlighten you for the rest of your days.

My grandfather drew in his breath as if he was troubled by a memory.

'Are you all right, Papa Leonardo?'

'Her last words to me—' He cleared his throat and pointed to a photograph. 'Pass it to me, Mia.'

He ran his finger over the surface, his face relaxing. 'I remember that day so well, all of us together for a picnic. Do you see, there is Bañu?'

At the front, a stiff little woman in a long black skirt and a white shirt was holding her hand across her face in a self-conscious way. Isabel was sitting on a rug in a white dress while Carlos stood at the head of the cart, with a glass in one hand and a silver-topped cane in the other. And there was Leonardo, a languid teenager lying on the grass with a dog draped over his chest. He was grinning into the lens but there was something else in his eyes as he gazed at the photographer.

'I remember Valeria trying to make Bañu smile,' my grandfather interjected. 'She failed, of course.'

'And that, I assume, is Luna?' I asked him, touching the image of the shaggy beast.

'Yes, that is my Luna, the most loyal dog in the world.'

There was another image of Valeria in her fencing kit standing next to the priest. Her mask was held beneath her arm and her astonishing blond hair hung loose down her back. She looked so sure of herself, so full of life.

'She was so beautiful,' my grandfather said with a sigh.

'She looks so utterly alive,' I replied, feeling my chest swell.

There were more photographs of Padre Alvaro, her parents and Bañu. Favourite horses and ponies were snapped in abundance, and, of course, her friends, but none as much as my grandfather. There were shots of Leonardo riding Saturno bareback, his body low over his neck as they galloped along, his long hair tangled in the wind. There was Leonardo dressed in formal Spanish riding costume doing a dressage demonstration in Jerez.

One made my lips twitch in amusement. Valeria had obviously given her camera to the priest, because she was fencing with Leonardo. From their stance they looked such a graceful pair, but you could almost feel the tension between them.

'She always wanted to beat me,' my grandfather clarified.

Valeria had either considered her boyfriends to be unworthy subjects, or she had discarded the photographs because the next large tranche was from her trip to Florence to stay with her cousin Elena. There were dozens. Every vista in Florence had been recorded for posterity, every statue. There was one of her cousin Elena standing beneath the nude statue of David. She was laughing, and the photograph was slightly out of focus. It was easy to guess why. There was another of Elena sitting on a low wall with a view of Florence behind her. Fiesole was written on the back.

'Do you know what happened to Elena?' I asked. 'She was obviously important to Valeria.'

My grandfather gave a small grin. 'She is still very much alive and is now a matriarch in Florence; she writes to me occasionally.'

My heart quickened; the next shot was the interior of the *Farmacia di Santa Maria Novella*, the shop where she had taken Valeria to buy her scent. All the pieces of the puzzle were slotting into place.

I was making my slow but steady way through the photographs, when the tone changed. Each image had the place and date on the back. At first there were weddings, funerals, civic events in Seville, but as the months crept by, they were harsher, starker, brutal images of war. They showed her determination and her courage, I could feel her emotions spanning the intervening years. There were photographs of young republicans, their gun barrels pushing through barricades, others of women soldiers punching their fists in the air. Another taken in May 1937 was labelled *The Siege of Madrid*. The photograph showed the *Plaza Red de San Luis* during an attack from the air. A man was crouched on the floor of a tram, his face gaunt with terror, while two republican militiamen lay dead on the ground outside. You could almost hear the sound of running feet on the cobbles as bombs exploded overhead. When I came to an image of a little child lying in the rubble, her dress rucked around her chubby thighs, I put my head in my hands.

'Too much?' my grandfather asked gently.

I nodded, putting the photograph back in the box. 'But I have to go on for Valeria.'

I sifted through the remainder on my lap, hurrying through the images of children, killed or maimed, steeling myself to continue. There were distressing pictures of mules rotting on the ground, maggots crawling from their eye sockets; a group of soldiers from the International Brigades, smiling into the camera, a long way from home. Valeria had brought the seasons to life. You could almost feel the heat and the dust of the high summer, and the freezing cold of winter. I could even imagine the rain beating on my face. My grandmother had captured the death and destruction with gritty realism.

I was nearing the end when I picked up a photograph of an adolescent boy standing on a barren hillside facing an execution squad; he couldn't have been more than fourteen. I handed it to my grandfather, unable to grasp the reality. 'How could this happen?' I whispered. 'He was just a boy.'

My grandfather winced, tears springing to his eyes. 'Terrible things happened every single day, atrocities that made me ashamed to be alive, but I never killed a child. I would have died rather than harm a defenceless child.'

By the time I had finished, the photographs were scattered around me. The ordeal had exhausted my grandfather and I took his shaking hand.

'It's all right, Papa Leonardo,' I said. 'It was not your fault.'

'But it was, Mia. Don't you see? Valeria followed her conscience and her heart; I did what was expected of me. Padre Alvaro's murder was the catalyst, but I quickly realised I was fighting on the wrong side. The republicans didn't stand a chance. Much of the world turned away, letting the fledgling democracy die.'

I could see that my grandfather still carried his shame, but there was little I could do to help him. When the photographs had been returned to the box, he handed me the envelope.

'The originals from your Leica, Valeria's shots of the German planes,' he uttered, his voice gruff with emotion.

I pulled out the photographs, my hands trembling. I had thought I had exhausted my emotions, but obviously not. The images were stark, immediate. You could almost put out your hand and touch the planes. I shuddered, thinking of the risks Valeria had taken to get them.

'These are extraordinary,' I whispered.

'That is a Heinkel He 111 bomber,' my grandfather pointed out. 'That is a Dornier 17 and, lastly, this one is a Messerschmitt 109. Your grandmother climbed onto the wing of the Messerschmitt to get the last shot of the cockpit interior. It is also where she fell and alerted the Germans.'

He tapped an image of a young man in a boiler suit with dark, untidy hair, a crooked nose and a great smile. A camera bag was slung across his shoulder.

'If she hadn't fallen and had arrived at the meeting point moments earlier, Walter would have got away.' He sighed, repeating the long-ago story told to him by Valeria. 'She never forgave herself, said it was her fault. She blamed her insatiable desire for that last image of the cockpit.'

'*Dios Mio*, Papa Leonardo. Did they make any difference – the photographs, I mean?'

'No,' my grandfather said with a sigh. 'The British wished to appease Hitler at all costs. They had no desire for war, nor to be considered to be in bed with communist Russia. So no help came from that direction.' He cleared his throat, running his hand across his eyes. 'And Valeria was pregnant at the time.'

My thoughts were churning. Walter had died for nothing. Valeria had risked her life and the life of her unborn child to show the world what was happening, but the world had turned away.

As I gazed at the Messerschmitt 109, an idea was forming in my head. If one person today was affected by her work, one child turned away from hatred and violence, then Walt and my grandmother's sacrifice would not have been in vain.

My grandfather coughed. 'Do you realise, Mia – these photographs have been in your Leica for over sixty years. I believe Valeria never developed the last images of the cockpit interior because of Walt. They are quite unique.'

He passed me a newspaper article written by the British journalist, Jeremy Page, and I read it out to him. The strapline read: *Extraordinary photographs revealing the German involvement in the war in Spain.* But it was the editorial that made my mouth go dry: *Two photojournalists risked their lives to bring you these photos showing Nazi involvement in the Civil War. Isn't it time that Britain stepped up?*

My grandfather was looking at me intently. 'Quite something, unseen photographs from the Civil War. I bet there are a lot of people who would love to get their hands on them.'

'It is quite something, Papa Leonardo.'

I was mulling over the possibilities when my grandfather pulled the last two photographs from the envelope. The first was dated August 1938 and had '*Rafaela*' written on the back in a bold hand. I held it for a moment, gazing at the tiny little infant in the crib. There was a smile on her face as she kicked her chubby legs, innocent of the events around her, unaware that she was only days away from losing her mother.

He then passed me the other. 'Juan took it,' he whispered. 'It was the last photograph of my beloved Valeria.'

Leonardo's arm was draped around Valeria's shoulder in the garden of the hacienda. They were facing the camera with a look of optimism and hope in their eyes.

'It was taken the day before she died,' my grandfather uttered, his shoulders drooping. 'At least we had this last time together, but it was not enough, Mia. It was never enough.' The anguish on my grandfather's face was unbearable and though I longed to comfort him I resisted. The floodgates would open, embarrassing the frail old man.

I was clearing up around him, shaking up his pillows, anything to lighten the mood, when he caught my hand. He took the rest of the newspaper cuttings and the notebook from his bedside table. 'Take them, Mia, read them at will. I have told you everything, so the worst is over for me.'

'Rafaela?' I queried.

'She needs to come here, Mia,' he replied.

Chapter Sixty-three

That night, sitting in bed with my grandmother's notebook, I was immersed in her writing. Words had occasionally been crossed out, scratched with a black pen, and there were gaps between the entries. It was a hurried, immediate journal and I was once again caught up in her world. As I turned the thumbed pages, I read her thoughts and her frustrations:

No fuel to heat the office and difficult to concentrate when terribly cold. Mama sent me her old fur coat, which I sleep in at night. Walt worries if I wear it in the street, so today it was four jumpers layered beneath my jacket and Papa's balaclava! Food situation is dire, nothing apart from beans and watery soup. Walt, in true British style, never complains; he procured a bar of chocolate last week, but refused to tell me how! It is only his laconic humour that keeps us on track. He is the best possible comrade in these terrible times.

Treated to supper by an American journalist at the Hotel Florida. The food was diabolical but there was plenty of bread and wine.

Mama keeps begging me to go home. I am tempted, but then I remember the reason I am here. While the republic is being left to die, I have to get the evidence to the world.

Electricity is down again so am writing this by the light of a kerosene lamp. It smells disgusting.

Ilaria, a telephonist I knew at Madrid Telefónica, was killed today. She refused to leave her post, despite the Junkers bombing overhead. She obviously believed that informing the International News Service of our plight was more important than her life. Sometimes it's all too much!

Walt managed to get some controversial images through the censor today; he even managed to charm Señora Deleon! Thank God we can offer the images to the International Press. Walt says a picture tells a thousand words.

As I leant back against the pillows, I pictured Valeria climbing through the ruins of Madrid on her way to a smoke-filled bar. I could feel her apprehension as she drove through the night with Walt, press passes at the ready, using up their meagre petrol allowance to get to the front line. I could even feel her despair as she wept over the death of a friend.

It was well after midnight when I turned out the light. My thoughts were beginning to focus. Valeria had achieved the extraordinary. I had witnessed the horrors of the *Guerra Civil* through her eyes, but now her incredible work needed to return to the public domain. So much had been subdued over the years, so many of the atrocities hidden as one government, then the next, had chosen to suppress the truth. As I mulled over the possibilities, it occurred to me that an exhibition would be easier than getting the photographs published in a newspaper or magazine. But would my grandfather ever agree to share Valeria's legacy?

*

The following afternoon, I rode Lyra into the hills. With all this information to digest, I welcomed being on my own. As I let out the reins and cantered along the ridge, the photographs kept returning to my mind. I hadn't yet broached the subject with my grandfather, but the more I thought about Valeria's work going on public display, the more excited I became.

If an exhibition could bring about any kind of reconciliation, if it could heal any of the wounds of the past, we would be giving Walt's and Valeria's dreams the recognition they deserved. As I reined Lyra in and gazed out over the winter landscape, I pictured Valeria. She was a truly modern woman in a bygone age. She had defied her father and she had put herself in peril every moment of the day. She had risked everything to tell the world what was happening in Spain. But it seemed, back then, that the world had chosen not to listen. I would do what I could to make people listen now.

When I turned for home, I was still in a reflective mood. Valeria's photographs and her notebook had affected me more than I could say. Her courage and spirit shone through them, and now all these years later, if my grandfather allowed, I would let her shine again for the world.

Felipe was getting out of his red Seat Toledo when I rode into the yard.

'Oh, it's you,' I said, looking down at him.

He came towards me. 'Is that a good thing or a bad thing?' He ran his hand down Lyra's neck and she nuzzled into him.

'Lyra seems to think it's a good thing,' I remarked with a smile.

'So I have an ally, Mia,' he murmured, following me as I returned Lyra to her stable. I didn't reply, aware only of him watching me as I took off the bridle and undid the girth. When I passed him the saddle, he hung it over the stable door.

I was brushing Lyra with long, even strokes when he came up behind me and put his hand over mine. I stopped when he whispered in my ear.

'You are inside my head, Mia, you are—' His close proximity and the feel of his breath on my neck melted any resolve. Before I could help myself, I had turned and moved into his embrace.

Later that afternoon, we walked up to the old tobacco fields, soon to be planted with the Picual variety of olive. I reminded him of the day we had imagined the whole estate replanted, row upon row of olive trees stretching away into the distance.

'I suppose I have to acknowledge this was your idea,' I teased.

'Would that be so difficult?' he replied.

'A little,' I said, and I grinned.

Felipe laughed, and it was so good to hear his laughter again. He put his arm around my shoulders and I was filled with elation.

'Just think,' I murmured. 'When all these barren fields have been replanted, it will provide work in the community.'

'And your grandfather will be able to direct operations from his wheelchair,' Felipe chuckled. 'Seriously, what you are doing is amazing. Franco's senseless notion of destroying the ancient olive groves in favour of soya is being put to rights. Apparently, your grandfather bought some of the land back for a fair price.'

'You seem to know everything,' I grumbled.

'Only what your grandfather told me,' he said with a smile. 'I know he is very proud of you, Mia.'

'But we wouldn't have been able to do any of this without the money from the auction. And that was down to you.'

As the sun lowered in the sky, we discussed his idea of forming a co-operative that would encourage other farmers to join us on the adventure, pooling resources and making money into the bargain.

'One day, perhaps, my mother will come and live here. Who knows, Poppy may come too.'

Felipe laughed and put his fingers on my lips. 'You are getting a bit ahead of yourself, Mia.'

'Probably,' I said with a laugh, finding it difficult to imagine my stepfather agreeing to live in Spain, but at that moment anything seemed possible.

Chapter Sixty-four

Two things happened at the beginning of December. The first, our purchase of a wheelchair-accessible van was life changing for my grandfather. He now had the freedom to go anywhere he pleased. After his initial reluctance, he wished to go everywhere. The local supermarket attendants became used to the elderly gentleman with long grey hair, scooting down the aisles. At the bar in Cazalla de la Sierra, he was welcomed back with open arms. On the day he insisted on going to the Ortega auction rooms in Seville, Ramon and Lucia took him, but I stayed at home.

The second was life changing for both of us.

It was a crisp sunny morning and my grandfather was feeding Lyra a carrot when I broached the subject.

'What would you say if we did something amazing with Valeria's photographs?'

He looked at me for a moment with his penetrating eyes while Lyra nuzzled his hair. 'By something amazing, you mean that you wish to hold an exhibition?'

I laughed. 'Am I that transparent?'

'To me you are.'

'That is only if you want to, Papa Leonardo. I realise it may be too difficult for you—'

My grandfather interrupted me. 'Yes.'

'You mean yes, it is difficult, or yes to the exhibition?'

'The latter, Mia. It is time the world saw Valeria's photographs. They have been locked up for too long.'

Once my grandfather had agreed, we spent an entire day trawling through the possible venues with Ramon. Seeing the photographs together had changed everything for both of us. He became interested in every detail of the project and it quickly became my obsession. I wanted to complete Valeria's journey. If I could make any man, woman or child turn away from hatred and war, I believed I would have fulfilled her life's work. I felt so close to her in those days, as if she was spurring me on.

It was also a gift to spend time with my grandfather with no secrets between us, no more lies. I noticed he had his sparkle back, charming the curators wherever we went. Finally, we had narrowed it down to two locations. The first was the *Casa de la Provincia*, situated on the east side of *Plaza del Triunfo*, between the cathedral and the *Alcazar*. This imposing former government building, now a museum, had the advantage of its incredible position, which we judged would attract the widest audience. It didn't take long to change our minds when we crossed the river and saw the Andalusian Museum of Contemporary Art on *Isla de la Cartuja*. The museum had two former lives, first as a Franciscan monastery, *Santa Maria de las Cuevas*, then, in the nineteenth century, it was converted into a ceramic factory by a Liverpool merchant. Now the original brick kilns had been incorporated into the most astonishing museum spaces that I had ever seen. The setting was truly breath-taking; a stunning combination of the ancient monastery with the contemporary. As we wheeled my grandfather towards the porticoed entrance, I was overwhelmed. The reflection of the cream stone façade, with its exquisite domed chapel and terracotta roof tiles, shimmered in the water below.

'This may not be so central, but what do you think?' I asked, feeling a little emotional.

'Can you believe I have never been here before?' Papa Leonardo murmured, his voice hushed.

Inside, we were no less amazed and I could already see Valeria's photographs hanging on the walls.

We were greeted by a tall, slim woman, in an elegant trouser suit and white silk shirt. Her dark hair was drawn back in a glossy ponytail that swung as she walked. Her features were elongated, glorious, straight out of a painting by Modigliani. At once my flying jacket over jeans seemed highly inappropriate.

She went first to my grandfather and put out her hand. 'Señor, welcome to our museum. Your granddaughter has given me an indication that you might like to hold an exhibition here?' Her voice was strong and low, and she raised one perfectly shaped eyebrow at my grandfather.

My grandfather smiled. 'And you are?' He was obviously enjoying the attention.

'I am Gabriela Montes de Oca, the curator here. And I must tell you that I am interested to see what you have brought us.'

My grandfather pulled some of the photographs from a new leather folder and handed them to our host.

When she gasped, Papa Leonardo gave me an imperceptible wink.

'Where did you get these?' she stuttered, her perfect face turning a little pink.

'Mia's great-aunt, formerly known as Val Saint, took them in *la Guerra Civil*; she was a photo journalist.'

'Well, then, Señor Palamera de Santos, Señorita Mia,' she was almost genuflecting now, 'we would be so honoured to host you. We pride ourselves on honouring artistic endeavours now and from the past. But these photographs are unique.' She stopped and raised her hands in the air. 'These photographs are miraculous.'

It was easy after that. Not only did she offer the museum, but she said she would help us with publicity and with the launch. I would sort the photographs and bring them to her in the next few weeks.

'I would propose April as a possible date?' she suggested to my grandfather. 'It will give us time to get maximum exposure and publicity.'

My grandfather looked across at me. 'Mia, it is your exhibition and your decision.'

When Señora Montes de Oca had recovered her equilibrium and poise, we said our goodbyes and Ramon wheeled my grandfather back to the car.

'A good outcome, Señorita Mia, is it not?' Ramon said, his taciturn face breaking into a smile.

'A good outcome,' I agreed.

Chapter Sixty-five

A week after our excursion to Seville, my mother called me with the news that they were all descending on us for Christmas. Papa Leonardo looked a little apprehensive, but I was thrilled.

'You have to tell her about Valeria sometime,' I said to him. 'Better when there are distractions, Papa Leonardo.'

Manuela immediately went into a flurry of baking *pestiños* and other Christmas luxuries. There was an enormous goose to pluck, which she delegated to Ramon, as well as various kinds of stuffing to make. It became a military operation ordering all the food until I teased her it was not a national crisis, just a family Christmas. Papa Leonardo and Ramon spent hours planning the wine. My grandfather obviously believed that he would have wholesale dispensation with regard to alcohol at Christmas and I didn't like to disillusion him.

For weeks I had wracked my brains to come up with a suitable present and when Tajo, my employer, pinned a flyer to the bar, it seemed the perfect solution. Ramon and I would take my grandfather to the Christmas display at the Royal Andalusian School of Equestrian Art, in *Jerez de La Frontera.* When I told Poppy, she immediately gate-crashed my plan and before I knew it, the little outing turned into something of epic proportions.

Even Lucia insisted on coming, but, to my surprise, my mother informed me Peter had declined the invitation.

I had another idea for Dante.

'Someone needs to remain in charge of the horses,' I apologised, handing him an envelope.

'Tickets to visit *Yeguada de la Cartuga*?' he asked, his face lighting up. 'For me?'

'For both of us. I know you have always wanted to visit the breeding stud, and we might even choose a foal.'

Before I telephoned the box office in Jerez, I made a call to Felipe. My heart was fluttering a little as the receptionist took my name.

'I am sorry, Señorita Ferris, he is in a meeting at the moment. I will tell him that you called.'

Besieged with misgivings, it took Manuela ten minutes to calm me down.

'Of course he will ring you back, though I really don't know why!' she smirked, handing me a cup of coffee.

Fortunately, I didn't have to wait long.

'The thing is,' I stuttered, 'I am taking Papa Leonardo to the horse display in Jerez and I wondered—'

I didn't get any further. 'If you are asking me to join you, then I would love to, Mia.'

'It is a Christmas surprise for my grandfather,' I interrupted him. 'So it's entirely my treat.'

'I am not averse to being a kept man,' Felipe chuckled at the end of the phone.

When I explained to the man in the ticket office that they were for my grandfather, a renowned horseman, he asked for his name.

There was a pause at the other end of the line. 'Not *the* Leonardo Palamera de Santos?' he queried, his voice hushed. 'One of the finest horsemen of his generation?'

'One and the same,' I replied.

*

Now my grandfather was in better health, he was raring to go, wanting to make up for lost time. When he wasn't out in the cart with Felipe, or inspecting the land being prepared for the olive groves, he was giving unwelcome instructions to Manuela for the Christmas festivities. We spent hours in the study working on plans for the exhibition and selecting the photographs. It was cathartic for both of us. When he announced that Ramon was bringing him to the bar in Cazalla de la Sierra to check on my waitressing skills, I saw straight through his ruse. It was an excuse to have a night out with Ramon, but I knew his former comrade-in-arms would keep an eye on him. While I flitted between the tables of the hot, smoky bar, I could see them, heads bent together, lost in their own world. How different from Ramon's visits to the hospital only a few months before.

Before I knew it, 16 December had arrived. Ramon went to pick up the family from the airport and collect Great-Aunt Gracia from her flat in Seville. As my grandfather and I waited in front of the enormous Christmas tree in the hall, I adjusted a lopsided bauble, remembering the copious amounts of sherry Manuela, Lucia and I had consumed the night before.

'An essential ingredient in the *decoración de este árbol magnífico*,' Lucia had assured me, as she wobbled up the ladder to put the star on the top.

These days, Lucia was a changed person. I would often hear her humming in my grandfather's bedroom as she made his bed. Perhaps it was her passionate affair with Tajo, the owner of the bar, that had made her so happy, but I like to think being part of our crazy and unusual family had something to do with it.

As the car swept up the drive, and Ramon climbed out, I imagined a Christmas in another age, when a small boy and girl had waited on the steps for a car to return from Seville. I tried to picture Valeria throwing herself into her father's arms and Leonardo holding back.

'A penny for your thoughts, that's how you say it in England, no?' My grandfather was looking at me, a quizzical expression on his face.

'I was thinking about you and Valeria, waiting on this step for Carlos to arrive.'

He nodded his head. 'Strangely enough, so was I.'

It was wonderful to see my mother and Poppy. My stepsister flung her arms around me with her usual enthusiasm.

'You have no idea how much I have missed you, Mia.'

'And I have so much to tell you,' I revealed.

'Keep the interesting stuff for later,' she whispered in my ear.

My mother linked arms with me and led me towards the drawing room. 'Your grandfather looks so well, *querida*, I can see I made the right decision leaving you in charge.'

'For the first time in my life I think I have made a difference, and it has been a good feeling.'

'You have made a huge difference, I just wish …' My mother's voice trailed off.

'Is everything all right, Mama?'

'Yes, of course it is, darling,' she said a little too brightly.

I hugged her hard. 'Well, I can tell you one thing, you have been the best mother in the world.'

We had an early supper, a feast cooked by Manuela that seemed to go on and on. We finished with her famous *Crema Catalana* with a dollop of pomegranate sorbet on the side. When Peter started pontificating on the merits of the early release of the convicted gangster Reggie Kray, so he could die at home, my grandfather yawned.

'Time for bed,' he said with a sly wink. Ramon, Lucia and I all rushed to help him to his room.

'Will you tell your mother that I'd like to talk to her?' he asked me, catching hold of my hand. 'In ten minutes, after Lucia has sorted me out.'

'It would take a lifetime to sort you out,' Lucia retorted with a grin.

My grandfather looked at me, eyebrows raised.

'I'll tell her, Papa Leonardo.' I kissed his forehead and murmured in his ear. 'Don't worry, it will be absolutely fine.'

'I just want to get it over with,' he said, with a nervous smile.

For at least an hour I could hear their voices coming through the door, until my mother came out, her face white.

'He's told you?' I said.

She nodded. 'I need a drink, Mia.' She took my hand and dragged me through to the study, where she slammed the door and poured herself a glass of brandy.

'It's all right, Mama,' I reassured her. 'I know it's a shock and it's all come as a great surprise but—'

At this her shoulders started to shake, and she laughed hysterically. 'Oh my darling girl. Don't you see it is not a shock? Most of my life I have waited for my father to tell me. I have known about Valeria since I was fifteen.'

'What,' I gasped, 'you already knew?'

She started to pace the room. 'It was after my mother, I mean Paloma, had her first bout of cancer. Papa Leonardo was staying in the hospital and asked me to get some of her things. I was going through their cupboards when I found the box. I shouldn't have looked inside, I know, but I couldn't help myself. I opened the copy of *Romeo and Juliet* first, saw her signature, and that's how I realised the box was Valeria's. Then I looked at the photographs. I was aware she was a photographer, but these—' My mother exhaled. 'I was about to close the lid when I saw the image of Valeria holding a baby in her arms. It had slipped down the side. The shape of her face, her eyes . . . It was like holding up a mirror. Suddenly everything made sense. Paloma had dark hair and was shorter, her character was so unlike mine. Afterwards, I read every notebook, every editorial. When I thought of this brave, incredible woman, whose memory had been kept from me, I was filled with a terrible rage.'

My mother looked at me for a moment and took a slug of her drink. 'My father had concealed it for all those years. I wouldn't have minded, Mia, if I had been told the truth, I loved Paloma completely and I would have understood.' She sank down on the sofa and put her head in her hands. I sat beside her.

'That is why I ran away to England with your father. I was furious with Leonardo. I had so much pent-up anger, I just wanted to hurt him. In the end I think I broke his heart.'

I refilled my mother's glass and decided I needed one myself, gasping as it hit my throat. I looked at her, as the realisation sunk in.

'If you minded so much, why did you never think to tell me?' I asked.

'I couldn't, Mia, it was your grandfather's story to tell, not mine and it was undermining to Paloma. Of course, I hurt her too when I left.'

We were silent for a moment, staring into our glasses.

'Until today I didn't know the full story,' my mother said at last. 'I didn't know about his real father, nor did I think of the consequences of his love for my mother. I was thinking only of how it affected me. That poor little boy, he must have suffered so much, then he risked everything after the *Guerra Civil* to keep us safe. He was a wonderful father and I was mean to him. I have to make amends.'

'I think the fact that he has told you at last is enough for him. He was so frightened of telling me, telling us both. He thought we would hate him.'

Tears slipped down her cheeks. 'So many years wasted, Mia,

so many years lost. And to think I ran away to punish him when he had already been punished so much. My marriage, all of it, was to hurt him.'

I took her hand. 'I am sure you being here is enough for him, Mama.'

When we had finished our drinks we returned to my grandfather's room. He was staring at the ceiling when we arrived. I lifted the back of the bed so that he was facing us.

'So?' He looked at us both, but his lip was trembling.

'It seems, my beloved Papa, we have a hell of a lot of catching up to do.' My mother went towards him, putting her arms around him.

A tear slipped unchecked down his wrinkled cheek. 'I was so terribly afraid,' he whispered.

'There is nothing to be afraid of any longer, Papa. I only hope you will forgive your wilful daughter. I will make it up to you, I promise.'

'Forgive you?' he shook his head as if unable to comprehend her words. 'There is nothing to forgive.'

'I think there is,' my mother replied, 'but we shall not argue about that.'

She sat on one side of his bed while I sat on the other, each of us holding a hand, until he finally fell asleep.

Poppy and I had planned a Spanish sleepover, so after sneaking down to my grandfather's cellar and procuring a bottle of his finest Rioja, I pushed open her bedroom door with my foot, the bottle in one hand and two glasses in the other.

She put down her book and grinned, the lamplight casting a halo about her red hair. I flopped down on her bed and she plumped up the pillows. Now was the time to tell her everything.

Chapter Sixty-six

Dawn broke in Andalucía and the sun rose in the sky, burnishing the mountain tops with liquid gold. It was the perfect weather for our trip to Jerez. After I had ridden with Dante, and Felipe had arrived, we piled into the two vehicles, Manuela for once adhering to the instructions to follow Ramon.

We were entering the town through an avenue of jacaranda trees, when my grandfather awoke. He gazed about him, recognition dawning in his eyes.

'Jerez,' he murmured. 'I used to come here as a child.'

Soon my mother and I were bombarding him with questions. For the first time we were learning about his early childhood.

He told us about the horse fair in May, when the jacaranda trees were heavy with purple blossoms. He described the old farm wagon rumbling into town with the horses for sale tied to the back. I could feel the anticipation of the young Leonardo wedged on the seat between his mother, Adrianna, and his father, Esteban.

He portrayed the streets packed with horses, livestock, carriages and carts, the señoras, clad in their finest flamenco dresses. Adrianna came to life in flamboyant red with a crimson rose in her hair. I could see her dancing in the middle of a circle, her body alive with the music. His depiction of himself as a

seven-year-old boy on a huge white horse, one hand on the reins, the other on his hip, parading in the traditional way, brought a lump to my throat. He told us of the deals done, the promises made and Esteban haggling for the best price for his horses.

My grandfather's voice was thick with nostalgia as he remembered the wagon driving away from the town, and a small boy resting against his mother's shoulder, his head filled with dreams. He coughed, and the images faded away. 'Sorry, I must be boring you.'

'No, Papa, far from it.' My mother was leaning towards him taking in every word. 'Please tell us more.'

'There is not a lot to tell.' His voice was soft, his mind still far away.

'Did you come again with Carlos?' I asked.

He nodded. 'I was sixteen and, on this occasion, it was a Rolls Royce pulling our trailer; they were very different times.' He grinned suddenly. 'The girls thought I was quite a catch.'

'I am sure you were, Papa.' Rafaela squeezed his hand. 'You still are,' she teased.

My grandfather looked at his daughter suspiciously. 'What are you after, Rafaela?'

After parking the cars we went through the bustling streets of Jerez, to the gatehouse on *Avenida Duque de Abrantes*. Poppy, Lucia and Manuela entered into the spirit of the occasion, their arms linked around Ramon. When my grandfather observed Felipe holding my hand, he winked, and I wasn't the least embarrassed. It was so good to see him having fun. As my mother wheeled him through the main iron gates past the stately nineteenth-century palace, he gestured to Ramon.

'Do you remember?'

'I do, señor.'

'And, of course, we went to the Cartuja stud many times.'

As his excited comments continued, we approached the entrance of the elegant and iconic school.

'If you think this is impressive,' he informed me, 'wait till you get inside.'

And it was true, the arena with its circular windows that cast pools of light on the sand below, the pillars and colonnades, proved to be a magical backdrop for the famous horses.

'I think we are in for a wonderful evening, thank you, *querida* Mia,' Felipe murmured.

'*De nada*,' I replied.

My grandfather was placed at the end of the front row in his wheelchair, my mother next to him.

'Ramon and I came here shortly after it was founded in the seventies,' he whispered, 'by invitation of the founder, Don Alvaro Domecq Romero. They had just been awarded the—' He looked frustrated for a moment. '*Maldición*, what was it called?'

'*Caballo de Oro*,' Felipe reminded him.

'Yes – yes, of course, sometimes my memory lets me down.'

'Mine too,' Felipe answered with a grin.

My grandfather put his hand over his mouth, lowering his voice. 'Alvaro and I were in the war together, same regiment. Two years before Franco's death he invited me here to see the school. Even then I could see that Alvaro would achieve something extraordinary and I was right. It was a talisman for the future, a jewel in the crown.'

My mother leant across and kissed his cheek. 'Well, then, we have a real delight in store.'

As we watched the *Sinfonia al Caballo*, and the evocative music echoed through the school, I was filled with wonder. Occasionally, I glanced at Felipe and I could see his eyes were sparkling too. Aunt Gracia and Lucia were equally overwhelmed with the beauty of it all. Observing the magnificent animals performing their equestrian ballet in the packed arena was one of the most moving spectacles I had ever seen.

'Are you enjoying it?' I leant over my mother as ten grey horses, their riders in eighteenth-century costume, did their exquisitely choreographed *Half Pass* across the school.

My grandfather nodded. 'That is an understatement, Mia. It is sublime.'

When a beautiful grey stallion performed the *Posada*, rearing onto its hind legs and holding the position, my grandfather leant towards me. 'That horse, he is just like my Saturno.'

As our little party made its slow way from the palace back to the car, my grandfather looked up at me. 'You have given me a new memory to cherish. Thank you, Mia.'

Felipe had been invited to stay by my grandfather, so after a glass of champagne with the family, I showed him to the guest room upstairs.

'*Buenas noches, querida*,' he murmured, drawing back my hair and kissing my neck, making it hard to pull away.

'See you in the morning,' I replied.

I somehow got to my bedroom and leant against the door, not wanting the evening to end. I imagined his arms around me, his lips on my skin, but after all we had been through, I was scared. I sat on the edge of my bed, wondering if Felipe felt the same. Before I could change my mind, I slipped my kimono over my Winnie the Pooh T-shirt and tiptoed along the corridor to his room, trying to avoid the creaking boards. It was after midnight when I tapped on his door. It swung open immediately and his face told me everything I needed to know. I was no longer apprehensive as he drew me inside.

'I was hoping to see you,' he murmured into my hair as he closed the door.

'I thought you might need some company,' I whispered.

'Definitely,' he breathed.

'That you might be a little lonely.'

'Terribly lonely,' he replied.

I let the kimono slide to the floor and he took in my white T-shirt.

'I have to admit, I have never been seduced by a girl in Winnie the Pooh before, but you manage to make it look incredibly sexy.'

'I am not trying to seduce you,' I argued.

'Umm, I may be wrong, but you have come into my room in the shortest T-shirt that shows off your incredibly long legs, wearing delicious scent, and you are not trying to seduce me?'

Before I had time to argue he silenced me with a kiss.

As I stood in the moonlight, I lifted my arms and he pulled the T-shirt over my head. 'I think we might do without Pooh,' he said.

Chapter Sixty-seven

From Christmas, Felipe and I spent every available moment together, becoming the best of friends. Our relationship was being built on a solid foundation with mutual respect, and through it I learnt the true meaning of love.

Papa Leonardo obviously approved because he was always commenting that it was he who had brought us together, which was true, in a way.

'If it hadn't been for me, there would be no you two,' became his favourite expression of the day.

The *pièce de résistance* was my birthday, in February. As a child living in London, I had hated birthdays, knowing I would wait for a present from my father, and it would rarely come. As I got older, I tried to let them slip by unannounced, but my mother and Poppy invariably put a spoke in the wheel. Without fail there would also be a card and money from Papa Leonardo.

This year I was woken early on Saturday by an orchestral rendition of 'Happy Birthday' outside. I rushed to the window and there was Felipe standing by his car with the CD player blaring, his arms full of red roses.

'Shh,' I giggled. 'You will wake Papa Leonardo.'

'I'm already awake,' we heard him bellow. 'Manuela, for goodness' sake let the poor man in, before he frightens the horses!'

By the time I had cleaned my teeth and brushed my hair, Felipe had reached my room carrying the roses and a box.

'Happy birthday, *mi amor*. For you, Mia,' he announced, raising his eyebrows at my fetching plaid pyjamas. 'A very good look,' he observed.

'If I had known you were going to turn up, I would have put on something more suitable.'

'Don't just stand there, open the box.' He shook his head in exasperation.

I unwrapped the paper slowly and lifted the lid to reveal the most exquisite wisp of blue silk. With a gasp I let it unfurl to the ground.

'I hope you like it,' he said, looking suddenly unsure. 'Poppy helped me, and it is your size. *Jesús del Pozo* is a name I know you admire—'

'It's beautiful,' I exclaimed, placing the dress on the bed and walking into his arms. 'So this was a conspiracy,' I murmured.

'Definitely a conspiracy,' he agreed. 'Now you had better try it on.'

I slipped out of my pyjamas and with Felipe watching, I put on the dress.

'Could you do up the little buttons at the top?' I murmured, feeling his hands on my back, the whisper of his caress.

I turned to face him, and I could feel his eyes on me as he looked me up and down, '*eres una mujer hermosa*,' he uttered, his voice low. 'You should be aware that every man will want you, Mia, including me.'

'So you want me, do you, Felipe?' I asked, returning to him, letting him slip the straps from my arms.

After breakfast and telephone calls to both my mother and Poppy, I had to do a parade for the household. Manuela whistled, Lucia clapped, and my grandfather gave a wistful smile.

'Beautiful, *querida*, I only wish I still had the family diamond necklace; unfortunately, I sold it long ago.'

There were more cards and presents, followed by a joyful ride in the cart with my grandfather and Felipe. Manuela cooked all my favourite things for lunch and, as far as I was concerned, the day couldn't have been better. I soon learnt there was more to come.

At four o'clock, Felipe drove me into Seville with my new dress safely stowed in the boot, and we went to his apartment to change.

'So now for our final destination,' he announced, as we stepped from the taxi in front of the *Teatro de la Maestranza.*

As I looked up at the theatre, my eyes were shining. Felipe was taking me to a performance of *Swan Lake.*

'Your grandfather told me you once wished to be a ballerina,' he revealed, guiding me up the stairs to the elegant foyer.

'Thank you, *amado*,' I replied, gazing at my handsome boyfriend. 'This is the best present in the world.'

We were sitting in our seats when he took my hand and whispered in my ear.

'So what happened to the dancing career?'

I giggled. 'I danced like a heffalump, that's what happened.'

'Impossible,' he murmured, caressing my arm beneath my shawl.

Throughout the exquisite production I was conscious of Felipe beside me, of my hand in his. Occasionally, I glanced at his face and could see that he was equally moved. As the spirits of Prince Siegfried and Odette ascended into heaven in the final scene, there were tears in our eyes.

When we came out of the theatre, a mist had come down, giving our drive home a dreamlike quality, almost an echo of what we had seen. I leant over and kissed his cheek.

'This has been truly the happiest birthday. Thank you, Felipe.'

'*Es un placer*, Mia.'

Chapter Sixty-eight

Spring came with a profusion of wildflowers. There were pastures filled with daisies, wild orchids, cistus and violas. It was a time of rebirth and renewal and a time to get my grandfather outside.

As I wheeled him down the track one March morning, I stopped for a moment and put on the brake, taking in the glory of our surroundings. In normal circumstances, this was not a gentle landscape, it was harsh and barren in winter, hot and dusty in summer, but in spring its beauty was unsurpassed. Ahead of us in an old tobacco field, clumps of narcissus fluttered in the breeze. Everywhere the colours were exuberant, the birdsong loud. It was my favourite time of year.

I had turned for home, the wheels bumping over the dusty ground, when a butterfly alighted on my grandfather's arm. He looked at it for a moment and a smile lit up his face.

'*Euchloe crameri*, or in layman's terms, Western dappled white,' he pronounced.

My grandfather never ceased to amaze me, and as I watched the delicate creature unfurl its precious wings to fly, I was reminded of the day in Kent when I had chosen a verse from *Winnie the Pooh* to read at my father's funeral.

'How does one become a butterfly?' Pooh asked pensively.

'You must want to fly so much that you're willing to give up being a caterpillar,' Piglet replied.

'You mean you die?' asked Pooh.

'Yes and no,' he answered. 'What looks like you will die, but what's really you will live on.'

I could still remember my feeling of numbness, of separation from the sea of faces in front of me.

My grandfather coughed, breaking the silence between us. 'You're thinking of the funeral.' It wasn't a question.

I cleared my throat. 'I can never see butterflies without thinking of Ashley. Some people thought it was a strange choice of poem, but I knew that he loved it.'

'You read it brilliantly,' he murmured.

'It was easy, Papa Leonardo, because I was saying the poem to my father.'

We walked on, the hum of insects pulling me back to my childhood.

'I know Ashley would have been proud of the woman you have become,' he said at last.

I stopped in my tracks and leant forward.

'Are you getting soft in your old age, Papa Leonardo?'

He laughed gently. 'I may not have seen eye to eye with your father, Mia, but if he did one incredible thing in his life, he was responsible for you.'

I couldn't speak, and my grandfather patted my hand.

'Don't be sad, *querida*, I am sure he is looking down on you now as you prepare for Valeria's exhibition.'

'I only wish both my parents could have known her,' I said with a sigh.

*

We returned home, and I left my grandfather in the garden with a cold drink, his reading glasses, his book of *crucigramas* and a pen for the crosswords. After planting his hat firmly on his head, I fled before he could think of anything else. At last, I was able to pack up the photographs. Our selection of images had been enlarged, and I couldn't wait to deliver them to the elegant curator. I remembered my second visit just after Christmas. On that occasion I had chosen my clothes with care and my mother's old Armani trouser suit had seemed to fit the bill. As Señora Montes de Oca had shaken my hand, I had realised she could spot a label from twenty feet, I only hoped she couldn't guess the year.

While Ramon fetched the car, I ran upstairs to change. Today, it was the turn of my Balenciaga miniskirt and black pumps.

The traffic was light going into Seville, so we reached the museum in record time.

'I have ordered a new suit for your exhibition,' Ramon confided as he turned off the engine. I had only ever seen Ramon in one suit, so this was a revelation. 'I need to be smart for such an event,' he qualified.

'I am honoured,' I replied, slightly lost for words. Throughout my life Ramon had been there, solid as a rock, saying little, but his loyalty and friendship were unquestionable. Now this affirmation from the man who had helped my grandfather through his darkest hours, meant so much to me.

Gabriela was waiting for me when I reached the other side of the causeway.

'So, Mia,' she said, proffering her hand as she greeted me, for we were now on first-name terms. 'I have been counting off the days.'

I handed her the box and followed her immaculate silk-clad posterior through the entrance hall and into her office. It was a sophisticated space that suited her, with rough grey-plastered walls, which were hung with contemporary art, and a huge black desk. As she lifted off the lid, her polished veneer crumbled and she looked exactly like an excited child.

'*Increíble*,' she gasped, picking up one photograph after another. 'These are even better than I had imagined. They will make an extraordinary exhibition.'

With the photographs arranged on her desk, we decided on a simple black box frame with ivory mounts for the whole collection. We had put a date in the diary for my next visit, when I broached the subject of my speech.

'It may be uncomfortable to those who fought in the war,' I suggested, 'but I want to speak freely. Are you happy with that?'

Gabriela sat down on the corner of her desk and lit a cheroot. She offered me one, but I declined.

'It may ruffle a few feathers, Mia, as you know deep divisions still exist in this country. You just have to look at the Catalan independence movement and the recent bombings even here in Seville. The hatred didn't go away with Franco's death, despite the *Pacto del Olvido*, memories of the atrocities linger on. Remember it wasn't just Franco's nationalists, there were dreadful acts committed by both sides.'

Gabriela glanced at her watch and stood up. 'Forgive me, I have a meeting at five.' I picked up my bag, looking at Valeria's precious photographs and notebook one last time.

'Take care of them,' I pleaded.

She put her hand on her heart. '*Puedes estar segura de eso*,' she promised.

The next few weeks gave Gabriela ample time to advertise and promote the exhibition, and apart from a few last-minute hitches, we were ready for the opening night. Monday, 23 April arrived and I was glad we had chosen Shakespeare's birthday for the preview, knowing how much his work had meant to Valeria.

My mother had flown in over the weekend with Poppy, and

before an early lunch at the hacienda, I intercepted her on her way to the kitchen.

'Shall we go and visit Valeria?' I asked.

Together we walked arm in arm through the stable yard, and up the white dust track, past the family chapel to the graveyard beyond. The lavender was in bloom and at once I realised the significance of the sprig of lavender in the little silver tin. We were opening the gate when Ramon came towards us. I raised my hand, our eyes met, he nodded and hurried past.

When I saw the freshly cut roses on Valeria's gravestone, I was able to add one more to the list of selfless errands he carried out for my grandfather. I realised now it would have been Ramon who had placed flowers in the room at the end of the corridor. Ramon, who, refusing to retire, continued to do so much.

We stopped at the most recent gravestones, Carlos, Isabel, Bañu. Lastly, we came to Valeria. Pinned to the roses, was a small message written in my grandfather's wavering hand.

'Death lies on her like an untimely frost
Upon the sweetest flower of all the field.'

'*Romeo and Juliet,*' I murmured with a lump in my throat.

My mother looked at me and drew me close. 'Valeria has not been forgotten. She may be buried beneath our feet, but her spirit lives on.'

The afternoon sped by and after a trip to the hairdresser's, my mother, Poppy and I changed in the luxurious cloakroom of Hotel Alfonso III.

'So, this is the famous dress,' my mother murmured, doing up the back. 'Felipe and Poppy chose well.' As I twirled in front of them, my reflections spinning away from us in the mirrors, my confidence grew.

'*Courage*, my beautiful sister.' Poppy kissed my cheek and followed my mother to the bar.

I was on my own when I took the small bottle of *Acqua di Colonia Melograno* from my bag.

'Never forget that you are your own splendid person, Mia,' my grandfather had said as I had unwrapped his present. 'You may resemble your grandmother, but you have an identity all of your own. Wear this in honour of her, not because you are trying to stand in her shoes.' Now as I breathed in the heady fragrance, I knew my grandfather was right. Though Valeria would be with me, supporting me through the evening, I had my own message to give.

We were just finishing our cocktails in the American bar when Gracia hurried through the door.

'*Lo Siento*, the traffic, it was awful, Mia.'

'There's no hurry,' I replied.

At last we piled into a taxi for the short distance to the museum. We stepped onto the causeway, and gazed at the monastery ahead of us, the golden stone glowing pink in the setting sun. We were quiet for a moment, lost in our own thoughts.

My mother spoke first. 'The perfect location, my clever girl.'

'Astonishing,' Poppy sighed.

We all linked arms and walked towards the entrance, the reflection of our dresses rippling in the lake below.

Gabriela was there to greet us at the entrance, looking more like Modigliani's muse, Jeanne Hébuterne, than ever before. This evening her abundant dark hair was held back in a clip and she was wearing a sweeping floor-length gown. She put out one long and elegant hand.

'Señora Palamera de Santos, so good to meet you at last, and you must be Tía Gracia. And you could only be the gorgeous Poppy.'

Poppy laughed but I could tell she was pleased. She turned to me last. 'And you, Mia, wearing an exquisite Jesús del Pozo, if I am not wrong?'

Throughout the week I had been helping to hang the photographs, but tonight, with the lighting levels adjusted to perfection, I could hardly breathe. I went from one framed image to another, trying to stem my tears. It was more than I could have dreamed of, more than I could have possibly hoped for. Now I couldn't wait for my grandfather to arrive.

My mother took her own time going around the rooms. When she returned, her lip was trembling. 'I am a little overwhelmed,' she whispered. 'I only saw them on that one occasion, but in the trauma of the moment I had forgotten how extraordinary they are.'

'This is your mother's achievement, Mama,' I affirmed, comprehending fully the impact these photographs must have on her.

'What an inspirational woman, and I never knew her,' she uttered, grief etched on her face, and for the first time I truly understood her loss.

She took my hands. 'But I have you, Mia, and it is my belief that much of Valeria lives on in my daughter.'

'She lives on in both of us,' I vowed.

At precisely seven, my grandfather arrived, wheeled in by Ramon in his smart new suit, with Manuela, Lucia and Dante following behind. Papa Leonardo looked so handsome in his dinner jacket, his shaggy silver hair tamed in a ponytail.

My mother kissed his cheek. 'I am going to let Mia show you around, Papa.'

'I would like you to come too, Rafaela,' he instructed. 'She was your mother, after all.'

Soon the guests were wandering through the rooms. I weaved my way through the crowds, hearing enthusiastic comments and words of praise. There were journalists, curators from other galleries and museums, celebrities invited by Gabriela, and, of course, there were our family guests.

I found my great-aunt standing beneath a poster of Valeria.

The photograph showed my grandmother leaning against a crumbling wall, wearing light trousers, a white shirt and a cap, which was pushed low on her forehead. Her Leica was hanging around her neck.

Tía Gracia looked first at the photograph and then back at me. 'For years I have wondered, and now I know the truth, you are the image of her, *querida*.'

'What are you saying, Gracia?'

She laughed softly and shook her head.

'You have all been so thoughtful to me, so kind, but perhaps tonight the world should know who you really are, who your grandmother is. You have the opportunity to put things right for Valeria.'

'Papa Leonardo wanted to protect you; he never wanted you to think that you weren't part of the family.'

Gracia's shoulders shook as she pulled her handkerchief from her bag. 'Leonardo wanted that?' she asked. 'I thought he didn't care for me.'

'Of course he does, it is just his little game. You are our family, Gracia, and I couldn't have got through the last year without you, nothing will ever change that. Paloma meant so much to my mother and you mean so much to all of us.' I hugged her. 'If you will excuse me, I need to talk to Papa Leonardo and my mother. My speech is in a few moments.'

I found them with Ramon, who discreetly slipped away.

'Gracia knows,' I said, taking my mother's hand. 'She believes I should tell the truth, but you and Papa Leo must tell me what to do.'

They looked at each other, then my grandfather spoke with a firm voice.

'If it is all right with Rafaela, then, of course, Mia. I believe it is what Valeria would have wished.'

I was about to dive into the cloakroom for a last look at my notes when Felipe hurried towards me, having arrived straight from work.

'You are an amazing girl,' he uttered, taking my face in his hands and looking into my eyes.

'You think so?' I questioned, biting my lip.

'I know so. And my family will think so too. They are already here; I will introduce you to them after your speech. Now go, get on that stage and show the world who you really are.' He brushed a strand of hair from my forehead and Gabriela swept towards us, her green silk dress shimmering beneath the lights.

'I think we should begin,' she interrupted. 'Let's go, Mia.'

The gathering parted as Gabriela led the way, and after climbing onto the podium she gazed at her audience. 'Welcome everyone,' she began.

The rest of her introduction passed in a blur, and as I made my own way to the steps, my grandfather caught my hand.

'Everyone is wishing you well, *querida*, and I know Valeria is looking down on you.'

Suddenly the light was shining on me.

'Please may I present Mia Ferris, who, with her grandfather, has made this remarkable exhibition possible.'

As the guests clapped, I adjusted the microphone.

'Thank you so much for being here. I did have a speech prepared, but at the last moment something happened, making much of it irrelevant. So please forgive me if this is not polished, but I will speak from my heart.'

My great-aunt was staring up at me from the front with my mother and Papa Leonardo. I glimpsed Poppy and Felipe standing at the side. I could feel them all encouraging me, and my fear dissipated.

'We all know the Spanish Civil War was catastrophic for Spain; it tore the country apart. This exhibition is my family's attempt to show the futility and the ferocity of war; the evil deeds of which this divided nation was capable, and which must never occur again. We need to understand how son could rise up against father, brother against brother, why even women, the bringers of life, could kill. I am asking you as an audience, some of whom may have supported Franco, to look at these photographs and take some responsibility for them, so that it never happens again. As most of us here will know, the terror of Franco's regime didn't stop with the end of the war, but continued for years, during which time citizens feared their fellow citizens.'

There was a murmuring in the audience, but I continued, realising my words might cause discomfort, but knowing they had to be said. 'The younger generation, *my* generation, should know what our forebears were capable of, so that we understand how to guard against it now and in the future. And perhaps we can even forgive. If the images you see here today can, in any small way, help heal the wounds of the past, then my grandmother's work and that of her associate, Walter Mayhew, will not have been in vain.'

Once again there was a stirring in the audience, Gabriela's eyebrow was raised. 'Grandmother?' she queried audibly.

'Yes, Valeria was my grandmother. For many years another story has been buried, but tonight I am able to speak the truth. Valeria Palamera de Santos, or Val Saint, as she was known, was pregnant when many of these photographs were taken. For her entire life she had been in love with one man, my grandfather, who at fifteen was adopted by her family and so a lie began. Tonight, I want to celebrate her work, her life and her devotion to my grandfather. I want the world to see her bravery and her sacrifice. Her diary is also on display; you will be able to look at some of the excerpts written during the war.

'This is not about sides or blame, it is about creating a better world for the future generation, it is about understanding and love. I think Valeria's message would be that we are all Spaniards and there is more to keep us together than there is to pull us apart. Thank you.'

I stepped down to a round of applause and immediately found myself surrounded by journalists all clamouring for an interview.

'Perhaps you should speak to my grandfather,' I suggested. Soon we were both the object of their attention, and it became obvious that Papa Leonardo was enjoying himself immensely. For much of his life he had been forced to guard his secret and now I could sense his relief that it was out in the open.

When a journalist from *The Times* asked him a question, he gestured at me and grinned.

'It was my granddaughter's perseverance that has brought this story to light, her sheer tenacity that made the exhibition possible,' he said, finishing his glass of champagne. 'I am extremely proud of her.'

I left him with his audience. He was having his moment and it had been long enough coming. Ramon was standing protectively behind him.

'Look after him,' I whispered.

'Of course, Señorita Mia, and may I offer you my congratulations. I am sure your grandmother would have approved.'

When I leant forward and kissed his cheek, he blushed.

I found my mother sitting on one of the steps that separated the galleries. She was gazing at the photographs. I sat down beside her and she stroked my cheek. 'I am in awe of you, my darling, but you must forgive me if I am a little emotional.'

'Would you prefer to be on your own?' I asked.

'Would you mind, darling?' she replied.

As I walked away, I could see Poppy amongst a circle of admirers, but I was not looking for Poppy. Felipe came up behind me, putting his hands on my shoulders, and I spun around.

'Well, was it OK?'

Felipe smiled. 'I suppose you want me to say that you are the most incredible woman I have ever met?'

'Naturally,' I said with a nod.

'I admit you do have certain admirable qualities.' The way he looked at me made my knees go weak.

'My parents are longing to meet you. Just so you know, they are putting on a good show of togetherness for this evening.'

I followed him towards an elegant woman who held out her hand. 'Mia, what a superb speech, and you are every bit as lovely as my son promised.'

'Thank you.' I glanced at Felipe, hoping my embarrassment wasn't noticeable.

'It is a pleasure to meet you, señorita.' His father, a tall, refined gentleman with a Roman nose and silver hair, smiled at me. 'I agree with my wife; that was indeed impressive.'

I was introduced to two of his three sisters who both shared Felipe's colouring and were pretty in different ways. They were warm and effusive, and I was basking in their attention when Felipe's grandfather came towards us.

'I have been mesmerised by the exhibition, the photographs are remarkable, Mia, if I may call you that. Your grandmother must have been an exceptional woman. To take up the republican cause when her family were nationalists, is a feat in itself, but as a woman … extraordinary.'

'You are right, and it is wonderful to be able to exhibit her work at last. I am truly glad you are here, señor.'

'I would not have missed this occasion,' he replied.

'Please may I introduce you to my grandfather?' I suggested, a sudden opportunity springing to my mind.

The old man hesitated for a moment and then he laughed. 'Now that is an interesting idea,' he said. 'Reconciliation at your exhibition would make a marvellous story.'

As we walked across the room, I knew I had to record this

for posterity. I collected my camera from the concierge at the desk and returned to Señor Ortega.

'Come with me,' I said, taking his arm.

My grandfather looked up as we approached. The crowds around him had begun to disperse and I noticed he looked a little tired.

'Papa Leo, please may I introduce Felipe's grandfather, Señor Ortega. He was a colonel in the republican army.'

The old man limped towards the wheelchair and I could see my grandfather's expression change. For a moment the two men stared at each other, as if a thousand memories were going through their heads, then my grandfather slowly raised his arm. As the two men shook hands, tentatively at first, and then with a firmer grip, I removed the cap from my lens.

'I hope you will accept my apologies,' my grandfather uttered. 'It was a despicable war and I am ashamed of my part in it.'

Señor Ortega smiled. 'At my age one does not expect apologies for the past, but it means a lot to me. Thank you, señor.'

'May I ask how you received that injury?' My grandfather pointed to Señor Ortega's leg.

The old man leant forward on his stick, lowering his gaze to meet my grandfather's eyes. 'A cavalry charge at the Battle of Alfambra,' he explained.

My grandfather drew in his breath. 'Until my dying breath, I will never forget the slaughter. I have no right to expect your forgiveness.'

Señor Ortega shrugged. 'There is no point carrying your anger, because the only person to suffer is yourself.'

While the two men conversed I took photographs. The camera came alive in my hand. I caught the expressions on their faces, and amongst photos of death and destruction, I saw the possible dawning of a friendship.

Chapter Sixty-nine

I was woken by the buzzing of my mobile phone.

'Mia, a triumph,' it was Gabriela's gravelly voice. 'You should see the public pouring through the doors.'

After her call, there were messages from guests thanking me, and one from Felipe's grandfather saying that his meeting with Papa Leo had been a defining moment in his life. Then came Felipe. I was beginning to know every nuance of his voice, every subtle change. 'I will see you later this afternoon,' he promised. 'After I have supervised the hanging of a picture sale.'

As soon as I heard the crunch of tyres on the gravel, I rushed down the steps to greet him.

'Let's go for a walk,' he suggested, putting his arm around my shoulders.

We ambled up the track and stopped at the olive trees now planted and flourishing in the temperate spring. He stood behind me and put his arms around my waist and we gazed across the landscape. In the foreground the young branches were heavy with clusters of creamy white blossoms that trembled in the early evening breeze.

'Beautiful,' he murmured.

'I presume you're talking about the blossoms and not me,' I said, nudging him.

Felipe laughed, and I rested my head against his chest.

'I can't stop thinking about last night.' I broke free and skipped away from him. 'And one of the best parts was introducing the two veterans from the Civil War. You should have seen their faces.'

'We were talking about it earlier. My grandfather suggested you should write an article. He was sure the newspapers would publish it.'

'An editorial on the exhibition, or his meeting with Papa Leonardo?' I asked, my imagination immediately running away with me.

'His idea was mainly about the reconciliation. I saw you taking lots of photographs, and I am sure you could present it to *The Times*, just as your grandmother did all those years ago.'

'Surely that's aiming a little high? Do you really think they would publish my article, Felipe?'

Felipe threw his hands in the air. '*Confianza*, *Mia*. You have just helped to organise an incredible exhibition, and you gave an amazing speech without using notes.'

'But this is different.' I looked away from him.

'*Ridícula*, last night your speech not only captured the essence of your grandmother, but it highlighted the undercurrents in Spain. Everyone in the audience was spellbound. You have to write about it.' His voice softened as he cupped my chin, looking into my eyes.

'I have chosen this spot because I want to ask you something important.'

'What?' I asked, holding my breath, all thoughts of editorials, newspapers and exhibitions disappearing.

Felipe pulled a box from the pocket of his linen jacket and handed it to me. It was too heavy to be a ring, and I experienced a moment of disappointment. I looked at Felipe then back at the box.

'Why don't you open it, Mia?'

I took off the wrapping paper and gently lifted off the top. Inside, nestling in dark blue velvet, was the Fabergé egg.

'I don't understand,' I stammered.

'I bought it for you.'

'You spent all that money on me?' I gasped. 'That's the most thoughtful present in the world.' I leant forward to kiss him.

'Well, open it,' he suggested, his face anxious.

'What do you mean?'

'Press the jewel!'

My hands were trembling so much, it took a few seconds for the lid to open. What I was not expecting to see was the sparkling of diamonds around the tiny foal's neck. Felipe retrieved the ring and picked up my hand. I looked at the antique square-cut diamond surrounded by baguettes and my eyes filled with tears.

'What would you say if I asked you to be my wife?'

I swallowed hard and sniffed. 'I'm completely lost for words.'

'Well, that's a first,' he replied. 'But is it a yes?'

'Of course,' I responded, my heart leaping, as Felipe slipped the ring on my finger. When we finally drew apart, he smiled, an achingly wonderful lopsided smile.

'So you really want to spend the rest of your life with me? And you won't run off and leave me at the altar?' he asked.

'Felipe Ortega, I give you my word.'

'Well, then, I think it is time we told your grandfather you have agreed.'

As we approached the terrace I could see Papa Leonardo watching from the loggia. I ran towards him waving my hand.

'So it seems I am not only gaining a grandson,' he winked at Felipe. 'But a fellow horseman. What more could I want?'

Champagne was ordered for the entire household, as well as a biscuit for Dante's dog. Before the toast, I telephoned my mother to share the news.

'I am so thrilled, Mia, Felipe is the perfect man for you.' There was a pause and a slight giggle. 'I will, of course, disinherit you if you ever get on his motorbike again.'

After she had promised to fly out the following week, I telephoned Poppy.

'Oh my God, Mia, I can't believe you're marrying that gorgeous man! If I'm not your bridesmaid, I'll never speak to you again.'

'Of course you will be, silly. Can you come over with Rafaela? I can't wait to show you the ring.'

'I'll bunk off law school, but only if you promise to invite some of Felipe's handsome friends.'

Later, as I lay in Felipe's arms, the moonlight streaming through the bedroom window, I could hear the high and low sweet notes of a nightingale.

'Are you happy?' he murmured.

I leant on my elbow and looked into his face. Not only was I going to marry the man who shared my passions and dreams, but I was also on the verge of a new life with him in Spain, full of purpose and determination. Valeria's photographs and diaries had inspired and enlightened me. It was as if the spirit of my grandmother was working through me, guiding me forwards to my future.

'*Completamente*,' I whispered.

Acknowledgements

If you have reached the acknowledgements of *Shadows Over a Spanish Sun*, I can only hope that you have read my novel and indeed enjoyed it, because without you, the reader, there would be no stories to tell. I want to thank each and every one of you, and I hope you were able to remove yourself for a moment to the hot days and balmy nights of Andalucía. It has been a joy to write and has been inspired by my love of Spain and its rich and diverse history, by my love of horses and by the joy of writing. My husband has always said that horses only kick at the back end and bite at the front, but fortunately there are millions of people out there who would disagree, which brings me to my wonderful friend Carl Hester.

When I first saw Carl ride, I realised I was watching something extraordinary, and the moment has remained with me ever since. His bond with the horse is unique and magical and has inspired the main character in my novel, Leonardo. I am extremely lucky that Carl has remained my great friend throughout his ascendency to the very top of his profession. Bless you, darling Carl.

When I embarked on a love story set in the Spanish Civil War, Patrick de Pelet and John Mackay Adam, two learned historians, scholars and friends, pitched in to help. What they must have thought, I have no idea, but they did it with such good grace and indeed promised they had enjoyed the experience. Patrick told me the only novels he has ever read are mine! Thank you for always answering my questions and for our many lively discussions on the politics of Spain, how fortunate I have been. John lives in a hacienda near Seville, and with his intrinsic understanding of the Spaniards and their history, he was able to point out any obvious errors in the extremely complicated and controversial arena of the Spanish Civil War. They gave me their incredible knowledge and their time, and for that I am truly grateful. If I used author licence occasionally and have not always followed your guidelines, I hope you will both forgive me.

Christopher Yeates, who is married to my cousin, trained as an engineer but seems to have a knowledge of everything. In *An Italian Affair* it was blowing up trains and siphoning fuel from one motorbike to another, in *Shadows* we discussed a range of topics, from cavalry charges to steamy bars in Madrid, all in the context of the Civil War.

Also to Heleen Schierbeek, who has lived most of her life in Madrid. She was not only happy to read the manuscript but also to check my use of Spanish. I am so grateful for your corrections and for your appreciation of my story.

To Elise Smith, who gave me so much of her time when I was writing my first draft. Your contribution, advice and reassurance was invaluable. Thank you so very much.

My deepest gratitude must go to my wonderful husband, Conroy Harrowby, who has been my staunchest ally and support, always providing a shoulder to cry on when my confidence was flagging. 'If JK Rowling can do it, so can you,' was his rally to arms! Together we explored the glorious cities of Granada and Seville, and his training as an architect and love of Moorish design made for an enchanted trip. I could never have done this without you.

So many thanks go to Victoria Oundjian, my previous editor at Orion, for her vision for this novel and for setting me on this exciting journey. Huge thanks go to lovely Olivia Barber, for your truly beautiful editing and your extraordinary keen eye for detail. You have a great gift for cutting the unnecessary and driving the story forward. It is such a pleasure to work with you. My thanks go to the rest of the Orion team, because it is not just the editors, it is everyone behind the book, thank you so much.

To Cristine Mackay Adam, who I met by chance at our hotel in the Jewish quarter in Seville, and who I emailed with questions throughout the writing of this novel.

To Bernadette Hewitt, Pink Harrison and Gina Blomefield, who have always been ready to listen when I needed an ear. To Louise Harwood, Jo Frank and Caro Sanderson, my brilliant author friends, who provide huge inspiration and copious amounts of laughter.

To my gorgeous daughter Clementine for your continuing belief in your mother.

To Nicola Finlay, who has been incredible in helping me with my edits. Nicky, you are a saint and I appreciate your support and patience so much.

I want to thank my agent, Matilda Forbes Watson. What can I say? You are remarkable, brilliant and amazing, and I would not want to do any of this without your unbelievable guidance.

Lastly, my fabulous family who have put up with me and my writing with unstinting good humour and love – well, most of the time anyway. My thanks go to each and every one of you.

Credits

Caroline Montague and Orion Fiction would like to thank everyone at Orion who worked on the publication of *Shadows Over the Spanish Sun* in the UK.

Editorial
Olivia Barber
Victoria Oundjian

Copy editor
Marian Reid

Proof reader
Rachel Malig

Audio
Paul Stark
Amber Bates

Contracts
Anne Goddard
Jake Alderson

Design
Rabab Adams
Joanna Ridley
Nick May

Finance
Jasdip Nandra
Afeera Ahmed
Elizabeth Beaumont
Sue Baker

Editorial Management
Charlie Panayiotou
Jane Hughes
Alice Davis

Production
Ruth Sharvell

Marketing
Lucy Cameron

Publicity
Ellen Turner

Sales
Jen Wilson
Esther Waters
Victoria Laws
Rachael Hum
Ellie Kyrke-Smith
Frances Doyle
Georgina Cutler

Operations
Jo Jacobs
Sharon Willis
Lisa Pryde
Lucy Brem